**Daniel Chavarría** is a Uruguayan writer. His novels, short stories, literary journalism, and screenplays have reached audiences across Latin America and Europe. Chavarría has won numerous literary awards around the world, including the 1992 Dashiell Hammett Award. For years, he was a professor of Latin, Greek, and Classical literature, devoting much of his time and energy to researching the origins and evolution of prostitution. Serpent's Tail publishes *Adios Muchachos*, Chavarría's first novel in English translation, *The Eye of Cybele*, and this, his third novel, *Tango for a Torturer*.

**Also by Daniel Chavarría and published by Serpent's Tail**
*Adios Muchachos*

'Pulp fiction in Castro's Cuba, A picaresque novel with sex, scheming, and, well, more sex' Martin Cruz Smith

'Out of the mystery wrapped in an enigma that, over the last forty years, has been Cuba for the U.S., comes a Uruguayan voice so cheerful, a face so laughing, and a mind so deviously optimistic...Welcome, Daniel Chavarría' Donald Westlake

'If for no other reason than Daniel Chavarría and his novels of money, sex, and crime in Havana, the U.S. embargo against Cuba must end forthwith' Thomas Adcock

The beautiful Alicia hatches a plot to ensnare the wealthy foreign visitors to Castro's Cuba with an elaborate scam involving a broken bicycle and her voluptuous charms. Taking choreographed spills in front of expensive foreign cars, Alicia squeezes the maximum sympathy and cash out of her clueless, yet sexually aroused, victims. However, when she attempts to trap Victor, a convicted bank robber masquerading as a Canadian businessman, they quickly realise each other's nefarious motives and embark on a misadventure of sex, cross-dressing, kidnapping and death by olive.

*Adios Muchachos* is a dark, erotic, brutally funny romp through the underworld of post-revolutionary Cuba. It is the first English translation of a brilliant new voice in Latin American fiction.

# tango for a torturer

**daniel chavarría**

**translated by peter bush**

A complete catalogue record for this book can
be obtained from the British Library on request

The right of Daniel Chavarría to be identified as the
author of this work has been asserted by him in accordance
with the Copyright, Designs and Patents Act 1988

Copyright © 2002 by Juan Daniel Chavarría
Translation copyright © 2006 by Peter Bush

First published in Spain in 2002 as *El rojo
en la pluma del loso* by Mondadori

First published in this English translation in the UK in 2006
by Serpent's Tail, 4 Blackstock Mews, London N4 2BT
website: www.serpentstail.com

Typeset at Neuadd Bwll, Llanwrtyd Wells

Printed by Mackays of Chatham, plc

ISBN-13: 978-1-85242-874-7
ISBN: 1-85242-874-0

10 9 8 7 6 5 4 3 2 1

Translation funded by the Arts Council of England

To Hilda, pilot and boatswain of this vessel

# author's note

I have never brought charges or been charged legally in Cuba. I've never been to a trial. In terms of laws and procedure, I know the necessary, which two lawyer friends have taught me; but no doubt in the relations that exist between the police, the public prosecutor and the courts, I have surely committed errors that run counter to the usual practice between jurists and delinquents. My apologies in advance to all concerned.

# contents

# Part I

# 1 wheel and thumb

Where did he learn to move it like that? Fact was, for a gringo he danced great. Fifty-five, and so youthful and strong. He was a real good-looker. But above all very kind and tender.

They were already into their third delicious day together. Bini felt she was being treated like a bride-to-be, an' not like a pick-up you pay for. An' Aldo, considering his age, wasn't a bad fuck. An' soon came back for more…You know, better than most thirty-somethings.

Another stylish thing about Aldo was his way of handing out dollar bills. He was no scrooge. And it was no big deal. He paid for Juanita's flat, just to please her; but kept his room at the National Hotel, which he hardly used. Style galore. And ever since they'd met on O Street, they'd never been apart.

But what Bini most liked was the patient way he taught her to drive; and even when she skidded, he wouldn't take fright like that bastard François or shout at her like Rafael. Aldo was fun…

On the other hand…she couldn't entirely forget the progress

she'd made at the wheel with Alberto…Now she did almost do everything right.

An' fact was, she loved driving. In a car of her own, she'd spend the day careering up an' down, if only just to be on the move.

Yes, guy, what she did most was move it; speaking of which, she now found discos a drag. Why don't we go to the cabaret at the National Theatre? Tonight César López was on with the Habana Ensemble.

Yes, a saxy friend of hers, a great kick. Yeah, come on, my lovely *papi*, an' slavering an' nibblin' his neck, an' biting the lickle lug'ole of her rubadubduckie, making him laugh, come on, *mi amor*, take me.

What she wanted was to dance into the early hours.

But he didn't, he'd had enough.

Aldo had been drinking from early on, and knew if he downed a couple more glasses, he'd be zonked on the floor. And in that state, no way could he drive…

An' Bini offering to drive.

An' he no-no.

An' she in a tantrum.

An' he no way in the dark.

An' she threatening him, if he didn't let her drive, she not give him his titfeast come mornin'.

An' he tittered an' promised to take her to the beach come mornin' an' there he'd let her drive to her heart's content, an' she slaverin' an' lickin', an' come on, *mi amor*, only a bit, an' finally givin' in, lettin' her drive a bit, but only part of the way, 'cause round Fifth Avenue, cars went very fast, an' till she was more experienced, driving at night was what you call dangerous.

Aldo drove them from the disco at the Comodoro Hotel. And when they reached 60th Street in Miramar, he turned left. On the corner of First and 60th, opposite the Aquarium, he let her have the wheel.

She gripped it lustily. With that wheel between her hands she was transformed in her own eyes into a character from a novel. Life looked like a film.

Bini drove along First to 10th Street.

She drove well, calmly and confidently, at the right speed.

Aldo praised her. He said she only needed to do a little bit more and she could take her test.

Bini turned into 10th in the direction of Fifth Avenue.

Aldo tried to take back the wheel, but she begged him to let her cross Fifth Avenue. At that time of night nobody was driving there, not even the police.

Aldo let himself be persuaded.

And also let her persuade him where 10th crossed Seventh.

'Oh, *papi*, don't be mean.'

An' *papi* wasn't mean.

An' he also let her, a last lickle last touch, cross the Iron Bridge. An' right after, another lickle favour, drive up 17th Street, and as far as Vedado.

In the end, Bini drove to the corner of 21st and N.

'Oh, guy, just one more lickle, lickle thing, *por favor*.'

And he let her drive the car into the building's communal garage.

She parked easily.

'You see, *papi*, all present and correct?'

An' *papi* saw. An' nodded distractedly.

He was sure Three-O was hiding in Havana under the name of Alberto Ríos. Ever since he'd arrived, three days ago, *papi* could only vamp and revamp his plan to kill him. This time he wouldn't let him escape.

That night, he was asleep soon as he hit the sheets.

She went to the bathroom for a quick shower. Took a toothbrush from the shelf above the basin, basted it with handsoap, and started rubbing the thumb of her left hand. Rubbed the nail with particular care. Then rubbed all along to where it joined her palm. Scrubbed like a maniac. After five minutes, she washed the toothbrush, put it back in its place, and returned to the bedroom.

She picked up an Italian magazine and started to leaf through it, sitting on the bed, next to Aldo. While she read, she started sucking her freshly cleaned thumb with gusto.

He'd begun to snore, and was now purring very gently and pursing his lips slightly, as if pouting for a kiss. His style even went that far.

Aldo's mouth fascinated her. It reminded her of Pepito's, the even teeth and deep red lips... That was probably why she liked him so. Yes, right from the start. Then she really loved to hear his Argentine lilt.

She also liked the fact his mouth never stank. On the contrary, his breath was always scented.

What she most hated, when she went out with fellows, was when they kissed her.

But kissing Aldo was heavenly. She just shut her eyes, and it was like kissing Pepito.

Yes, she felt fine with Aldo. If only they were all like Aldo.

How long would he last?

After a time, Bini was bored by all those men. And she dropped them, even though they treated her like a queen.

# 2 neither the pantheon nor the coliseum

Aldo could say he was thirty-eight, though he was fifty-five. And if he claimed to be thirty-five, people also believed him.

Aurelia had got to know him two years ago in Rome.

'Gonzalo, you sure that's his real age?'

'Of course, Aurelia, Aldo and I grew up together.'

What a fine monument to conservation! Almost an insult. Such skin, such firm features...Did he dabble in cosmetic surgery?

'The fact is he looks after himself...' Aurelia finally groused.

'Yes, I should be looking after myself as well...but not now. I'll put myself on a diet, when we get back to Cuba. But now I'm on holiday and want to enjoy myself...Don't be a spoilsport, my love.'

Aurelia soon blushed when she recalled her first negative impressions of Aldo. And she didn't just envy his perpetual youth. She was riled by his success. There was something seriously fake about him: the way he looked at you, his over-concerned politeness towards Pia and herself. For the first few weeks, Aurelia kept her defences up.

Aldo had invited them. He'd paid both their fares, though his friends had set Gonzalo up with lectures so he could earn money at various universities and Italian cultural centres. And even that generous welcome sparked her mistrust.

Charismatic, handsome, a public relations star, in 1982 Aldo had married Giuditta, a Roman beauty and daughter of the owner of a real-estate company.

Within three years, he'd saved his father-in-law from bankruptcy and taken charge of the business. By 1990, somehow or other, he'd bought the company out. Soon after, he extended and merged it with a more powerful enterprise; by '96 had turned himself into chief executive and main shareholder. He quickly accumulated a small fortune. He once confessed to Gonzalo that Pia's dad, namely his second Italian father-in-law, had helped him well before their marriage.

Aldo always slipped easily into high society. He was a Don Nobody in Buenos Aires yet got to be a member of the Jockey Club.

'He always went down well,' Gonzalo recalled. 'He inspired trust.'

He welcomed them at Fiumicino with hugs and kisses.

'Pia is really crazy about meeting you,' he told Aurelia. 'She's sorry not to be here at the airport, but she had prior engagements... You know what it's like...'

She took that to be in deference to Gonzalo. She usually found a surfeit of effusive warmth stifling.

When they were in the arrivals lounge, he took her hand luggage, grasped her by the arm, then outside he opened the car door and offered her the front seat. He pointed Gonzalo into the back.

No Cuban would ever dream of putting an old friend's wife and a complete stranger next to the driver's seat.

Nonetheless, Aurelia kept her defences in place.

When she learned about Aldo's successes, she commented to Gonzalo how she'd didn't trust the honesty of very nice, handsome men who had super-rich in-laws.

'Do you find him that handsome?'

'Way over the top.'

And of course he was: one metre eighty-four tall, with dark wavy hair, blue eyes, a manly jaw, broad chest, flat stomach, perfect teeth, and a voice that would be the envy of any professional newscaster.

'It's in his blood.'

And Gonzalo told her that his mother, born in northern Italy but brought up in Buenos Aires, was a beautiful woman.

'A drunken poet who propped up the bar on the corner called her La Botticelli and wrote poems to her. Everybody made eyes at her, and flirted with her.'

'And what was she like?'

'A very proper lady who never strayed from home, but really vivacious. I remember how she once came home laughing her head off because one of the layabouts on the street corner called her "a little porcelain doll from the Columbus Emporium". She really did have an adolescent's skin. She also concealed her age. Just imagine what she was like when she passed the fifty mark, and did herself up and went out on the arm of one of her sons – she looked like his girlfriend…. And Daddy Bianchi as well was older than her, but a well-preserved, ripe old fruit. That's why I say: Aldo is champion pedigree.'

'And he looks after himself,' Aurelia insisted.

Indefatigable in her struggle against her husband's obesity and alcoholism, Aurelia would have no truck with any genetic fatalism.

As for the successes of Aldo, who had risen from penniless immigrant to millionaire industrialist, Gonzalo cleared him right away of all suspicion.

'He was a very decent young man, very Catholic into the bargain…'

'Weren't there communists in his family?'

'His father and brothers were, but he followed his mother, in every way…'

'But he looks after himself.'

Aurelia could really harp on.

In Rome, Aldo accommodated them on the top floor of his palazzo. From the terrace, adjacent to their bedroom, they could see the interior garden and swimming pool. Aldo had cut a three-hundred-metre path that snaked between gnarled trees and served as a running track. Every day he would run four kilometres, and immediately swim thirty lengths of twenty-five metres.

Gonzalo and Aurelia were witnesses to his self-discipline. In the month they lodged with Pia and him, he didn't miss a single day.

He'd come down for his run at 8 a.m. His guests watched him jog along, while they breakfasted on the terrace.

'Do you see?' bitched Aurelia.

'Yes, I can see,' rasped Gonzalo, angrily buttering his toast.

Aldo, on the other hand, showered and then vertically breakfasted on fruit juice and coffee, and went to work at 9.30.

On rainy days or the harshest days of winter, Aldo had at his disposal a very well-equipped gym. Naturally he kept his blood pressure and cholesterol at just right the level.

'And his bilirubin and triglycerides and even his conscience,' commented Gonzalo. 'That's down to his red wine intake. Did you know it prolongs life?'

Aldo divorced Pia at the beginning of 1999. She was his second Roman wife.

A winner on every front, intelligent, companionable, rich and available, Aldo soon became a good match, even for wealthy young women. There was much conjecturing in the clubs and salons of the cosmopolitan society where he mingled.

Since his divorce he sported various possibilities on his arm, ever more beautiful and high ranking, but he stayed single.

Until one day he fell in love and announced he was getting married.

He fell in love in Havana.

He fell in love with Bini, a little twenty-seven-year-old whore.

'A stupid, thick mulatta,' commented Gonzalo after meeting her.

Bini caught one's attention not for her beauty as an individual, but because of her rough-and-ready Creole look, nobody could catch sight of her front carriage and sexy strut and not turn round to give her posterior the once-over. Tall, curvaceous and feline; but Aurelia and Gonzalo would have ruled her out as bait for the sophisticated, worldly Aldo Binachi.

'Skin-deep beauty…and compared to Pia, a disaster,' was Aurelia's verdict after meeting her.

As a psychiatrist, Aurelia drew various hypotheses, but she lacked data to confirm her diagnosis.

As a fifty-plus, she felt let down by Aldo.

'What an asshole!'

And as a Cuban, she couldn't avoid feeling ashamed, as if her country was to blame.

'Fancy hooking up with that little hussy…'

Gonzalo and Aurelia were very grateful to Pia. She acted like a sister during their stay in Rome. She devoted a whole week of her summer holidays to driving them to Florence, Bologna and Venice.

Pia worked in a museum and was the best possible guide, well versed in art and history. And she was a splendid human being, transparent, helpful and quite unaffected. Her warm gestures communicated simplicity and goodness. And as a wife, she had a good relationship with Aldo.

Aurelia the psychiatrist knew nobody should be influenced by appearances; that every marriage is a Pandora's box…but fuck, it was as painful as it was unexpected when Aldo abandoned his thirty-four-year-old wife, a polite, cultured, witty, elegant, classical beauty, to hook up with trash like that.

Of course, neither Aurelia nor Gonzalo imagined Aldo was

a monogamous little angel. But neither was he a whoremonger. Married or single, he always had a legion of women in train, and they both imagined he must be promiscuous. Promiscuous with good taste and discretion. And never with women who were stupid and coarse.

In May '99, Aldo announced his first trip to Cuba. He would fly on Thursday the sixth. Gonzalo let him know in advance he wouldn't be able to meet him, because he would be chairing an exam board at the time. (He taught literature at the University of Havana.) But he said Aurelia would be there.

Aldo answered not to worry. He'd take a taxi to his hotel, rest a while, and eventually ring them and fix dinner.

But he didn't call that evening. He called the following midday, to apologize and say he'd just met someone, a fantastic romance...

He didn't reveal any details. He seemed in a hurry. He asked them not to worry on his behalf. He felt very well and looked forward to seeing them. If he didn't call them tonight, he'd be sure to in the morning.

But he didn't.

He saw Gonzalo on his last day, when he only had ten hours left in Cuba. They chatted frantically in a bar in Vedado.

Aurelia was pleased she couldn't go. Better that way.

'What do you think he's playing at, *chico*? Do you reckon it's right to abandon your friends to go whoring?'

Determined to change the subject, Gonzalo told her that among other things, Aldo wanted to tell them about the interests of his real-estate company, which specialized in condominiums. Architectural complexes, he said. And recently they'd been building hotels. Consequently, he intended testing out the terrain in Cuba. In his opinion, the hotel industry here looked ripe for development. The American blockade wouldn't be eternal. He trusted his nose for business, which never let him down; perhaps his firm could open a new line of investment.

That was the main reason for his trip. The idea had come to him suddenly and he'd decided to take five days' holiday. He'd also get to know Havana and see his friends.

But after getting waylaid by the girl he did none of that.

'Or perhaps it was the best business he'd ever done.'

'For Christ's sake, how could you, Gonzalo?' Aurelia protested.

Gonzalo went on the defensive. 'He said that, not me. You should have seen him talking about her, endlessly, like an excited boy. Piling on the superlatives…He's totally infatuated and says it's serious. He's even talking about marriage…'

'What's she like?'

From Aldo's description, Gonzalo imagined a mulatta from Oriente province.

'How did their paths cross?'

'He spotted her near the National Hotel, invited her for a beer, and then they headed straight to a flat of a friend of hers.'

'And he'd only just got to know her? He didn't know who she was? He's raving mad…'

'He says he'd never felt so sexually aroused…He even confessed that he's been suffering from impotence for several years; that in bed, of a night, he rarely made it more than once. Often not even that. In his best performances, when he'd taken Viagra and was sleeping with women he desired a lot, he sometimes managed two orgasms a night. But with Bini he came five times in four hours.'

Aurelia chortled contemptuously.

'And, as he told me, he upped the figure with his open fingers, and stared at me intently, to see whether I believed him or not.'

'Didn't you laugh in his face?'

'I couldn't. He was dead serious. I just stood there, suffering liporis.'

(Liporis was a term invented by a colleague of Aurelia's, to make up for the paucity in modern languages of words to describe our embarrassment when other people make fools of themselves.)

'He said it was a lifetime record. When he was twenty, he'd never hit such highs.'

With each number Aldo added, Gonzalo's liporis count went from strength to strength.

'And that night, after the fifth fuck, he went on a binge with her. Can you imagine?'

'He must have been including her climaxes....'

'No way; he was quite serious about his five orgasms.'

'How ridiculous! Well! He's a real disappointment...'

'He kept repeating he'd never had it off so much even in his twenties...what a night it was, what a fantastic time, and that's why he forgot to call us. Oh, and he said the next day he was a bundle of energy, like never before...'

'Naturally, and he beat his breast like Tarzan ...'

'...and when she woke up, he was waiting for her like a stud in springtime: three times in the morning, two in the afternoon, once at night.'

'Don't ass around, Gonzalo, you're taking the piss.'

'Cross my heart, Aurelia, and guess what his tally was over the four days?'

She shook her head silently.

'Twenty-one! And he reckoned that by the last clinch, before he left, he'd make it to twenty-three or twenty-four...'

Aurelia just gawped.

'I must have gawped at him like that,' commented Gonzalo. '"Don't you believe me?" Aldo asked very seriously.'

'And did you?'

'How do I know?...I didn't recognize Aldo in that guy notching up the numbers. Even if he wasn't lying, it saddened me. I think something's wrong with him...That's an incredible total...'

'Twenty-five times in four days? Wild animals might.... I suppose Aldo's telling the truth....That's a whole lot of passion! Even a galvanized pussy would be hard put to...'

She put on her psychiatrist's hat and diagnosed a Pygmalion complex. She couldn't say for certain, but it was possible.

'I'd have to see them together to be certain, get to know the girl, observe how he performs in public; but it is one possible explanation.'

Gonzalo was acquainted with the myth and knew it represented a psychiatrically pathological state, but wasn't familiar with the small print.

Aurelia explained how it was emotional behaviour associated with the natural conflicts that came with old age. It usually appeared in men over fifty. Sometimes, a man feels attracted by a young woman who could be his daughter or granddaughter. The first step in the genesis of the complex is the psychological sleight of hand by which the old guy spares himself all self-criticism. To that end, he denies any real interest. He admits to being seduced by the young girl's original sense of humour. Or her unexploited, natural intelligence. Or her sensitive temperament. Or her artistic talent, which deserves to be nurtured.

'Didn't you say he praised her gifts as a storyteller?'

'Sure, he says she sings and dances well, and is quite an original in everything she says and does...He's mad about her.'

'That's how this complex works; in order to justify such an unequal partnership, the old guy says he will devote himself to her education. He dons a professorial disguise. And seeks out an altruistic motive: the talented girl deserves help. She's destined for stardom. And, of course, worthy of the old man and his milieu. Thus he fulfils his desire to make her his lover.'

'And erases any sense of the ridiculous?'

'Naturally, he'd make fun of any other such unequal partnership. He'd be merciless in his criticism. But the pathology stems precisely from the method the old man employs to sidestep any self-criticism. He tries everything to persuade himself that his is a valid relationship; and via that mechanism of self-deception, he has to exaggerate or invent the young thing's virtues: he's sure the raw diamond, once cut into a jewel, will love him for ever, will be faithful and grateful to him even in his dotage. Got it now?'

Gonzalo was quite suspicious of the one hundred per cent correctness of psychiatric diagnoses; but he thought in Aldo's case Aurelia was possibly right. It was the only way to explain his absurd choice.

Aldo also commented how his four days in Havana were astonishingly active, and not only on the sexual front. They walked a lot, went to restaurants, discotheques, nightclubs, the show at the Tropicana, and were even present at a *bembé*.

Bini the whirlwind. She introduced him to her voodoo godfather, a *babalao* from Regla. She introduced him one evening, when her godfather was presiding over a session with the dead. That night, Bini, daughter of Yemayá, goddess of the sea, was possessed by a dead person. She danced wildly to the beat of drums and sound-boxes. She rolled around on the earth floor, flailing her limbs, convulsing, next to other people in a trance; and she walked several times barefoot on the hot coals cooking the broth, and got not one blister on the soles of her feet. Aldo drank a lot of rum, got drunk, and when the rumba finally kicked off, he danced into the early hours. In all that dancing, he lost his wallet, almost eight hundred dollars and his credit cards. But one of those present found it and handed it to the *babalao*. And next day, when Aldo woke up next to Bini in the room they'd been allotted, the old man returned everything.

The *babalao* threw down and read the bones, and everything he said about his past was quite true. According to what he told Gonzalo, Aldo reckoned it was impossible they'd played a trick on him. He hadn't told anyone in Cuba what the *babalao* told him.

'Not even us or Bini,' said Gonzalo.

Aldo was very struck by the old black man, the vitality of the ritual and the excellent drumming of the previous evening. He praised to high heaven the affability of those people, who were at once simple and childlike. He ended up showering five hundred dollars on the *babalao* and promised he'd come back and cook them some Argentinian pasties, something he did with the help of several women there. The *babalao*'s family came and some twenty godchildren. Then came the rum and the rumba and Aldo put his life and soul into the party. He praised the old *babalao*'s dignity and manliness; he professed an enviable ethics in his very elemental exposition: for a man to be a man, he must be a good son, a good father and a good friend.

'It's not bad as a code of ethics,' commented Gonzalo.

'Yes; and it gives you the freedom to be a thief, murderer or profiteer, like my uncle Eduardo.'

Gonzalo and Aurelia understood how the *babalao* and atmosphere had dazzled Aldo. They were well aware of how the magic of Afro-Cuban drums and songs, plus rum and the contagious euphoria, by the side of a wild, beautiful female, can liberate repressed passions.

Gonzalo remembered how Aldo, when very young, had shown a propensity for magic.

In Buenos Aires, Gonzalo had in fact been a friend of Pepe Bianchi, Aldo's older brother and his contemporary. They went through primary school together, then met again in the ranks of the Communist Party of Argentina.

When he left the Catholic Church, Aldo got into theosophy, yoga, Eastern mysticism, which for Marxist–Leninists like Gonzalo and Pepe was esoteric nonsense, a way to escape reality. Pepe in particular joked cruelly at little Aldo's expense.

During the dictatorship Gonzalo emigrated and they didn't see each other for many years. In '88, they met by chance at the house of a common friend in Italy. Gonzalo discovered there that Aldo was still very interested in Oriental philosophies.

*

Aldo met Bini in May 1999. And on three subsequent visits, he told Gonzalo and Aurelia about her, but never introduced her. They wanted to meet her, but refused to force a meeting. They waited for Aldo to suggest one. But the opportunity didn't present itself till July.

On the 20th, Gonzalo celebrated his sixtieth birthday. His wife had devoted the six previous months to a clandestine labour of love. She intended to surprise him with a colossal party; something he wouldn't get a whiff of. On the sly, she drew up a list of his best and oldest friends, in and out of Cuba. She located four in Argentina, and another twelve surfaced in Mexico, Colombia and Europe. She got in contact and persuaded seven to travel to Havana around 16 July. From Cubans and foreigners resident in Cuba, she invited another thirty people whose company Gonzalo enjoyed.

Aurelia planned and acted cautiously, secretively. Gonzalo didn't suspect a thing. Nor did he imagine that Aldo was helping her.

Gonzalo hadn't celebrated his birthday since he was a child. Sometimes, Aurelia and his mother-in-law, an inspired Creole cook, took the initiative and he celebrated at home with a special lunch and lashings of rum.

For his sixtieth, she suggested organizing a meal with a dozen guests. She took it for granted that Gonzalo would censure any party that went beyond the family circle. He wasn't at all amused to be hitting sixty.

'It's like getting a certificate for being ancient.'

'That song again!'

Why did he complain so? He went on bike rides, on twenty-kilometre hikes with close friends, downed rum like a Cossack, and even though he was old and fat, women still fell for him... Why else did he get so much of the come-on from the goers in the faculty?

It wasn't quite like that; but Gonzalo, down in the dumps as he was then, didn't get her drift.

Yes, Aurelia tried to flatter him. And he perked up when reminded of his good health and physical virtues; but that imminent six-o, which would stay with him for a decade, called for an attack of amnesia and no partying. As a child, he'd thought sixty meant decrepitude. And it was difficult to cast off childhood convictions. Ever since he'd made fifty-eight, the prospect of crossing the dread threshold filled him with feelings of guilt and embarrassment. (Sorry, ladies and gentlemen, I didn't intend growing old…It took me by surprise.)

They agreed his birthday would be celebrated as he wanted, namely a simple family affair: his in-laws, La Molina and nobody else.

Mid-July, Aurelia telephoned Rome to make sure Aldo was coming. He confirmed that he'd travel on the 17th and would stay till the end of the month. He'd be sure to come to the party. He'd bring Bini along.

He phoned Gonzalo shortly after arriving. He invited him to lunch with his fiancée on the 20th. But, under orders from Aurelia, he didn't mention the birthday party.

Busy with the last touches of party preparations, Aurelia excused herself on a work pretext and didn't go; but she insisted Gonzalo accept. It would do his current depression good; meeting the girl would be a little light relief.

The lunch with Bini was a ruse to take Gonzalo out of circulation, while Aurelia welcomed secretly one last guest.

At 2 p.m. Aldo picked him up in his Cuba-Auto Toyota. Bini was at his side. She presented a soft, warm hand and smiled at him shyly, not saying a word.

For the moment, she was a sleek-haired mulatta, all gleaming shoulders and slender, long neck. Her profile was beautiful, rather aquiline.

She didn't open her mouth on the drive. Just stared at Aldo's every movement as he steered the car.

They got out at the Two Gardenias, a restaurant in Miramar.

19

When he saw her head to toe, Gonzalo shared Aldo's enthusiasms. He hadn't exaggerated. Her looks from the front, broad face and prominent cheeks, didn't belie her profile.

Gonzalo would have preferred her not to be mini-skirted. That slim waist, come-on bum, shiny legs dimpling wonderfully at the ankle and behind the knee were too in your face. She only had to smile and show the slant in her dark eyes to be sexy. She'd have been more provocative, more chic, in loose-fitting clothes and a low-cut blouse.

Before they entered the restaurant proper, Bini said she was thirsty and Aldo invited them for an aperitif.

They sat down at a table in the bar and asked for mojitos.

Aldo and Gonzalo started to converse politely.

Suddenly, Aldo stretched his neck and stared inquisitively behind Gonzalo.

'What's the matter?'

'It's fat Villarreal…!' exclaimed Aldo. 'A spitting…'

Gonzalo tried to turn round…

'He's gone now,' said Aldo. 'But he was a spitting image of Villarreal, when he was thirty…you remember Taf,* don't you?'

How could he not! Fat Villarreal was a good friend of his, and a man worshipped in the barrio.

Aldo hadn't seen anyone: the fat Villarreal simulation was part of the intrigue organized by Aurelia. The idea was to stir Gonzalo up; to provoke memories of old childhood friends; to encourage him to wonder about them and their fates; to build up the surprise at the imminent reunion.

Aldo artfully aimed his darts and reminded him of four of the Argentines who were already in Havana. Gonzalo would encounter them that same afternoon. And at no time did he mention his birthday.

Suddenly, Blini interrupted them to announce she was going

---

* 'Taf' as in 'versere', is a form of River Plate waterfront *lunfardo* slang, in which words or syllables are spoken back to front.

to call Carlitos. Aldo lent her his mobile and she went to the back of the bar. She came back euphoric after two minutes.

'Carlitos is back. Why don't we go and eat there?'

'He's open again? Wonderful,' Aldo agreed. 'He's the best chef in Havana. Don't you know him?'

No, Gonzalo didn't know him.

Nor could he possibly. Carlitos the chef didn't exist, and had reopened no restaurant. More subterfuge and intrigue, which even Bini was party to.

Aldo paid, and while the waiter was bringing the change, he started to whistle one of Gonzalo's favourite tangos: 'El bulín de la calle Ayacucho'.

'You still dance tangos?'

'I love dancing, but here it's almost impossible to find anyone to dance with. The Cubans are full of rhythm but tango is about timing, and they leap and kick the floor when they dance: hopeless…'

Aldo explained to Bini that Gonzalo was the best dancer in his barrio, that the girls were always after him at the hops…

'Oh, great, teach me, Gonza!'

They hadn't exchanged a couple of words and she was already shortening his name. This chick wastes no time!

As they walked to the car park, Bini hung on Aldo's arm and began to stroke him, and whisper in his ear. Aldo laughed and swayed his head.

'No, Bini, not now, don't be so manic…'

'Oh, *papi*, don't be nasty…It's only round the corner…'

'That's enough,' replied Aldo, digging into his pocket. 'You want to get me put inside?'

'Too right, *papi*, then you'll never leave Cuba again.'

When Aldo handed over the keys, she gave a little jump and ran out to the car. Like a little girl being given a treat.

'There's no stopping her! She's learning to drive and it's driving me mad…'

'You're not kidding,' said a frightened Gonzalo.

'She's pretty good at it now…'

Apart from a jolt when she started the engine, she drove smoothly, like someone in the habit. She turned down Seventh Avenue, round a corner a few blocks on, and parked in front of an elegant two-storey colonial mansion. There was a well-kept garden in front and a lawn at the back.

'Here we are,' said Aldo.

Bini tittered. Gonzalo thought this was down to her good parking.

Aldo went through the wrought-iron gate, and when they were in front of the high wooden door, they made sure Aldo was in between them.

Aldo rang the bell and, to Gonzalo's surprise, they began to hear an accordion and guitar playing 'El bulín de la calle de Ayacucho'. It wasn't a recording. Live music? What was all this about?

Fat Villarreal opened the door.

Yes, it was him.

'Happy birthday, kid,' and he hugged an astonished Gonzalo.

'But…how come you're here, Taf?' Gonzalo burst into tears and hugged him desperately. 'We saw you in the restaurant a few minutes ago.'

He understood nothing. Could it be a dream?

Fat Man kept a tight hold and led him into an enormous room, dominated by a photo three metres by two, from when Gonzalo was five years old, wearing a velvet suit, and with a small quiff.

The accordion and guitar stopped, and smiling faces, contrite faces, began to appear, biting their lips, wiping their tears away.

It was them…they were…lifetime friends, lost over many years and continents. And dozens of Cubans, and other Latinos, people he loved, being resurrected from every corner of the mansion. A stack of people. He sobbed and throbbed. He stiffened. Was dizzy.

'You...bastards!' and he sought refuge with Aurelia. 'Look, what a trick they've...'

He still didn't understand.

'I almost had a heart attack,' he'd blather, when he'd come to his senses.

Just then the 'Cumparsita' by D'Arienzo struck up, and in the greatest of all resurrections Nena Pacheco appeared from behind a column, on cue, according to Aurelia's libretto.

La Nena danced towards him in tango time.

Gonzalo had to pinch himself to believe this.

Partnering this woman, Gonzalo had won his first tango competition in Puente Alsina. She'd emigrated during the dictatorship, married a Mexican and lived in Monterrey.

Now she planted a kiss on his cheek and led him on to the dance floor. Close together as in their youth, cheek to cheek, tears streaming down mid-tango.

When Gonzalo finally looked up, he saw that everybody was crying. Bini as well, floods of tears.

Gonzalo ordered a treble shot.

Ever cautious, Aurelia gave it to him straight. She knew he was in for lots of toasts.

Then his friends began to hug him.

'I said all kinds of idiot things,' he'd recall the next day.

He was drowned in emotion; he couldn't breathe, as if he were under a waterfall.

The accordionist who'd come from Buenos Aires was Tito Perluffo, a retired pro whom Gonzalo only recognized close up. (Aurelia would later confess that Aldo had offered to pay for four tickets from Buenos Aires.) Tito had seen a hell of a lot of carnivals. It showed.

And to counter the fresh pangs, another straight.

'That's three,' Aurelia reminded him, bottle in hand.

Sergio Vitier, a virtuoso Cuban guitarist, an excellent tango player, was also an old friend.

Aurelia was the only one who didn't cry. She confessed

she'd already cried enough in the preparations, imagining the meetings and exchanges.

It was the most beautiful party Gonzalo had ever had. He drank and drank, and within two hours was declaring he was embarrassed to be so happy.

As soundtrack to the succession of cardiac-arrest reunions, there was a discreet set of tangos played by Troilo and Grela, with a repertoire by Discépolo, Contursi, Homero Manzi, Cátulo, Celedonio — all the greats. Aurelia had prepared cassettes with all Gonzalo's favourites.

When Peluffo and Vitier played a duet, Gonzalo danced again with La Nena. They were startling. Bini observed them, incredulous and admiring. She saw tango being danced for the first time with all its twists and feints. She couldn't keep still. Applauded and cheered.

The portrait gallery was riveting. Grouped under large numbers, from zero to five, they paid homage to six decades in the birthday boy's life. It comprised photos, some blown up to a colossal size, drawings, oil paintings and caricatures.

While Gonzalo reviewed the long wall where Aurelia had hung the exhibition, Bini stood by his side. Overwhelmed, she took one of his hands and kept a hold.

Gonzalo stammered something. He couldn't think what to do. Since he didn't know Bini very well, he was initially embarrassed. It was the kind of thing she liked to do. Perhaps it was one of her childish, fresh reactions, which so infatuated Aldo.

Aurelia took stock and raised her eyebrows sarcastically.

Emboldened now, he squeezed her hand and quite openly began to stroke her fingers. He realized his rum intake would lead to insanity. But now he was in his sixties, he could allow himself a little freewheeling. Didn't the justified drunkenness and festive atmosphere allow for that as well?

Dangerously uninhibited, halfway through the evening Bini had contrived to interrupt conversations and force everyone to dance salsa with her. She then demanded silence and told stupid, obscene stories she'd heard from a third-rate Miami comic. And finally staged a pathetic song-and-dance routine.

In other circumstances, her hyper-kinetic youthfulness among so many old-timers would have seemed trying rather than entertaining, but the Argentines, all hyped up and emotional, smiled and listened benevolently.

Aurelia confirmed that Bini was a stupid, crazy little hussy. And to judge by her repertoire and over-hit delivery, no Pygmalion could cure her terrible taste; particularly when she imitated those awful singers who always exaggerated body gestures to reinforce their stupid lyrics. How could Aldo ever have fallen for such an idiot!

A torrential liporis rained down on the Cubans. Dr Livia Molina, creator of the term, was soaked to the skin. When she sang 'my heart is yours/oh, my beloved sun', Blini underlined the image by pretending to pluck the organ out and hand it to Aldo.

'A pair of tits have more pulling power than a cart,' a Cuban whispered to Gonzalo, and lipped that message to Aldo, who smiled, highly flattered.

By now Bini's performance was arousing patriotic embarrassment and La Molina, with the excuse that she had to make an announcement, wrested the microphone from her.

'Dear guests, in spite of the fascinating beauty of our magnificent Bini, we must not forget that this party is in honour of an Argentine, and the members of the organizing committee are calling for a new session of tangos.'

That eight-roomed mansion had two bathrooms upstairs and one downstairs. Aurelia had hired one that size, thinking she would be gathering together some fifty guests. And at the very moment Gonzalo was leaving one of the upstairs bathrooms, Bini came out of the other and saw him. She tiptoed down the passageway behind him and nibbled his back.

Gonzalo turned round quite brusquely, rather afraid.

'You're a good dancer. As soon as I saw you, I wanted to

bite you…' she declared, the underlying assumption being that biting was her way of expressing admiration.

Gonzalo forgot her stupidity, bad taste and relationship with Aldo. He was driven by an urgent, burning desire for that crazy mulatta. Her elemental, primitive bite had swept away any complex about his being ancient.

'I also want to bite, eat and drink you, but not here,' he whispered, pinching her on a buttock.

The incident occurred in front of a balcony open to the warm night air; and she pointed out a dark spot, at the bottom of the floodlit garden.

'I'll be waiting for you there,' she told him, as she rushed downstairs.

They disappeared for ten minutes. After hasty caresses from hands and mouths, she lifted her skirt up and received him as if under starting orders for the hundred metres. And they both came in ten seconds flat.

As he tidied his clothes, he wallowed in the euphoria of someone spliffing coke.

After all, it's not every day you have a birthday among friends who've come from the ends of the earth.

And it's not every day a twenty-something goer offers herself with no self-interest or money in mind, from pure passion, to a fat, sexagenarian dancer.

When they returned separately to the main room in the mansion, Aldo, glass in hand, was staring at the floor. He looked quite out of it.

'He must be dead drunk,' commented Aurelia.

But Aldo wasn't drunk, simply engrossed in thought.

He was turning over an idea he'd had in the course of the party. He'd already proved his suspicions beyond all possible doubt: Three-O and Alberto Ríos were one and the same. And at that moment, Aldo was perfecting his revenge. He'd been waiting many years for this opportunity.

*

The party finished very late in the early hours.

Aurelia put her foreign guests on a coach she'd hired and sent them off to their hotels.

Aldo, in his cups, was too far gone to drive. Bini started an argument with Aurelia and La Molina. She wanted to drive at any cost.

'Look how fit I am,' she said, biting her tongue and turning like a model.

A Cuban finally drove them both to Vedado.

The next day, Aurelia and Gonzalo commented on the preliminary arrangements for Aldo and Bini's marriage.

'He says he's taking her to Italy in a couple of months.'

'She's a walking disaster area…'

'I'm not sure, Aurelia, we should get to know her better… You never know…'

But Gonzalo did know.

He knew that if Aldo took Bini with him, in a few months he wouldn't be able to walk under any arch in Rome, or enter the Pantheon or the Coliseum. His cuckold horns would be too enormous.

# 3 not a ripple

Alberto Ríos descends through the silent atria. The beckoning fingers of the coral reefs invite him to enter their sumptuous biological mansions, children of the tides and the centuries. Alberto lights up cauliflower-eared corals with yellow foliage and gigantic green leaves, and swims, head down, towards the nocturnal forest of polyps.

It is the time when the coral has just been feeding. The colonies withdraw to rest and digest in their edifices of stone and water, while they wait for the shadows to redescend.

He advances, gently propelled by his fins, between deer antlers, the labyrinthine horns of the coral jungle; and slips down a slope of purple cylinders, shimmering like cloaks, as if blown by the wind. Alberto recalls the magic carpets in some streets of Buenos Aires when the jacaranda sheds its flowers. And then come roses of stone, wrought in gold, and cameos, green-grey discoid brooches evocative of jade; and Muñoz tries to catch a red-backed squirrel-fish bristling with spines in the mouth of its cave, from where it points a round alert eye at you, before disappearing into its labyrinth. And then, a sudden close-up, a soldier fish that's also red and shiny; and behind, strange undulating creatures; and Alberto films a spotted drum, all yellow head, black fins, blue crest, a starlet proud of her graceful style; and then a *chivirica*, which sidles over its flat black body to look at you on the sly; and the horrific great barracuda, which Cubans call a *picúa*, voraciously picking fights, continuously on the move and displaying its sharp teeth; but Muñoz has taught him that a swimmer must never retreat, because then it gets bold and attacks; and they also capture images of the amiable nurse shark, which spends its time lying on the white sands of the seabed, a sociable, welcoming fish, which when visited by humans interrupts its rest and starts to swim and weave, dodging in and out, pirouetting, and causing a fuss so they chase it, or playing at hide-and-seek in the deep caves; and on the other side, the majestic, limpid blue school of a hundred barber fish, with their transparent tails, armed with sharp razors; and a parrot fish, red belly, green fins; and a trumpet fish, as stiff as a soldier on sentry duty, endlessly immobile, poised almost vertically; and a porcupine fish, annoyed by the powerful torch with which Muñoz dazzles it, puffing out threateningly; and they also film *gorgoniae*, with their intricate corneas, dancing in fans of greyish mauve, which for millions of years have been swaying to the to and fro of the deepest currents; and medusas rising, more transparent than the sea at dawn, great jellied mushrooms; or bladder-shaped, opal and turquoise, the ones called 'evil waters' in Cuba; or the mimetic purple flounder, whose flattened body adopts the bumpy forms of the floor of the reef – moving only on one side, both its eyes appear on the other; and a shoal of sardines, which swim almost on the surface and make a great seething mass. And the seagulls, whirling sharp eyed, spot them and swoop down to gorge on them.

And Alberto Ríos smiles contentedly.

He is no idiot, like the sardines, which offer themselves up to their enemies. He lives in Havana and doesn't cause a ripple or a stir. He's got a new look that renders him unrecognizable. He's got a new name and forged but perfect papers. He's a resident foreigner, with everything in order, a well-stocked bank account, dedicated to a business that is honest and profitable. None of those who want to assassinate him would ever think of going to look for him in Cuba.

# Part II

# Part II

# 4 figueredo

Figueredo growled again. The driver looked at him angrily.

'A fucking downpour and you decide you want to have a piss…'

For a twelve-year-old, Figueredo was still a compliant, sociable companion. His only quirk was quite recent: when he felt like a piss, you had to let him run for it right away. He gave you one or two warnings, and at the third, he'd lift a leg and unload wherever. Urinary incontinence, according to his vet's diagnosis. Quite normal at his advanced age.

'Don't be mean, boy,' said his assistant. 'Can't you see he can't hold it any longer?'

The driver suspected the youth wanted to relieve himself as well and was using Figueredo. He remembered how in Sancti Spíritus they'd both eaten fish, drunk lots of water and had now been on the road for eight hours.

'With all this goddam rain, he'll get his paws all muddy and get the lorry all shitty…'

When he crossed the lights at La Giraldillla, the downpour

turned to drizzle. The driver decided to stop at a crossroads, where he saw a zinc roof, next to the cobbled entrance to a large mansion.

If the dog went and pissed under the roof, he'd only run over cement and wouldn't get so muddy.

'Go on, let him out.'

His assistant opened up and when Figueredo had jumped out, he swung round in his seat and started a hot piss.

'Look at that!' protested the driver, pointing at the dog.

Rather than run on the cobbles and shelter under the roof, Figueredo was heading across a mud flat towards a tree.

The driver took out a packet of cigarettes and offered his assistant one. Just as he was about to light up, he heard Figueredo barking.

By the tree, not assuming any micturating stance, he kept jumping up and down and looked away from the road. He alternated a stream of barks of alarm and little nervous jumps and short little runs on his way back to the lorry, as if asking for help.

'Something must have frightened him.'

His young assistant rolled up his trousers, took the torch and jumped down from the lorry.

When he was by the dog, he half turned and gesticulated dramatically at the trucker. Urged him to come over.

The trucker, a paunchy fifty-year-old, stiff after the long trip, jumped down, his curiosity aroused.

Figueredo was still barking and the assistant, crouching down, stroked his back, trying to calm him.

When the driver was some three metres away from the tree, his assistant lit up a shape on a stretch of slime. As he drew near, the trucker made out the body of a man, stretched out full length, one side of his shirt soaked in blood.

The driver walked over briskly and put the back of his hand on his neck.

'He's cold….'

His assistant shone his torch at a spot where something glinted. When they got nearer, they saw the twisted frame of a bicycle.

On Sunday, 18 July, at 6.11, the main switchboard at the National Revolutionary Police station rang on the number 82-0116, one the population of Havana has memorized for emergencies. It was a male voice, which refused to identify itself: 'Ten minutes ago, I was driving along the Southern Motorway from San Agustín. Three or four blocks before the Muñeca crossroads we saw a dead cyclist. As you come into Havana, you'll see the corpse lying on the right, among some bushes, next to a tree.'

The informant hung up.

The trawl for the call, a routine operation in homicide cases, indicated that it came from a public telephone on Fifth Avenue. The recording reproduced a rather cracked drawl, an Oriente accent, of a man the right side of thirty. He stammered and panted, obviously in a state of distress. He hung up immediately.

An NRP radio-patrol car got to the spot at 6.18. The rain was pouring down, but they easily located the body. They took as their reference point the tree mentioned by the informant, combed the area round about with a mobile spotlight and the bicycle frame soon glinted.

They found the corpse a few metres away. They collected from the clothing one hundred and twenty-three pesos, fourteen dollars, identity documentation that testified to the man being Baltasar París Pérez, forty-six years old, married and living in San Agustín, a baker by trade.

A cloth bag hung round the corpse's neck. Inside they found two cold, stodgy pizzas, and a plastic bottle almost leaking its cheap rum bought from the barrel.

They managed to detect on the highway, in spite of the rain, slight evidence of sudden braking that had taken part of the turf with it. It all suggested that the driver had steered to the opposite side of the highway to avoid a collision. The front left wheel had stopped on a heap of mud next to the edge of the roadside gulley, which was deep at that point.

Two policemen sat and waited for the forensic experts, who got there at 6.50. First of all, they took photos of the tyre marks that were quite clear on the layer of mud by the edge of the road. They took measurements, looked for footprints thereabouts, took samples of earth, and arranged for the bicycle to be taken to the laboratory.

The wretched task of notifying the victim's family fell to Pedrito, the sergeant who worked as deputy to Captain Bastidas. The latter hated doing such things. When faced with the relatives' doleful reactions, he never knew what to say or what expression to adopt. Pedrito, on the other hand, even managed to find words of consolation, patted people on the back and expressed his sympathy for their sorrow most professionally.

On his return, Pedrito informed him that Baltasar París had left a widow and two daughters, eleven and eight years old.

At the Bread Roll, they told them Baltasar had finished his shift at four. After preparing pizzas for his daughters that morning, he stopped to drink rum with two bakers on his shift. They sat on a small roofed terrace by the entry to the bakery and waited for the rain to stop.

According to the two colleagues who saw him leave, Baltasar zigzagged slightly as he pedalled, but wasn't that drunk.

It was already 7.30 and the head of the forensic team hadn't arrived.

By 8.50, Bastidas had received only the preliminary report. He passed over the legalistic preamble, looked for what was of most interest and started to take notes:

…almost instant death, around 5.15…
…the deceased, who had imbibed a considerable quantity of alcohol…

Significant details observed on the slimy, ungrassed

surface, four different sizes of footprint (indicated on the attached diagram as A, B, C and D) and, similarly, the paw marks of a dog (P).

It is evident that A and B were there before C, D and P, because in some cases it is evident that C, D and P are super-imposed on A and B. It is clear that A crouched next to the body (as revealed by very distinctive marks of the balls of feet in two places where there are no heel-prints); and one can conclude that when he had seen the cyclist was dead, he returned to his vehicle and took flight.

The B footprints belong to a smaller foot, almost definitely a woman's, and come from plimsolls or some sporting shoe.

C and D correspond to work boots. C to the smaller foot of a thin individual; and D to somebody weighing more than two hundred pounds.

All the prints, including the dog's, show how their owners came and went. Those of A and B indicate they came from the NW (see attached map). They start from the place where the car that flattened the cyclist braked, and return to the same spot. On the other hand, footprints C and D and the dog's come from the SW and return there. This suggests that A and B were travelling in the vehicle that killed the cyclist, and that C, D and P were those who found the man and reported their find, an hour or so after his death.

It is to be regretted that because of the rain and constant flow of heavy traffic at this hour that there are no traces of shoe-prints on the highway.

# 5 the florsheim shoes

As soon as he finished reading the report, Captain Bastidas received a call from the control centre.

'Yes…yes…uh-huh…thank you.'

As he listened, he scrawled something on a piece of paper, which he handed to Pedrito.

As he hung up, he jumped to his feet.

'Get to the office and circulate this car registration. It's probably the one that knocked the cyclist over.'

At 7.35 that morning, somebody had notified a police station in the Calvario neighbourhood of the theft of a Moskvich Aleco.

'Fuck, Captain, what a hectic spot of duty.'

'Hey, come on; and cheer up,' commented Bastidas.

Pedrito stood up and stared at him, and didn't see anything to be cheerful about.

Bastidas detested Sunday shifts of duty.

It was his day for friends and family, for fuck's sake.

It was his day set aside for drinking.

On the one hundred and eighty square metres of his terrace, where Bastidas had put an awning over one large corner, he could fit tables for forty people. A cool breeze always blew and he'd set up a bar and a cooking area. It was the place to meet up with his sons, who were both musicians, and with their girlfriends. Bastidas invited his relatives, friends, neighbours there, and partied almost every Sunday.

Bastidas was a good singer and accompanied himself well on the guitar. Beatriz, his wife, on the piano, and a neighbour on the congas, guaranteed a hot tempo.

Some regular visitors did their bit by bringing provisions: a bunch of bananas, a pig's head for the broth, a shoulder of mutton, a sack of yucca, and a range of rums, sometimes from a dollar-shop or barrel, get your knickers off, gut-rot, etc., at twenty pesos a bottle, but which also raised spirits and nurtured fraternity.

Rum, rumba, the cult of friendship and lasting peace with his sons, who for years wouldn't forgive him for his divorce, were the only means by which he could fulfil himself, feel happy with himself and recharge his batteries.

His father also visited on Sundays.

But, above all, it was the only day of the week when he allowed himself to drink to his heart's content and felt no remorse.

Years ago, Bastidas had been a Russian-style alcoholic, of the kind who started drinking at ten in the morning. Because of rum, he'd had to abandon his post in the State Security Department.

For three years he followed a cure, and was obliged to ingest a pill that made him vomit. He knew that if he combined it with alcohol it would bring on convulsions if not death. His doctors told him to persevere for a couple of years, by which time he would start to feel indifferent towards alcohol and finally would hate it.

Nothing of the sort. When he stopped taking the horrible chemical, he began to feel the urge to drink once again. Every day in ten years of total abstinence he'd wanted to drink alcohol.

Then, one 1 January, he could bear it no longer. He decided that if he couldn't have a swig, he'd rather have a bullet.

And he signed a pact with himself, man to man. He'd drink moderately, and only from time to time.

'He's fucked himself,' his friends said.

They all warned him against it. His wife was horrified. A doctor friend tried to dissuade him. The only person who was of any help was Black Azúa, who was a kind of witch-doctor, who gripped his hands, looked him in the eye and predicted he wouldn't waver.

And so it was. He started to drink, but only on occasions that merited it.

And the best occasion was Sunday, on the roof terrace of his house.

He sometimes downed a shot he hadn't programmed. As part of the deal, to overcome some momentary stress, exhaustion or depression, Bastidas would grant himself a maximum of eight ounces of distilled alcohol which he could drink slowly or in a single sitting.

And much to the surprise of the doubters, he kept it under control. He was now into his eighth year and not one step out of line…But he needed those Sunday drinks at home…They were his weekly stabilizer.

The greatest danger he confronted was a Sunday on duty with little or nothing to do: the desire for those drinks he couldn't gulp down at home on that Sunday, driven by boredom and frustration, metamorphosed into a searing pain. His whole organism rebelled and endangered his pact.

Luckily for Bastidas, Sundays were days of tragedy, disorder and disturbances; he rarely had an inactive Sunday on duty. But he feared them.

In truth, Bastidas feared himself. At the age of forty-eight, he wouldn't let himself relapse into alcoholism, and thus be reduced to a paltry thing, a candidate for suicide.

★

'Yes, Captain, they stole it from that carport.'

The informant was a giant, almost two metres tall and weighing in at two hundred and eighty pounds, who identified himself as Lázaro López Carranza, a mechanic by profession, and forty-nine years old.

The vehicle's owner was a well-known, popular pianist, a childhood friend of Carranza's. And whenever he was travelling abroad, he would entrust him with his car to give it the once-over and repair whatever. Naturally, the musician also gave him permission to drive.

On Saturday, the night before the accident, after a row with his wife, López Carranza decided to sleep at his mother's place, in El Calvario, which he planned to leave the following day at 8.30 a.m.

'I was going to earn a few pesos driving a family to Santa María del Mar, and, you can imagine, I left them completely in the lurch.'

It was a family of friends who were renting a house at the beach for a fortnight; and they'd invited him to spend Sunday with them.

The so-called *carporche* (mangled Cuban for carport), with its rusty tin roof and grille on its last legs, perhaps acted to protect the car from the sun, but not from thieves. Bastidas saw it would need only the lightest touch to push it over.

According to Carranza, before going to bed he'd switched on the powerful car alarm; but, inexplicably, the thieves managed to deactivate it. The two women who slept in the house, and the neighbours, were definite they'd heard nothing – no alarm, no suspicious noises.

'And that alarm always goes off?'

'Well, it has always in the past,' replied Carranza thoughtfully. 'The thing is, sometimes I don't remember if I connected it or not...'

'And are you sure this time?'

'Fact is, Captain,' Carranza smiled embarrassedly, 'I'm never sure of anything.'

Bastidas nodded. He was convinced by the man's straight delivery. He was the same. By midday he didn't know whether he'd taken his blood-pressure pills or not; and sometimes, as he went into his office, he couldn't remember whether he'd switched off the bathroom heater; and as his wife left very early for work, he had to curse his way back home more than once to avoid a possible catastrophe.

As Bastidas predicted, the search for the Moskvich gave almost immediate results. They hadn't even changed the number-plate. It was located at 8.40 in the district of San Miguel del Padrón, near the Virgen del Camino.

At 10.10, after the tyres had been examined, and evidence revealed of a collision with the front mudguard and bumper, Captain Bastidas already knew, beyond a shadow of a doubt, that that car and no other had knocked down Baltasar París.

They discovered that the people responsible for the death of the cyclist left no finger- or footprints inside the car. It was clear they'd removed them on purpose.

From the perspective of police investigation routine, López Carranza the mechanic was technically under suspicion, and Bastidas should investigate him thoroughly, but his intuition told him the guy was clean.

According to his statement, he reached his mother's place at around 6 p.m. on Saturday. He played dominoes in the neighbour's doorway and had a few drinks till about 11.30 p.m., when he went to bed; but his mother and one daughter couldn't act as witnesses. When Bastidas questioned them, they both stated they'd fallen asleep in front of the telly. And neither saw him walk by to the little room where he said he went to bed.

Thus, Carranza had no way of proving that he was sleeping there at the time of the accident. The business about the alarm wasn't very convincing either. But there was no evidence to accuse him of lying about the theft, or motives to suspect him of being guilty of knocking the cyclist over. He lacked a criminal record, and the reports from his neighbourhood were excellent. His past was a past of enormous revolutionary solidarity, in the militia, as a soldier and internationalist volunteer.... But the real reason to lead Captain Bastidas to exonerate him was the size of his feet: he wore a broad size 45, and a 46 in some styles; the biggest size found near the body was a 42.

Despite the US blockade of Cuba and the bad relations between the two governments, the main crime-solving institutions in both countries collaborate amicably.

The powerful Federal Lab in Washington, DC, close to the FBI, which supervises the activity of all the laboratories in the Union, has worked for several decades with the CCL (Central Crime Lab) in Havana; and vice versa. Thanks to this link, some dollar counterfeiters, and various US escapees, criminals, fraudsters and drug dealers, have been captured in Cuba.

The examinations of the body and bicycle, carried out at the CCL, gave no leads as to the slayers of Baltasar París.

Nevertheless, when the footsteps near Baltasar París's corpse were detected, a specialist in legal photography did capture, inside the A footprints, two interesting inscriptions. The first, on a right heel. They were faded letters inside a rectangle and, when enlarged, the following could be discerned:

TM———OES

The central part was an illegible, single blur. The first two letters were open to interpretation: they could be TM, TH, IH or IM. The mud was too soft and retained only a hazy imprint. The second inscription was more valuable. It also corresponded to a right footprint, but on firmer, smoother mud the heel hadn't flattened. In this case, it was in relief, imprinted from the hard sole formed by the curve where the foot arches, and read most clearly: 'Bg & Wh 345/95'.

After searching their shoe catalogues, the Cuban experts decided that the first imprinted text perhaps corresponded to 'The Florsheim Shoes', the inscription carried on all heels of shoes belonging to this brand.

On 20 July, the specialists sent the Federal Lab both texts, together with a detailed description, by Internet. Their colleagues specialized in footprints and shoes, recorded in the annual catalogues from all US producers of shoes, and faxed an answer on the 23rd. They confirmed that the letters in the box were part of 'The Florsheim Shoes'. And among the sets stored on the lab's computers, number 345 corresponded to a model sold on the market in the summer season of '97. It was a two-tone design, with a heel and pointed toes and in very light chestnut, almost beige kid; the white part comprised a plaited sheepskin ... They sent a drawing, in which one could see the design and the distribution of the embosses on the two beige-coloured areas.

It was a novelty manufactured only on special order, for aged folk with brittle skin. 'Brittle skins and powerful purses', commented the colleague from the lab. In effect, according to a recent Florsheim catalogue, a pair cost twelve hundred dollars. And they added the fact that the white area corresponded to a WMH-1009 tone and the caramel of toe and heel to a BBC-3261. (That was how both colours appeared in the World Colour Convention on their computers, which record sixteen million shades.)

Not only could they discount López Carranza as a suspect because of his huge feet, but also almost all Cubans living during the Special Period. Given the general lack of economic means, it was difficult to imagine anyone wearing such expensive shoes. And even more absurd to imagine that anyone who could afford them would be out there stealing cars.

'A bad start,' murmured Bastidas bad-temperedly.

The car thief must be a Cuban criminal quite inconsistent in his range of felonies. And as it was quite impossible that anyone could move around consciously wearing the world's most expensive shoes in a second-hand tinpot Russian car, Bastidas conjectured that the car thief and cyclist-slaughterer didn't realize what kind of shoes he was wearing. He wasn't just shod in a millionaire's shoes. He was walking on a time bomb, because Bastidas would haul him in very quickly precisely because of the shoes. He was sure of that.

That same afternoon, Bastidas took the initiative of circulating the security officers in sixty-seven Havana hotels with the following note: 'Inform Homicide, IBL 341, immediately of the presence of two-tone men's shoes in white and a very light brown, almost beige'.

He also ordered his assistant to ask central office to include the term Florsheim in the Red Alert section of their Brief Report.

'And send the hotel note to all nearby stations as well...'

He went silent and sat thoughtfully nibbling his pencil for a few seconds.

'And ask for a slot for me with the graphics department,' he ordered Pedrito.

That same afternoon he met up with a big-nosed artist, a close friend of his, who promised she'd prepare a coloured drawing that would match the sketch sent by the lab people. But following Pedrito's advice, he emphasized to the artist that she should try to get the exact shade of the very light beige, from toe to heel, and passed on the chromatic reference number taken from the World Colour Convention.

As Pedrito confessed to him, he was also crazy about two-tone shoes and had recently ordered a pair to be made up. And he knew that when Cuban artisans crafted made-to-measure two-tone shoes, they always used dark brown. He was sure that beige would catch the eye in any part of Havana.

On 24 July, twelve colour photograph copies of the Florsheim designs were sent to the police stations nearest to the spot where they had located the stolen Moskvich; and an equal number were distributed to those responsible for security in hotels.

According to Bastidas's reasoning, the car thief and slayer of Baltasar París was a brainless swine.

'You bet if he abandoned the car there, it's because he lives round about.'

Bastidas took it for granted that in San Miguel del Padrón and neighbouring districts, there were enough fans of two-tone shades for the Florsheims worth twelve hundred dollars not to pass unnoticed. And in all probability, the police wouldn't be immune to the admiration they'd arouse.

Two-tone Florsheims (rebaptized *florichéins* in Cuba) not only appealed to old gents with iffy feet and millionaires possessed of good taste. Because of their high price, they were also the fashion among gangsters in gringo films, the ones Cuban wide boys and criminals imitated in the fifties.

# 6 velasco and company

All police units in Havana prepare a Brief Report on the new criminal activities they encounter daily, and forward it to the offices of the Technical Investigation Department. The reports must be logged before nine, and the hard disk of the main computer receives the information, which is then printed for distribution.

On the morning of 5 August 1999, the captain who heads BICTAD (Libraries, Scientific-Technical Information, Archives and Distribution) received the diskette put together by the compilers and keyed in the Red Alert programme before putting the new info on her hard disk. Exclamation marks appeared on the screen to indicate Alert, next to the name of a petty criminal, a pharmaceutical product and the Florsheim brand of shoes. The captain printed out the three reports, took them to her superiors, finished eating her roll and shut herself in the bathroom to smoke a cigarette.

That same afternoon, around four, Bastidas received a call from the Comodoro Hotel. The officer responsible for security remembered a pair of white-and-beige shoes that had caught his attention. He'd seen them perhaps a month before receiving the image from Bastidas. A tourist he couldn't identify was wearing them. He was certainly a tall and fair-haired foreigner, but he couldn't remember any more details, and was unsure as to his nationality. From his appearance, he could be Spanish, Italian or even Latin American.

Bastidas had just hung up when he got another call. A citizen of Sweden, on Guanabo beach, had just reported the theft of a camera, and a small case containing his papers, air tickets, some money, credit cards, clothes and some Florsheim shoes that – 'fuck the bastard!' – were black patent leather.

A waste of time.

But it's a queer world…and incredibly, that same day, Bastidas got a third call, at 17.15, this time from central office: a policeman on duty in El Cerro had recognized some two-tone Florsheim shoes, identical to the ones he'd just circulated on colour prints.

El Cerro! Incredible! Bastidas thought the shoes would be meandering somewhere in the vicinity of San Miguel de Padrón, where the prints had been handed out.

'What happened, Captain,' explained the policeman who'd spotted the shoes, 'is that I worked in San Miguel right up to last week.'

'A providential transfer to El Cerro!'

A guy by the name of Velasco wore the shoes, a sixty-eight-year-old tobacconist with no criminal record.

Bastidas decided to question him but had few hopes in that direction. A citizen with no criminal record, resident in El Cerro, doesn't steal cars at two in the morning in El Calvario. Anyway, he went through the motions, called El Calvario, and that same night went to see Velasco in his abode on Tulipán Street, along with Pedrito and the policeman who'd spotted him in the locality.

The man seemed shifty and frightened; a normal state for intelligent, civilized people when visited by a policeman.

The size, design and colour of the shoes matched those of the model circulated in line with the Florsheim catalogue.

The first thing Bastidas did was to scrutinize the curve of the arch. There he could make out quite clearly the number 345 and the same letters. As the high part of the sole didn't come into contact with external surfaces, the characters were still legible.

Beyond a shadow of a doubt, Bastidas was holding the shoes that had left their mark by the body of Baltasar París. He also looked at the heel for the remaining letters of the Florsheim brand name; but could see only what seemed like a single relief, as if the letters had been soldered together. At first sight completely illegible.

Only eighteen days had passed since Baltasar París's accident, and it didn't make sense if he couldn't see what the forensics people had seen.

'Perhaps they used a magnifying glass', he thought.

In any case, the 345 stood out clearly, and the colours and design coincided with the lab description. No doubt they had been next to the body. But could they really be the murderer's shoes?

'When did you purchase them?'

'Not very long ago, Captain,' and he placed his cigar between his teeth and counted on his fingers; 'a fortnight or so.'

Bastidas did a quick calculation: it was 5 August; so if Velasco was telling the truth, he must have purchased the shoes on 21 or 22 July; that is, three or four days after the accident.

That is, if he was telling the truth.

He'd have to really grill him.

'And how'd you get them?'

'A fellow sold them to me, in…'

'In where?'

'Vedado, around Nineteenth and E, I think, or on the corner of F, I don't really remember…'

'And what was the individual's name?'

'Oh, I definitely never knew...'

'Not even a nickname?'

'No, Captain, it was the first and last time I ever saw him.'

'And what did he look like?'

Velasco looked up again, trying to remember.

'He was a light-skinned mulatto, around the forty mark...'

'And are you always so trusting with guys doing business on the street?'

'Fact is, I was crazy for those shoes, Captain, and the man seemed straight enough...'

'You haven't seen him since?'

'No, captain, not once...'

'And how much did you pay for the shoes?'

Velasco started to turn the dead end of his cigar between his fingers, and looked embarrassedly at Bastidas. 'A thousand pesos.'

A bargain, thought Bastidas. At the present exchange rate, bought new, they'd be worth some twenty-four thousand Cuban pesos.

'And how come you struck a deal?'

'You know, I was just taking a stroll in Vedado, and the fellow came over to me. When I was young I always earned good money in my trade, and I liked to look smart, you know the kind of thing, and I always wanted shoes of that make; and in those days, two-tone *florichéin* were the height of fashion, and they'd always been my heart's desire. And now they just fell from heaven...on me. I couldn't let the chance slip, Captain... How else would I ever get clobber like that in this day and age? And they looked really new...Then they fitted just right, so I bought them and that's...'

The guy was lying and Bastidas was in no mood to waste time.

While he organized his next raft of questions, he opened his notebook and made a few quick notes.

'Look, Velasco, I don't think that's how you bought those shoes…'

'Well, Captain, what must I do to convince you?'

'…and I don't think you'd spend a thousand pesos just like that, if you didn't know the guy…'

'You know, Captain, a thousand pesos is only fifty dollars…'

Bastidas stared at him and the man returned his stare.

'That's your story, Velasco. I can only say that these shoes are implicated in nasty business, and if you can't remember who sold you them, I have no choice but to suspect you are hiding something very serious…

'Cross my heart, Captain, it's the truth…'

'…because the man who wore these shoes on the eighteenth of July, eighteen days ago to the day, killed somebody. And if you can't prove you didn't buy them after that day, I will be forced to arrest you on suspicion of murder.'

'What!!! No, no way! Well…Wait a minute…If that's the situation, look…'

He took a deep, deep breath, emptied his lungs and stared at the ground. He'd decided to confess, but still didn't know where to start.

'If you want to know the truth, Captain, I'm a cock-fighter…'

Fuck me, that's why you didn't want to tell me where you got the shoes.

'…and I bought the shoes at a cock-fight last Sunday. As far as I…'

Bastidas quickly glanced at the small calendar in his notebook and saw that 1 August had been a Sunday.

'…I don't know how to put this, Captain, but, you know… cocks are everything to me, the thing I most like in life…But I'm an honest man – and a revolutionary, and…'

And he started to recount how he was already selling raffle tickets for the '26 July Revolution' in 1958. He was threatening to embark on the history of the universe. Bastidas looked at his watch and pretended to yawn.

'Hey, I'm here because of the shoes. I'm not interested in your fighting cocks.'

His prompt produced the goods: 'I bought them at a cockpit in Guanabacoa.'

A guy called Mantecao had them and he sold them for a thousand pesos.

No, Velasco didn't know where he lived; but everyone who lived near the bus terminal knew who Mantecao was.

That same evening Bastidas phoned the NRP station nearest to the Guanacaboa bus terminal. And was in luck. They knew Mantecao only too well – ex-jailbird, pickpocket, a regular customer at the station, who'd been arrested by chance that morning for suspected robbery. His real name was Julio Valencia Romero.

Mantecao was questioned the following day at 9 a.m. in the Guanabacoa station.

Bastidas had to listen to Mantecao repenting his past. Captain, he was a good boy now, was looking for work, even with the government.

'I found the shoes in a trash can.' He nodded warily. 'Fact is, Captain, people have gone crazy. Fancy throwing out such a fine pair of shoes, almost new…'

After hearing him lie for five minutes, Bastidas repeated the argument about being suspected of murder, and that if Mantecao couldn't show that by 18 July he hadn't yet come into possession of the shoes, he'd find himself well and truly in it.

'And for murder, with your extensive criminal record, you'd get twenty years in the can.'

Mention of twenty years also had the required effect.

'I got them from Felo, an old black shoeshine who works in Cotorro; and it was after eighteenth July.'

And in order to queer Velasco's pitch a bit more – he'd informed on him – he modified his statement: the sale of the shoes had taken place at an afternoon cock-fight when Velasco's rooster had won him a ton of pesos.

'As soon as he saw me wearing the *florichéin*, the old man went mad. He went out of his mind. I'll give you a thousand, he said, and then he upped it to fifteen hundred and two thousand. And you know, Captain, a man has got family obligations, little kids, and for a couple of thousand smackers I'd cut a leg off and sell it, let alone my shoes.'

Pedrito couldn't restrain himself and burst out laughing.

People were always setting up and taking down clandestine markets in different parts of Guanabacoa. One of the officers in the local unit, present at the questioning, asked where that cockpit was and Mantecao reminded him he was a thief, not a nark. And if he'd mentioned the market it was to show that old Velasco was no cherub.

'And I told him straight that the shoes were hot property in El Cotorro; because I might have my problems and things, Captain, but I'm a serious guy; and I didn't want Velasco walking around El Cotorro in those shoes, because someone would steal them from him.'

Bastidas reckoned this wasn't so, but that he wanted to shovel shit on Velasco to make him seem like a fence.

By eleven o'clock, that same morning, Bastidas and Pedrito were parked next to Felo's house in El Cotorro. They found him shining a customer's shoes in the doorway to his house.

Felo explained how besides his shining shoes in the armchair, some neighbours would drop their shoes by in the morning and pick them up in the afternoon. He'd always put these shoes on the pavement, next to his dais, so he could give them a shine when he had no customers in his chair.

He described the thief as someone with the same features as Mantecao.

'He parked his bicycle at the side of the road and sat on the chair to have his shoes polished; when I'd almost finished, the fellow acted as if he felt sick. He looked fish-faced, his eyes squinted, and he told me he had heart problems and needed a glass of water so he could take his pill. And when I went inside to get him some water, the guy grabbed all the shoes within hands' reach, jumped on his bike and rode off.'

'And do you remember the date?'

'Of course I do! It was the twenty-seventh of July, a day before my daughter's birthday…And I was trying to get a few cents together to give her a little present. Imagine the palaver… and afterwards, I had to tell my customers their shoes had been stolen. The ones I was most upset about were Colorado's *florichéin*, wonderful shoes. Just imagine: when I was a kid, a pair of shoes cost you four pesos, and *florichéin* a cool twenty-five or thirty.'

Colorado, well into his forties, and red haired, as his name suggested, worked in the gourmet trade and took the theft calmly. He knew that Felito was incapable of pulling a fast one.

'Don't worry, guy,' he soothed. 'More was lost in the war, for fuck's sake…'

Felito went with the two policemen at midday to see Colorado, who lived three houses away. They found him eating by himself. At the same time he was moving chess pieces on a board, in a mood of total concentration. He wore slippers and shorts. Friday was his day off.

'No, no, comrade, you finish your lunch in peace; we'll wait in the doorway.'

The policemen sat down in two rocking chairs and Colorado's wife brought out two cups of coffee on a tray.

Within five minutes, now wearing a shirt, Colorado joined them.

After thanking him and praising the coffee, Bastida launched into his questions.

Colorado revealed how he'd bought the shoes the night before he'd taken them to the shoeshine.

'I didn't even have time to try them out.'

'And how did you come to buy them?'

'I swapped them for a pair of Italian moccasins.'

'And who did you swap them with, comrade?'

'Manolín, my chess instructor,' and he pointed his nose in the direction of various boards with Capablanca endgames that he'd painted on the wall.

Colorado was a local star and played for the municipality of Cotorro. His instructor had more status: he played for the Havana provincial team, and gave classes twice a week to a small group in a club in Vedado.

'And how come Manolín swapped the shoes?'

'Apparently, they were on the tight side; and I had some size forty-four moccasins that were too big…I always had to stuff a rag in them to wear them. And as the twenty-sixth of July is a holiday and I wasn't working, Manolín called me early in the morning to see if I was at home. And he was here in a jiffy suggesting I swapped them for the *florichéin*. I tried them on, they fitted and I accepted the deal.'

'You have any idea how he got them?'

'Not at all, Captain, but he's an honest man…'

'Of course he is…Do you know where he lives?'

'More or less; but I always call him at the watch-shop where he works. Is there some problem with those shoes?'

'Yes, there might be.'

Bastidas looked at the time: ten past one.

'Do you think he'll be at work now?'

'Well, I imagine…'

Manolín had left work early in order to finish a job in a customer's home. Bastidas found him in the chess club at four.

'My mum gave them to me.'

'Your mum?' asked Bastidas, surprised.

'Yes, my mum…and she got them as a present from a hooker.'

Half an hour later, in her own home, Josefina Albarracín, or Fefita, a maid working at the Triton Hotel, confirmed her son's statement: 'Yes, comrade, I got them from a…how should I put it?…a young woman, one who escorts tourists…'

'A hooker, Mum,' rasped Manolín.

'Well, if you like…the thing is, Captain, I don't like to speak ill of folks, and less so if they've done me a favour, but…yes, it's true, that's how she looked…'

'And how come she gave you them as a present?'

'She told me they gave her nightmares…she worries about such things and persuaded the gentleman she was going with to throw them out. And as I don't believe in any of that nonsense…'

'And do you remember the girl's name?'

'She told me at the time, but I can't remember it now. Do you want me to find out for you?'

'If it's at all possible…'

The woman stayed silent for a few moments and then looked at Bastidas: 'Look, Captain, you've got to be very careful with the business of presents you get from tourists, because they're very strict in that hotel. And when the girl gave me the shoes I told her that I was going to hand them to the management. And she came back at me: "Come on, love, don't be silly, if you like the shoes, keep them. And if you get any complaints, go and see Pepe Jaén who works for the management, and he's a real close buddy of mine. You just go and tell him that So-and-so gave them to you as a present, and if they're suspicious tell him to call me and I'll give it him straight."'

'Wait a minute,' Pedrito interrupted her, and turned the cassette over.

Bastidas squashed an impulse to bark at him – he was so keen to record everything that he'd interrupt folk and they'd lose their flow.

'And what can you tell me about the man whom she was escorting?'

Fefita wrinkled her brow as if to make an intellectual effort. 'I can only recall an older man…'

'How much older?'

'Fifty-plus.'

'Do you remember his nationality?'

'No. I only saw him a couple of times and didn't hear him speak, but from his clothes and looks I'd say he was a foreigner. I just remember he was tall and well built…'

'Could you remember his features so we could make a photofit picture?'

'No, I couldn't at all, I always saw him from a distance. What I do remember is that he wore a little white goatee beard and very long hair that was white as well. They stayed in room three hundred and twenty-two. I haven't forgotten that because I see to the third floor.'

Bastidas and Pedrito exchanged hopeful looks.

'And when was that?'

'Now that's difficult, it's a few days ago…'

'It was July twenty-fifth, Mum,' interjected Manolín. 'Remember how it was the twenty-sixth the next day and I used the holiday to go to Cotorro and take them to Colorado?'

'You're right, you know,' concurred Fefita.

Bastidas jotted a note down and, before saying goodbye, looked at his watch. It was 17.20.

'One last favour,' he asked Fefita. 'Please call the hotel and if Comrade Jaén is there, ask him what the girl's name is…'

Fefita got up, took a few steps and was about to dial when Bastidas warned: 'Call on your own behalf, don't mention me…'

Fefta nodded, dialled the number and stood there waiting.

'Norma? Josefina here, the third-floor maid…. Yes, dear, I'm fine, how about you? I just wanted to speak to Pepe Jaén. Thanks, Norma.'

Fefita covered the mouthpiece and whispered to Bastidas: 'Yes, she says he's in his office,' and then: 'Hallo. Yes, comrade, Fefita here, I'm sorry if I've dragged you…It's just I'm trying to locate a friend of yours who sometimes comes to the hotel… Yes, she's a tall, slim mulatta, who does her hair in a ponytail and plait, like a dancer...It's just she said you were a friend of hers...What? No, she told me another, shorter name...What? Uh-huh, Bini, yes, that's the name she said, but I just couldn't remember...'

Just then Fefita saw Bastidas pass her a piece of paper on which he'd written: 'Ask him for her address.'

'And do you know where she lives...? Uh-huh...uh-huh...'

Bastidas stood waiting, pen at the ready to write down the address, but she shook her head. Then he grabbed the phone.

'Good evening, comrade,' said Bastidas. 'This is Captain Ignacio Bastidas, from the Ministry of the Interior...'

Jaén refused to see Bastidas in the hotel at 18.30. He alleged he already had a meeting at that time. And suggested seeing him at eight.

'Fine, thank you, I'll come to the hotel at eight.'

As soon as Bastidas hung up, Jaén called Chacha, Bini's cousin. She must track her down right away.

That policeman had him worried. Not for his own sake, but for Bini's. He must do everything to warn her the police were after her. But after calling ten times he angrily slammed down the receiver. Calling a 40 number was one big pain. You only had to dial a four and the line would go dead on you.

He decided to use the direct method. He went into the hotel car park, leapt on his motorbike and twenty-five minutes later was parking in a street in Víbora.

Chacha told him Bini was with a friend in Pinar del Río.

'They left on Friday morning and said they won't get back till Sunday night.'

'You don't know which part they went to? Pinar is a big area...'

'She fancied horse riding and they went to Soroa or Viñales.'

'Didn't they tell you which hotel they'd stay in? What's the guy's name?'

'Hey, kid…what's the problem? You're not her husband to come asking so many questions.'

'Help me find her, Chacha, it's really urgent…'

'If you won't tell me what it's about…'

'I shouldn't tell you but I will…we must warn her the police are asking after her…'

'Ay, Pepe, has she got herself into another mess?'

Jaén managed to find out that her companion for the moment was Aldo Bianchi, a loaded Argentine, who must be putting her up in the best hotels.

'You know the lifestyle my cousin's fond of.'

From the conversation with Fefita, Bastidas had a clear picture of Bini as a mulatta with a good head of hair, styled like a cabaret dancer's, tall, slim, vivacious, slim waisted, pretty, a pert little bum, a good bust, very chatty and jokey. Fefita remembered she had a gravelly voice and tended to shout when she spoke.

On their way to the Triton, Bastidas and Pedrito mulled over what they'd found out: 'I don't get why they knocked a cyclist over in an old Soviet car…No foreigner ever drives in that scrap metal…even less so if it's stolen goods.'

'And I don't get why a hooker is going around giving thousand-dollar shoes away as presents, just because a spirit appears in her sleep and tells her to chuck them…'

'She has no reason to know how much they cost, Pedro; but he must…'

'He's probably a believer as well, Captain.'

'Right you are…'

And Bastidas pursued a monologue, on subjects worthy of Ripley* that happen in Cuba, where after forty years of

---

* Ripley was an American cartoonist, whose comic strip, 'Believe It or Not!', featuring strange, unexpected events, was syndicated to newspapers worldwide, including the Cuban daily *El Mundo*.

considerable cultural advancement, there are people who not only adore Afro-Cuban deities but catechize foreigners, and get them to spend fortunes on *santería* rites.

'Your gut's rumbling.'

Hungry and exhausted, not far from the Triton, Bastidas parked the car opposite a stall where they were selling home-made pizza and ham and cheese sandwiches.

'You get out, kid,' Bastidas told Pedrito, handing him a fifty-peso bill. 'Get yourself whatever you fancy and bring me a pizza and a cola.'

It was starting to drizzle. Several people were huddled under a zinc roof waiting to be served.

Bastidas reckoned Pedrito would be a few minutes and wondered whether he should allow himself a shot of rum.

What for?

Extreme exhaustion after a long day that still hadn't come to an end, and the need to be clear-headed in order to question that Jaén.

Honest?

Honest?

OK.

He opened his case and took out a canteen and a glass, which he filled to the brim. And he visited it once, without taking a breath, his Adam's apple gently rising and falling, as he tossed down the full throat-burning measure.

When Bastidas drank to overcome exhaustion, he always did it Russian style. According to him, there was no marijuana, no cocaine, nothing that could raise your spirits like a full measure of rum downed *da kantsá* (in one go).

People not in training had to learn to control their breathing, to drink with relaxed muscles. If you had a healthy stomach, the body quickly reacted to the impact. And ecstasy was immediate: when the liquid reached the bottom of the stomach, one levitated blissfully.

Bastidas returned the glass and the bottle to his case and leaned his head back.

His neck began to dissolve on the heated seat plastic, now smelling sweetly of soft chamois leather. Millions of bubbles, bearers of euphoria, burst in his veins. His revitalized blood now buzzed round his body.

A pity it lasted only a few seconds.

If God existed and was, as they said, so merciful, Bastidas would beg him for three hours a day of that buzz. And he'd be the person most blessed in the universe.

When he looked in the direction of the pavement, he saw that two people were in front of Pedrito in the queue.

Now the ineffable buzz had gone, Bastidas let the gastric heat produced by the rum rise to his chest. And as usual, when it reached his throat, he repressed his desire to jump and roar like a bull on the taiga.

He smiled. His brain now rushed round in refreshed circles, teemed with dancing neurones and welcomed the vapours rising up from his throat.

That's right, they flew straight from throat to brain, according to the anatomy of euphoria.

He closed his eyes and breathed in deeply.

When he opened them again, he was at peace with himself and the world.

Ready to go.

Now he was serene and full of energy, a man of optimism. And would be for the next fifty minutes. That was how long the rum effect lasted. And in fifty minutes his working day would be over and he'd go to bed.

Twenty years earlier, as a member of the secret police, Bastidas had formed part of a Cuban trade mission to Moscow, where every afternoon he would go to a gym club and practise karate. A Russian doctor went to the same Muscovite club, at the same time of day: in his sixties, strong and well built, a second dan, who moved with incredible energy and litheness for his age.

And that Russian, who turned out to be a professor of nutrition, told him once that if someone was capable of downing every day a single full-measure glass of vodka, rum, etc., *da kantsá*, it would do his intellectual and cardio-vascular activities no end of good. But whoever did so ran the risk of yielding to the euphoria the draught provoked, similar to the effect of cocaine or other hard drugs. The wonderful impact of the first glass called for a second and a third...

'That's why we have so many chronic alcoholics in the USSR.'

Bastidas proved the doctor wasn't lying. He so took to this drinking habit that he became a horrific sponge for two years: a piece of almost human detritus.

According to the mother of his children, that Russian doctor was Satan, who'd infiltrated the USSR.

Pepe Jaén welcomed him into his office at the Triton at eight. He looked to be around twenty-seven. He was a handsome mulatto wearing an elegant red-and-white striped shirt. He welcomed them without the usual anxiety or feigned relaxed manner the police officers were used to. He described Bini in the same terms as Fefita, and said he'd known her from secondary school where they'd been friends.

'Did you know she was whoring?'

'Yes, of course, I've seen her with guys; sometimes she even introduces them to me...'

Bastidas was surprised by the casual manner in which a hotel employee spoke of his relationship with a hooker. He showered her in praise: a loyal, sincere, helpful, generous sort. He regretted she'd been put inside because of a brawl in the street.

'She did a year and a bit.'

According to Pepe Jaén, it was also regrettable she'd taken the path of prostitution, because she was a generous person, but such was life...

The mulatto seemed to be telling the truth. Bastidas was highly impressed by the fact he wasn't afraid to disclose his solidarity with a hooker. The shit from that fan can always hit a hotel employee. But when Jaén embarked on a dangerous digression about the Special Period, his difficulties, young people going off the rails, destiny, life, and so on, Bastidas cut him short: 'Now you must tell us who occupied room three hundred and twenty-two in the last ten days of July.

'Of course, straight away,' Jaén replied. 'What details do you need?'

'Just names and nationalities.'

Jaén repeated the request down the line to a woman in reception.

While he was waiting for the information, Bastidas copied down the little map Jaén did for him showing where a cousin of Bini's lived in Víbora. It was a difficult place to get to, down a street Jaén knew how to locate, though its name escaped him. It was where Bini lived for most of the year when she wasn't entertaining a client.

The print-out mentioned only five names of people who'd occupied room 322:

> July 18/23: Luis Silva Pla and Marta Ruiz Soto, Spaniards.
> July 24/26: Alberto Ríos, Argentinian.
> July 27/31: Ingrid and Gissbert Punkenberg, Germans.

It was pitch dark at 21.15 when they entered Immigration. A young lieutenant who said she was working till late agreed to wait for them. She also told them that the Spaniards Luis Silva and Marta Ruiz, as well as the Punkenberg couple, left the country in early August on Iberia and AOM flights. Alberto Ríos, on the other hand, had been residing in Cuba for almost a year.

Bastidas wanted to see a photocopy of the Argentine's passport.

As soon as he got his hands on it he smiled and handed it to Pedrito.

The photo showed a good-looking, sprightly old man, with a beard and long white hair.

Bastidas requested a photocopy of Alberto's file and as soon as the lieutenant brought it he started underlining what was of most interest:

Argentine passport no. 3,675,165...
Place of birth: Corral Quemado, province of Tucumán
Date of birth: 12 June 1944
Entry into Cuba: 2 June 1998
Resident from: 18 June 1998
Migrant status: Temporary resident
Occupation: Investor and director of Texinal
Residence in Cuba: Calle 206, no. 20674, Atabey, C.
    Havana
Home telephone: 24-4576
Office telephone: 24-5671

At 21.40, Alberto Ríos had just had dinner at home and was getting ready to watch a film on video when the telephone rang.

'Hello?'

'Señor Alberto?'

It was a female, rather bellowing voice.

'That's me. Who are you?'

'I'm Anita, I'm a friend of Bini's.'

'Oh, how do you do, what's happened to that ungrateful bitch who's never rung me back?'

'The fact is...'

And the line went dead.

Alberto tapped the telephone receiver and then hung up. She'd call back...

'Another of Bini's little whoring friends.'

And he decided not to switch on the video till the girl called back.

At the other end of the line, the blonde with the rank of lieutenant looked at Bastidas knowingly. 'Yes, Captain, he knows Bini.'

'What did he say?

'That she was ungrateful because she never called him back.'

At 22.20, while his wife was practising a sonata, Bastidas was spooning down a chickpea stew, confident that Alberto Ríos was the owner of the Florsheims worn by individual A on 18 July. It was very likely that A and Alberto were one and the same. He now just needed to know whether the B footprints matched Bini's feet.

He smiled at the coincidence that A and B might be Alberto and Bini. And at the same time, he thought how absurd it was that a foreigner as well heeled as Alberto Ríos should be travelling in an old, battered car that had been stolen in the outlying area of Calvario.

# Part III

# 7 the hairy hand

When he woke up, he caught her sucking a finger.

He found it very arousing and pretended to be asleep for a while, in order to spy on her.

Bini had put the whole of her right thumb in her mouth and was sucking energetically while watching telly.

Naked, sitting on the bed in front of Aldo, she kept her legs crossed, like a yogi.

His eyes half closed, Aldo was driven ecstatic by the motion of her lips, swelling out and puckering. *Madre mía!* The almost spherical shape of that big dark mouth round her straightened thumb produced his first erection of the day. What got him going most were the two dimples the rhythm of the sucking formed in both her cheeks. And her eyes lengthened slightly, giving her an oriental look.

On Aldo's various trips to Cuba, Bini had never presented him with such a childlike, lascivious, beautiful vision.

Suddenly she spotted him spying on her and blushed. She giggled and hid her thumb between her bare legs.

But he said no, no, carry on sucking.

'If you like it, it does things for me as well. Take a look.'

And he uncovered himself to show the effect.

She gripped him with her left hand, but he asked her to do it with the other, the one with a thumb that was still red and wet.

And she started explaining how she came from a family of finger-suckers.

'When he got into bed, my cousin Pedro used to suck his two middle fingers and he'd pull hairs out from down here with his other hand, and give you a grim, ugly look as if he were scolding you.'

Aldo looked at her incredulously.

And Chacha also used to thumb-suck, but she was filthy and never washed it.

'And as she sucks it, she raises her eyelashes with her little finger; like this.'

And when he saw her twist her hand to imitate Chacha, Aldo guffawed.

'On the other hand, Lulo sucks his little finger and scratches an ear with his two big fingers till it gets red and sore...'

And Bini stood up, imitating her finger-sucking relatives, and Aldo ran to the bathroom so as not to piss himself, and when he got back, she was leaning on the bed, stroking herself while he titfeasted.

And then she leapt on and bit him on a shoulder.

Oh, Aldo's cologne drove her crazy.

And she was at it again, biting Pepito's lips like crazy, sucking them, and he, fucking hell, coiling back like a spring, tee-hee-hee, a young lad, and easing himself up on the pillows to see how she was kissing him, she, with his cocketycock between her hands, bang bang, like a sharpshooter, and now kneeling on the floor, and aiming at the window and ceiling, aiming at him, bang bang bang, you're dead, kid, and him opening his arms and falling backwards, and her bang bang in a round of fire, starting to shoot at every corner of the room, full of enemies, and now, balancing the pistol on her tongue, she shoots herself with a final shot and drops dead, stiff, face up, and he goes on with the game, throws himself on the floor, and she checking it's still hard as rock, who'd have thought it, and sitting up, wanting her to perch on him again, but she gets on her knees, crouches down, turns into a lickle rabbit, and flaps her ears at him and pouts her lips to show him her snout and sharp little teeth, and kneels on a cushion on the ground, so he can slip in the rabbit from the rear, and him panting, *ay dios mío*, what is this, my Lord, and then resting and laughing again, and hugging her round the waist, and lifting her whole body up, twisting her round, shouting like a little boy.

And sunbathing on the terrace, and not letting him drink his whisky, and he complaining, and she upsetting him, sticking her finger between his lips, she wanting to drink first and give it to him mouth to mouth, and suddenly, *ay*, you scratched me, look at those long nails of yours, and she, taking her bag, getting out small scissors, a file, nail-cutters, obliging him to let her do his feet, and he refusing, it's tickling me, she naturally carrying on for she was an expert, for fuck's sake, you won't believe it but I'm a chiropodist, I did a course, got a diploma, the works, cutting his cuticles, and filing his nails, while she told him about her cousin Chacha's husband breeding rabbits, and one day after a row with her mum she went to live at Chacha's, and suffered so to see the little rabbits shut in a cage, and when they told her they were going to kill one for Sunday lunch, she couldn't sleep she was so sad, and just imagine, I opened the cage and all the rabbits escaped, and my cousin's husband wanted to kill me, me, yes, kill me, kill me, and I put a knife in his hands, but I knew the bastard wouldn't hurt me, and Aldo wanting to know everything, and where did I live at the time, and she saying she didn't live with her mother no more because she was very strict and was a pain, and always rowed, she could never do anything right; and then she went to Grandma's, Chacha's, or to other relatives' or friends' houses.

'And what about your dad?'

'I adore him, and we get on really well, but we hardly ever see each other. He's on his fourth marriage and has a pile of children, but earns very little.'

And when Bini started whoring with foreigners she did it to get dollars and buy her own clothes, her sports shoes – in a word, to get her independence.

'No, I was born in Havana. My family come from Oriente.'

Her grandfather was a poor peasant, who rebelled with Fidel in the Sierra, and after the victory, the whole family came to live in Havana.

'All very revolutionary, 'cept my mum. Dad went off to fight in Angola and Ethiopia, but Mam never liked the Revolution. An' is very strict and kept me on the straight and narrow, my daddy couldn't stand her any more 'cause she argued an' liked Miami an' he went off to live with an army captain.'

Her mother then lived with a succession of guys, each more brutish and more of an asshole than the one before, but she deserved them because she was as bad.

Bini never got on with her. When she was little, her mother was always threatening her and frightening her, and went into a rage if she cried.

'An' was a right bastard, 'cos when I were three or four Mam cooked something up with my Aunt Celia, who lived next door, an' the two made a glove with long, black hairs, which they got from a pig, an' told me it was the hairy hand that came to take off cry-baby girls.'

And when Bini started to cry, they put her out in the yard, and Aunt Celia would walk the hairy hand across the top of the dividing wall of the other house and let out horrible screams.

'I shat myself I was so scared, but I never cried.'

And if it wasn't the hairy hand, they frightened her with the dead and with ghosts and the headless horseman, and the mourning lady, and a series of scares they believed in, and which they swore appeared to them in the Sierra Maestra every night; and because of what they did when she was a kid, Bini never forgave her mum or her aunts, and to avoid living with them, she spent year after year in government-paid hostels.

'An' they put me inside because I helped a girlfriend of mine.'

She got three years but did only fourteen months. But she wanted to forget that now, and all her woes; she blamed her mum and her stupid aunts, but she worshipped her dad, and he her, and he even forgave her for whoring...He was so understanding...

# 8 worst luck

Pepito was one Bini's great admirers. Unconditionally loyal ever since she gave him a helping hand years ago, at secondary school.

Like many young people of her generation, Bini identified the good and bad sides of the Cuban revolution with the defects and virtues of the teachers, education administrators and even her own companions, leaders of the Federation for Secondary School Students that luck sent her way; and she was very unlucky.

That child, daughter and granddaughter of rebels, who learned to love Martí and Fidel as a kid; who every 28 October cast flowers on the sea, to honour Camilo Cienfuegos; and who in her young pioneer's uniform would swear every morning before the flag of the fatherland 'We will be like Che', turned into a demoralized adolescent, a couldn't-care-less adult, into a main chancer, ready for jail and whoredom.

In first year she had a young teacher who threatened and mistreated the children. To get her on their side, mothers had to give her little presents; soap, talcum, underwear, a bag of coffee, chocolates…

The bitch and a half loved coconut sauce, and Bini's mother made it real good. But Bini, at the age of six, got on the wrong side of her schoolmistress. When she saw her get in a rage and pinch the girl who sat next to her, Bini intervened. She bit her hand hard. And even drew blood.

When the headmaster chided her, Bini said the teacher wasn't like Camilo and Che. She lied to her pupils. She pinched them.

It was a serious accusation, and if proved would have meant the teacher's expulsion from the national education system; but Bini was unlucky with her headmaster, a gallant cock just twenty-five years old, who was making eyes at the teacher, though to no avail. And the pedigree stud saw that episode as an opportunity to further his urges with his inferior, a highly edible item.

When he'd managed to lay her for lunch, he called up Bini's mother and advised her to switch to another school. Really, Bini required a special regime; she was very conflictive, etc.

Bini's mother, on the other hand, never inflicted anything on anyone, outside her home and marriage. As good as gold. And after the drama over Bini, she calculated she'd need mountains of coconut sauce to pacify the pinching mistress; so she switched her to another school.

By the age of fourteen, Bini had already been kicked out of two other primary schools and finally out of one secondary school.

Pepito was handsome and the best dancer in the secondary school. The girls were crazy about him, including the president of the Student Federation, a big-nosed fatty, who became infatuated with him.

With very little likelihood of attracting him physically, Fatty tried to have him always on hand. She sent him on errands, and

Pepito went along with her for a time; but when he saw how Fatty got more and more lovey-dovey with him, he started to cut loose.

On one occasion, Fatty summoned him to a cubicle where the Fed. was meeting. She engineered it so she was alone with him, locked the door and started to touch him and arouse him and strip off in front of him. And Pepito would have rubbed her off to be done with her, but Fatty's breath always smelled so bad, and that day it was awful, girl, as if she'd swallowed a rotten corpse.

Pepito saw he wasn't going to make lift-off and tried to dissuade her, but Fatty fell on him, wanted to slaver all over him, and he finally pushed her over and made a run for it. She put on a show of wailing and howling. When the others came running she was shedding big tears and stared at her comrades, terror-stricken: 'Pepito tried to rape me.'

The school staff couldn't believe their ears. Pepito was a very polite, gentlemanly pupil. But the next day, Fatty's mother, another fat blonde, came stamping high-heeled down the corridor in her Ministry of the Interior strip, a personal appearance to demand that the degenerate who tried to rape her daughter be expelled.

Bad luck had it in for Bini. Her Fed. Pres., who should have been an example and a beacon to her comrades, turned out to be a total harpy as well as the mediocre, opportunist fart they all knew, and Fatty's mother was a fool blinded by maternal love, unable to realize that a handsome, easygoing lad like Pepito had no need to go around raping squinty eyesores like her daughter.

The fact is that Fatty set up a big intrigue in order to kick Pepito out of the school. When his teachers questioned him, he just said it hadn't happened like that. But it was his word against the word of the Fed. Pres. For her part, the headmistress began to be discreetly leaned on by the Ministry of Education, where Fatty's parents kicked up a fuss. The headmistress sympathized with Pepito and detested and feared Fatty at the same time. And she suggested the students themselves should consider the case in a sovereign assembly, and take a decision she would then accept.

Confident that her influence and power would intimidate the student body, Fatty accepted the idea of an assembly, and got two followers to testify to Pepito's other misdeeds.

One pupil asked to speak in order to argue timidly that Pepito was a good, polite, well-disciplined, hard-working student; and he couldn't accept that he'd done something so objectionable. Another flourished subjective opinions that contributed nothing to Pepito's cause.

Halfway through the assembly, the headmistress and four other teachers, who attended as observers, predicted that, when it came to a vote, Fatty would get a majority to expel Pepito.

Suddenly, as the headmistress was speaking, Bini got up to interject: 'But, just take a good long look, Headmistress; first at Pepito and then at this fat lump…'

There was a ripple of repressed guffaws…

'Sit down!' ordered a teacher.

Bini was frightened and felt like pissing herself, as if she'd seen the hairy hand, but her rage got the better of her and she ignored the order. 'Come off it, Teach'! You gonna tell me this handsome lad fell on this fatso? Take a good look, Teach', you as well, look at the fat-ass…'

The warning shouts, calls to order, for respect, for a language of moderation, were of no avail in silencing the chorus of uproarious laughter, or Bini's honking voice, now on a roll: 'Just take one good look at him, take one good look…'

'She was the one who tried to rape me,' Pepito dared shout as cries of support went up.

In the midst of the tumult and hoo-ha, Fatty realized that Bini had turned the assembly round, and that she'd now lose any vote. She opted to pretend she was outraged, burst into tears and withdrew from the meeting, which was finally suspended. No vote was taken that afternoon.

But Fatty had had the assembly recorded, and the next day her parents attached the cassette to the complaint they presented to the Legal Department of the Ministry of Education.

Bini was the one expelled. It was recommended she be transferred to a special school.

She didn't want to go to any more schools; but at the time she had nowhere else to go: she'd broken definitively with her mother, and her father was living with an odious woman in Grandma's house. She took shelter at her cousin Chacha's, at the time packed with relatives from Oriente. Bini had to sleep on the floor, in a corner, and food was in short supply. In order not to suffer more hostility from the rulers of the roost, she was persuaded by her father to go on studying.

Pepe Jaén went to see her in her new school, and rested a fraternal forehead on her shoulder. She gave him a big hug.

'I'll do anything you want,' he stammered in her ear, whispering conspiratorially. 'From now on you are more than my sister. You can rely on me for ever,' and he kissed his crossed fingers; 'I swear by my dead mother.'

Bini cried; and felt life wasn't all shit; and that friendship was the noblest of sentiments. And to ensure she kept him as a friend, from that day on she decided not to desire Pepito as a lover ever again.

He stayed in the same school to final grade and after a few years got a degree in economics. He maintained an unwavering feeling of gratitude towards Bini. He never failed her as a friend. Although he pretended to tolerate her whoring, he suffered for her sake, and harboured secret dreams of redeeming her one day.

When Bini was interned in the 'Nut House' she was just sweet sixteen.

The Nut House is the Havana Psychiatric Hospital.

The Carlos J. Finlay Special School didn't really deserve the nickname the girls themselves gave it.

As a centre for the rehabilitation of adolescents with behavioural difficulties, it was a model for Latin America. Naturally, there would be aggressive situations between very difficult youngsters, but the Nut House was never a madhouse for children or a prison den to turn offbeat girls into hated delinquents, or prostitutes or drug addicts, like all other similar spots on the continent.

But Bini's bad luck continued in the Nut House. She got on the wrong side of Bleacher, the eponymous leader of an inside gang.

Fortunately, the Bleachers weren't lodged in the same wing as Bini; but, under strict supervision, they shared the same yard and ate together in the refectory.

Her dormitory companions warned her to be extremely careful when in the yard. To keep her wits about her when they walked near the Bleach. Never get distracted or move far from the monitors. In the refectory, she'd run no danger if she sat well away from them.

Bini took no notice and was soon in a confrontation with Bleacher herself, who wanted to turf her off a low wall where she was sitting and watching people play volleyball. Bleacher claimed it was her place and nobody else could sit there. Bini gave her a mighty push and a scuffle started which didn't escalate thanks to the monitors' immediate intervention.

Shortly after, Bini couldn't down her pea soup, which tasted slightly burnt. She was famished. She grabbed the roll she'd been served and took a big bite. She suddenly felt something hard and then realized that it had been half cut open.

When she opened it, ugh!!!, she'd bitten a cockroach!

She saw two other dead roaches inside.

Bini choked down the sick and her desire to blubber. Her disgust provoked slight breathing difficulties. She got goose pimples. She felt her bones setting and her body go stiff, and she couldn't bend. Then a pain surged in her solar plexus and paralysed her breathing for a few moments. What usually happened when she had a panic attack...

Suddenly, a shout went up and Bini was charging at the meal trolley, at a titchy blonde who was taking the rolls round. She was a Bleach and helped the sergeant in charge of serving out food. She weighed barely fifty kilos. Before any monitor could react, one hand was wrapped round her neck, while Bini's other went between her legs. And electrically powered by fear and hysteria, Bini hoisted her shoulder high and dipped her head into the pan of peas.

The girl's face was disfigured for life and Bini spent six months in a reformatory for minors. She never set foot in another classroom.

When she left reform school, a brother of Mireya, the scorched blonde, tried to stab her, but Bini escaped miraculously. Her father, who was working in Oriente at the time, took her with him, and Bini lived in Baracoa for two years. There she married a young lad her own age. Within a fortnight they'd had their first fisticuffs and in three months the marriage was over.

Bini soon became infatuated with a fifty-plus witch-doctor and went to live with him. She went all religious. But he was bossy and a drunkard and they also ended up fighting.

Finally, when her father was moved back to Havana and started living with his unbearable wife again, Bini started spending periods with her cousin Chacha and periods with her grandma, according to the ups and downs of the family thermometer.

By the age of nineteen, she had begun whoring very unprofessionally and behind her father's back; he was a tolerant, ingenuous guy, who still thought of her as a baby, and loved her remorsefully because he'd abandoned her when she was five years old.

He regretted that his daughter had paid the high price of eight years without a father, so he could go fighting apartheid and the CIA in Africa; though sometimes his guilty conscience reminded him that his move to the front as an internationalist soldier was largely an evasion; he was frightened of himself; one of those days he would shoot Bini's politically treacherous mother between the eyes for being such a domestic pain in the arse. She was constantly shouting and squabbling, reducing him to a sullen silence; or she exhausted him and he gave in out of exhaustion; or he got all heated and was forced to walk out, slamming the door behind him, only to lose himself in alcohol and the plotting of his revenge.

The person who most hated Bini, even more than Fatso Carmita and Blonde Mireya, was Rosa de la Caridad Menéndez y Padrón, alias Shake It Rosy.

On her father's side, Rosy was the daughter and granddaughter of Asturian communists. She owed her names to Rosa Luxembourg and the Virgen de la Caridad del Cobre, whom her mother, a black from Contramaestre, worshipped.

Born like Bini in 1972, she never knew her father, who died that same year in a border skirmish, when he was splayed with bullets during a raid by an armed launch from Miami. Nor could she remember her mother, who died in '77 from leukaemia.

In fact, Rosy was legally registered but her parents never made it to any altar. The fruit of ephemeral love and disturbed times, she was brought up by her black family in a house in Santiago de Cuba. By the age of eleven, she already had a fine body. And her precocious gifts as a dancer earned her the nickname of Shake It Rosy.

Too much, some women thought.

'Let she move it: it be hers to swing, cha,' chorused the drunks, entranced by her bum in action.

By thirteen, she was a rotund beauty, gypsy-like, with a manly voice, vivacious, haughty, and one metre seventy tall. By thirteen, she was also the unchallenged captain of indiscipline in her secondary school.

The others, both males and females, were scared of her. Shake It didn't hesitate before she bullied or beat up anyone who didn't carry out her orders.

She was expelled from that school, where she'd terrorized the student body for almost two years, because she slashed the face of a boy who mistreated one of her followers.

She made it to fifteen in Havana, where a local pimp taught her how to whore, and taught her minimal techniques for dealing with foreign tourists. But she soon got into the scene, rented her own room, made friends in bars and hotels and had a big public fall-out with the pimp, and secretly threatened to pay someone to kill him if he continued fucking her up. She was earning enough money to hire a killer.

But he was a stubborn pimp, and she got him punctured three times in the belly.

She was also going to kill Bini.

Klaus Werner, a very rich German who visited Cuba on business, after professing lots of love for Shake It, wanted to take her to Stuttgart, to buy her a flat and put her in charge of a school for tropical dancing. Shake It built up great hopes. But on his last trip, Klaus hadn't rung her and started going out with Rita, a gorgeous chorus girl and friend of Bini, who at the time was dancing in a cabaret in Guanabacoa.

As soon as Shake It found out, she went after her in Guanabacoa, accompanied by two women and a man.

Rita was ready to start her show, dressed in her rumba outfit, in a little bar next to the dressing rooms.

Shake It introduced herself as one of Rita the chorus girl's friends and they pointed her up some narrow spiral stairs, so she could climb up to see her.

She decided to go up alone. In fact she didn't need help from anyone. The others weren't accompanying her as an escort, but as witnesses to the exemplary lesson Rita was about to be given.

Yes, all the whores in Havana should know what to expect, if they got involved with Shake It Rosy's clientele.

When she reached the bar landing, she saw that three tables were occupied. She went over to the nearest, where two girls were chatting, one dressed for rumba.

'Where can I find Rita?'

'That's me,' replied the rumba dancer.

Without a by-your-leave, Shake It pulled over a chair from another table, sat down next to Rita, opened her bag and took out a knife.

'Don't you know who I am, you fucking bitch?'

Rita and Bini looked at her, terrified.

Knife in hand, Rosy brought her chair right up close and rested the knife-point on Rita's naked navel, underneath the table.

'If you don't want me to put the knife in and scrape the lips of your pussy, so you'll never hump again, just get down them stairs and into the street with me, and explain what the hell you're up to with Klaus Werner...'

Shake It got up, so in command of the situation she even put the knife back in her pocket. Rita also got up, stunned by fear, both hands clasped over her belly. She was trembling and crying.

When Bini saw her obey and head downstairs in front of the other woman, she saw red and grabbed the vile bitch's ponytail from behind and wrapped it round her wrist.

Then she pushed and kneed her downstairs. Her firm grip on Shake It's hair stopped her from turning round and defending herself, though she was taller and stronger.

Between the three of them, Rita leading the way, weeping and bellowing, Shake It in the middle, her hair being pulled and getting pummelled, and Bini shouting insults, slut, queer, who the fuck do you think you are to come and mistreat my friend, they created such a kerfuffle that the music stopped and the customers all stood up.

Bini kneed Shake It in the back and pounded her neck right down the thirty steps. And it was impossible to stop the fight from in front, because nobody else could fit on the narrow staircase. The people upstairs, a waiter and a few artistes, saw that their colleague was being well defended, and leaned on the bar and enjoyed the fight.

Immobilized by the double grip on her ponytail, Shake It could only curse, I'll kill you, I'll gouge your eyes out, and Bini was just making fun, oh oh oh, how scary, and bang bang, another knee in the back, another bite, and when they landed on the cabaret floor, Bini sunk her teeth into her skull, and fingers when Shake It tried to scratch her, and two men couldn't separate them. The bartender called a radio cop straight away.

Shake It fell face down, pretty much out for the count, with Bini astride her back. She held her ponytail with two hands and began to flatten flagstones with Shake It's nose. She shook her head like a rag doll's, and spread blood over her face, cheeks and jowls.

The waiters tugged timidly and couldn't break them up. Everybody tried to keep out of the fray and thus avoid being splattered in blood. Seeing Shake It in such a bad state, one of her friends fell on Bini's neck, but another rumba dancer shouting wildly at the ringside, kicked her off, and the woman's guy kicked in and a second colleague attacked the dancer, although two customers joined in on her side in a second scrummage.

After an attempt to grab a table leg, Shake It broke a bottle, and a piece of glass from the bottom buried itself in an eye.

When the radio patrol arrived, two policemen got Bini by the armpits and lifted her up, but she still hung on to the ponytail, and the two women fell down again and Bini bashed her on the floor again, and the police wrestled with her, and the other fight was still going on but they had no reinforcements, and now Bini was biting one of Shake It's ears and pulling, trying to take it out, dead to the feeble blows Shake It was flailing at her. Seeing that Bini was about to lop off a lobule which was hanging by a thread, a policeman got Bini by the hair, and dragged her sharply back, thus ensuring Shake It definitively lost a lobule, and the power of his movement sent the two police and the two women flying in opposite directions, helter-skelter to the other set-to, and Bini spat the lobule out at them, hey, get that bit of ear, and stick it back on tomorrow, and they knocked over another table, till finally, as entangled as a ball of snakes, they catapulted out into the garden at the entrance, to the clatter of broken glass and shattering of ornamental plants.

A bunch of onlookers followed them out, keen not to miss the finale.

Bini came out of her rage only when one of the policemen shot into the air twice.

When the police took them off separately, Rosy Shake It's ear was ripe with clotted blood and she covered a very painful eye, but let rip a string of curses, wait till I get my hands on you, you bitch, I'll pulp you.

The policemen took her to the nearest clinic, where they could do nothing. The injury to the eye was serious.

Soon the much-bruised witnesses to the exemplary lesson Shake It had planned turned up, and found her crying in pain, crushed, battered, dirty, soaked in her own blood, blood clotted on her skin, in her hair, no sight in one eye, short of a piece of one ear, bereft of honour.

She was moved as an emergency to the Pando Ferrer Eye Hospital, where she was given an emergency operation, but it was too late: the beautiful mulatta lost her right eye.

During her convalescence, Shake It Rosy spent her days bitterly plotting her revenge. Bini had trampled on her prestige, the only thing she had in life. She hated her and began to plan her death.

Until the marks from that drubbing disappeared and they fixed her up with a false eye, she didn't dare show her face in public. After three months, back on the street, she broadcast her death sentence against Bini to the whole of Havana.

But her bad luck would have it that around then they caught

the murderer of her smart-ass pimp. And the guy informed on her. He confessed he'd done the job for three hundred dollars.

After all, Rosy couldn't consummate her revenge, because she was totally broke, among other things.

They sentenced her to eight years in prison.

For her part, Lázara Sabina López Angelbello, arrested the day of the row and tried shortly after, was sentenced to three years' deprivation of freedom.

After several weeks of appeal, on 9 August 1997, she entered the New Dawn, a jail for women, where she did only fourteen months because of good behaviour.

Alberto Ríos met Bini in October '98. Rita, the chorus girl from the Guanabacoa shindig, introduced her to him.

Rita, who did her primary and secondary education at a swimming school, was an excellent diver. Her new Brazilian lover, who'd taught her to windsurf, was amazed how quickly Rita caught on. After a few weeks she was better than him.

The forty-year-old Brazilian theorized about the body control in the air that divers develop; and, clearly, considering the rhythmic gifts every dancer's feet had, Rita's aptitude was logical enough…

'And youth? Doesn't that count?'

Rita reckoned men deserved to be treated badly. That made them cling more. And that's how she acquired an illusion of autonomy.

Soon after, on a weekend in Varadero, Rita challenged another Brazilian, who was a young surfer.

They put out buoys as markers, agreed to go there and back, and the other people on the yacht placed bets.

Rita won easily. The Brazilian bathed her in champagne and gave her a hundred and fifty dollars, as a commission from his own winnings on the bets.

According to the calculations of someone timing the regatta, Rita discovered that when she went westward ho, despite the choppy sea, her board reached a speed of thirty-eight kilometres an hour.

Someone else commented that, with a south wind, at that speed, she could have disembarked in the United States in four and a half hours.

Rita proposed that when the next wind came from the south, she'd have her board and sail to hand and wouldn't stop till she hit Miami.

In time, she found out that the previous year two lads from Santa Fe had crossed the ninety miles of the Bahamas Channel before being picked up very near Key West by a US Coastguard launch.

And one day she outlined a plan to a very enthusiastic Bini.

'I'll get you to learn how to surf with my friends in the Hemingway Marina. And when you're ready, we'll wait for a south wind and off to Florida we'll go.'

From the day Alberto Ríos met Bini, he felt very attracted. But she didn't like him.

'*Ay, chica*, you've got to stick with him...'

Alberto was central to their plan. Apart from lending her a surfboard and teaching her to pilot his yacht, he let her practise driving in his car, so she could actually learn.

'What I like most about him is his driving lessons; and the fact he only humps once a day.'

'And he keeps you in bucks, and is not bad looking...'

'I don't like him; but, don't you worry, I'll go on milking him.'

'And what is it you don't like about him?'

'He's too sarcastic and sometimes I don't understand him. He's odd, like that rooster tattoo of his; but the worst thing is his tool, darlin'...'

Rita gave her an amused look.

'He's got a twenty extra-long, king size thing. He really hurts me...'

Bini wasn't such a skilled surfer as Rita and no way could handle the wretched sail. It was easier driving the yacht and car...She suddenly had a brilliant idea. One day when Rita and she were in the yacht, they could work together, give Alberto a KO, tie him up, and turn the prow northwards.

It was a deal: onward to enjoy democracy and human rights.

A foreign journalist and occasional client of Bini's was very worried by her lack of knowledge and took it upon himself to explain to her how in Cuba there was no democracy or human rights as in Europe and the United States; and proof of that she could see on television: refrigerators full of food, well-dressed people, fine houses, black and white women driving beautiful cars, and everyone with a credit card to buy whatever they wanted.

A few days later, however, Bini met Aldo Bianchi, who started to talk to her about marriage and taking her to live in Italy.

Now her plan to pirate Alberto's yacht didn't seem such a bright idea.

'Just think, Rita, if we steal a yacht, use force and get to the US of A, we'll rot in the can, if they catch us...'

And Bini knew all about being banged up.

Besides, Aldo came every month, gave her money, treated her properly...

And after Aldo's third visit, Bini eliminated Alberto. She ignored his calls and the repeated messages he sent to Chacha's.

Aldo had many good points. He was almost all good. The only bad thing was that he lived perched on top of her. He was insatiable.

And it wasn't that Bini didn't fancy Aldo.

What she didn't like was having it off every day with the same fellow, even less if he kept coming back for more, like Aldo.

She got bored. Needed to ring the changes.

And if one day she married Aldo, and went off to Italy, land of so many tasty men, she'd find it difficult not to help herself.

Bini knew she had a defect: when she had the hots for a fellow, she couldn't rest till she'd pulled him. And one day, married or single, in Rome or Havana, she'd put the horns on Aldo. What would he do, when he found out?

That would be Aldo's problem.

# Part IV

# 9 no storm clouds

The waiter, who was new to the hotel, brought him his coffee and made a couple of comments on the weather.

Alberto Ríos went on reading, and didn't say a word.

The waiter saw he was reading something on underwater life.

'That looks really interesting.'

'Go away and don't talk to me,' rasped Alberto.

The youth walked off, angry and humiliated, but what could he do? He remembered how difficult it had been to get this little number with dollar tips…He wasn't going to get the chop because of that asshole.

After his first rebuffs, nobody now tried to make friendly conversation with Alberto. And, besides, his sarcastic protests about bad service, and a couple of complaints to top management plus his hefty tips when he got treated properly, ensured that the whole staff dealt with him efficiently, quickly and fearfully. But he never said hello, thanked or smiled at anyone. He soon became the best-served but most hated customer at the Copacabana Hotel.

On the other hand, his fellow *frontón* players got the changing-mood treatment. One day he was charming, chatty and witty. He captivated them with his conversation, good humour and anecdotes, and paid for their drinks. The following day, if someone came over, Alberto froze him out: he had reading to do. It was enough for someone to get that reaction once never to dare to approach him again.

He enjoyed seeing people move silently round him, on the alert for a chance to hear him joke, suggest a game and invite them for a drink. But they feared his rebuffs and ill temper, of which he'd already given them several samples. And they soon got used to the fact that if he didn't take the initiative, better leave him alone and not talk to him.

Ever since his arrival in Cuba, and for the whole of June '98, Alberto Ríos devoted hours to reading and briefing himself on textile questions with a Uruguayan specialist. He had to avoid anyone spotting he knew sod-all about the industry. Within a couple of weeks, he'd memorized the names of the machines used in the factory, of certain techniques, and the basic trade vocabulary.

He was entranced by the white Ford the firm put at his disposal and asked whether he could have it permanently. He'd never before dared to drive around in a convertible. It would have been like putting his head on the block for his enemies.

Now cruising through Havana in a coupé stoked his enjoyment of his new freedom. The yacht arrived in the first days of June and gave wings to his limitless passion for a sea that was unrivalled in the tropics for its light, its colour, the benign temperature of its waters, its coral reefs, and the teeming variety of underwater species.

By the age of twenty Alberto Ríos was already a good yachtsman and an accomplished waterskier. He'd learned in Punta del Este, Uruguay. But it was in Punta del Este, Cuba, on the Isla de Pinos, where he developed his passion for the submarine world.

The yacht *Chevalier* was an excellent buy. It was most seaworthy, and Nene, the mechanic, jack-of-all-trades and helmsman, proved to be a real find. Alberto very quickly tested out his abilities and honesty; but to fashion him entirely to his liking, he inspected him daily and asked trick questions.

'You think I'm dishonest?'

'Don't ask idiot questions, kid,' replied an annoyed Alberto. ''Course you're dishonest...Nobody is honest; I'm not...Go on, fetch me my slippers.'

He'd be forever setting him some humiliating chore, while he stretched out on his lounger and drank, without ever inviting him.

When he was sure that Nene detested him and was starting to fear him, Alberto felt content. That was the relationship he required with his employees.

For a hundred dollars a month, Nene kept the yacht in first-class condition, acted as helmsman, and didn't dare steal a crumb.

Thanks to his good physical shape and long experience as a waterskier, Alberto learned very quickly to use a surfboard and sail. In order to learn, for the first few days he'd ordered Nene to surf around the yacht, and observed his movements. But he never received any advice or asked for any. Despite being fifty-plus, it was enough for him to imitate how it was done; as soon as he'd learned the basics, he made progress by himself.

He never gave Nene any space. To keep him hard working, honest and at the same time submissive, he preferred to pay him well. But never be nice or friendly with your employees.

In September '98, Nene got an unexpected rise. Alberto began to pay him one hundred and fifty a month; but assigned him an extra task, that of getting whores who'd come on board outside Cuban waters. The Cuban authorities wouldn't let them embark on the quayside.

\*

Alberto loved the sea, but hated sand. He couldn't bear it between his toes. Someone recommended to him the Copacabana Hotel, on the Miramar coast, with its natural salt-water swimming pool and small reef. From there bathers could dive into an open, clean, lively sea, and didn't have to step on a molecule of sand.

Alberto turned that hotel into his general headquarters. He'd go there to swim, play *frontón*, read, take aperitifs, and sometimes would stay for lunch, a siesta or to read on a lounger.

Before downing the salad the chef learned to prepare just so for him, and which was his usual lunch, he'd jump in wearing snorkel and flippers for half an hour's underwater swimming.

Life was beautiful.

His brother Tomás's advice had been spot on; now he was tirelessly insisting he should try to set up a permanent residence in Cuba.

In November '98, when Tomás came on his first visit, Alberto took him out in his yacht without Nene – to ensure no slip in their conversation revealed he was a relative and under an assumed identity.

And he took him way out to sea, to talk by themselves. In the presence of third parties they addressed each other very formally and always pretended to be engrossed in business talk.

The yacht trip was partly to boast to Tomás about the thirty degrees, and the absolutely calm sea.

'Didn't I tell you? A fantastic climate,' commented Tomás.

'And just when winter is beginning.'

'Fucking hell, Butcha'…The fact is life is a tango,' sighed Tomás. 'Who'd ever have predicted you'd feel so good here?'

'Do you know something?' Alberto smiled. 'It's not only nature. I even like the social climate.'

'Just tell me, Butcha': you goin' bananas or have the communists brainwashed you?'

'Don't be barmy, Masito, you know they can't scratch what I've got in my brain even with a wire brush. But onions is onions: there's no street violence, no drugs, no poverty like you get in other countries…'

'Fuck me! They have brainwashed you…' joked Tomás.

'They just wash my prick.'

They bantered on for a while.

Butcha' was also delighted because of the better selection of women.

'When I was in hiding, I had to accept what came. Now I'm free, I can chose them off the peg, you know?'

'Yes, you're like those old biddies who like to give what they're buying at the market a good feel.'

'And even taste before buying.'

Alberto started to speak in praise of Cuban whores.

'You won't believe this, but they're very different, very sure of themselves…'

'You ball-crusher, you, a whore is a whore is a whore…'

'You don't get me, Masito…The Castroites and all their nonsense about emancipation put love-dust in their maté, and they couldn't care less if you're the king of spades, a beachcomber or an ambassador. They give you equal treatment…And that way, they're hot cooky, and you're not next to a pile of rent-a-pussy…'

'Don't make me laugh, *che*, it never bothered you if the ass you were fucking was rented or came of its own accord…'

'Don't believe me, but I get extra crack from these girls. Some have been to university and boast about being emancipated… And I fuck them and tell them that, according to Marx, people think as they are, and that they, consequently, think like whores… Oh, and I always pay before I get my prod into them. I get them to grip the bills tight and count them, so they know I'm paying for their pussy, not their intellect, and then, when I've crash-landed them, I get more out of fucking them…'

'You bastard! You're evil! Ha ha ha…'

'Last week I had one who was in her third year of psychology, and while I fucked her she kept on about Freud…'

'Don't make me laugh so much, Butcha', I'll sick my food up…'

'…and I had to tell her: "Let Freud be and swing that butt, you fool…"'

Tomás choked on a guffaw, coughed and went on laughing… When he got his breath back he poured himself another glass.

'You've obviously got a special line to enlightened whores… Last night I had the stupidest, skinniest…Imagine how thick she was – she was amazed because I speak such good Spanish.'

'And what did you say to her?'

'That I'd taken a correspondence course…'

'You need to try some others. There are some who leave you cold with their patter. A few days ago I took home one shitty black woman I'd fished out of the sea…'

'Out of the sea? You hooked her?'

'Yes, it's a trick I invented; because they're campaigning against prostitution here, and don't let Cuban women on the yachts from the quayside. So I told Nene to get me whores who can swim and I meet them a mile from the coast…'

'That's original. And what happened with the black woman?'

'She started talking and I realized how intelligent she was. And it turned out she sings opera, jazz, boleros, whatever…She was five years at the conservatoire and now alternates art and fanny. She said it's a laugh, a nice little earner and she meets people. She holds forth on history and philosophy, and makes sense…And when I went to pay her, I showed her a hundred-dollar bill, but acted absent-mindedly and dropped it in the sea. Guess what she did?'

'Dived in?'

'Naturally, if there are dollars floating they jump in even if they can't swim.'

'Take care, Butcha', one of these days a black tart will drown on you and you'll be in the jug…'

They dined that night in El Tocororo, where Alberto reckoned they worked wonders cooking fish and shellfish.

A starfish hung on one of the walls in a pretty frame.

'Isn't that nice,' commented Tomás.

'They look like innocent little stars, but are really frightening,' explained Alberto: 'They're the big deep-water predators…'

As he said this, he looked at the starfish passionately. He could get obsessed with underwater issues. Later on, when they served up red snapper, he started on a lecture on tropical ichthyology.

Tomás was pleased at the success of his suggestion that he should hide in Cuba. He'd adapted magnificently; better than he imagined. And he even felt proud at pudding time when he heard him relate his summer trip to the Isla de Pinos.

He'd met Darío Muñoz there, a young Cuban ichthyologist and marine specialist with whom he went on a cruise in the yacht *Chevalier* to waters off Punta del Este.

'I think this trip marked me deeply.'

'How come, Butcha'?'

When he described his entry through the coral wall and passage into the reef garden, Alberto's eloquent enthusiasm made him see Technicolor.

'I went back five times, and decided to write a book.'

'No kidding, *che*. On which subject?'

Muñoz had shown him a video in which an octopus imprisons a lobster in its tentacles; and after biting it between head and neck, sucks all the white flesh out of the crustacean till its carapace is empty.

The scene made him think of the eternal laws that had guided the evolution of the world for millions of years.

'I've never mentioned it, but I've been wanting to write a book on cruelty for a long time.'

He'd tried, in an essay, to study the horrors of nature that ensure life and perpetuate the species in its biological cycle. His book would be entitled *Fruitful Cruelty*.

Perhaps, at heart, he was really a scientist.

And soon after his encounter with Muñoz, Alberto got to know other marine scientists through him, including Raquelita, a biologist who became his friend and the main adviser for his book project. They frequently sailed in the *Chevalier* and snorkelled in different places. Sometimes Muñoz would join them or other marine professionals. They all used his yacht to get research material.

On Raquelita's advice, in December Alberto bought professional cameras and equipment in order to record scenes of marine life.

In May of the following year, Tomás viewed all the material filmed by Alberto and his advisers.

'Fantastic, *che*, fucking brilliant! What are you going to do with all this?'

Muñoz suggested employing a good editor to produce a scientific short that, in his opinion, would sell well. But Alberto wasn't interested. It wasn't worth it from a business point of view, and above all, he didn't want to release information and images he preferred to keep back for his book.

The idea of writing a book about cruelty gathered strength. Already by July, particularly with the help of the providential Raquelita, he had acquired a wealth of texts and knowledge, hours of video, extraordinary photos, which enabled him to write two chapters: the first, a very strong one, in which he described mastication by carnivorous mammals as a loathsome, cruel act, even more so when executed by a human being, the most rational and subtle of them all; and a second, in which he tackled Catholic communion and other religious rites associated with the phenomenon of cannibalism. And he was now sketching out a third he would devote to insect cruelties; in particular, those spiders who immediately follow up the act of fertilization by eating the father of their children.

Tomás saw that he was serious and refrained from any irony

at the expense of his brother's scientific dabbling. He recalled his childhood experiments on cats.

Let him get on with it, if it made him happy. One man's meat...

'And what do you do at night? Take out your swimming whores?'

'Not at all.'

To avoid problems with moralistic Cuban society, Alberto tried to project an image of an orderly person, as he partly was: he had aperitifs and lunch almost always in the Copacabana; at night he dined by himself, in his house, on what his cook had prepared; and every once in a while, he invited Raquelita to a good restaurant, but rarely other women.

'And do you fuck Raquelita?'

'You're kidding. She's like a sack of potatoes...'

In her forties, probably lesbian, Raquelita lacked sex appeal, but made up for it, according to Alberto, with her vast, sophisticated knowledge of the biological world.

Apart from that, Alberto never went to cabarets or discotheques. If he were in need, he'd shut himself in at home with whores and transvestites, without any house staff to take a peek, as they always left in the evening. Nobody ever saw his bouts of drunkenness or disorderly behaviour.

His life was prospering in Cuba.

On the one hand, the company was growing and promised to become a gold mine. And thanks to Alberto Ríos's simple, clear attitudes, he lived without storm clouds on the horizon. He lived in a state of euphoria, because he'd recovered his freedom of movement and could dispense with his armed heavies.

In peaceful, unpolluted Havana, perfumed by tropical vegetation and sea breezes, he could finally lead a healthy, productive life. His book and projects enthused him. For the first time in his fifty-five years he was a man content with his life as it was.

Every day he got up at seven, and at 7.45 parked his convertible by a local public track, between Fifth Avenue and 60th Street, where he jogged four kilometres. On the days when he didn't have to go to the Texinal offices or factory, he'd go straight from the track to the Copacabana Hotel, only a few blocks away, where the parking guy had a spot reserved for him in the shade.

Twice a week, Nene would come in the *Chevalier*, and would hove to two hundred metres from the Copa. Alberto would swim over and then practise surfing or underwater fishing for a couple of hours.

He didn't jog on Saturdays, because he'd meet up with some youths he'd met at the hotel, good *frontón* players, in the gringo-Cuban mode of the Basque ball game, with an open hand. Three-walled *frontón* was essentially the same game at which Alberto had excelled as a young man, when he went to Euskal Erría, in his own country. Three decades later, under the sun of the tropics, and against young arms used to baseball, *frontón* was the most exhausting physical activity he practised in Cuba. Three doubles of thirty points, playing from the baseline, left him on his knees.

Whether he came from *frontón* or jogging, he reached the swimming-pool area dripping in sweat, and dived into the open sea, for a half-hour swim. When he got out he had a shower and changed in the booths next to the cafeteria. In sandals, shorts and loose towelling sweatshirt, he'd sit down for a second breakfast: fresh fruit and two cups of strong black coffee.

The waiter would bring his breakfast and the case he'd left in the cafeteria when he'd come in. He'd packed it with his reading materials, pens, an electronic notebook and a small cassette recorder.

Seated at the same table where he breakfasted, under a multi-coloured umbrella, he'd read and take notes till 12.30, when he went back to the sea for a quick dip. He'd follow that with a couple of aperitifs and a half-hour nap, on his lounger.

He interrupted his routine sometimes for several days, to go out diving in his yacht with Raquelita and other seafaring friends. He listened to the young scientists, gathered material for his book and became intoxicated on riddles about the void and immensity of space.

On Saturday, 12 June 1999, Alberto and his usual *frontón* partner, a seventeen-year-old, won a hotly contested third double to enter the semi-final of a tournament improvised by weekend players, who frequented the courts in Miramar.

Exhausted by those never-ending ninety points, Alberto didn't go for his usual swim. He took a dip in the sea. The sun was burning down and it was thirty-two degrees in the shade.

He was very pleased they'd won their game and invited several tournament players to have drinks at the poolside, where they put several tables together and engaged in animated conversation.

This was another of his new pleasures in Cuba. He didn't know why, but for some time he had been enjoying the company of young people and chatting about sporting trivia with whomever. Perhaps it was a little relaxation, acknowledging his recovery of freedom. Up to a few months ago, any stranger was a source of fear. He dealt only with his brother Tomás, his bodyguards, a couple of employees, his servants, and a few very trusted people. He practised sport in clubs rigorously checked out by his staff or in his fortified mansion or in houses of people he could really trust, and always under escort.

That day, after downing three mojitos, his tiredness after his day on court brought on sleep. He called the waiter and paid the bill. Someone wanted to pay for another round.

'No,' replied Alberto. 'Off you all go, because I want to sleep...'

He let down the back of his lounger, leaned his head back,

shut his eyes and put a towel over his eyes. He was asleep in two minutes and enjoyed a longer than usual siesta.

When he woke up, the others had gone. It was 14.40.

He was always cheered to find that in Cuba one could sleep like a cherub, in the public light, and completely safely.

His sleep had been so deep and angelical that he hadn't noticed when a stranger came over to his table and put five fingers in his empty glass. He then splayed them out, lifted it upside down and carried it off covered in a straw hat.

# 10 a saturday party and a sunday riddle

Could Raquelita be a lesbian?

She was certainly an odd woman.

She had several brothers and sisters and a large family, but she saw only her mother, with whom she lived. All her usual friends were former fellow students of marine biology, work colleagues or fishermen.

Alberto Ríos merited her friendship in that last category as the owner of a yacht.

But Raquelita didn't take an interest only in his yacht and its potential. She appeared to display a certain amount of affection towards him. Not long ago, she had presented him with a *majagua* hardwood carving of a barracuda, with black lacquer veneer. It was a metre twenty high and flashed a fine array of teeth in a lecherously cruel gesture.

Alberto was delighted and gave it pride of place in his living room.

Since childhood nobody had ever given him anything for his birthday. According to Raquelita, it was a gift from a sculptor friend. A refined, very expensive present; but her mum was terrified by the malign expression and didn't like seeing it in her living room every day; and Raquelita's packed little bedroom had no space to share with that strange character.

Unless it was carnal commerce, sometimes nakedly commercial, Alberto didn't do female friendship. Rather than lesbian, Raquelita seemed asexual; she was his ideal adviser; he could suck from her all he needed to know about the underwater world, like an octopus with a lobster.

Raquelita shared a skill with Alberto that he found rare in other people: she knew how to integrate knowledge from dissimilar fields. She wasn't content to juxtapose the disparate pieces, like most people.

Alberto immediately put his yacht at her disposal; and from the first day tried out all his arts of seduction. He transformed himself into the charming gentleman who could speak up for himself when he needed to; discreet, respectful and, just in case, an outright bachelor, to avoid her getting emotionally attached to him.

But it never happened.

Well, perhaps she was a lesbian. Just as well. A woman with men on her mind wouldn't have helped him so much with his opus.

Raquelita was the daughter of an idiot who'd been tortured and killed under the Batista dictatorship. And politically and philosophically she too was a hundred per cent idiotic. Fortunately, she never got into politics with him. Alberto tackled only scientific issues with her, and preferably marine biology.

As soon he started his book, he'd see her every week and go over a series of queries he'd noted while reading. Raquelita would take Alberto's sometimes superficially banal questions as a challenge to her wisdom. And when she started, it was a delight to listen to her.

At times, Alberto put her in a tight corner. One day he

wanted to know what in essence is the biological process that makes it possible to transform a habit, acquired over millennia from the need to survive, into a hereditary ability incorporated into a species' genetic code.

'I don't know,' she answered frankly.

And she'd embark on a long disquisition: if there existed an answer, it'd give him the key to understand, at least biochemically, the mysterious evolution of the species. An intelligent question which, according to her, related to enquiries into unknown processes that took place in the kernel nucleus of God the fuck knows what…Chromosomes and so forth…

Alberto understood little about biology. His real interest lay in the social behaviour of animals, but as he didn't want to come up with anti-scientific nonsense, he checked out everything before daring to put forward his personal perspectives.

Yes, Raquelita was a jerk, but she didn't fly kites and was very knowledgeable. The wisdom and information he extracted from her for his book weighed more in the balance than all the deference, time and feigned affection that Alberto dedicated to her.

Between June and July '99, Alberto sketched out the fourth chapter of his book, this time focused on birds and their unusual 'pecking order' as he denominated the basic model of social organization within a flock, where each individual is equipped to peck holes in any other bird below it in the hierarchy, without fearing any fight back, and in turn lets itself be pecked by its superiors in a most disciplined way.

Raquelita was very actively helpful and introduced him to ornithologists in the Biology Faculty and the Academy of Sciences.

From his observations of cruelty in the animal kingdom, Alberto was intending to draw valid sociological conclusions for human groups. Indeed, wasn't the right to peck, found in migratory birds, a paradigm for military discipline? Nonetheless, in order to extrapolate scientific data, he needed to seek advice from someone well versed in natural sciences, but expert in philosophy and history. Once more the providential Raquelita lent a helping hand. She promised to introduce him to Dr Pazos, a prickly character, a teacher in whose lectures one could hear flies fly, a somewhat aloof forty-year-old, a good biologist with humanist interests, and very au fait with the philosophy of science. And to set the contact up, she decided to invite them both to a party at her place on 7 August, her birthday.

Alberto arrived at 18.30, after all the other guests. They introduced him to Pazos and some ten others. He knew only Muñoz, the underwater specialist from the Isla de Pinos, and his wife.

Raquelita was decked out in an uglier, more mannish fashion than usual, in jeans and a check shirt.

The Oklahoma Strong Man, thought Alberto.

And he started to look at the women there to guess who might be Mr Raquelita's lover.

The remaining guests that afternoon were almost all under thirty. Alberto calculated he hadn't been in such a meeting with strangers, who were young to boot, for thirty years. But recently he'd relaxed on the social-mixing front. In Cuba he seemed to have got more tolerant when playing the game of being polite and showing an interest in any boring, stupid item of conversation. Although here it was an imperative, not a little game. He no longer had the choice between surviving in open society or shutting himself up in an ivory tower. He had perforce to adapt in Cuba – among other reasons, to validate his act. That was what he decided to do as soon as he landed. And as he got skilled in the gymnastics of adaptation, he began to find it tolerable, and sometimes even amusing.

On the other hand, now that he no longer needed to make a career for himself, he found it easier to be more moderate; though he regretted renouncing the pleasure he found in distancing himself from others and generating fear.

His progress in the exercise of tolerance was particularly

surprising. When he was fifty, he still abstained from parties and meetings, because he couldn't control his sarcasm or impulse to compete fiercely with the first successful cretin he bumped into. All that aggression did him harm. If he hadn't been like that, he'd have climbed to the highest reaches in…

But that was past history, pissed on and in the pot.

Another thing he learned with age was to avoid excess in the pleasures of sex and good cuisine. Now he was an old tiger, living contentedly, and saving his energies. His hedonism still included a discreet measure of violence, compliance in which he rewarded handsomely.

Life gradually became a highway without potholes, where everything rolled by at his pleasure.

'This is Alberto Ríos, my Argentine friend,' Raquelita introduced him.

'He's too elegant to be a sea-wolf,' joked one guest.

'If she told you that, she's wrong,' advised Alberto. 'I'm really a barfly, and I'm thirsty. Pour me a drink, Raquelita.'

Alberto went down well at the party.

Pazos lowered his guard from the outset, and they began a lively exchange, warmed up by a few rums.

Alberto was jovial and witty, and displayed his River Plate *bonhomie*, which in Cuba, and generally in the rest of Latin America, either appeals or goes down like a very wet blanket. Though Alberto knew from long experience that he always appealed, when he put himself out.

Raquelita's guests were all ingenuous dupes, after the manner of Darío Muñoz, almost all scientists, young intellectuals, but none with that intellectualism in relation to life's practicalities that so got to his balls, particularly among writers and artists.

Alberto drank, danced, told stories…And acted as the deferential student, all ears, when at the end Raquelita provoked an argument about plant-eating fish stocked in a reservoir.

People drank a lot and there weren't enough savouries. Mine host, who had a few lobsters, asked Alberto to cook them according to a gringo recipe, as he had done days before on his yacht.

'He does them in breadcrumbs and they're delicious,' opined Raquelita.

'Sure, but I need a syringe,' said Alberto.

A recipe he'd learned in Panama: he boiled the pieces of lobster for a few minutes, injected them at various points with a mixture of garlic, oil and lemon; then basted them in flour and eggs, and added a pinch of pepper. Once they had been fried, he let them cool slightly, and before serving them injected them again, this time with white wine.

In response to the general enthusiasm, he donned an apron, took some dollars and his car keys from his pocket, and asked someone to go and get more rum, whisky and white wine, and kicked the women out of the kitchen.

The lobster deserved plaudits. Pazos licked his fingers and wanted to take down the recipe.

'Naturally, Doctor,' answered Alberto obsequiously. 'I'll give you a demonstration whenever you want.'

After the party, Alberto drove back home several guests who lived far off.

When he got home himself, well past eleven o'clock, he found a summons. It was a summons to go to an office of the National Revolutionary Police, the following day, 8 August, at 11 a.m.; there was a telephone number to ring to confirm his attendance or to suggest another time, if that wasn't convenient. He could leave his message at any hour of the day or night, to be passed on to Asdrúbal.

He couldn't imagine what this could be about; but it must be something urgent if they were calling him in on a Sunday.

Perhaps he'd not paid all his traffic fines?

No, they wouldn't summons him on a Sunday for that.

Had some whore died? Or one of the queers that used to come to his place?

He decided it was useless to play guessing games. The riddle would be solved the following day. It couldn't be anything serious; because in Cuba, were he to commit a single crime, they'd not interrogate him in a police station, or even in the Investigations Department, but in Immigration Headquarters or State Security.

But he'd arranged his *frontón* finals game at eleven in the Copacabana.

He called straight away and left a message for Asdrúbal. He said that at eleven he had an unavoidable sporting engagement at the Copacabana Hotel.

But he'd be free by lunchtime and invited Asdrúbal to meet him at that time in the hotel cafeteria, by the swimming pool; or at two, wherever the policeman suggested.

# 11

## mistake or bullshit

On the night of Friday the sixth, just after the exchange with Bastidas, Pepe Jaén phoned a relative in Pinar del Río, to get them to find out where an Argentine tourist by the name of Aldo Bianchi was staying in Soroa or Viñales.

Like Chacha, Pepe didn't know that Bianchi was travelling on an Italian passport. And nobody could know that Aldo and Bini had decided against Soroa and Viñales, where there were few rooms available that weekend. They'd followed some advice and gone to the Parque de la Güira, a place with isolated log cabins, from where you could go on long hikes, horse-ride or reach, a mere five kilometres away, the sulphur thermal baths of San Diego de los Baños.

And only on Saturday night, when Bini decided to call her cousin Chacha, did they discover that Pepe Jaén was looking for them urgently.

'But what did he tell you?'

'Only that a cop was asking after you.'

Chacha couldn't tell her anything else.

And Pepe wasn't on the phone at home.

Aldo suggested they shouldn't wait till Sunday afternoon to go back as they'd planned. And by Sunday lunchtime, Bini was finding out about Fefita from Pepe himself.

'She called me at the hotel? Fefita, the maid?'

'Yes, a policeman asked her about some shoes she had had at home…'

Bini realized that if Fefita was mixed up in this, the police were a step ahead of them.

'We mustn't wait for them to come for you,' said Aldo, when he found out. 'You must go and present yourself now at the nearest police station and volunteer a statement…'

Bini understood. It wasn't the same if they extracted information from her about what happened to the cyclist after she'd been arrested on suspicion than if she presented herself of her own accord to make a statement of the truth.

It was vital to beat them to it.


When Bastidas summoned someone on a Sunday, he did so to suggest it was really urgent and thus scare the person involved, without saying a word. Intimidation, no doubt, but it brought good results. When people got the willies, they usually said the wrong thing.

He sat down to drink a few beers in the hotel and observe the man Alberto Ríos; especially as that Sunday he was bound to be bored stiff at home as there was going be no fun and dance. Building workers would invade the place mid-morning to put up four pillars for a conservatory and build the wash-place his wife needed.

Bastidas took it for granted that Alberto was the slayer of Baltasar París: or at least, had travelled in the car stolen from Carranza, as the *in situ* prints from the Florsheims indicated.

He also thought that if the man were guilty of homicide, when he saw the summons for a Sunday, he'd try to see Bini.

If he were a cautious type, he wouldn't ring her. And when Bastidas asked him about her, if he denied that he knew her or said he'd not seen her for a long time, he'd have him by the short and curlies. That way he'd save on time and sweat.

Out of sorts and half asleep, Pedrito drew up next to a little park at 6.30, some two hundred metres from Alberto Ríos's house. He was riding a motorbike, ideal for giving chase.

Alberto left in his car at 7.35. When he headed towards the sea, Pedrito guessed he wasn't going to Bini's place. To go to La Víbora from Atabey, you have to take the highway.

But Alberto kept on down Fifth Avenue to the church of San Antonio.

'The target parked on sixtieth between Fifth and Third, opposite the church. Over.'

'Keep an eye out to see if he goes in and prays, or whatever the fuck he does. Over.'

'Understood, over and out.'

If he went into the church, Pedrito would follow him. She'd probably be waiting for him inside.

But Alberto didn't go into the church. He crossed the street and went into a sports ground. There, after a brief warm-up, he started to run in two-hundred-metre bursts. Pedrito counted twenty.

The apparent failure of this tailing put Bastidas in a bad temper.

At 8.10, Alberto went to the Copacabana Hotel, where he dived into the sea, swam for five minutes, got out and took a shower. In shorts, sandals and an elegant towelling shirt, he sat down to breakfast in the cafeteria. He started to read and take notes seated at the same table.

'All right, go and have a rest and pick me up at home at ten thirty. The beers are on me.'

Bastidas and Pedrito turned up at the Copacabana at 11.05,

well in advance. The appointment with Alberto was at midday, but before they questioned him, Bastidas wanted some sun and a few beers.

Once inside, they located Lieutenant Ramos, responsible for security in the hotel, and coordinated the operation. But they wouldn't be seen together till it was time to question him.

Alberto and his partner had won again and were well happy. Now spectating, each armed with a can of beer, they cheered on the other duo from the Copacabana playing in the second semi-final of the day.

When the tournament was over, winners and losers gathered at a festive table, by the swimming pool.

Dressed in plain clothes, Bastidas and Pedrito sat near by and ordered beer.

With an excellent self-critical sense of humour, Alberto Ríos told a joke about Argentines, always characterized by Cubans and other Latins as loud-mouthed megalomaniacs.

'A guy from Buenos Aires enters the Paris Ritz, and fills in the form, puts his name, Juan Pérez, and where it says nationality, Argentine, and where it says sex, writes in capital letters: HUGE...'

Alberto was a witty storyteller and the circle greeted his patter with guffaws of laughter.

What a nice guy, thought Bastidas.

And what a great time he was having. He conversed excitedly, was the soul of the party. Got up, gesticulated, enthused over what he said and rocked with infectious belly laughs. Clearly, he was not over-worried by his imminent appointment with the police.

Bastidas could see him from behind, slightly at an angle. He could see him easily, without being seen himself.

If that guy's good mood was genuine, he was not the one who knocked over the cyclist. Or he was downright irresponsible...

If you are aware you've killed a cyclist, only a fool or

someone irresponsible could be so euphoric when about to be paid a Sunday call by the police.

No, he was not irresponsible. People who worked for prosperous commercial enterprises weren't irresponsible. And prosperous businessmen didn't knock over cyclists in stolen cars.

Bastidas didn't notice him look round once in the fifty minutes he scrutinized him. He was not interested in the nearby tables.

Anybody, knowing that the police were coming to see them there, would take the odd furtive glance, if only for curiosity's sake.

That live-wire jester was evidently without a care and was not what Bastidas was expecting. His years of experience indicated that he should be seeing a guy who'd slept badly, who was trying to control his nerves, a taciturn fellow incapable of laughing like Alberto, and one keeping a close eye on his immediate environment.

Besides, Bastidas's conjectures about complicity with Bini had begun to wane from early on when he found that Alberto made no attempt to locate her.

Perhaps the business of the Florsheim shoes wasn't as he'd imagined. Perhaps Alberto wasn't trying to get rid of them, but a nightmare really had persuaded Bini to bin them.

Alberto's table remained lively till 11.35, when some people began to leave. But Alberto hadn't looked at his watch, as if he'd forgotten the appointment with Bastidas.

Suddenly, the guests began to argue over paying. But Alberto wouldn't let anyone pay. The expense was his. And he gave strict instructions to a waiter. Make sure you don't take money from anyone else.

He paid the bill at 12.10, said goodbye to the few still at the table and began to move towards the exit, accompanied by his *frontón* partner and another competitor.

At that very moment he was accosted by Lieutenant Ramos. Bastidas and Pedrito were waiting a few steps behind.

'Señor Ríos, by any chance?'

'Yes?' Alberto frowned at the lieutenant.

'Could I please have a word in private with you?'

Alberto's companions knew that Ramos is the hotel "security" and melted away discreetly.

The lieutenant introduced himself and reminded him of his midday appointment.

Alberto hit his forehead and looked at the time.

'Right, I was expecting you! Forgive me, I'd completely forgotten.'

Bastidas looked on from three metres away.

Alberto's manner when he turned round on hearing his name, his surprised look, annoyance, apology, was so genuine... Could he really not have thought the appointment important? He'd forgotten? Very strange in someone guilty of murder!

Was he really guilty?

Or was he a bastard and an excellent actor?

The lieutenant showed him his identity badge in his narrow, rather uncomfortable office in the hotel. Bastidas also presented his credentials.

'Well, please do tell me...'

A rush of doubts to do with his real identity, with his fraudulent papers and passport, emerged from his disturbed memory. But already, the night before, Alberto had told himself repeatedly that any fear in that respect was totally unfounded.

His disguise was perfect.

Nobody could detect him.

There was no reason to lose his calm.

Bastidas opened his case, took out an opaque nylon bag and put it on the table.

He also took out a photo of Bini which he handed to Alberto.

'Know her?'

Alberto smiled. Looked surprised.

Ahh! What a relief. It's not you they want. What's that mad hussy got up to?

'Yes, of course, it's Bini,' and apparently anxious, 'Has something happened to her?'

Bastidas realized his concern was a pose. But Alberto's genuine smile and real curiosity disconcerted him. They were not the reactions of someone suddenly confronted with the photo of his accomplice in a homicide.

And his doubts returned as to the shoes that Bini had given to the room maid.

Perhaps they didn't belong to the guy opposite…

Bastidas walked a few steps and stood with his back to the office's only window. He needed light to see his reactions better, the pupils of his eyes if possible, before coming out with the news that was sure to disarm him.

'Sabina López Angelbello is implicated in a collision, knocking down a cyclist.'

'Phew…'

Alberto slowly and automatically puffed out his lips. He whistled.

He was surprised. No doubt about that.

His mouth, the way his eyebrows arched, his wide-open eyes, all indicated that.

And Bastidas faced the same dilemma: a brilliant actor or the victim of a mistake?

Alberto now frowned, but said nothing. He passed a hand over his head and slumped back in his chair. He sat looking at the police, waiting for more information.

Bastidas extracted the Florsheim shoes from his bag. He got up, walked three steps, held the shoes in one hand, bent down, placed the shoes on the ground next to Alberto's feet, and stared at him.

Alberto returned his look unperturbed, another question set on his face.

'Recognize them?' asked the captain.

'Recognize what?'

'These shoes as yours.'

'No, I don't recognize them at all. I've never seen them before. And please be a little more explicit. Am I under suspicion for something?'

'We suspect that you were in the same car as Bini on July eighteenth when the cyclist was knocked over.'

Bastidas now saw the first look of alarm on Alberto's face. But then, who wouldn't be scared to hear something like that?

Nevertheless, Alberto quickly switched from an expression of alarm to a sarcastic smile.

'Of course,' and he theatrically tapped the face of his watch with his index finger, 'and you want to know now, on August eighth, what I did on July eighteenth...'

'That would be perfect.' Bastidas smiled jokily back at him and waved his hand obsequiously, like a courtier doffing his hat before a superior.

Surprised by the policeman's versatility, Alberto looked at him, tugged at his beard thoughtfully, and looked back at his watch.

'What day was July eighteenth?'

'Sunday,' replied the lieutenant, pointing to a calendar hanging on the wall.

The eighteenth fell three Sundays ago.

Alberto cheered up when he recalled that he went out sailing with Raquelita and Darío that Sunday...He smiled.

'Well, my dear friend, on that Sunday I was sailing with three people who can support...'

'At what time?' asked Bastidas, taking notes in his diary.

Alberto waited for a few seconds. He was seeking an exact answer.

'I think we left at around eleven and came back at dusk ... There must be a record in the control office at the Hemingway Marina?'

'And don't you remember what you were doing on Sunday the eighteenth, at about six a.m.?'

Shit.

He was asleep then.

And had no witnesses.

He remembered how Jasmine and the other rent-boy came to his place at about eleven, on the Saturday night; they left around one o'clock, or perhaps two; and he went to bed straight away…

Alberto looked at the floor for a few seconds. Finally he shrugged his shoulders.

'I was asleep at home,' he replied calmly, very poised.

Could Bini have knocked over Baltasar París by herself? But …what about the Florsheims in that case?

'Were you sleeping by yourself?' asked Bastidas.

'Yes, I always sleep alone; and none of the servants stay at night.'

'What time do they leave?'

'At eight o'clock; but I give them the day off on Sundays.'

Bastidas stood and stared at him. Alberto stared back, frowning. He now looked impatient and bad tempered. Bastidas confirmed his initial impression that the man wasn't lying. But the evidence against him was very strong…

'Are you sure you never wore these shoes?'

'If you ask me the question again, I suppose it's because you think I'm lying or am an idiot. How should I take it?'

'I can assure you I don't think you're a fool.'

'I appreciate your courtesy,' he riposted, and laughed sincerely, as if wanting to make peace. He finally bent down, took one shoe, rested a foot on his other knee and measured the soles. 'I think they'd be a perfect fit, but I detest showy, two-tone shoes.'

'But someone said Bini gave them to her as a present, when she was staying with you at the Triton Hotel.'

'Bullshit; I only do women in my house.'

'Or in your yacht…'

'At any rate, on my own ground,' admitted Alberto laconically.

'Nevertheless, the computerized records at the Triton show that Alberto Ríos, Argentine,' and he read from a slip of paper he took from his shirt pocket, 'on an identity document for foreigners number 43082324421 stayed in Room 322, from July twenty-fourth to the twenty-sixth this year.'

'Total bullshit,' protested Alberto, standing up and staring at Bastidas.

'Calm down,' advised the lieutenant, also getting up.

Alberto scrutinized Bastidas through half-closed eyes, as if trying to guess what he was after. He shook his head. Pressed his lips together incredulously and diverted his gaze to the wall. He remained undecided for a few seconds.

The others said nothing.

Pedrito changed the tape in the cassette recorder and the lieutenant lit a cigarette.

Alberto looked down and raised both hands, asking for a truce.

'All right, I'll take that back. Perhaps it's not bullshit, just a mistake. Let me think aloud what might have happened. In the first place, I certainly know Bini and have been with her several times in my house and on my yacht.'

'And in your car?' interjected Bastidas, deliberately trying to trip him up.

'Lots of times,' agreed Alberto, not wavering or seeming worried by the question. 'Not just that; I also let her drive, because she wanted to learn...'

'Did you ever give her your car?' asked the captain in alarm.

'Of course not,' replied Alberto. 'When she drove I was always next to her and we went to out-of-the-way places.'

Bastidas walked a few steps, his head lowered, and said: 'I take it that your relations with her were only...sexual?'

Alberto focused on the wall again, smiling sarcastically. 'And what kind of relationship does one have with a whore?'

'Yes, but if one's teaching a woman to drive...'

'Yes, I understand, there may be other interests...But not

in Bini's case. I go with her because I like the way she fucks, and apart from that, she's as mad as a hatter and the things she does and says make me laugh. I just invite her to go for a ride, or have a drink, for light entertainment, and when she's with me in the car, she always wants to drive, and I let her drive for a while. But that's as far as it goes. I'd never have dreamed of shutting myself up with her in a hotel. That's not my style, I can assure you…'

'And I can assure you your name appears on the records of the Triton Hotel; and the number of your Cuban identity card, and the photocopy of your picture…We've checked everything.'

When he said that, Bastidas saw Alberto's face light up.

'My Cuban ID? Now wait a minute: I lost my residence card last month, and was given a new one the following day. You can check that I asked for a replacement.'

'You suggesting someone checked in using your name?'

'That's right, but I've thought of another possibility: if you take the trouble to go the Argentine embassy and consult a telephone guide to the federal capital and Greater Buenos Aires you'll find a dozen or more subscribers called Alberto Ríos. And one could reckon on another such number living in the interior of the country. So I can think of two possible responses: either someone used my previous card to check in at that hotel, or a fellow countryman of mine caused this confusion.'

'What about the shoes…?'

'I can only repeat they're nothing to do with me. I've never seen them before.'

Alberto spoke steadily. Now more confident of himself, he smiled serenely as he gave his explanations.

And Bastidas pondered: if Fefita, the room maid, hadn't seen him in the Triton and described Bini's companion as 'a tall man with a small beard and long hair', if Pepe hadn't confirmed that, after checking him in at hotel reception, if the Florsheims weren't his size, one would have to accept he was innocent.

The card could be a coincidence or a trick; but two witnesses who had no relationship with Alberto Ríos remembered him personally. Why would they lie? That was the most incriminating evidence of all. Nonetheless, Bastidas would keep it up his sleeve for the moment. For now, Alberto would not know about Fefita and Pepe Jaén's statements. Bastidas wouldn't play all his trump cards till he'd questioned the Bini woman.

That afternoon Bastidas needed a siesta, but it was impossible at home with the builders banging on the roof. Next to him Pedrito was yawning away. The early rise and beers were taking their toll. Bastidas took pity on the youth and let him off for the rest of the day.

As soon as Pedrito had left, Bastidas made another attempt to communicate with the Hemingway Marina.

Not a word. They weren't responding.

Half an hour later, he walked into the office of the duty officer in Security, who at the time was dealing with an incident in the port.

When he finally located him, Bastidas brought him up to speed on the situation. The man, a lieutenant, was already familiar with the case.

For the moment, they should be on high alert. The Argentine owner of the *Chevalier* might try to sail off early the next morning.

'Should we stop him?'

'No, but the coastguards should be ready. He's now more likely than ever to try to escape. Tell them not to let him out of their sights.'

Back in his house, Bastidas wondered whether he might not be exaggerating. The coastguards weren't going to sleep that night. And if the colonel found out he was mounting such a fuss over a case of manslaughter, he might get riled at him. Only premeditated murder or crimes against the security of the state warranted so much vigilance and activity. But Bastidas felt particularly hostile towards hit-and-run drivers.

He had quite enough with the evidence already collected to hand Alberto Ríos over to the public prosecutor. But his intuition and experience told him that, despite the overwhelming evidence, that guy might be innocent. And he decided to delay posting the order a couple of days more.

Besides, it would be wrong to hand him over to the prosecutor before questioning Bini, who was also under suspicion.

# 12 the pure, whiter-than-white gospel truth

Alberto Ríos didn't board the yacht *Chevalier*, as Captain Bastidas had feared, early on Monday morning, but later. He turned up on the quayside at 10 a.m. with a woman he'd already been seen on board with several times.

Bastidas was sent the information by a security officer who relieved the lieutenant at the marina. He also checked that one of the armed patrol boats was patrolling the outlying area at the time. Everything was in hand.

And at 10.15, he received an unexpected piece of news from central control: the previous day, at 11.30, while he was preparing to question Alberto Ríos by the Copa swimming pool, citizen Sabina López Angelbello, alias Bini, daughter of Lázaro López Carranza, had gone to a police station and confessed that, on 18 July, she was riding in the car that knocked a cyclist over on the southern highway.

Fuck, Carranza's daughter! Was it the one I questioned in El Calvario?

Bastidas remembered the mechanic's daughter; a nice piece of mulatta who'd said she'd gone to sleep watching a film with Grandma. That was why she couldn't tell him anything.

At the time, it never entered Bastidas's head that she was involved in the theft.

Now that same mulatta, or one of Carranza's other daughters, was the one who'd informed in Miramar on the killer of París the cyclist, one Alberto Ríos, an Argentine citizen, who was teaching her how to drive.

According to the Bini girl's statement, Alberto was driving the car she'd taken from Grandma's house, while her father was sleeping.

Bastidas deduced that on Sunday at 11.30, when Bini was spattering him with shit in the Miramar station, Alberto Ríos still didn't know why the police were summoning him.

No doubt on the advice of some lawyer, Sabina López came forward to make a statement, in order to diminish her complicity in the crime. And clearly the little move had worked wonders for her, because according to HQ, she could remain free. She must have made a good impact at the public prosecutor's office. Otherwise why hadn't they immediately arrested her as a preventive measure? That was the routine. When a homicide took place, even though unpremeditated, anyone suspected of complicity was automatically placed under arrest and held till the trial.

Bastidas went off in hot pursuit, determined to question her straight away.

Accompanied by Pedrito, he first went to La Víbora, to her cousin Chacha's place, following the map sketched by Pepe Jaén. But they said they'd not seen her since the previous week.

Nor could they find her in El Calvario, where she used to stay.

The grandma confirmed that Bini was one and the same girl they had seen and questioned in her house, the day they went to see her son Lázaro.

'Let's see... Yes, she came by here on Thursday, to order a goat and pigeons...

'She bought them from a neighbour who sold animals for sacrifice.

'...and she left me money to pay for them when he brought

them; and asked me to keep the animals in the yard. Yesterday, right early in the morning, a gentleman came in a truck to pick them up, because Bini's godfather in Regla was putting on a *bembé*.'

She also told them that Bini sometimes stayed at her godfather's house for several days; but she didn't know the name of the street where he lived.

'I only went there once, when Bini pledged herself to the saints.'

She did recall that it was a large wooden house with a huge yard, near the cemetery.

'And her godfather's name?'

'I don't really remember, but I think it's Pedro Pablo, or Juan Pablo, or something of the sort, but Bini just calls him "my godfather".'

Juan Pedro lived near the cemetery, in a wooden two-storey, eight-roomed house, with a yard full of mango, mamey and banana trees.

As they were going to a *babalao*'s house in Regla, Bastidas and Pedrito dressed in plain clothes.

The man was well known in the area and proved easy to find.

They knocked at a door with only one leaf. The other looked as if it had been yanked out at a stroke, judging by the gaps in the jamb, where hinges once hung.

'Mitch,' commented Pedrito.

'Yes, the hurricane ravaged wooden houses.'

'What do they do at night? I expect they tie a dog up...'

'No need, *chico*, they're protected by the saints.'

Two children were watching telly in the living room and ignored the knock.

Bastidas's knuckles rapped on the leaf again, and one kid, annoyed by the noise, howled: 'Graaandmaaa!'

A minute passed and nobody appeared.

Pedrito had stepped inside to talk to the children when a

partition door opened and out of the darkness emerged an aged mulatta tottering along with the help of a stick.

'We'd like to speak to Bini,' said Bastidas.

'Who are you?'

'Captain Ignacio Bastidas,' and he showed her his badge, but she didn't take a look.

The old lady didn't seem at all worried. She inspected them for a moment and beckoned them in.

'Take a seat. I'll see if she's in. There are so many people in this house one never knows…'

'But…haven't you seen her?'

'Yesterday she was at a saint's ceremony we had, but I don't know whether she slept over or left. Wait a minute while I go and ask Juan Pedro.'

After a few moments, a sixty-year-old black walked in, on the bald side and looking daggers at them.

'Bini twisted her foot dancing and it's very swollen,' he told them. 'She says you can go into her room.'

They followed him down a passageway, to a room right in the outbuildings.

When they crossed the back yard, the police saw a man stretched out on a sofa, and a fat woman on a hammock. Both seemed to be sleeping.

For an August day it was surprisingly cool. Bastidas noticed it clouding over. Soon it would be raining. A stiffening breeze was rustling the foliage in the yard.

'It looks like a north wind is blowing up,' commented Pedrito, as the *babalao* walked silently in front.

At a nearby table, under a wooden awning protected by the centennial trunk of a mango tree, several men played dominoes and drank rum from the bottle; a *danzón* tune was thundering away.

When she saw them come in, Bini leaned back on her bed.

'Oh, it's you again,' she said, almost as if displeased.

'Yes, we met in your grandmother's house,' said Bastidas.

With her hair dishevelled and naked shoulders, her youthful beauty had acquired a wild jungle allure. She'd just woken up. She covered herself with a frayed, yellowing bedspread which she gripped in her armpits to hide her unprotected breasts.

'You'd prefer not see us again…?'

'I'm a bit embarrassed, because that day I…'

'Spun us a few lies.' Bastidas smiled indulgently.

She said nothing. She arched her eyebrows above closed eyes, pressed her lips together and swayed her head slightly. Hardly an expression of repentance. Perhaps a degree of disappointment.

When she stretched a hand out towards the bedside table to get a hair clasp, the bedspread slipped down to near her nipple, but she readjusted it elegantly and unhurriedly.

She looked thoughtful. Didn't seem worried by the presence of the policemen. In order to fix her ponytail without exposing her breasts, she held the overlay between her teeth. She performed naturally. Didn't try to show off by stripteasing.

Pedrito unzipped a bag and switched on the recorder.

Sitting on a rickety armchair, her godfather watched warily from the doorway.

'Don't get upset, Godfather, let us be. I told you…'

The old man got up and stood by the door, undecided, for a few moments.

'Don't worry,' retorted Bini. 'I'll do what you say…'

The two policemen looked at each other furtively.

The old man nodded reluctantly and departed.

'Did Alberto tell you we wanted to question you?'

She shook her head.

'No, but the dead man did,' she replied, and sighed.

Bastidas put his guard up. He sat back in his chair again.

Pedrito gaped at her.

'He's been keeping me awake for over a month. He appears in my dreams every two or three night. Riding his bicycle, crying, scratching his face, and moaning at me for what we did to him, and yesterday I could stand it no more and told all.'

'And this time you're going to tell us...?'

'The pure, whiter-than-white, gospel truth, the truth, *Combatiente*...'

'Captain,' Bastidas corrected her.

*Combatiente* was the term used by prisoners when addressing their guards.

In five minutes, after a weep and several interruptions, Bini confirmed what the room maid had said.

Yes. Just after they knocked the cyclist over, Alberto Ríos stayed in the Triton Hotel and she spent three days there with him.

'Tito was the one who wanted to get rid of the shoes...'

'Tito?' repeated Bastidas.

'Yes, Alberto...I always call him Tito.'

Bastidas nodded and scrawled something in his notebook.

'I took the shoes out in a bag to chuck them; but then I just couldn't...They looked so pretty...And were almost new. So when I saw the maid, I called her and gave them to her as a present. She looked after me very well...When we met in the corridor, she always smiled at me; so I gave her the shoes. But the truth is I've soured poor Tito's life...'

Another bout of weeping.

'All my fault...because I wanted to learn to drive...'

After another tear-jerking interlude, when Pedrito handed her his handkerchief so she didn't keep drying herself on the overlay, Bastidas resumed his questioning: 'And how did you manage to take the car without anyone noticing?'

'Oh, easy-peasy, Captain: my grandma's deaf, and Dad's a deep sleeper. When he starts snoring it's not easy to wake him up: you have to shake him, pinch him...Get me? An' at about three, I took the rubbish out, an' as I didn't see any neighbours around, I went to his bedroom, took the keys he always leaves on his bedside table and the remote for the alarm, and off I went.'

After pushing the car back to get it out of the shelter with the engine switched off, she went and practised elsewhere. She had a few dollars, bought plenty of petrol and drove for two hours by herself. She was in San Agustín and about to return home when it started to rain and she got on to a mud flat where she manoeuvred poorly and slipped down a slope, and didn't know what to do to get the car out of the dip. She was very worried because it was getting late; she walked to La Giraldilla restaurant, and a nightwatchman let her use the phone. Then she called Tito to get him to come to help her.

'When he arrived, he looked for some branches, some guano stalks and stones, and soon got the car out…'

'And how did he get there?'

'In a taxi.'

'Why not his own car?'

'Because he didn't know the way…'

'And did he call for the taxi?'

'How do I know? You ask him…'

'And you don't remember what the car was like?'

'Fuck me, I was hardly going to bother about that? Forgive me, *Combatiente*!'

'All right, go on.'

'Well, OK; it was raining a lot and he refused to let me drive; and when we were on the highway, we suddenly saw a cyclist, no lights, nothing…Just imagine, Captain, Tito did all he could not to knock him over, but there was a tremendous wallop, and the man and his bike flew up like toys. Tito and I got out straight away to help him, but the poor fellow…' and her thumb simulated a beheading.

After the interview, Bastidas asked her where she could best be located, in case he needed to see her.

'The best place is my cousin Chacha's, in the morning, though at the moment I'm staying at a friend's flat in Vedado.'

'What's her name?'

'Juanita, but I don't know her surname.'

'And what's your relationship with her?'

Bini responded brazenly: 'I meet my Italian friend there.'

'And what's the Italian's name?'

'He's really Argentine, but an Italian national. And his name is Aldo Bianchi.'

(Aldo had told her to give whatever information they asked for about him, and the flat on 21st Street. He thought it inevitable the police would investigate his most recent relationships, and it was best not to hide anything.)

'And how long's Aldo been in Cuba?'

'Ay, Captain, I don't remember. I got poor Tito in a mess because of Aldo.'

'And how come?'

'You know, Captain, this is what happened: Aldo my boyfriend arrived in Cuba the day before; and I went to meet him at the airport, but he told me that night he couldn't go out with me because he had a business dinner; and that he was tired after the flight from Italy; and he was going to go early to his hotel, because if he stayed with me at Juanita's, I wouldn't let him sleep and... You can imagine; he was right. And as I'd had a row with Chacha that day, I asked him to leave me in El Calvario before going to his hotel, where you were at my grandma's place; I went to sleep early, and woke up at three, feeling hungry and bored, and it was then I thought of going for a little ride. And that's why I say that if Aldo had taken me out that night, I wouldn't have caused Tito this problem.'

'Let alone the cyclist and his family...'

'Ay, the poor guy...' and she grimaced in concern.

'Well, where is Aldo now?'

'He's still here. He's staying at the National, though we almost always stay in Juanita's flat.'

They were in the *babalao*'s house for half an hour.

Bini's confession tallied with various conclusions drawn by the forensics people. The tears, coursing down her face at various times, had the speed and volume of ones provoked by real anguish. She seemed to be telling the truth.

Nevertheless, Bastidas smelt a rat with the business of the dead cyclist visiting her in her dreams. Her precision in the small detail also made him suspicious.

He didn't know what to think.

'The Argentine is fucked,' pronounced Pedrito, at the steering wheel. 'His fancy woman's statement has well and truly done for him.'

'True enough,' agreed Bastidas. 'But before I give him over to the public prosecutor, I want to question him again. And her as well; and also that Aldo Bianchi guy.'

That same Monday, in the afternoon, Bastidas visited the coastguard office and the head of the unit gave him a verbal report.

Alberto and the woman with him, a buxom blonde, on the robust side, had started to deep-sea dive three miles from the coast. Only the helmsman stayed on the yacht. They both emerged after two hours and, with the young guy's help, they hoisted up three cages, each with several compartments of differing size, in which they'd caught samples of marine fauna. After a while, they started to sort out the fish, put them in glass bowls and plastic bags.

'They had some drinks, and chatted.'

She spent a long time showing him something in a bowl. It didn't seem much like the actions of a fellow preparing to flee the island.

'We saw her spread some cream on and stretch out to sunbathe on the deck, and he went back in on a board and started to surf.'

'What time did they return to port?'

'Around four.'

The marina authority informed them that, apart from Alberto's white convertible, they were also met by a truck belonging to the

Texinal company, on which the driver and his assistant loaded all the glass containers.

The woman and Alberto left in the convertible, followed by the truck.

The marina security officer said that the woman was Raquel Hurtado, a researcher at the University Institute of Maritime Biology, and authorized by the Ministry of the Interior to fish anywhere in Cuban waters and bring the specimens caught to wherever she thought fit. Captain Bastidas shook his head: only a very cold-blooded person could have acted as Alberto Ríos did that day, only thirty hours after being questioned as a possible accomplice in a homicide.

At Immigration, Bastidas checked what Bini had said about Aldo; he had landed in Rancho Boyeros on Saturday, 17 July, was checked in at the National; but when Bastidas went in pursuit, nobody answered from his room, nor when he was called over the Tannoy.

He then called the number on 21st Street.

'Hello?' It was Bini.

'You got back so quick from Regla?'

She didn't seem frightened or bothered when Bastidas asked to speak to Aldo in private.

'Please, wait in the lobby, by the phone. I'll be there right away,' Aldo greeted him affably.

And in fifteen minutes he confirmed what Bini had said.

Bastidas asked about the people he had had dinner with on the night of Saturday 17th.

He gave him the names of a vice-minister for construction and an important civil servant in the Ministry of Tourism. And added that he'd gone back to his hotel shortly after midnight because he was exhausted by the long journey and extended dinner.

The following day, the vice-minister confirmed his statement. And that, one could see at the dinner table that Bianchi really had been tired out by his long journey.

# 13 precautionary measures

On Tuesday, 10 August, at 10 a.m., Bastidas was issued with an arrest warrant.

He consulted Security at the Copacabana Hotel and learned that the target was busy with his books at a table in the swimming-pool area.

Bastidas and Pedrito arrived at eleven.

When Alberto was informed they were coming for him, and saw the older officer waving a yellow envelope at him, his first reaction was one of incredulity. That could in no way be an arrest warrant...Well, maybe they needed to question him again, and hence the bit of paper; but it couldn't be that they wanted to arrest him...Him of all people?

Standing next to his table, by the edge of the pool, the officer told him that Sabina López Angelbello had confessed all.

'All what?'

'That the cyclist was knocked over by the vehicle that you were driving.'

'That I…!!?'

'Yes, you; two employees at the Triton say they saw you with her in the hotel. I'm sorry, but you must come with us.'

Surprise and incredulity turned to fear. Lots of fear. Fear of the worst.

'You are allowed to read what Sabina stated, or hear the recording, if you so wish…'

Fuck! Fuck! They're on to me, he thought.

Only his usual enemies could have set this trap. The same people who mounted the two attacks in Montevideo. It was both unexpected and horrific.

His head slumped and he sank his face into his hands.

Bastidas and Pedrito looked at each other. Would he cry? He seemed about to faint.

'Do you feel ill?'

'Just give me a moment,' he managed to say, lifting one hand up.

The news was a punch to the kidneys. It made him feel queasy. He took a deep breath to control his heartbeat and breathing difficulties. And made an effort to calm down.

'Please give me two minutes,' he said, his face still in his hands.

'Can I get you some water?' asked Pedrito.

Alberto didn't respond. He shook his head and breathed gently again.

So that fucking bitch Bini was working with them…?

How did they recruit her? When?

If it were true, why didn't they kill him and get it over with?

What were they waiting for? What did they expect to get from this bullshit about knocking over a cyclist?

Suddenly his fear and indignation disconnected. When separated, they no longer overwhelmed him. He could finally take a deep breath. He rapidly assessed his position: he shouldn't let panic force him into wild conjectures. And despite his heart, which was still thudding away, he looked up and asked to see the arrest warrant.

Under the multi-coloured parasol he read the paper quickly and handed it back. He took his glasses off, closed his eyes and squeezed his nose. He already looked in better spirits.

'All right, what can one do?' he said finally, grimacing in mild displeasure. 'Give me a few minutes to get dressed.'

He didn't ask a single question.

He gathered his things together and went into a cabin, which he left almost immediately, preceded by a blast of eau de cologne.

He wore a blue appliqué T-shirt, pearl-white trousers and black moccasins. He was carrying a huge tooled leather case that was also black, in which he kept his books and writing materials.

There was a moment of hesitation as they left the hotel.

'Couldn't I follow you in my car?'

'I'm sorry, that's not allowed,' replied Bastidas, pointing him towards the patrol car.

Alberto sat behind, next to Pedrito, with Bastidas next to the uniformed driver. They drove in silence to the station.

Alberto decided not to say a word till he'd heard Bini's statement. He'd listen to her attentively. She was bound to contradict herself at some point and then he'd refute her.

By the time they entered the aged building, he felt much better. But the corridor, packed with wan faces, eye-bags and long-suffering women, was depressing.

'Follow me,' said the younger policeman, and took him into a room where they asked him for his personal effects: the case, keys, watch, pen, glasses, documents and money.

A very young, pallid and short-sighted corporal, who was having a snack at the time, took his things. He sealed the case with tape and piled the rest on his desk. He placed a sheet of paper in an antediluvian Underwood and started typing with one finger. Bent forward in order to see the keyboard. Screwed his eyes up with a similar effort in his approaches to his omelette sandwich, making sure his bite hit true.

When he'd finished the list of things requisitioned, he gave it to Alberto to read. He signed a receipt and went out accompanied by a policeman who led him to an office. Captain Ignacio Bastidas (as he read on a small acrylic card placed on his desk) was waiting for him.

According to Bastidas, Alberto had the right to hear the witness's statement. And he listened to every word in a haughty silence. As Bini explained what had happened, he blanched in rage.

What the policeman really wanted was to observe Alberto's reactions as he heard the details. And once again, what the veteran policeman, confident in his intuitions, saw wasn't the expression of a guilty man; these weren't the shifty eye movements of someone who realizes he's been caught, but flashes of indignation. It was the disarray of an innocent.

And Bastidas then thought of Azúa the black.

It's madness, he told himself.

At any rate, he would speak to the black.

Done.

He would declare the investigation over and put the Argentine into the hands of the public prosecutor. He couldn't keep hold of him any longer.

Alberto was still listening transfigured: '…just imagine, Captain, Tito did all he could not to knock him over, but there was a tremendous wallop, and the man and his bike flew up like toys. Tito and I got out straight away to help him, but the poor fellow…'

'That's enough; I don't want to hear any more of this rubbish,' said Alberto, putting his face in his hands again.

At a signal from Bastidas, Pedrito switched the recorder off.

'Have you anything to add?'

Alberto looked at the ceiling and breathed deeply.

'Nothing to add or take away: after such slander I just want to tell the people at my company to find me a lawyer.'

He couldn't detect any holes in Bini's confession. Could she possibly have cooked that up by herself? So much bare-faced cynicism bewildered him.

When they brought him out into the yard, where two blacks were whispering to each other, his spirits sank once more and he had another attack of fear.

Unexpectedly that recording had revealed a master storyteller.

Who, then, was Bini?

No *felacia*, for sure, as he'd labelled her. Who the fuck was this Cuban Mata Hari, weaver of the lies about the shoes, stealer of his ID, actress in the hotel wings, who so realistically and in such detail related the accident of the car in the mire and Tito's collision with the cyclist?

But...the car business was true. She stole it from her father...The police had proved that.

What doubts! What confusion! What a daughter of a thousand whores! Who could have imagined that Bini would put him in this scrape! What a cunt! What a piss-pot! He'd let a shitty little slut sweep the carpet from under his feet.

A policeman removed the two blacks and Alberto was left alone on the bench in the yard. He tried another route to relaxing and managed to think more objectively, more dispassionately.

No, no, no, Bini was not and could not be a Mata Hari. Or a Sarah Bernhardt. Bini was Bini. The one he knew. It was absurd to endow her with the ability to organize this puzzle in a few days; or to imagine her working for his lifetime enemies.

All things considered, this wasn't their style. If it had been them, they'd already have killed him. It would have been easy for them to knock him off in Havana, where he moved around unescorted. And besides, what could his real enemies get from setting up this trap to put him inside for such a footling thing?

No. They'd never allow such a light sentence. They'd want to see him dead; first tortured, beheaded, and then cut into little pieces. If they'd seen he was such an easy catch in Havana, they wouldn't even have shot him. They'd have kidnapped him, and one day his mutilated corpse would have appeared, either bloated in the sea, or in a field with a mouthful of ants. And *chao*.

Then he saw the captain's aide at the other end of the yard. The youth signalled to him to follow him and took him back to Bastidas's office. The Texinal lawyer was waiting for him and he'd just read Bini's statement.

'Coffee?' asked Bastidas, as he saw him come in.

'No thanks,' replied Alberto, even though he felt like some.

All in all, this cop was amiable enough. During the interview, at his request, he'd informed him that, for a hit-and-run job, someone like him, with no previous record and a foreigner, would get a maximum sentence of two years; perhaps less.

After switching on the recording, he'd agreed to telephone the lawyer for him; and now he was giving up his office so they could have a private conversation.

The lawyer had soaked up every detail of the accusation and didn't believe he was innocent. He didn't even try to raise his hopes. He stated solemnly that the evidence and statements against him didn't allow him to be optimistic. Alberto should anticipate the worst. If there was no way to prove that at the time of the collision he was somewhere else, or that he hadn't stayed at the Triton on those dates, it would be very difficult to defend him.

But he promised to ensure that Texinal engaged a defence lawyer from abroad for him as soon as possible.

That same afternoon, Alberto was placed at the disposal of the public prosecutor.

At five o'clock, they took him in a prison van to Combined East. He went in as a temporary inmate suspected of murder, waiting for his trial.

The following day, on the orders of the public prosecutor, Sabina López Angelbello was also placed under precautionary arrest.

# Part V

Part V

# 14 that night, on O street

And you don't only remember the magical encounter on O Street: you see yourself on the plane. The Cubans have gone wild now they're arriving. You join in and sing along when they sing *Guantanamera, guajiraguánnn tanamera.* There are such nice guys, painters and sculptors from Santiago who've just put on an exhibition in Rome, and a festive band has formed round them and their bottle. When they finish their rum, you buy them another bottle, and an ode merchant appears, the Cubans call them *repentistas,* and he starts improvising verses for everyone, and some of them have a drop too much; but you're as right as rain.

You are rather sad, and you never get drunk in that state. You can't see anything through the windows; only darkness, a scattering of small lights, as in the countryside. The plane begins to buck as it loses height.

You're tired.

And depressed. You'd planned this trip with Pia.

You're upset by the separation. She was fantastic with

you, but it didn't work, and, as usual, it's your fault. Your conscienceonometer had plunged out of sight.

Let's hope you can have some fun in Havana. You really deserve a rest. Pity it's only four days. On Sunday the ninth you've got your return flight.

You can catch some sun on a beach. They say the May sun is very bright in Cuba.

Ha…Nobody can know how much you need this rest after the picnic in the office over the last few days…You regret the arrangement with Gonzalo and Aurelia. You want to fall on your bed as soon you've checked in at the hotel.

Look, look, the landing signs are on…

You bid farewell to the group – well, see you in Cuba, Aldo Bianchi, pleased to meet you, and they all exchange names and offer you their houses, and you go back to your seat in first class, and put your belt on and try to see something, but it's pitch black…

The plane is still losing height.

They say landing will be in a few minutes.

You insist on looking out of the windows but see nothing, total darkness.

Fucking hell, you don't like landing and not seeing…And when you're a hundred or two hundred metres from the ground, you begin to make out the airport buildings, and some dull lights, and in the other direction four or five planes, and then you spot the landing strip. You're about to touch down.

You sit back in your seat and shut your eyes, and wait for the bang, bang, bang, three bumps and applause.

Your seat is the second in first class and you've hardly got any hand luggage. You wait in front of the door, and when they open it, shuaaaa, the warm, scented air from a hairdryer, just like Bahía and Cartagena.

It's like a syrup oozing into your lungs.

You have a good memory for smells and the tropics are unmistakable, smell the same everywhere.

The downside is that you get used to it in half an hour and no longer feel...

Ah, the transfer bus is at the bottom of the steps...

You're one of the first to leave Immigration, and Customs lets you through without checking your luggage.

You reached the National Hotel in twenty-five minutes. A fine pile of antiquated, lordly brickwork. Must have built it in the forties. French Rivièreish, high ceilings, lots of class, good service, the sea in front, an enormous inside garden, lofty palms, a swimming pool...And right in the centre of Havana. The bonus of a city with sea.

The perfumed, humid heat of night transforms you into an exotic character, the protagonist of an adventure. It excites you, like in the carnivals of your childhood, with the sweat of women and smell of ether. Suddenly, your tiredness has dissipated. You want to walk for a while around the city, meander, fill in time till you phone Fatso.

You take a shower, put lighter clothes on, and back in the lobby buy a map and a guide to Havana.

It's five minutes past eight. As you leave the hotel, to the left, you see more movement and start walking down a street on the slope. When you look at the street name you see a circle, but nothing indicates whether it is a zero or the letter O. That wretched gringo mania for giving numbers and letters to streets.

You cross over to the opposite pavement and start down the street and two chicks are arguing in front of you: 'No, no, I mean no, girl...' And so on and so forth...And now they stop halfway down the block. The taller one, a vivacious mulatta, a real scorcher, is gesticulating and talking at the top of her voice. She's in a blind rage, lets her words out in rushes, swallows her S's, swallows complete syllables, and though you catch her drift, you miss some things. She suddenly says something you didn't expect to hear on the streets of Havana: 'A *felacio*, that's what your Rodolfito is, a fucking *felacio*, and the best thing you can do is send him packing right now…'

Did you hear right? Was it a Cuban word? Could Three-O have been here? Could she have learned that word here? And you can't avoid the undesirable vision of Three-O, his voice, his laughter, the glint of the revolver he put in your mouth, on the corner of Lavalle and Talcahuano.

Three-O in contact with that chick?

Don't be barmy. A stupid idea. It can't possibly be.

You're angry, you're upset and at the same time saddened, but you get closer, stand on the kerb so you can hear what the big girl is saying; she's still gesticulating, and affirming that a guy like that will always cause you problems.

'With a *felacio* like that best you…'

With her index and long finger she scissor-slices the air.

The other, a blonde little something, argues that Rodolfo isn't evil, that he means well…

'I don't say he's evil; but even if he's got the best of intentions, he's always going to hurt you.'

And you frowning, unable to breathe, the word shatters you, bites into you, rings in your ears…You've relived so often the incredible scene, the emotions, the quickened pulse.

Till then, you thought '*felacio*' was a term invented by Three-O, in order to make fun of your Gelasio. Once you even looked the word up in an ordinary dictionary and in medical dictionaries, and it didn't exist. Three-O was making fun of you, bust his gut laughing: 'But, *che*, what an idiot your dad was; or he must have been pissed when he went to the registry. How could he give you such a crazy name? And I bet they spelt it wrong, because what you are is a real *felacio*, ha, ha, ha…'

In fact, they added on the Gelasio because your grandma insisted, in honour of St Gelasio, who appeared on the saints' calendar for that day; and that's when they nailed that moniker…Bad luck.

And now, standing in front of these chicks, in Zero or O Street, you're still wondering whether Three-O hadn't been to Cuba. It was he who probably taught them the word.

Could it be Cuban slang? Judging by the woman's strong tone, it could have a very similar meaning to the one intended by Three-O.

You move nearer to the taller one, ready to dispel doubts: 'Señorita, I'm sorry…'

They both gave him welcoming smiles. They're giving you the come-on.

Are they hookers?

And as you can't think of another way, you just fire your question at her: 'Please explain what *felacio* means in Cuba?'

They both roar with laughter. Double over. The little'un covers her face, to hide a gap in her teeth.

Finally, Big Browny asks you whether you're Argentine…

'Yes, how did you know?'

She's shocked: 'How come you don't know what *felacio* means? It's a word from your country. Another Argentine taught it to me…'

You get a needle-point in a vein. Suddenly become fevered and lucid. Get flash images of Three-O, his violence, his henchmen, and in a second decide to invite that chick out, to court her, to shut yourself up with her wherever. Anything to find the Argentine who taught her that word. You must grill her, but without alerting your prey.

It seems fantastic, but there was nothing to prevent Three-O from coming and hiding in Cuba. Through a mad coincidence, someone who learned it from him could have taught it to her; or else, once minted by Three-O, perhaps it had prospered and spread in Argentina, and entered some people's vocabulary.

At any rate, this girl was the end of the skein. And you have to start with her to get any results.

'Alberto is the name of the guy who taught me,' she adds. 'Do you know him?'

You make it clear you don't, and naturally show no signs of interest.

'...and Alberto taught me it to stop me from swearing, and in the end I also started to say *felacio* and *felacia* to everyone, and, just imagine, joking and fucking around, all my friends learned it; and now none of us says *comepinga*, which is what we Cubans call that...'

When she hears the swear word, the other girl starts to split her sides. A pedestrian stops and looks at them, highly amused.

Now, Browny also catches it, and as they laugh, they both almost double over at a right angle.

The littl'un makes obscene gestures, putting the fingers of one hand into the hollow of the fist of the other. What a rude pair. They must be whores, but you now ask them what *comepinga* means; and they fall apart again, and you end up inviting them for a drink, and when they sit at a table in a bar, they both start to explain that *comepinga*, well, how to put it, here you call any asshole, idiot, imbecile a *comepinga* but the pretty brown thing, now quite shyly, reveals that it is also a very rude way of saying *fellatio*.

The fact that the chick used that technical word not only surprises you but, emanating from her soft, wet, fat lips, it unexpectedly arouses you, and her mischievous, cheeky eyes attract you. The strange situation, the heat and humidity, provoke you, and you invite Browny. Only her.

You've suddenly seen her as desirable. She must be twenty, tall, slim waisted, beautiful teeth, sleek skin.

And you feel like having a fling on that May night, getting drunk on the heat of the tropics.

And it will probably work wonders for you.

For she's a sweetie...A chocolate sweetie, soft lips, wicked butt...

What if you no can do?

Well, what the hell, idiot. Besides, you lose nothing by trying...If it doesn't work, she's only a hooker. All that matters is keeping sight of her, becoming her friend, and today, or tomorrow, or the day after, extracting information from her about this Alberto...You must track him down, set your eyes on him...

'I'm inviting you to dinner,' you tell her.

The girls exchange professionally understanding looks. The white littl'un looks at her watch and shouts 'Hey', and bids a rapid farewell, yes, *chao*, pleased to meet you, she's got a date.

Browny is called Bini. When you're alone with her, you grab her hand and she grips you tight.

Fucking hell! What's this chick doing to you? On the one hand you only want to find out about that Argentine, but the mere thought it may be Three-O makes you really horny for a fuck. How twisted!

When you get up and leave the bar, you start to fly. Instead of walking, you pedal backwards, in reverse on an airborne bicycle.

How much upset for a word...For that word, Three-O's trademark. And you've not taken any stimulants. And you're not drunk. Did anything similar ever happen to you?

Bini refuses to go to the National, she says the porters there are right *felacios*, ha ha ha, and that they won't let her in, she takes you to a nearby building, a tenth floor, belonging to a friend of hers who owns a next-door flat she rents by the hour.

As it's only two blocks from the National, you raise no objections. And as soon as you're alone, she bites you on the chest, and unbuttons your shirt, and trousers, and you, erect as never before, astonished at yourself, let her do what she fancies, and she loosens your belt and pulls down your trousers, and swings you round, voraciously bites your buttocks, and kisses you, and tells you she is a *felacia*, and when you asked her about the little word, you gave her a look that made her wet, wet, wet. You fall flat on your back on the bed, and she doesn't even undress, and in seconds gives you a blinding orgasm, and then

155

she strips off and takes you by the hand, and leads you to the shower and washes you, and strokes you and offers you her breasts, and kisses you and drags you back to bed, and makes you kiss her and has a quick orgasm that arouses your second, and almost immediate third erection, something you didn't think you had in you, in a mere four hours you achieve quantitative miracles. And still don't feel at all tired, and she's a laugh, you see her playing with you, say things a ten-year-old would say, and the guy Alberto was Ríos by name, an Argentine who lived in Cuba, a yacht owner, she'd been with him several times, but hasn't seen him for some time, a strange guy, a rooster tattooed between his thighs…And your heartbeat races again, your solar plexus contracts, because now you know for sure: the *felacio* word and now the tattoo mean you can be sure that Alberto Ríos is none other than the Three-O man, and when you realize that, and imagine you're going to take revenge for what he did to you, you get hornier, how terrible, it's never ending, and she says you're very sweet and gentle, and you see Teresita surrounded by Three-O and his gang, young guys, smiling, not a hair out of place, in stylish gear, scented bastards…And curiouser and curiouser, this time the vile memory doesn't inhibit, on the contrary, it turns you on. For God's sake, what's got into you?

You want more breast, more thigh, to cling to life, and you kiss her and penetrate her more lustily, and she groans sordid, affectionate indecencies at you, and causes you a total orgasm, like you've not had since you were a kid, and when you drop down on the bed on your back, she gets on top, and leans her head on your chest, and you hug her silly, that slip of a whore who's just entered your past, and you slide your hand over the nape of her neck, down her back, and let yourself be driven by filthy pleasure, and you slaver, as if she were a sugary cake, because you now know very soon you can rid yourself of the need to settle accounts with one big, big bastard.

★

Twice you had him in the firing line and your people let you down. He realized it was a miracle he wasn't killed. And understood that his retirement to Montevideo and hired gunmen could no longer guarantee his safety, so he preferred to take himself off. But life takes such strange turns...look at the ridiculous way you came across him...

You would proceed very cautiously so as not to frighten him off.

At first you weren't sure. At times, you wanted to murder him with your own hand, split open his skull with an iron bar. But then told yourself: 'Hold off, *che*, don't rush things...'

'First make sure that Alberto Ríos and Three-O are one and the same...'

'More proof?' you got impatient. 'Isn't it enough that the fellow talks about *felacio* and he's got a rooster tattooed between his thighs? What more proof do you want? These can't just be coincidences...'

But you couldn't kill a guy without being totally sure. And you mustn't ask Bini anything. They were probably better friends than she let on, and maybe she'd tell him another Argentine was around and asking after him. If you put him on his guard, you can bet he'd take off again.

There were hours of endless, sterile monologue. You couldn't make your mind up. Didn't know what to do.

You thought of making a few enquiries at the Argentine embassy...

Dangerous. Better to wait till she made another mention of this Alberto. And then you could get her to talk, just casually. She really liked gabbing away...

At her cousin's place, she didn't shut up for a moment; and at the theatre, when you were listening to the singer, she hummed and chatted away; and just the same when you went to her godfather's: you were incredibly interested in what the guy was telling you, but Bini kept interrupting him, wanted to give you her own advice, until the old fellow lost his rag and told her to shut up, ha ha. He was certainly a fantastic guy, in a fascinating, crazy set-up. He said that non-believers lived in darkness. Just what you told your brother and Gonzalo when they mocked your faith. And after the rums you downed at the godfather's place, you really felt like going to the beach at midday, and stretched out on the beach, you remembered the yacht Alberto Ríos owned, and you threw out bait to Bini, said that you fancied a bit of sailing. She bit right away: said you could hire a yacht at the Hemingway Marina, but then she took it back and suggested another wharf. She didn't want to meet up with Alberto, who'd start complaining because she'd never called him back, or gone sailing again in the *Chevalier*...

'*Chevalier*? How nice...'

That day, at 6 p.m., you went back to her godfather's house for the *bembé* that had been announced. It was wonderful, so vital, drums, choruses, dances; and cheap, warm rum, in that dirt yard, tasted better than the seven-year-old stuff.

In the early hours, when Bini was very aroused and wanted to be with you, her godfather wouldn't allow you to go. He said it was an insult to the saint, and insisted you slept in a room he'd order them to get ready for you; and the grandma, who'd seen ninety-four carnivals, gave them for their only bed cover a Russian flag somebody stole from a boxing tournament, and as they were short of blankets in the house...And you stifling your laughter, but the old lady wasn't so off the rails, because despite the May heat and intense amorous activity, at 4 a.m. a most irritating breeze slipped through the cracks in the wood. And you had to have recourse to the flag, and at seven Bini was sound asleep, and you tiptoed out and went off to look for a taxi.

You rented a Toyota from the Cuba-Autos office for the three days you'd got left in Havana. And after buying a few bottles from the hotel shop and everything necessary for a spaghetti feast, you slammed your foot down and reached the Hemingway Marina in half an hour.

You immediately found the *Chevalier*, a small yacht under a French flag, moored at one of the jetties. You didn't see anyone on board.

On the pretext you'd like to buy it, you went to the port authority for information on the owner. You spoke like an Italian, because if Three-O found out an Argentine was after him, he might take fright. And that was how you found out where he lived, his home and work telephone numbers. Ready. Everything you needed.

Bini was waiting for you in Regla, sitting on the bed and sucking her finger.

A half-drunk bottle of rum survived on the bedside table which she'd taken to the room in the early hours.

Her godfather and his family welcomed the heap of food and drink you took them. They also welcomed the three blankets you gave them, and, above all, the crockery. When you were shopping, you remembered they only had three deep plates and two glasses. They drank rum either from the bottle or cardboard cups, and in order to eat the broth they made from a hog's head for the party they would wait for someone to finish with their plate, wash it and lend it to someone else. What a shambles! But it was a moving, cheerful poverty without complexes. When there is, there is; and when there isn't, you're fucked. That's what they said. And then you bought them four sets of crockery, the cheapest going, each for six places. They were very pleased. Now they could have get-togethers with lots of people.

And then you reckoned up again. You had forty-eight hours left in Cuba. You had to use them to confirm that Alberto Ríos was Three-O. And the only way was to see him with your own eyes.

Then crazy, hectic days would follow.

# 15 rigoborio and camberto

Thirty-four degrees on that 5 June in Havana, with ninety-eight per cent humidity, beat you down more than forty-three in a dry city.

Sweaty, ruddy-faced tourists took photos of each other, removed clothing and scratched their naked bodies. They enjoyed or pretended to enjoy. In any case, islanders saved energy in the shade and made careful calculations before undertaking to cross a street.

When Luis Julián left home, at 5.30 p.m., the heat persisted. Luis Julián had begun to walk down Patria Street when a Russian jeep hooted and braked next to him.

'Where you off to, Lucho?'

A soldier in uniform got out and kissed him.

'Fuck, Rigoberto, it must be ten years since I last saw you!'

'But you know how much I love you, dear Uncle…'

'Fuck, nephew, I'm not so sure now…'

'Oh, Uncle dear, you're not going to say a silly, silly thing, like I don't visit you? You know what it's like: children, the wife, work, university…where you heading? Can I give you a lift somewhere?'

'No, lad, I'm only going a block, to a friend's place. And what are you doing round here?'

'I came to talk to you.'

On his way home, accompanied by his nephew, Luis Julián discovered the reason for his visit.

'Someone in the area is putting horns on a buddy of mine…'

'Now, my lad, so what; cuckolding is the culture of today…'

Rigoberto ignored the joke.

'…and I owe this buddy a very great favour; and, you know, he's asked my help to catch the bastard in action, with proof, so he can make sure of holding on to his children.'

'An' what can you do?'

'You know, he's setting him a trap, and needs some fingerprints. He says it would be easy to get the guy to put his fingers round a glass or a bottle, get what I mean? What my buddy needs is to prove that the lover goes in his house when he's not there. But we don't know how to record the prints…'

For thirty-five years Luis Julián had been a specialist in the fingerprint department of the Revolutionary National Police. He'd retired the year before and spent his time reading novels and watching baseball games.

If it hadn't been his nephew, he'd have refused the request. Police who'd retired from specialist technical activities weren't allowed to put their expertise at the disposal of individuals.

But Rigo wasn't any old individual. He was his nephew, for fuck's sake. His own blood. Impossible to refuse.

'But you know nobody must find out that I…'

'Fuck, uncle, of course! I'm a policeman as well…'

'All right, but I'll need a good camera…'

'I've got a Kodak I can lend you.'

'All right, but don't bring me any prints before Tuesday…'

'Don't worry, my man, this can wait for a few days, till my friend gets them…What he needed was to know how to get them…'

Luis Julián went on talking to himself thoughtfully, not hearing him:

'…because I'll have to go to the laboratory to see if I can get some white lead and a drop of ammonium sulphide…'

'Yes, I'll be in contact with him, and I'll bring them as soon as he gets them…'

'If you can, bring them, at the latest, two hours after they've been left. Then it's all much easier.'

'And if we can't?'

'Bring them all the same, even if they're several days old; but if they're fresh, everything is easier and quicker.'

He then set about showing him how to handle the material without impacting on the prints. If it was a glass, you had to pick it up by introducing your five fingers parachute style, and open them up once inside. He should then press the backs of the fingers and nails against the glass. If it was a bottle, then pick it up by the bottom, with the fingers flush with the surface where the bottle was standing. No way should the material be carried in plastic, paper or cloth bags. They should make a container out of hard cardboard or wood to hold the glass or bottle by its base and the opening, without making contact with the sides.

Twelve degrees centigrade in Montevideo on that 15 June, lashed by a hundred-kilometre-an-hour wind from the pampas, which had been flooding the city for the last week with sheets of rain, would suggest holidays in Brazil, not sitting unheated in front of a computer belonging to the electoral register.

Even the telephone spluttered when it rang.

'Hello?'

'Good morning. Can I please speak to Dr Felipe Almanzor…'

'Indeed, I am he, and who's that?'

A hoarse voice chorused a song from Andalusia down the line: '"The Moors left Spain only/the tale of the Caliph's kniving…"'

Felipe smiled and sang the other two lines of the verse: '"…two moccasins, the Tower of Gold/and a tradition of skiving."'

'Oh, Camborio, old and hairy one. Where have you been?'

That song, which they'd used as a password in their old clandestine revolutionary organisation, reminded him that Camborio worked as a presenter on a Montevideo radio station.

In spite of the gusts from the pampas, they met in a café in the centre of town.

Camborio explained how he'd already spent more than a week looking for a guy's fingerprints.

'I tried to get them from a bastard in Foreign Affairs, who'd promised to collaborate, but then backed out.'

And he handed him the paper with the prints.

Felipe was a lawyer working for the Electoral Office. There they held the National Citizens' Register, with the fingerprints of every voter.

'I'll have to nick the prints myself, but it's no big deal,' Felipe assured him. 'People are so dopey with this cold that they haven't the faintest idea what everyone else is doing. I'll get you them today. Come to my office tomorrow, after nine, and ask for Rosalía. She'll have them in an envelope carrying your name.'

Rosalía did indeed hand him a tightly sealed envelope, on which it read: Antonio Torres Heredia, F.H.H.A.

El Camborio didn't know what F.H.H.A. meant.

'It means "for his hands alone",' explained Half-Dead.

'I'd imagined you'd turned into an ink-spreading bureaucrap.'

El Camborio was a past master at wordplay. In 1970, when he and Half-Dead spent two months shut up with a ransom victim of the Org., they'd invented a little game to fight off boredom: 'Don Quimancha de la Xote', 'Wottle Limen', 'The Cabigari of Dr Calinet', 'Jasonauts and the Argon'.

That very afternoon they enlarged the prints of the thumb, index and big fingers to the size of a duty sheet, as they'd been asked. And the six sheets were faxed from Montevideo to a telember nuphone in the city of Rome.

# 16 now is when

Going to see the godfather, so he talked to Rigoberto, and Rigoberto talked to the fingerprint specialist – it was an act of pure Christian charity on his part. And way over the top, because by then he was quite sure that Alberto Ríos was Three-O. After seeing him, and being very close; hearing the same voice with its loathsome resonances, recognizing his gestures and cocky stance with his one stiff leg and the other splayed out, why did you bother checking out his fingerprints?

Fucking hell, way over!

That Saturday, from your seat on the terraces at the *frontón* court, you saw him playing; and, no kidding, it was him. And when he dived in for a swim and emerged with his hair stuck to his skull, he was like he used to be with his crew cut. The same youthful face...How could there be any doubts?

That day you should have sent another fax to El Camborio telling him not to bother chasing Three-O's fingerprints in Montevideo. You didn't need them now. There he was. Right opposite. He was burning your eyes. Besides, he was the very same man who told Bini about *felacio*, and she'd told you he had a rooster tattooed in his groin.

For heaven's sake!

One can't be so short sighted.

Short sighted and irresponsible. You ran a needless risk in the swimming pool. Anybody might have seen you carrying his glass off.

And now the guy is in the can you must be more wary than ever. You'll have to prepare Bini down to the last detail. She can't put a foot wrong in the trial. One slip by Bini and your whole plan goes down the pan.

# 17 the immaculate preparation

You contemplated the sea that night, its pitch blackness behind the lights on the Malecón, the starry sky. You were planning to buy a house on a beach in Cuba, to have a tree-lined patio, a yacht. You did your sums. If you retired from business, just from the sale of the building on Monte Mario, without touching your shares in the company, you'd have more than enough to live for several decades on the island. After all, one day you'd stop toiling…and what better retirement than enjoying Bini and the delightful mess at her godfather's…Dancing, listening to music, communing with eternity via rum and drums, going deep-sea fishing; namely, moderate hedonism to round off life; and as the Andalusians say, summer in the shade and winter in the sun.

You hadn't been to hot climes for several years, since your visit to Maracaibo. And when you breathed the same sweet, salty air, you brimmed with adolescent happiness; and in the marrow of your bones, that electric heat of Buenos Aires in carnival time.

When you got off the plane in Rancho Boyeros, you remembered the ether bottles that perfumed your barrio; the smell of women aroused, who disguised their voices, provoked you with masks and half-masks, and you wanted to go on a drinking spree and a love-in…and it was just the same with Bini; or not with Bini, but perhaps her party moods, her climate, her temperature, her own carnavalesque irrationality.

Who at your age wouldn't fancy treating themselves to a retirement in a climate like that, your arm round a young waist, firm thighs, with a boat to explore those fantastic seas…

And according to Gonzalo, you needed only a couple of tricks up your sleeve in order to live in Cuba, and with a thousand dollars a month you lived more than decently; and you reckoned that with five thousand – that is, half what you spent in Rome – you'd live *de puta madre*, as the Spanish say. And your capital would grow and grow and never be a headache…

But in your heart of hearts, you realized those plans were mere idle daydreams. They'd never come to fruition; because you weren't equipped to survive without work. Soon after embarking on your Cuban-Andalusian fantasy, with the sea, palm trees, ancestral drums, carnival irrationality and a bevy of sirens like Bini, you'd be bored to death.

You knew only too well that you couldn't live without something to worry about. Your dramatic scheme for settling accounts with Three-O could give you headaches. The simplest and least dangerous option, in order to abide by Teresita and your conscience, would have been to shoot him in the street and *chao*, forget the bastard for ever. But you prefer headaches. Therein lies the problem.

When you received Three-O's prints from Montevideo and confirmed they matched those on the glass, you started to refine your ideas, which were still rather hazy.

Three-O drove around the whole of Havana without a bodyguard, like a fish in water, crying out to be killed. A couple of shots to his head would be a piece of cake. But at the same time just shooting him was a waste. That kind of death wouldn't make him pay for his crimes. And if Cuba offered facilities to set up a long-drawn-out affair, you weren't prepared to let the wretch die from a single bullet. You wanted him to suffer, to feel terror. And for the suffering and terror to haunt the rest of his life. An eternity in hell wouldn't pay for what he did to you. And like Neruda with Franco, you wanted '…a river of severed eyes to flow by staring at you, interminably'.

After a couple of days of hesitation, you thought of impaling him.

'Stinking sputum, dung of sinister sepulchral fowl', went the poem against the Generalísimo. And your sombre mood over those days also turned you bilious. You mixed up Neruda's hatred with the black humour of Prince Vlad, who liked to banquet and entertain his guests in the middle of a circle of torches. Except that the torches alternated with sharpened pikes where a few impaled fellows were always agonizing. The prince would say the plaints of the dying were the best condiment for their feast.

You would opt for a more technical impaling. You'd look for premises with a high ceiling, from which you'd hang a few pulleys. Then you'd tie Three-O's feet to the end of a plank of wood, so that they were some fifty centimetres apart. Like that, gagged so his screams couldn't be heard, tied hand and foot, you'd hoist him up three metres with his legs apart. Then, you'd start sharpening the pike in front of him, to see him suffer. And would kill him gradually… The first day you'd stick it in only fifteen centimetres, then farther and farther until forty-five centimetres were in; but ensuring the whole thing didn't slide in, so he stayed alive for at least a week, while you took lots of photos, even a video, to send round to the mafia of all his buddies.

That onanistic biliousness lasted a single day; but finally upset your stomach. You could eat nothing that day. And convinced yourself you were neither Prince Vlad nor the Marquis de Sade.

You would impale no one, nor pluck their eyes out, nor their nails.

The only thing you could do was execute him. You owed that to your dead. And that's what you'd do.

But then you had another problem: how to get a firearm in Havana?

Importing one was a huge risk. If they caught you carrying it, even though you hadn't shot one bullet, they'd put you inside for several days and never again give you a visa to enter the country; and goodbye Bini, and goodbye to all your plans.

It would be stupid to ask someone to bring one in for you. You couldn't expose any of your friends to such a risk. And dealing with European or Latin American petty criminals, who would do it for money, could generate blackmailing in the future.

Try to get one in Cuba?

Even more difficult. You'd have to deal with dangerous hoodlums. Cuban criminals had sometimes acquired the few firearms they had by killing and robbing policemen. And the price for that was the death penalty. Negotiating for a weapon from such underworld guys, who could be caught tomorrow and implicate you, would be stupid.

You then thought of poisoning him, or stabbing him, or smashing his skull with a baseball bat, or drowning him out at sea, or knocking him over with a car. But all these variations implied physical proximity, and so felt loathsome. To have to foresee every detail, imagine them, depressed you. You became, in your own eyes, a hideous wretch.

You finally rejected any brutality. You weren't any good at that. All you could do was shoot him, and you were back in the impasse of how to get a firearm in Cuba.

And during those days of uncertainty, Bini woke you in the early hours. After landing in Havana that afternoon, you'd seen her for only a few minutes, while she accompanied you in a taxi. You'd left her at her grandmother's, because you had to dine with government functionaries and she'd be out of place. Besides, you'd finish very late, and you were already dropping from exhaustion.

But Bini phoned you around 3 a.m. She was stuck in a mud flat driving her dad's car; she needed someone to give her a hand. She agreed a rendezvous in the entrance to La Giraldilla restaurant. You'd just arrived and still hadn't rented a car for your stay, so you went there by taxi.

You managed to drag the car from the mud quite easily and get it out by driving through an area that was flooded but driveable.

Just then, the rain poured down. And there was incessant thunder, with deafening blasts that terrified you. Bini looked fearfully at the sky. With each new crack, she closed her eyes, sobbed, sank her head between her shoulders and covered her ears. She asked you to hug her. Finally she pulled you inside the car and hid her head between your legs. She was like a small scared animal. She asked you to hug her harder, harder. With her eyes moistening, she started to tell you how a flash of lightning killed a cousin of hers in Oriente. And you caressed her, and she clung to your waist, curled up.

When the electric storm stopped and the thunderbolts faded into the distance, it was very late. Wouldn't her father have woken up? She insisted he always slept like a log, and that, in order to wake him, she sometimes had to hit him. Besides, he had gone to bed sozzled, because the neighbours he was playing dominoes with always pumped the rum in. That's what she said.

When you joined the highway, you were at the wheel. She wanted to drive, and you didn't let her; it wasn't a good time to practise. She started to moan and weep and say that nobody would teach her to drive, nobody would help her, and now she was going to stand on her head, and start playing the naughty child, flouncing around inside the car, and you laughing, and she put her feet on the ceiling and her head on the seat, and then stuck her tongue out and said *felacio*, and put a trainer over your face so you couldn't drive, and you removing it, trying to see through the rain still pouring down, until suddenly, whack, she jumps into the back of the car and starts tickling you and covers your eyes, and her childish pranks make you laugh more and more, you can't stop, you can't control her playing, till she begins to tickle you again and feel your crotch, and undo your belt, and the zip and, you, an itinerant erection, under the rain, a new record, you finally let her get on with it, and lean back, and quite out of her mind she gets on you from the back and unbuttons your shirt, almost pulls it off, and slips her head down your chest and starts nibbling your nipples, and you're just as irresponsible, laughing fit to burst, surrender to her, do whatever you want, and she keeps on down, until bang, a cyclist turns up on your right, and however much you try to avoid him, you hit him head on, the poor fellow and his bicycle and everything rebounded against a tree five metres from the roadside, and you managed to brake the car in contra-flow gully. She was the first to get out. You felt his pulse, put your ear to his heart and zilch: he was dead. She was crying and wringing her hands, and begged you to take him to a hospital, but you persuaded her that would be silly. Nobody could do anything for the poor guy.

You finally left that spot and went somewhere in the centre where you made her get out and take a taxi to her grandmother's. You gave her the car keys and the alarm control, so she could put them back on her father's bedside table, whence she'd taken them. And you took the car to an out-of-the-way barrio and abandoned it; but first you cleaned anywhere they might find your fingerprints or Bini's: the steering wheel, gear lever, handbrake, dashboard, windows, mirrors and carpets.

The idea of dumping the collision with the cyclist on Three-

O came to you the day after the accident. And you imagined a grandiose schema. You'd get him put inside in Cuba, though it were only for two years and on any pretext.

You were overjoyed. The plan would really work. In the first place, because you'd make him pay for something he hadn't done, and that would send him into a rage, or at least make him suffer.

In the course of Gonzalo's birthday, you thought of how to find out where Three-O was in the early hours at the time of the accident. It was important to find out that he wasn't anywhere at the time where others could give him an alibi.

Now the details of the new plan flooded your mind. An intelligent move. A much more efficient punishment than all those you'd imagined before.

What about Bini? Wouldn't she put her foot in it?

No, Bini was an intelligent lass; you'd make sure she performed immaculately.

# 18 the tocororo

It was 6.30 a.m. on 22 July and Alberto Ríos had just got up. After switching off the air-conditioning, he picked up the intercom and pressed the button for the kitchen. His two maids arrived around six.

'Orange juice, mango juice, passion-fruit juice, coffee with a small spoonful of sugar,' he said, and hung up.

As he was heading to the bathroom, the phone rang.

At that time of day it might be a long-distance call from his brother...

'Yes?'

'Alberto?' He heard a woman's voice. 'It's Bini.'

'At this time of day?' But he was pleased to get the call.

'Yes, I dreamed about you and I'm desperate to see you.'

'Are you in need of cash?' Alberto went on the defensive.

'No, not at all, I'm calling to invite you to eat at the Tocororo, and I'm paying.'

'You won the lottery?'

'Something like that, and all down to you.'

'Down to me? All you can think of is having lunch with me?'

'Not just lunch, *felacio*. I want to eat every inch of you, from your toes...I don't know what's got into me, but I've been pining after you for days. And this time it won't cost you a cent. I'm paying.'

'If you're so desperate why didn't you call me at the weekend? You know they're the days I keep for you...'

'But I got fed up with ringing you...Last Sunday, I really wanted you at two in the morning, and I rang you, but you weren't in...'

'On Sunday? Don't lie, Bini. I was in bed at two in the morning...'

'Yes, with one of your whores sucking your ear off, because you didn't hear the phone...'

'You're wrong, kid; I was by myself, and it's not true you rang me...'

'I swear I did, Alberto, and I called you back at about six, and you didn't answer...'

'Look here, Bini, if you want to see me, you don't have to spin these yarns, or say you're going to invite me out. How much do you need?'

'I swear I want to invite you to lunch.'

'When? Saturday, Sunday?'

'No, it's got to be today. Do you fancy the Tocororo? I'll really pay, cross my heart, and I can, thanks to you.'

'But tell me, how come?'

'I'll tell you tonight in the restaurant. Eight o'clock all right for you?'

Alberto was very intrigued and accepted.

Anyway, he supposed he would pay. Sure, the little hussy rang him because she was short of money. And he'd give it to her, provided it wasn't too much. It was worth getting her back.

He'd not seen her for some three months.

Bini was by far the Cuban whore he most liked. And not only in bed; he also liked her brazenness, and that she whored straight, without saying she was a victim of the Cuban crisis, nor claiming to be an intellectual. She treated him as an equal. She could be as happy as a small child, and at the same time violent, mad and even rather dangerous. She'd been inside. And was also very proud: once, when he dropped a dollar bill on the floor so she'd pick it up, she left without charging him and avoided him for several weeks. Ever since, he'd treated her with deference, in order not frighten her off.

But something must be up, because he'd not seen her since May. Had she fallen in love? Perhaps she was no longer on the game?

And now, what had bitten her?

He didn't believe that she'd called him at the weekend; nor that she'd pay for his dinner tonight at the Tocororo; nor that she was so eager to eat him alive, as she claimed.

But her reappearance intrigued him.

At eight on the dot, Alberto took a table for two at the Tocororo. He chose the outside area, tucked away among ferns. He ordered a Chivas Regal on the rocks and looked around him. He was glad to be back at that restaurant. He'd not been there since May when his brother visited.

As usual, almost all the tables were taken, and mainly by tourists and foreign residents.

To his left, twelve or more people were celebrating something. And as part of the round of toasts, someone gave a speech in English, glass of wine held aloft. Alberto didn't manage to make out the words.

On the other side, a guitar trio was dedicating a *ranchera* to two polite, accepting, resigned Mexicans, who stoically chewed on their lobsters till the performance ended. When the trio was getting ready for another salvo, the diners tried to liberate themselves with a quick tip; but it wasn't that easy. They were so grateful for the tip they sang them a *corrido* and the poor guys chewed on in silence.

Alberto noted how Cuban trios were as predictable as ever. Where did they get the idea that tourists liked to hear their folklore being slaughtered?

After his initial clashes with trios, Alberto hid his Argentine accent in order to spare himself the inevitable Cuban-style tango.

When the trio left the Mexicans' table, they came over to enliven Alberto's solitude. He asked them not to disturb him because he was assessing a business deal that he'd have to discuss with someone in a minute.

'Music can inspire business,' suggested the most insistent of the trio.

'Yes, it's true,' replied Alberto sternly, 'but I like music so much I can't resist and start dancing by myself. And, you know, I forget my business deals as I dance.'

And he suggested they go and inspire the gringos on the table making all the toasts.

He soon realized it was 8.15 and took fright.

Could it be that screwball had stood him up for the fun of it? And at that very moment he saw her come in.

For the first time, she wasn't dressed as a whore. Every table turned to look at her. She was made up to the nines, and her hair was piled up in a bun. She wore a white linen dress, skirt to the knee, very tight waistline and delicate lace around the neck. She was showing off her perfect shoulders and neck and walked very slowly, looking around her as if needled by something.

Her eyes lit up when she spotted him at the corner table.

'How incredible, *che*, you've really changed!'

The elegant outfit didn't, however, change the wild cat that once wore miniskirts and cheap blouses.

'I was so desperate to see you, Alberto!' And she kissed him smack on the mouth.

Her thick, soft, hot lips, and hoarse, coarsely cadenced voice, worked their charm again.

'You'd forgotten me, you never call…'

Bini told him the reason for her call and invitation in a few words.

'The fact is I bet a hundred pesos on marbles last Saturday…'

'Marbles?' Taken aback, Alberto gestured with his thumb and index finger like a young kid playing at marbles…

'No, the lottery…We play the Venezuelan lottery here,' she added. 'And I just won seven thousand pesos.'

Alberto calculated that was worth three hundred and fifty dollars. He gave her a hundred whenever he saw her. What the fuck would she suggest now?

'What happened was that I dreamed about you on Friday night, and when I tell my cousin Chacha, she does a sum and says: "Put it on fifty-four!"'

'And what's my connection with fifty-four?'

'It's a sum she does: she adds together the letters of the name, multiplies them by seven and adds five. Alberto has seven letters, and seven times seven is forty-nine, and five more makes fifty-four. Get me now?'

Alberto could only shrug his shoulders and laugh.

'Cuba, crazy Cuba!'

'And then, I don't know whether it was because you made me lucky in the lottery,' Bini continued, having just put a naked foot on his knee, 'I really felt like having it off with you, like never before.'

He shifted his chair, took Bini's foot and placed it in his groin. She shut her eyes and bit herself lustfully.

'I tell you, Alberto…It was just like that. As soon as they told me the little ball had rolled my way I thought of you and went wet. It was around two on Sunday morning, and my cousin tells me: "Hey, girl, you just won yourself seven thousand pesos with that marble…" And do you know what I did then?'

'Yes, you went all wet; go on with the story,' and he undid

his fly so she could stick her foot inside. She slipped down her chair in order to meet his target.

'I love this fucking country,' cried a gringo at the next-door table.

'So do I,' added Alberto, gulping down a whisky.

'Yes, of course, I wet myself, like now, sweety…' and she pinched his rod with her toes; 'but that's the least of it…'

Alberto saw the head waiter coming over and sat straight in his chair. He ordered a selection of roast shellfish, a chef's special, and another couple of Chivas on the rocks.

'…and then, coming on like that, and the seven thousand pesos the ball boy brought me, I told myself: "I'm going off to jingle-jangle with Alberto"; and I picked up the phone and rang you, but you weren't there…'

'I told you, I don't believe you…'

She moved her foot away from his groin.

'Do you think you can call me a liar to my face?' And she looked at him in a rage. 'Not only did I ring you then; but I kept calling you, because I couldn't get to sleep…'

'But I was at home all the time. I swear I was in bed then, and didn't get up till six…'

'I don't know,' she replied, irritated. 'I might be a whore, but I'm no liar. And you'll just see how I'll pay for your dinner and how I didn't come to get bucks from you. All I want is to be with you, kid…Take a look at this.'

She opened her bag and showed him a wad of dollars.

'I changed what I won into dollars, so I could pay for your drinks and the meal.'

'You know I won't let you pay…'

'Yes, you will, because it's what my saints want.'

Amused and flattered by so much tomfoolery, he discovered that Bini's godfather, after consulting Orula, had ordered her not to touch a cent of the money she'd won in the Venezuelan lottery: she had to spend the whole lot on the man who'd brought her such luck.

'That's why, *hombre*, I can't let you pay…'

After a few hours in the flat on 21st Street, Bini took Alberto Ríos's identity card from his wallet and put it on the bedside table.

'He swallowed the whole story, Aldo.'

'Not Aldo, for fuck's sake,' he chided her.

'Ay, I'm sorry, Tito.'

She told him that, after making love, Alberto got up naked and went to the bathroom.

'And right there I took his wallet from his trousers and extracted his ID.'

Aldo smiled. His plan was gelling; when he knocked the cyclist down, Three-O was sleeping alone in his house in Atabey.

Now, everything was in place to set the sights on him.

# 19 combine, combiner

The East Combined was thirteen kilometres down the Monumental highway, at a spot that was ideally close to and far from the capital. It was inaugurated as a prison in 1977: near the coast, in a peaceful environment, no noise, pleasant to look at and plenty of fresh air.

Buildings 1, 2 and 3 and the disciplinary wing constitute the prison in itself, with beds for almost five thousand inmates. There's also the management building, which has spaces for services, administration, sleeping quarters for the guards, etc.

Building 2 is host on its first two floors to common criminals who present an average-to-high threat of danger. On the third floor, on the south side, are passive homosexuals, and on the north side the active brigade.

On the fourth floor, north side, there are all kinds of criminals, but none represents a tremendous threat to penitentiary coexistence. And on the south side, foreign inmates are incarcerated and enjoy more benevolent treatment.

The Combined owes its name to its double function as a jail

and plant for prefabricating CP 109, belonging to the Ministry for Construction.

Inmates who so wish can follow a rehabilitation project, which consists essentially of working. That allows them to obtain considerable remission. They reckon it alleviates the hardships of imprisonment, sweeps cobwebs from the brain and allows them to earn a little money.

Nevertheless, homosexuals don't join in the work in the prefabrication plant, because they always cause a ruckus, even if it's not premeditated. For the same reason, very dangerous prisoners or foreigners are not allowed in either.

Homosexuals and foreigners also labour and create art, but in their own buildings.

Alberto entered the Combined on 10 August at 6 p.m. He was joined in the prison lorry by two other prisoners who got on at the public prosecutor's office. All three were handcuffed.

One of them, an olive-skinned, very tall, muscular guy, nearing sixty, stretched out on one of the seats that had been let down, occupying the whole space. Alberto and the other prisoner sat opposite.

Not saying a word, as if the others didn't exist, the old fellow lay on his side, rested his head on a fist and shut his eyes.

Alberto sat opposite the old man's feet, by the van door. To his left, at the other end, leaning slightly on the bars between him and the driver's cabin, sat a very thin, fair-haired guy, whose age was hard to pin down; he was incredibly gaunt. The man stared at the little barred window in the door, smiling sadly and inconclusively. Alberto thought of the Mona Lisa.

The three didn't say a word on the whole journey.

Over the last few hours, at various, fleeting moments of despair, Alberto had taken refuge in the instinctive hope that he was living a bad dream. But now a very concrete reality, represented by the jolting lorry, its smell of poorly carburetted petrol and the baleful looks of the two criminals by his side, suggested that everything else was a dream. The tracks where he'd jogged early that morning were a dream; so was the routine of swimming and reading he'd enjoyed for so many months. His life was changing by the minute.

Now his immediate, definite fate was the East Combined. And there was a big question mark over his long-term fate.

How would it all end?

He decided not to think about the future; but he couldn't blot out his ominous present, fruit of his relationship with an enigmatic Cuban prostitute.

He shut his eyes and continued to ponder.

From the moment he was arrested, he'd consoled himself with the hope he'd find some way to prove his innocence.

He recalled how two days earlier, in the tournament, he'd played down the police's suspicions. Based on his erroneous registration at the Triton Hotel, and on shoes whose prints were found next to the cyclist's body, they were unsustainable. The mistake would become obvious at any moment. Everything would be cleared up. One way or the other, the police would discover he wasn't the Alberto Ríos checked in at Room 322 at the Triton from 24 to 26 July. And as he couldn't calibrate at that moment the size of the mess they were getting him into, he decided not to get distressed. Time would tell.

A few days before, when he couldn't find his ID, he hadn't suspected Bini. Now, however, after hearing the tape, it was obvious: she must have stolen it from him, in his own bedroom.

Perhaps with the idea of staying with someone else at the Triton…

With someone else?

Of course!

When the prison lorry swung round a sharp bend, it all became clear. Bini stole the car to enjoy a spot of driving; but then, by herself or accompanied, she knocked over the cyclist.

No, not by herself, she was certainly accompanied.

Yes; and her companion didn't want his dallying with a whore to be discovered; or to go to prison for being a drunken accomplice to a murder.

There was a companion. That was the key.

Perhaps it was some well-heeled guy; or a government high-up; or a foreigner, who suddenly found himself threatened with scandal and prison because he'd had a fling.

Yes, whoever it was must have offered her five or ten thousand dollars to come out with that string of untruths. What wouldn't a little whore like Bini not do for ten thousand bucks?

Obviously, once the cyclist had been knocked over, the guy must have reckoned quite logically the police would pin it on Bini. Several reasons would allow them to point their guns at her: first, because she was the mechanic's daughter and because in the early hours she'd been in the same house where the car was kept; and then because she was a hooker with a record and had done time.

The fellow must have been frightened that once they'd tracked Bini down sooner or later they'd get him. That was why he preferred to fabricate that story and blame the death on someone else. If they got her, she would do time without a doubt. But if the death were put on somebody else, at least she'd earn a packet.

Yes, but…why should they pick him out?

And how could they be so sure about his shoe size? Could it be that the same day Bini stole his ID she'd also stolen a pair from the enormous collection of shoes he rarely wore. But if the shoes were at the scene of the crime, she couldn't have got them afterwards…Yes, they must have fixed that before fingering him for the collision with the cyclist. It was all incredibly tortuous.

If they picked him, it was because it was Bini's idea; among other reasons, because she knew he never slept with anyone at his house. And as he had no alibi, he was the ideal candidate to pin an early morning road crash on. Whoever her accomplice was, he must have got Bini to steal his ID in order to use the shoes and hotel to frame him. It was a really clever operation.

Obviously, and to get into his place, Bini had spun him the tale of the Venezuelan lottery and subsequent randiness.

It was clear the imaginations of Bini, the hotel maid and the Jaén guy had been lubricated with lots of dough…

Alberto was relieved to think that his real enemies hadn't tracked him down.

In that respect, he should keep his cool.

To begin with, shock and fear had made him think of them. He was also depressed by the awful situation in which he found himself being questioned on suspicion of murder.

A sudden braking forced him to cling to the seat to avoid falling off. When he opened his eyes, he just caught sight of the old man sliding on his side. He had to put a foot on the floor so he didn't fall.

'Fucking cunt,' he shouted, looking furiously at the driver's cabin.

When he settled back, he twisted his handcuffs in order to put an arm over his eyes.

The other prisoner, up against the bars, rested his feet on the bench and hugged his knees with his handcuffed hands. He was so long and skinny he could easily rest his forehead on a thigh. Esconced as he was in the corner, the sudden braking had apparently not woken him up.

Alberto shut his eyes and continued to ponder.

Yes, they'd all been well lubricated.

He remembered how, when Bastidas offered to read him Jaén's statement, he had been quite overcome and asked him to sum it up in a couple of words; but the bastard insisted on reading the most scandalous paragraphs; particularly the one where Jaén had stated without hesitation at the sight of a photo of him from the immigration archives: 'Yes, that's him all right.'

'You absolutely sure?' they'd asked.

'Absolutely; I booked him into the hotel and he was right

opposite me. I can't be mistaken. That's the photo of Alberto Ríos.'

And the chambermaid described him as tall, over fifty, with a goatee beard and very long white hair.

They bought them. The bastards. They were happy to get rich by putting him inside.

Bastards, no: survivors. Another example to support his theories about survival and cruelty.

How many more had been bought up in that hotel?

Or perhaps they disguised somebody with a beard and long hair to look like him…

As for his ID card, Bini knew he kept it in his wallet, together with his money and credit cards, in the back pocket of his trousers. He remembered the time, when the asshole was next to him, when he had to get it out under protest, when a waitress asked for it. As they lacked equipment to check money, some shops and restaurants asked every customer who paid with hundred-dollar bills for an identity card. He also remembered how the last time he'd got out of bed naked to go to the bathroom she'd had more than enough time to take his wallet out of the trousers he always left on the folding table, next to his wardrobe.

He opened his eyes again, all agitated.

The fucking whore!

He tried to remember his movements on the 24, 25 and 26 July. Perhaps he could find some detail to undermine this nonsense about his stay at the Triton.

On Saturday 24th, bad weather had prevented him from setting sail. After a very windy break of day, with a rough sea, it had rained from mid-morning. On the Internet the weather looked very bad for small vessels. Fed up, he stayed at home all morning; and remembered various calls from wrong numbers, perhaps from Bini and her accomplice attempting to control his movements. At midday, he lunched at the Sevilla Hotel with Dr Pazos; and in the afternoon, he put the notes he'd taken during the conversation on to his computer. At night he watched videos until after one.

From early on Sunday he'd worked on his book; at around eleven, he went to Capdevila to play tennis. He had lunch in the club cafeteria. He took a short siesta, worked for a while, read for a couple of hours; from ten o'clock, he shut himself up with a woman he bade farewell to just before midnight. But nothing he did prevented him from being up to something with another woman at the Triton.

The bad weather continued on the Monday. Early in the morning, he couldn't go jogging or to the Copa. He took the opportunity to visit an art designer and talk about some prints he required for his book; at eleven he went for an appointment Raquelita had arranged for him with an ornithologist at the Biology Faculty. As it was a holiday and the man lived in Vedado, they met in the cafeteria at the Free Havana. In the afternoon he had to go to Fischer's place to sign some Texinal documents. At around five, when the weather improved, he went for a dip at the Copacabana, but had to miss out on that because it rained again. At night, at home, he dined on what his cook had left him and read in bed until late.

He supposed that Bini and company followed his every step over those three days.

In effect, none of his activities on those days gave him an alibi, because he could perfectly well have carried them out and stayed at the Triton.

Whoever had set him up knew what he was doing. The shit was getting to his brain. He should get it into his head that two years inside was the most likely outcome.

From that very moment, with the lorry on the move, he started to apply psychotherapy. First of all he shouldn't despair. He was going to lose this one. Bad luck. But two years inside wasn't the end of the world. No tragedy. There'd be better times. And meanwhile, he should keep cool and collected, like any intelligent person. Two years would fly by...As long as the conditions in prison were all right...If only he could get a single cell.

The van stopped in front of number 1 sentry box. Next to it, to the left, an electronic gate carried a notice: COMBINED EAST UNIT.

The guard accompanying the driver got out and handed over a sheaf of papers. Another man in uniform, carrying an automatic rifle, came out of the sentry box, climbed on to the back board of the prison lorry and inspected inside. He returned to his box, wrote something down, and a colleague picked a phone up.

Inside the lorry, there was a window that ran the whole length of the grille which opened up. The driver looked into the back and left the window open.

Alberto saw the number 1 gate slide open, and heard a thud in the sentry box.

He heard voices and laughter, but couldn't make out what they were saying.

The prisoner who was next to him, twenty-five years old perhaps, opened his mouth for the first time: 'Back on my patch.' He yawned, half sarcastically, half resigned, and lifted up his handcuffed wrists to stretch out.

The older guy reacted. 'What patch you mean? You've never been in here.'

'Oh no? What do you know about me?'

'Just looking at you, I know you're an asshole and a clown, and that this isn't your patch, because you've never been an inmate here.'

'Hey, let's show some respect or I...'

'And this guy's never been in the Combined either,' the old man's rough voice butted in, as he pointed at Alberto, not even bothering to look at him.

'You're right,' Alberto laughed. 'It's my first time.'

When he heard his River Plate accent, the old man was

transformed. His face lit up; he went doe eyed. He sat down for the first time, and pointed at Alberto again. He seemed in a state of wonder, as if he'd made a real find. He stopped arguing with the other man, who, feeling miffed and rather confused, was muttering 'balls' and 'fuck' under his breath.

The old man was around one metre ninety tall. He was sturdy, and had one bald patch in the middle of his grey hair.

'Argentine?' and he again pointed at Alberto.

'Yes, how did you work that out?'

'The way you gab, *che Garufa*,' and he thickened his Buenos Aires lingo.

'What's all this about the patch? I don't understand,' replied Alberto, who wanted to stoke the fire.

'Patch is house, pad, sack. Get me, *pibe*?'

And he started to sing by way of illustration, tunefully and in a good voice, a fragment of 'My Sad Night':

> *On my sack no more sign*
> *Of those pretty flagons*
> *Tied with pretty ribbons,*
> *Like when you here sighed…*

'"All the same design",' Alberto corrected the fourth line.

'Yes, you're right, "all the same design", *Garufa*…'

Now he spoke only with a broad Buenos Aires tang of the old school. A real caricature, but he thought he was good at it.

The other prisoner now smiled a wee smile again, though tinged with alarm.

'Tangos are my life…'

Each loony has his tune, thought Alberto, smiling.

The old guy let on that in the can they called him Gardelion, and Epilepsy as well, but his real name was Epifanio Salazar, and what he most wanted to do in life was go to Buenos Aires, the land of Carlitos Gardel, but he had hit fifty-three and it wouldn't be easy…

'I came here in seventy-seven. I'm one of the founding fathers, *Garufa*...And I even had to take up bucket and spade to finish off the building work, because I was in the can. I did twenty-two years; but this time it's only eight.'

And eight times he'd stabbed the sod who'd tried to stick it up his gal.

'But if it goes right, I only do a fistful.'

And at fifty-eight and with the pesos he was going to save in the can, he might even make it to La Boca, the Caminito, Calle Corrientes, Barracas al Sur, Tangolandia, and he launched into 'Mi Buenos Aires querido'.

He twisted his mouth and opened his eyes wide, just like Gardel; and did a perfect imitation of his overacted melancholy...But he felt something. That Buenos Aires he'd never known also belonged to him.

' "And the old coot can sing..." '

Suddenly the lorry stopped outside a four-storey building. They opened the door and told Alberto to get out.

'Epilepsy goes straight to number two building, and the other guy to one,' said one of the police, looking at a chart he was holding.

'*Chao*, Gardelion, thanks for the tangos,' Alberto muttered.

'*Chao*, Garufa, you'll be in number two as well; let's meet up, to gab in versere.'

Alberto waved goodbye.

Then he moved off with a policeman, pleased at his encounter with Gardelion. He hoped to meet up with him soon. If the tangophiliac had spent twenty-two years in that can, he must be well versed in the possible combinations of East Combined.

# 20 the merry widow

Ten p.m.

A hundred metres from his destination, the passenger says: 'Let me off here,' and hands the taxi driver a note from the back seat.

The driver takes it, and when he switches the light on his passenger has already got out.

The meter shows eight dollars forty cents and he's got ten. The driver has no time to thank him for the generous tip. He manages only to see his customer walking away from the back of his taxi.

He thinks he had an Argentine accent.

'Does Baltasar París live here?'

'He used to…He passed away a few days ago.'

''Oh, sorry, señora…I'm so sorry…'

'What can I do for you?'

The woman scrutinizes him, full of fear, and doesn't open the door wide…

'Well, I've just come from Argentina, and they asked me to bring this for him. Can I leave it with you?'

He's a tall, fat man with a white moustache. He's wearing dark glasses and a Basque beret.

The woman takes the bulky manila envelope rather hesitantly.

'On whose behalf…?'

'From Julio Rodríguez, an Argentine who made friends with him when he was passing through Cuba; and a little something for your daughters…That's what he told me.'

'Right… thanks very much, señor, but come in…' and she opens the door wide.

'That's very kind, señora, but some other time. I'm very tired after the journey and I've still got a few errands to run. I'm sorry about what happened. Goodbye…'

The man touches the top of his hat and walks off. She watches him walk quickly down the steps. A rare turn of speed, for someone so old and fat.

When he's in the street, the man walks a few metres to the corner; goes round, continues along the pavement to the next corner, goes round a second time, and gets into a car waiting for him with its engine running.

'Everything all right?' a woman asks from behind the wheel.

'Couldn't be anything but with the precautions we've taken, Aurelia. Now step on it.'

The vehicle has already gone three blocks, and París's widow is still opening the parcel. They'd put so many envelopes one inside another, with several layers of sticky tape, that it's difficult to open. She's thinking it must be some joke in bad taste.

At last, the final envelope contains notes.

Dollars!

Hundred-dollar bills!

Two hundred one-hundred-dollar bills!

The widow understands.

That's from no Julio Rodríguez.

It comes from the tortured conscience of the person who knocked Baltasar down. But as nobody can now return her husband, the widow will keep her trap shut. Nobody in her family, or Baltasar's family, will find out she's been given that money.

It's her first merry moment as a widow; which she will share with no one. She doesn't want the house full of relatives.

In the morning she'll go out and buy some clothes for the girls.

# 21 convict number fourteen

First they took him to an office, where he had to fill in forms and be given a yellow card. From there they walked him to an adjacent building to pick up his 'supplies': a grey T-shirt and trousers, a sheet, half a piece of coarse soap and a spoon.

He was surprised they let him wear him his own shoes and laces. Nobody allowed that in the prisons he was familiar with.

When they left, a policeman escorted him, also on foot, to building number 2. He was young and smiley. As they proceeded, he predicted he'd be put in a cell already occupied by three prisoners doing time for traffic crimes.

'Mariano will definitely put you with the traffic criminals. You'll be real comfortable.'

Major Mariano Robles Marín, who'd specialized over the years in foreign inmates, was in charge of south wing, on the fourth floor of number 2 building. He welcomed Alberto cordially into his office, and lectured him on the ways of that wing, which housed only foreigners.

'They're quiet folk, for what you'd expect in a prison.'

The really aggressive types, whether foreign or not, stayed in single cells in the disciplinary wing.

The 'nice' folk in south wing included seventeen murderers, some of whom were quite neurotic, escapees from the US, Mexico and the Caribbean, and it was best to keep your distance, but you couldn't call them dangerous...

Alberto informed him of his interest in writing a book, and that it would really help to have a single cell. After all, he had resources, his consul and friends at work could help him, and even help the jail, if they were short of anything...

'All right, Alberto,' Mariano responded, smiling. 'If you want a single cell, I can give you one, as I've got three available at the moment. You don't have to offer us anything. I must warn you that the jail is short on a lot of things: sometimes we're short on clothes, soap, toilet paper, and any assistance would be welcome. But we're not allowed to receive gifts from inmates. It's stupid, but that's the way it is. Anyway, foreigners can have anything they want for their personal needs; in the case of unpremeditated crimes like yours, you will get the utmost support from me and all the staff on this floor. Just tell us what you need...'

'Fine, Major, paper, writing tools, my laptop, and if possible a vegetarian diet, a few drinks...'

'The alcoholic variety?' asked Mariano.

'If at all possible, Major,' chanced Alberto, who till then had envisaged only coffee, mineral water etc.

'Alcohol is banned, but in single cells, with civilized people, who don't get outlandishly drunk, and don't share it round with other inmates, exceptions are always possible...'

From that first meeting, Alberto displayed his best wiles of seduction.

First of all, he wasn't sure whether that friendly prison guard was a shitty git he could put in his pocket, or a bribable brigand who knew how to play the game.

His first impression was that he was a git. Time would tell.

Alberto drew up a list of his needs on Mariano's desk. The prison office agreed to send a fax to Texinal. Alberto asked his partners above all for books from his library, a thermos, coffee, tea, and a range of whiskies from his place. He also asked them to come with the Argentine consul. Diplomats could visit compatriots in jail, whenever they wanted.

A terrific start.

The single cell Mariano assigned to him, nine metres square, was right at the end of the passage away from the entrance door, in the quietest part of south wing.

When he saw how his feet stuck ten centimetres over the end of the bed, Alberto couldn't not think how uncomfortable Gardelion must be. The shower and lavatory were mere holes in the ceiling and ground.

There was no sink or running water.

Mariano, who went with him to his cell, gave him some advice on how to make life easier.

Water was one problem they had in the Combined. The shower came out of a blunt lead pipe, and worked only for ten minutes from 18.00 to 18.10.

'Add a few plastic buckets to your list; tell them to bring five or six so you can collect plenty of water.'

Meanwhile, over the next few days, Mariano would lend him some family-size bottles of Tropicola. So he'd get through.

When he was by himself, he got that cold feeling of unreality once more.

Yes, he was in prison and this was his cell.

And it had happened so quickly…A raft of surprises over a few hours: shock, rages, scares, the arrest warrant, Bini and Jaén's cynicism, the prosecution and the handcuffs. And suddenly, what was he doing handcuffed between two jailbirds in a lorry? To think that that same day, till 11 a.m., he'd been a free man, reading under a parasol and taking notes for an essay by the pool in the Copacabana Hotel.

'Weeping behind the screen', hands on hips, he started to think how best to organize his space, when they brought him everything he'd ordered.

Like all the 'temps', Alberto had sparked some curiosity; but when people found out he was another traffic case, most lost interest.

The atmosphere in south wing wasn't much like a prison's. At least, not like the ones he knew. To his knowledge nowhere else in the world separated foreigners out. And obviously, the absence of local hoodlums and aggressive criminals allowed for a more benign regime.

His first surprise was the way his jailers behaved, usually very friendly and cheerful; and not only with him, but with most of the almost two hundred foreign inmates banged up in south wing.

When they were taken into the yard, however, they met up with around three hundred Cuban common criminals, lodged in north wing, on the fourth floor of the same building.

He hated that.

One of the guards informed him that the common element rubbed shoulders with the foreigners in the yard and also in the recreation area on the fourth floor, where they could watch telly and amuse themselves in other ways. And there were severe sanctions for attacking a foreigner. The Cubans were scared of Mariano, who went wild when any of his brood was touched.

The yard had a wall for *frontón* and fixtures for softball, volleyball and basketball.

As Alberto was interested in sports, he enquired whether it would be a problem if he wanted to watch them play.

The guard hesitated before replying.

'They're going to ask you for cigarettes, dollars... They may try to give you a fright: but if you're not frightened, they'll let you be.'

'Like dogs,' responded Alberto, developing the idea; 'if they sense you're afraid, they jump and bite you straight away.'

'That's right,' the guard went on; 'but if you want to play handball, it can be arranged through Mariano.'

That was great news…How wonderful if he could play handball or squash…It would keep him in good shape. And he could see that doing gymnastics in his little cell would be tricky.

'If you like, I'll mention it,' suggested the youth, a very wiry black, around thirty, who was muscular and athletic and looked like a *karateka*.

'Please, I'd be really grateful…'

'*Che, Garufa!*' he suddenly heard.

Alberto swung round and lifted a hand to his eyes, like a visor. He spotted Gardelion twenty metres away.

'Oh! So you already know Epilepsy?' the guard exclaimed, surprised.

'We came in the same lorry.'

When he saw him walk over, so sprightly, Alberto stretched out a hand and they shook.

'I'm so pleased, *che*…So they put you in number two building as well?'

'And in cell one thousand four hundred and fourteen…'

'Really, Gardelion? So you're convict number one thousand four hundred and fourteen, ha ha ha…'

'*Che-diddily-che, Garufa*…'

They went on joking in tango slang.

Gardelion was really pleased they'd met up. He slapped him on the shoulder like an old friend. As soon as he'd come over, he'd ignored the guard, who'd stayed next to Alberto. The old man was a head taller than both of them.

'Come on, meet my *radescom*, my partners,' he suggested finally.

Alberto looked askance at his custodian, who nodded imperceptibly.

A quarter of an hour later, after showing off with his cellmates, talking in Argentine port slang, Gardelion decided to pay homage to his new friend with a tango.

'What do you want me to sing? How about "Garufa"?'

'No, sing me "Convict Number Fourteen".'

Gardelion's mates were Nitrate and the Russian, two men sentenced to thirty years. A striking mulatto, El Guajiro, soon joined them, a big, red scar slanting across his face, from left temple to right jaw.

Fucking hell, a left-hander must have slashed him.

One eyebrow was sliced in half, his eye and nose had been destroyed and he made terrible faces when he spoke.

He looks like Frankenstein struggling to have a shit.

Gardelion was the only one of the quartet past forty. And you could see they all respected him.

When they saw Alberto in such company, the rest of the inmates started to look on the sly, but maintained a respectful distance. Alberto noticed the obvious curiosity aroused at Gardelion's free and easy manner with him. No doubt they were all wondering who Mr Newy could be.

In the afternoon, back in south wing, Alberto found out that the Russian was one of the hardest gang leaders. Nitrate and El Guajiro were his lieutenants, and Epilepsy a kind of adviser, the Russian thought of as a father.

He also found out that Epilepsy, after doing a thirty-year sentence, reduced to twenty-two, had only had a few days of freedom, enough to get back at another prisoner, a companion over years, who'd cuckolded him.

Epilepsy had declared his revenge and soon returned. He even informed the prison authorities. He wasn't in a waiting mood. He'd asked them to keep the same bed for him in the Russian's corridor. Before leaving, he'd entrusted all his belongings to Nitrate, except for his toothbrush. There wasn't much: two tango songbooks, a Carlos Gardel poster and a little picture, without glass, of La Pura. On the back, in childish script, Gardelion had written: 'My saint of a mother in 1933.'

He entrusted his toothbrush to El Guajiro, who never brushed his teeth.

So would never use it.

# Part VI

# 22 butcha'

Two sharpshooters took over the flat in the early hours of 3 December, 1998. They'd hide there as long as was necessary. And wouldn't leave until Three-O was dead.

The guy didn't even present himself as a target before the 14th. But they kept their positions, and never gave up their vigil. Waited for him, gun at the ready on its tripod. Telescopic lens and sights focused on the middle of the door. Which he'd have to go through when he decided to take a walk on the terrace.

Each worked a four-hour shift. One of the snipers was always behind the gun, keeping an eye on the house, a fortress where the bastard had holed up on his return to Montevideo over two years ago. He wouldn't be a real target until he showed up on the small back terrace. They'd thought it through. It wouldn't be impossible to get him driving down the street when he went out, but it would be very dangerous. His bodyguards inspired respect.

Three-O never left home on foot. And it was no secret his car windows were bullet proof.

The two marksmen maintained their vigilance. If they weren't short of one thing in life, it was time. Someone, with money enough, was financing the revenge, in the name of all three. They were also not short of images of horror and human wretchedness, lightning flashes of nasty memories, a past that would never be sufficiently remote to be forgotten. Gnawed by a loneliness they could never cast off, even when surrounded by their loved ones, their hatred came seasoned with a serene, obsessive patience wrought and perfected by ten years of prison and torture.

When the Tupamaros abandoned the armed struggle, they had accepted the order reluctantly; but passive resignation disappeared when the military torturers got an amnesty.

They bumped into each other one day in the street and talked. While Three-O and others of his kind lived unpunished, enjoying the oblivion and money they'd stolen from their victims, none of them could take a deep breath of fresh air, laugh cheerfully, play with their children, or have a moment's happiness in this piss-awful world.

Until Buenos Aires Man appeared, and then they reached an agreement. Yes, Orlando Ortega Ortiz, OOO, Three-O, Captain Horror, retired with a major's stripes, would be the first to be executed. And others would follow. They weren't short of time, patience or money to see to the liquidation of a goodly number.

They'd kill him as soon as he showed up on the terrace. He'd be in their sights the whole time.

One day he had to put in an appearance, if only for two seconds. Even though it meant waiting six months.

One day he had to take a walk through that green door.

It would be his last.

And after two weeks of waiting in vain, in that liquefying heat, they had an idea. Why not engineer a power cut in the barrio? The guy would soon gasp for fresh air, and decide to seek some out on his small terrace.

*

The heat of summer in Montevideo can exceed the forty-degree mark. And that 16 December, at one in the afternoon, Major Orlando Ortega was forced to interrupt his siesta.

'The power's gone? Fuck, fuck, fuck!' he protested.

Without air-conditioning or fan, the sacred siesta was impossible. His servant, Feliciano, rang the electricity board. He was told the area was affected by a fault in underground installations. It would take a couple of hours to repair.

It was a quarter past one. His brother Tomás would pick him up at four, to go to the lawyers and sign some Texinal contracts.

Ortega was intending to siesta until three, then shave and get dressed. And he needed that siesta. He had an idea that brought a smile to his lips. He ordered Feliciano and Juanita to create a draught from fans or pieces of cardboard, or whatever, while he slept in his bedroom.

It didn't work. The air generated by his sweating fanners was insufficient.

And what about a siesta on the back terrace? His hammock from El Salvador, with its wide mesh netting would be really cool. And at that time of day enjoyed shade. Perhaps there might even be a breeze…

'Yes, Major, there's a lovely little wind,' declared Juanita.

'There he goes!'

Beto Half-Dead (half a stomach, a single kidney and an escapee from two prisons), who at that moment was brewing his maté, dropped it on the table, moved aside the thermos that was very close to the gun, bent over the telescopic lens and…

El Camborio waited with bated breath for the shot that never came.

Half-Dead snapped white with rage: 'His bastard servant is blocking him.'

'Calm down, Beto, take it easy…'

Half-Dead watched his target sit on the edge of his hammock, unable to shoot, because the maid was in the way the whole time. As he let himself go, with all his weight on his back, Ortega made the hammock sink even farther down...

'Fuck! He's out of the line of fire...'

The motherfucker was protected by a small eighty-centimetre wall that acted as a parapet and a balcony to the terrace.

El Camborio urged him to keep calm.

'If you like, leave him to me...but keep calm, *che*. If you get mad, you'll only make things worse.'

Beto understood, nodded and made way for him. He grabbed his maté again, brewed up and grimaced in disgust. Shut his eyes and sighed deeply. He knew that all they could do was wait for Ortega to get up, and keep their sights trained on him.

'As soon as he gets up, he's a dead duck. Impossible to miss.'

Indeed, if the woman weren't in the way, he'd be the perfect target.

Time passed and Beto couldn't control himself. He was still very on edge. Brewed yet another maté. The spoon shook in his hands.

El Camborio, on the other hand, felt a degree of euphoria, which came with the conviction that it was going to happen. He knew exactly on which bit of terrace Ortega would resurface. And, inevitably, before he stood up, he'd first have to sit right in the centre of the hammock. His head would stick out, then gradually his whole body, as he sat up. And the spot where it would happen was already plumb in his sights.

Ortega couldn't get to sleep on the terrace. The breeze was too off and on and in the end kept waking him up. But he stayed on his back in the hammock for a few minutes more.

By the time the next power cut came, he'd have an enormous fan. He'd get one of those feathery ones, like Arab sheikhs have, in those films where a black eunuch dressed in red is always fanning. That get-up would suit the limp-wristed Feliciano, who was also black.

The business his brother was bringing him looked very promising. He could get a big return on a modest investment. And what Tomás guaranteed...

The bullet singed his ear.

It was a miracle he wasn't killed.

The nail on the wall saved him; it was supporting one corner of the hammock. When he sat on the edge, the wall gave, the nail came out, and the major was left sitting on the ground. As he tried to pull himself up, with his back to the street, he felt the bullet graze his ear and fell to the floor again. Sheltered by the low wall, he managed to drag himself off the terrace on his elbows.

Blanching with disappointment, Half-Dead and El Camborio saw the door open and shut.

'The fucking bastard!'

He'd escaped them.

And now, before the pigs got them, they'd have to collect their stuff and disappear for ever from that flat.

'The motherfucking bastard!'

At the age of fifteen, in 1958, little Orlando Ortega decided to become a doctor and began to study anatomy on his own initiative. He practised on cats. He donned a leather glove and baited them with bits of meat: 'Miao, miao, come here, my little pet, yum-yum for you.'

He'd strangle them with one arm aloft, as if giving a fascist salute, until the animals stopped waving their paws. After dismembering them, he'd put the organs destined for further dissection in jam jars, and hide the others so he could play hair-raising jokes on his neighbours later on.

Little Orlando's by then deceased father, a pastor in a Mormon parish in Montevideo, had collected funding over fourteen years in order to extend the church into the area of Malvín. Every year, the pastor would give alms to his most hard-up flock and add a few bricks to his church; but most of the collections would be shared out among his family. His children would get so many pesos a week according to their age.

In the last share-out, Tomás had got eighteen, Marujita sixteen, Butcha' fifteen and Adela thirteen.

Butcha' was little Orlando, and he owed his nickname to his uncle Lucas. After the pastor died, Uncle moved in with his widow sister; and as soon as little Orlando initiated his felinicides, filling the house with pots of cat organs and cremating the remains in the back yard, his uncle started to call him Buchenwald (pronounced Butcha'nval), which finally slimmed down to 'Butcha". And that was what his family called him from then on.

When he reached eighteen, before joining the Uruguayan police, Butcha' came into some money (nobody knows how), and went off to live in Peru for two years.

His house in Lima was home to eleven Indian women and two queers. They all met and worshipped his cock-a-doodle-do. Orlando boasted that it measured nineteen centimetres erect.

While he fornicated with a group of five of six Indian *cholas*, the others sang Mormon hymns he'd taught them. Grasping a bottle of *pisco* in one hand, he'd stand naked in the centre of the circle they'd form around him. He almost always did it clockwise standing up, and via the rear window.

Until well into his forties, Orlando was never sociable. He interacted with others only out of necessity. But when he wanted to, he could act pleasantly, even effusively, though it went against the grain.

He was a solitary wolf and, for years, a ferocious one.

He entered the Uruguayan Police Academy in March 1965

at the age of twenty-one. It was his first mature act, and came from a decision he'd reached clinically.

He'd just returned to Montevideo, after two turbulent years in Peru. Although his turbulent life had already started at fifteen, with his father and sister Maruja already dead, when he was expelled from the Liceo.

The trigger for his expulsion was Immanuel Kant, his philosophy teacher's idol.

By then Orlando had a pathological compulsion to devour books. And after reading *The Critique of Pure Reason* and *The Critique of Practical Reason*, he came to the conclusion that Kant was a dick-head. It wasn't long before his teacher, a skinny guy with horn-rimmed specs, shut him up when he was making some scornful aside and asked him sarcastically whether he thought he was more intelligent than Kant.

'Naturally,' replied little Orlando in the loftiest of tones.

And Orlando fired off at a perplexed thirty-five year-old teacher, a reverential Kantian and graduate of an institute of higher learning. 'Pure reason' and 'practical reason', converging as they did on the idea of God, were an intellectual product of little or no theoretical value, particularly if one thought how Kant always lived as celibate recluse, never going beyond the bounds of Berlin and Königsberg, wholly dedicated to a life of thought. And that was the end product? Ugh!

On the brink of apoplexy, the teacher, like a ruminant, couldn't prevent his neck and jaw getting into a twist. Impotent before such blasphemy, smoke poured from his eyes.

'Kant intelligent?' continued iconoclastic little Orlando. 'If you'd said Descartes, or Freud, or Einstein, or God knows who...If you'd said Heraclitus or Democritus, or Leonardo, or Galileo, I might have agreed. But Kant more intelligent than me? In all the time that geezer dedicated to masturbating on pure reason, I'd have produced something much more worthwhile.'

And he laughed in his face.

Still unable to reset his jaw, unable to speak, with no clarity of thought, without his glasses, which had dropped to the floor from pure fright, unkempt, aphonic and apoplectic, the teacher managed to grip the back of his chair and raise an arm with which to expel Orlando from the classroom.

The following day, as the blasphemous pupil refused to retract or apologize, he was expelled from the Liceo.

It was around that time his contempt for intellectuals gelled. Apart from a few you could count on the fingers of one hand throughout history, they were all idiots, fools, duped by the wet dreams of a dick-head like Immanuel Kant. And Kants were legion. Each century produced a plague of them, everywhere.

And when he found out that the act of cock-sucking was known as fellatio, he coined the word '*felacio*', which he'd applied ever since to most of humanity as synonymous with imbecile.

And at the age of twenty, when he tired of chaos, marijuana, of massacring riff-raff in Lima, and his daily excesses with the eleven Indian women he'd given a roof to, he returned to Montevideo with the idea of carving himself out a future.

He opted to join the military.

In a world replete with *felacios* he knew he couldn't stand any teacher of the liberal arts; and warmed to the idea of becoming a soldier. The military don't think. He assumed that in a regime of orders and obedience, he would be able to organize his life. But at the age of twenty, he wasn't old enough to enter the Military Academy and the officer class. On the other hand, he could enrol in the Police Academy before the age of twenty-one. And if he accepted the rules of the game, in a few years, with his brain and hormones, he would be flying high. So he drew a very enticing conclusion: he'd make it to captain in less than ten years. For every *felacio* with more stripes he'd have to tolerate without flinching, he could lord it over a thousand, from lower ranks to prisoners. And he never gave it a second thought.

Things went swimmingly from the start. Even when he was a novice and had the whole academy above him, he always found a way to survive boxing rings and tatamis. He would go and create riots in the barrios. Someone only had to look at him to spark off bloody fighting. Violence became a daily necessity. In time, it wasn't enough for him to beat or humiliate whomever he could. He was galvanised by the need to wax sarcastic in public, to exhibit his contempt for the *felacios* of this world.

He refrained from making friends with his colleagues in the whole first phase of his military life. At most he tolerated a few admirers whom he continuously mistreated. And he never gave up his habit of switching himself off and reading for hours on end. Even in the academy, he wouldn't go to the cinema or theatre on his free days. He'd stay indoors reading or go to the dances in poor barrios looking for a fight. He was wounded several times by knives or some such.

When he graduated in 1968, he was offered a teaching post in the academy; but preferred to work on the street and in prisons. He loved political prisoners. All his teachers regretted his decision; they were definite they'd never had such a brilliant pupil.

He was also a brilliant student of Dan Mitrione in 1970, on the Scientific Persuasion courses the CIA expert imparted in Montevideo for police officers and members of various paramilitary groups.

Uruguay was experiencing a deep crisis in government as a result of the actions of the Tupamaro guerrillas. In that state of emergency, Mitrione gave his first course on Techniques of Persuasion. Despite his very Italianate, at times quite incomprehensible, Spanish, the rigorous, objective focus of his specialist lectures aroused great interest in his students. In particular, the seminar on Inductive Persuasion was very fruitful.

At the end of the course, student Orlando Ortega Ortiz got top marks. In his report to the police hierarchy of Uruguay, Mitrione noted: 'He is one of the few pupils who didn't show signs of somatic rejection when the laboratory experiments reached the third degree of stimulation.'

As a result of Mitrione's suggestion, that year the paramilitary groups captured and distributed around different prisons dozens of beggars, alcoholics, beachcombers (whom Montevideans call '*bichicomes*'), in order to have more than sufficient material on which to experiment in the Techniques of Persuasion laboratories. Mitrione preferred drunks to political prisoners as his guinea pigs. Human dregs don't conspire against their governments. The inhabitants of drains, docks and bridges don't hide secrets that can be extracted under torture. Hence their usefulness: they make for uninterrupted teaching sessions and withstand 'the maximum degree of intimidation'. What's more, they die without anyone reporting them as missing or demanding compensation. Nevertheless, during his first and second Scientific Persuasion courses, little Orlando took it so far that one day even the gringo was disgusted: 'You's a fucking monsta,' he exclaimed. 'You do it to extract *la informazione,* not to enjoy yourself *bene.*'

And that day Butcha' thought how he'd love to stick the electric prod up Mitrione's ass. But then he'd learned to be a soldier and kept quiet. That was the deal and he respected it.

Orlando was contemptuous of Mitrione. He was a genuine torturer, who liked his trade as much as he did, but pretended he was a crusader for democracy, a good father, a religious man, kind to his dogs, etc. It was a load of crap. Besides he was ignorant. He knew a little anatomy, a little contemporary history, but if you got him off his home territory, he was a troglodyte. And a *felacio* who believed tripe about the free world and all that gringo baloney.

Nevertheless, Orlando was careful not to show any opposition and soon had him in his pocket. After passing him with the highest distinction, Mitrione recommended him for additional training in Devil's Den, Florida.

That was just what Orlando wanted.

In Devil's Horn, study was much more rigorous. Apart from persuasion, he learned anatomy, physiology, psychology, physics, economy, history and geography. He also learned to be surprisingly fluent and efficient in English. In the usual tests they gave people, he showed the highest IQ ever registered there: something unheard of, abnormal among Latin American torturers, who usually got the lowest scores.

He left that school in 1972, a qualified trainer; and on his return to Montevideo was involved in front-line action against communist and Tupamaro prisoners.

Employing the techniques of persuasion he had acquired and his innate lucidity, he obtained excellent results from some hermetic subversives who, at the hands of other torturers, withstood the electric prod, submarining, and didn't sing even when beaten to pulp. With Orlando they became 'fingerers', those who from behind smoked glass, pointed out their ex-comrades on the streets of Montevideo.

These results – which meant precocious promotion to lieutenant – brought him once more to the attention of the gringos, who gave him extra skilling in Fort Paramount, Georgia, in order to send him off to other countries to teach persuasion techniques. (There was a continental agreement, facilitating the recruitment of good persuaders from lower ranked officers in different police bodies across Latin America, and from the early seventies very quick promotions were agreed and granted.)

By 1976 little Orlando was already in Buenos Aires with the rank of captain. In his role as an adviser to the Argentine dictatorship he gave classes in the Navy Engineering School, the EMA.

One day, as he came out of a cinema, he felt aroused by some passing buttocks. He wasn't worried by the fact they were accompanied. His body wanted trouble. And a compliment wasn't slow to come: 'If I had that pretty little ass, I'd shit myself the whole day long.'

At that vile gratuitous remark, the boyfriend reacted quickly and angrily by kicking him in the groin. Orlando was caught unawares and doubled over in pain; but soon recovered, used his karate and massacred the young lad. With the help of a policeman, on the pretext that they were *montonero* revolutionaries on a wanted list, he arrested them and took them to the Engineering School. They gang-raped her. Attached her, almost fainting, to a machine designed in the United States and still at the experimental stage, which sucked the intestines through the anus till a handful was visible. Then mice were immediately let into the vagina, through a tube. They forced him to look on. He tried to stop them, offered money, begged, vomited, sobbed and fainted repeatedly.

Teresita didn't survive the pain and shock and died that same afternoon. He never saw her again. She reappeared only on the itinerant photos of the Mothers in the Plaza de Mayo.

The youth was terror-stricken and Orlando first forced him to pay respects to his cock-a-doodle-do, an iridescent cockerel, a pedigree Horpington, so he claimed, which he'd had tattooed on the inside of one thigh, its bright red comb and erect beak pointing towards his genitals. In the presence of O's juniors, and students who were enjoying the ritual, the lad was ordered to kneel, to salute the cockerel, to say cock-a-doodle-do, a-doodle-do, and repeat a whole liturgy Orlando rehearsed for him. Finally he had him handcuffed and sodomized him, in the middle of a circle everyone else had formed.

'What do you make of these *felacios*, then?' he asked mid-rape, to the guffaws of his students present. 'They act tough in the street but this is what they really like.'

Orlando Ortega spent twenty years visiting different prisons, but he was imprisoned only once at the age of fifteen. One day, when he was waiting at a bus stop, a young mother sat next to him with her five-year-old daughter, with beautiful curls, white ribbons and bows.

'Your daughter's really pretty, señora,' purred little Orlando.

The mother smiled graciously and started to read something; he stood behind the girl and busied himself undoing her bows. When he was on the fourth, he smiled gleefully when he spotted a dog turd in the shape of a horseshoe on the pavement. But just as he was trying to hang it on one of the girl's curls, someone grabbed him by the hair.

He had been caught in the act and had to spend several hours in the police station, listening to indignant reproaches from a self-righteous sergeant to whom he retorted:

'Why are you getting so worked up? It was only a joke…'

When Orlando was thirty-two, he reached the rank of captain, and entered holy matrimony with a Chilean woman from a very rich family, but they never cohabited. Their only child was born the following year. And while he was visiting Paraguay, Colombia, Guatemala and El Salvador encouraging disciplines of persuasion, he saw very little of the boy. But he ordered him to be sent to the Canal Zone for his school holidays. When he was eight, Orlando opted to give him a little educational guidance. And at their first breakfast together, he served up coffee and two round buns, which he attacked first.

'They've got cream inside,' explained Orlando, his mouth full. 'They're called friar's balls in Buenos Aires.'

When the boy bit the capsule of castor oil that his father had substituted for the filling in the second bun, he sobbed and was sick.

'First lesson: never believe anyone, not even your father,' Orlando pontificated solemnly, wagging an index finger in front of his eyes.

Once, when a colleague described him as abnormal, Orlando justified his behaviour by arguing that keeping your promises to your son, offering him protection and love, was to set him on the wrong track in life with false notions about reality. In order to immunize a child against the bastards he'd encounter in life, one had to imbue him with mistrust, and from the tenderest age. He shouldn't believe even his own parents.

In Montevideo Orlando Ortega was called Lieutenant and

then Captain Horror after the first syllables of his name. Others nicknamed him Three-O, after his initials.

He made money in Argentina by collaborating with an international network that sold the children of the disappeared to married couples in the First World. He also earned a bit from the traffic in organs, but didn't get too involved. He sensed it might be dangerous. And on the death of his wife, on the beach of Santa Marta in Colombia, properties worth almost half a million dollars came his way.

After that he didn't dabble in any more illegal business. His brother Tomás, who turned out to be a financial genius, and much richer than he was, advised him to make investments that, over twenty years, allowed him to increase his capital fivefold and ensure a substantial income. The Butcha' and Captain Horror became things of the past.

Major Orlando Ortega Ortiz returned to his own country after a plebiscite granted an amnesty to the whole of the Uruguay military, even the most persuasive among them. His return and the passage of time turned him into a pillar of society, the owner of a fine house in El Prado, of a yacht, and the recipient of an annual income of some four hundred thousand dollars.

The passage of time made him more sociable. He forced himself to be pleasant to distinguished folk, even though they were out-and-out *felacios*. He still had neither friends nor partner. He would adopt the necessary polite formulas and smiling face with his acquaintances, sporting colleagues and in the high-society clubs to which he belonged. It was true the planet was awash with *felacios*, but it didn't do him any good to proclaim it was so, so he began to find secret enjoyment in pretending to be just one *felacio* more, and in sharing more liberal attitudes regarding tolerance, human rights, etc.

He became a widower after only two years of marriage. His son lived in Santiago with his maternal grandparents and he never saw him again after that single encounter in Panama. His mother and siblings continued to live in Montevideo. But he kept them at a distance and accepted visits only from Tomás, his commercially minded brother.

Major Ortega didn't want to gather rust. He aspired to enjoy life for a long time and took care to look after himself. During the day he ate only fruit and vegetables and tried to keep himself on the move. He accompanied his frugal lunch and dinner, light on fat, with modest aperitifs and two glasses of red wine. He possessed an enviable video library which he constantly renewed with fresh titles, and at night, before going to bed, he'd see a film and down four to six shots of Johnny Walker Black Label.

He often read stuff written in English, and thanks to his huge satellite disc and growing fondness for the Internet, kept himself more informed on the world situation than many a professional journalist. Three times a week he would practise shooting and horse-riding in a club for retired officers; he devoted Tuesday and Thursday mornings to tennis and the afternoons to a bridge school, in his own home, or in a mansion in Carrasco; and just in case, his bodyguards went everywhere with him. He gave them leave only at weekends, when he went sailing in his yacht and waterskied at a prudent distance from the coast. The most expensive available call girls and rent-boys would visit his chambers on Saturday night, and sometimes midweek. You had to pay for the good things in life, and he was never stingy.

But Montevideo was a dangerous city and he had to live with his guard up. At home in El Prado, two bodyguards who went everywhere with him worked shifts and drove his bullet-proof car. And though he was past fifty and had moderated the hot rushes of blood of youth, his two maids, his gay butler and his cook were all given an opportunity to worship his cock-a-doodling rooster.

After the first attack, his two thugs redoubled their vigilance. They accompanied him on the high seas. On board *Chamamé*

*II*, they glared at the horizon armed with automatic rifles. As soon as they left the Buceo quayside, they kept a watch on any craft that tried to approach them.

Their precautions were to no avail.

On 2 February, he was attacked for a second time with long-distance rifles in a club on the Calle Yaguarón, when he was playing in a bridge tournament.

He'd taken his routine precautions and never imagined they might train their sights on that building.

He'd organize his usual bridge schools at his place or would go to a lawyer's mansion; a kind of castle in the elegant district of Carrasco, surrounded by two hectares of high-fenced gardens patrolled by private security night and day. Moreover, there were no high buildings in the vicinity and thick-foliaged acacias and eucalyptus walled off the big house. He didn't offer the slightest target when getting in or out of his car. Or in the rooms where he played, or in the dining room, or the bar he used to frequent.

As a real professional, the major knew that, to kill someone with long-distance weapons, it was necessary to know beforehand that the individual was going to put in an appearance. And he himself didn't even know till two days before that his championship game would take place in that central chess club. The speed at which the gunmen prepared their ambush was evidence of a spy among the bridge-playing fraternity, or some access to the information about the tournament. Otherwise, they couldn't have known with enough time in advance where and when he was going to compete. Once more they missed by millimetres. Chance saved him yet again.

He gave up bridge from that day and all contact with people connected to that world. It was the second attack in a month and a half. They'd had forty-eight hours to study the terrain and find a place to set up. He found out that the shot had come from some pigeon loft they'd improvised on a nearby terrace roof. No neighbour living in the thirty flats was able to give a lead on the gunmen. Nor could the police find anyone in the building or club who had been a political prisoner during the dictatorship.

That all showed they had an organization and informants. No doubt people ready to do anything.

That same day he decided to make a clean break. He'd not live in that continual nightmare any more, always on edge, fearing a shot from anyone who came near him anywhere. He'd change his name and appearance and would abandon that city, which was dangerous.

His brother Tomás had long ago suggested he should go and live in Havana. At first, the idea seemed ridiculous. He'd done in dozens of people on the excuse that they had connections or collaborated with Castro's Cuba.

Tomás insisted nobody would recognize him after so many years, with the natural changes brought by age, and a few tweaks to his appearance. He had gone quite grey, was a little fatter…If he let his hair and beard grow long, and wore dark glasses…

He was finally convinced. It was unlikely anyone would think of looking for him in Cuba. Besides, he adored the heat, which he'd already enjoyed in Panama, Honduras, Colombia and Florida. And also hot-blooded tropical wenches. In Cuba he could also indulge his passion for yachting, without bodyguards.

Three years ago the major had invested one hundred and seventy thousand dollars in Texinal, SRL, a small company formed by his brother Tomás, in partnership with another Uruguayan and two Panamanians. He did so on advice from Tomás. Major Orlando Ortega's name didn't appear in any of the paperwork and nobody in the company knew him. His brother appeared as managing director and the only investor – of a million and a half dollars, thanks to which the company started its operation in Cuba. In order to cover any fatal occurrence, Tomás took out life insurance for a million to be paid to Orlando.

Texinal started off by selling to Panama clothing and material brought from Hong Kong and other countries in the Far East. The initiative had come from Tomás himself, who used one Carlos Fischer, a friend from his young days and a professional footballer in the same team as him. In the sixties, Fischer was a trade union leader; then a militant for the Broad Front; and when the dictatorship came, he went into exile in Cuba for several years. He married a Cuban woman and, through her, established excellent individual and family relationships with a member of the Central Committee. Tomás persuaded him to mobilize his personal influence and goodwill with the Cuban government, and thus obtained authorization to create a firm to import textiles from Uruguay. Tomás had a long-term commercial vision, and knew that Uruguayan textiles wouldn't be able to compete on the Cuban market with textiles coming from Colombia and Panama, and aspired only to getting a foothold in Cuba, even though they might lose money for the first few months. And indeed, when he got permission to start operations, he made contact with two Panamanian importers of materials from Hong Kong, Singapore and other places in South-East Asia, and brought them into Texinal as industrial partners.

In its first year, with Texinal he processed eight hundred thousand dollars' worth of sales to shops on the Cuban parallel market; but in the second year, it was three million, and by the third year it reached four and a half million, with a gross profit at thirty-five per cent. Fifty per cent of the profits went to Tomás and Orlando, who'd made half of the capital investment. The two Panamanians took forty per cent for their administration and know-how; and Carlos Fischer, who'd not lifted a finger, ten per cent, which represented a hundred times the amount he ever dreamed of earning.

Already in its second year, Texinal began to incorporate other lines of business. Fischer started to represent an Argentine firm that manufactured kitchen products for the hotel industry; then a line in insecticides and another in raw materials for ice cream;

and finally, he got permission to operate in the Free Zone, created by the Cuban government, where Tomás's people bought containers of any kind of merchandise they could then resell, making an immediate, succulent profit on the local market.

After the shock of the first attack, Orlando dug himself in at home. He no longer trusted his bodyguards. He thought about it for two days. On the third, he sent his goons a cheque and sacked them without explanation.

And the same day he set sail for Argentina in *Chamamé II*.

He left home by himself, in his bullet-proof car. He went by a roundabout route to make sure nobody was following him and took refuge on his yacht. The following day, in the port of Carmelo, he registered his cruiser in Buenos Aires. At dusk on 8 February he anchored in El Tigre.

In Buenos Aires he tracked down El Negro, old Soria, his admirer and fan at the Navy Engineering School, a very funny, witty guy, who enjoyed any trick he played on the prisoners. He was the one who was most amused when mice were put into women via that tube. And one day he discovered that El Negro, who was a lieutenant, had been promoted to Colonel Primitivo Soria Pérez. After making a couple of calls to other colleagues in the inactive but united club of persuaders, he found him straight away.

Soria had retired from the army only three years ago and was still active with an important position in Foreign Affairs. Moreover, he had innumerable loyal buddies embedded in the whole apparatus of connections that thrived within the government of President Menem. And most important: Soria had secret access to a list compiled during the dictatorship of the names of the hundreds of disappeared who were never claimed. The paramilitary mafia of the day zealously kept hold of those names in case they ever needed to adopt a fake identity.

Thus, in twelve days, Orlando Ortega obtained an Argentine

passport in the name of citizen Alberto Ríos, born in Corral Quemado, in the province of Tucuman, in November 1942. In fact, the passport was forged, because it would carry Ortega's fingerprints and photo, and not those of the real Alberto Ríos. But in relation to the register of births, everything was in order: the passport corresponded to the registering of a genuine birth, properly recorded and archived, of a flesh-and-blood citizen; flesh and bone that had disappeared twenty years ago and was never claimed by kith and kin. And naturally, as there was no record of any demise, he was thought to be alive.

At the start of the process, Soria asked him to get photos taken for the passport.

'Not yet,' responded Ortega. 'You get on with the paperwork, but don't stick a photo in yet. I want a photo taken here with a beard and long hair.'

Ortega intended hiding for four months or so in Buenos Aires while he waited for his hair to grow shoulder length.

'Right. Good thinking,' replied El Negro. 'Bring me the photos when you've got them.'

While he waited, his brother Tomás visited him twice in his hiding-place. Orlando had instructed him to sell his car, the *Chamamé II* and rent the house in El Prado.

Buenos Aires was also a dangerous city and Orlando didn't want to make a present of himself. He spent most of his time shut up in Olivos, reading in his hotel room, which he left only in order to swim in the pool or go for a run in the neighbourhood.

As his goatee beard and long hair grew, so did his confidence. When his hair reached below his ears, he found it very uncomfortable, and tied it up in a homemade pigtail. But he let it down when he went out.

By the middle of May he was a different person, even to himself. He decided to test it out and fixed an appointment with old Soria in a café on Corrientes. When he entered and sat down at a nearby table, El Negro looked at him, hesitated for a few moments and reckoned it couldn't be him. Although he'd been alerted, he didn't recognize him. He was expecting someone long haired with a beard; but never thought he'd have such white locks. That misled him. The last time El Negro had seen him, he'd trimmed his hair down to a length of four millimetres and wore it chestnut red as the result of darkening shampoo he used. And now that gangling fellow, every inch a concert pianist, who limped in and sat down to read a newspaper without looking in his direction, could no way be Three-O.

'Fantastic, *che*! Not even Sherlock Holmes could sniff you out...'

A contented Orlando finally admitted that the new look gave him a distinguished air and softened some of the sharp edges of his angular face. His badly receding hairline, where a crew cut formed two partings, was now filled out with the strip of long, loose hair. That slightly round-shouldered fifty-plusser, weighing in at ninety kilos, with his nineteenth-century airs and greying, elegantly casual head of hair, was nothing like slender Captain Horror, with his crew cut, aged thirty-seven and weighing seventy-five kilos.

He was so confident of his disguise that one afternoon he went into the centre. He went to see the Mothers walking in the Plaza de Mayo. When he'd finished, he sat down in a café on the Calle Florida to enjoy his anonymity.

He was persuaded that he could now stroll unharmed anywhere in the world, even without glasses. Even down the 18 July Avenue in Montevideo.

As far as the Cuban authorities were concerned, Señor Alberto Ríos was a foreign expert who'd come to organize and manage a new line of business that, with due government approval, would be developed on the island by the Texinal company. It involved setting up a high-quality textiles factory.

In fact, a Uruguayan specialist who already lived in Havana

was carrying out this work from a more humble position. Tomás had seen to everything. Alberto would show his face only for protocol matters, but would never engage with customers; and he would only attend meetings called at the firm when it was indispensable.

Alberto disembarked in Havana on 2 June with a business visa; and immediately requested a residency permit. When the authorities had investigated his status as an immigrant, his solvency and projected activities, they granted him without hassle temporary resident status, renewable every two years.

On 18 June he got his foreigner's ID card.

It was all so easy....

While people at the firm searched for a house to his liking, by the sea, he spent his time driving around Havana in the white convertible they put at his disposal from the first day.

To begin with, it was a pleasure in itself just to be able to move around on foot or by car, without being afraid he'd be shot to pieces on some street corner, and he enjoyed it avidly and morbidly. He remembered one occasion when he'd had a leg in plaster for several weeks; when they freed him up, he couldn't stop scratching. The pleasure was so great he always drew blood.

Walking down the streets of a city was something he'd not allowed himself to do for ages, except for that single afternoon in the Plaza de Mayo.

Nobody would recognize him in Cuba.

As for the country, the climate and the sea...there were really marvellous. Chatting one day to Lazarito, a seller who worked for Texinal and was fond of underwater fishing, the brand-new Alberto Ríos spoke of his vocation for the sea, and how much he missed *Chamamé II*, which he'd left on the River Plate. And Lazarito knew a French diplomat who was selling his yacht at a knockdown price, according to him.

Alberto asked to be put in contact, and the next day they went together to see the *Chevalier*, under a French flag, and registered in Guadeloupe. It was a three-master, with a capacity of six tons, twelve metres long and very elegantly lined.

The yacht performed in sprightly fashion on a brief sail in nearby waters. It was a pleasure to be at the wheel. It was docile and very seaworthy. Alberto noted he could do U-turns in less than five fathoms. And the engine sounded good and powerful. The rigging, timberwork and metal fittings looked well worn but were in good condition. And the Frenchman was prepared to let it go for seventy-five thousand dollars, if he was paid cash.

After getting it inspected by an expert, Alberto bought the yacht a fortnight later.

# 23 his inexorable decline

The very day of the accident, Bini phoned you to say that after they'd found the car, the police turned up at her grandmother's house and questioned everybody, and they looked at your father and measured the shoes he was wearing, and you realized: 'Fucking hell! There must be footprints next to the body.'

Just in case, you decided to get rid of the incriminating shoes, although it went against the grain, because they were worth a fortune and were a present Pia bought you in New York.

It was then you thought of planting the shoes on Three-O and putting him inside. A silly idea, because Three-O deserved a much harsher punishment than being locked up for a few years; but suddenly you reckoned it wasn't such a bad idea. While they kept him for you in a Cuban prison, you could perhaps bring together the documentation to prove his crimes, and demonstrate who Three-O was. At best you'd get Cuba to condemn him to loads of years in prison because of his record of torture and crimes against humanity. And the next day you went to an international lawyer's office to make some discreet enquiries as to the possibility of denouncing a torturer from the Chilean dictatorship you'd thought you'd discovered on Cuban soil.

For twenty-eight dollars they informed you that the Cuban justice system tries crimes only against its own citizens; and in the case of foreigners, those exclusively committed on national territory.

But by now you were keen on the prospect of putting Three-O inside.

And in the middle of Gonzalo's party, while you were picking over the idea of making him do time for a crime he'd not committed, the concept of extradition came to mind.

You felt sure of one thing, without consulting anyone: if you managed to imprison Three-O for a traffic accident, and then presented convincing proof and witnesses of his past as a torturer, the Cuban government would be more than delighted to extradite him, once he'd done his time on the island.

Meanwhile, with the knowledge that he wouldn't escape you again for a long time, you'd have ample scope for reactivating your old project to denounce him in an international campaign. You could happily travel round Europe and do what Judge Garzón did against Pinochet.

You debated the new strategy in your head for several hours.

Would you find victims prepared to accuse him?

More than likely. You yourself knew *montoneros* and Argentine communists, children of Italians, Spaniards and Germans, who'd passed through the EMA. Perhaps there were victims of Three-O among them, and if you started investigating there might be one who'd taken out a European passport.

Your action would resonate echoing the actions of the Spanish prosecutor and help defeat compliant governments that amnestied their military; one more bell tolling against them consigned their crimes to oblivion.

It might be that others would follow your example so that the mafia of River Plate torturers would no longer live in peace, protected by laws they themselves dictated through threats and pressure.

With Three-O tucked away, you'd mobilize El Camborio, Half-Dead and the Argentines in the Memory Group.

Inevitably it could take you weeks or months to locate foreigners prepared to denounce Three-O. You'd have to initiate conversations with lawyers in solidarity organizations in different countries in order to promote the idea of creating a dossier against Three-O. You'd gather up eyewitness accounts from relatives of the disappeared, or tortured survivors from prisons where Three-O lectured. But none of that would be possible if he were free, because your actions would necessarily cause a stir. An international campaign of that size cannot be prepared secretly. It was inevitable that the paramilitary mafia on the continent would find out; and once Three-O got the first whiff of it, he'd be off again, perhaps for ever.

Yes, siree, a prison sentence in Cuba was the perfect solution; on the one hand, it would prevent Three-O from scarpering again; on the other, it freed you from the task of executing him yourself. You couldn't kill anyone in cold blood, not even Three-O.

And so, in the two or three days after the Sunday accident, you thought through your plan. But didn't get too enthusiastic till you were sure of Bini. Would she be prepared to lie to put Three-O in jail? If she accepted, it would be very easy to get him a sentence, even if only for a couple of years. Without Bini, you'd have to give up on your plan. You'd have no alternative but to execute him using your own means.

In the early hours after Gonzalo's birthday, Bini woke up in tears because she was dreaming of the dead cyclist. And that gave you an idea. At midday you phoned Gonzalo and told him a tall story about a girlfriend of Bini's whom you wanted to help. You asked him to find out what would happen to the lass, if she presented herself voluntarily at the police station and confessed she'd knocked over a cyclist and then made a run for it. What sentence would she get? The poor thing wanted to confess because the dead cyclist wouldn't let her sleep, visited her in dreams, etc.

Gonzalo consulted a criminal lawyer who was a friend, and thus you found out that if she wasn't driving, she would get only a few months inside, for not helping the victim; but if she came forward voluntarily to confess, because of her troubled conscience, it was most likely she'd get off scot-free.

That night you thought through the detail. Bini had a friend at the Triton Hotel. And when she needed a room to disguise herself as a foreigner and 'whore from the heights', that friend forged a check-in.

And in a right whirl, once you'd decided on your plan, you sent a fax to Rome that afternoon and asked your fixer friend who worked for the RAI to DHL you in Havana a white wig and goatee.

Bini had a militant sense of justice. You knew that. But you also knew she was prone to a lack of forethought. Would she be able to put on an act before the court?

Mid-afternoon on the 21st, still hung over from the birthday party, you spoke to Bini. You told her what happened on that dire day in Buenos Aires which changed your life. You started with that fellow, who talked dirty praising Teresita's bum...And you told her some of the macabre details of what happened in the Navy Engineering School.

When Bini found out that Teresita died on a torture table, and was immediately disappeared, she started to sob silently.

For fear of muddying your relations with her, you hid your own tragedy and the way Three-O humiliated you. And at the end you revealed who the character was.

'Alberto Ríos?' she shouted in horror.

You told her his real name was Orlando Ortega Ortiz.

When Bini learned that you had sworn to the spirit of Teresita that one day you'd revenge her with that scum's death, she commented that the angry saints had led Alberto to her, so you could find him and make him pay for his crime.

'His crimes,' you explained, and you informed her fully about Three-O, master torturer and sinister individual.

Bini wrapped a sheet round her and started to hop around the terrace, and to think of various acts of vengeance. She'd speak to her godfather, to Pepe Jaén, would get together a gang ready for anything, *abakúas*, rough people.

'And we'll cut that bastard to shreds.'

You let her give vent before bringing her back to reality. You convinced her that a savage revenge would make no sense.

By midnight Bini was agreeing to collaborate in your scheme. You insisted on the need to proceed cold-bloodedly. She would have to become an actress, and make false declarations before the courts and Three-O himself.

She smiled.

'Just like in the films!'

Her role in the plan delighted her; it wasn't only about doing justice, but playing a game. In no way would she lose her cool and take risks, provided she could fuck over that shit.

The following day, Bini stole Alberto Ríos's ID card; twenty-four hours later, you received the disguises you'd ordered. With the complicity of Pepe Jaén, you checked into the Triton Hotel on 24 July with Alberto Ríos's ID. Bini arrived soon by herself; located the maid servicing the floor, kept a sly watch on her, and you let her see you only a couple of times, when you were wearing dark glasses some way away.

That same night you went to visit Gonzalo and Aurelia. You'd decided to tell them about the accident and your plans to put Three-O behind bars. You imagined they would back you; and that later on you'd need them. Apart from Bini, they were your only close friends. But when you told them the details of the accident, Aurelia reacted unexpectedly: she was very scared, and started to say you should go to the police; and to criticize you harshly because you'd not helped the cyclist; and she'd piled the blame on Bini.

Aurelia disappointed you. You no longer trusted her. In order to placate her, you emphasized that you were sure the cyclist was already dead; that his wrist and jugular had no pulse beat; that you had to kneel in the mud in order to listen to his chest; and when you left him, you were certain he'd died instantly. What was Aurelia after? For you to go and confess to manslaughter? For you to spend two years inside for something you weren't to blame for?

The body reeked of rum, and only a drunk could have ridden on to the highway like that... Your conscience was clear. You'd make sure the widow and her daughters were compensated, but it would be idiotic to give yourself up.

Gonzalo listened to you calmly and expressed support; but Aurelia's attitude took away any desire you had to tell him about Three-O and your plans against him.

On the second day, Bini gave your Florsheims to the maid.

You were sure that those shoes, plus Bini's confession and Alberto Ríos's name on the Triton's records, would incriminate him in the collision with the cyclist. And if that weren't enough against him, there would also be eyewitness accounts from Pepe Jaén and the maid.

You felt that Pepe Jaén's relationship with Bini was rather dubious; but they had a close friendship and that wasn't usual between a man and a woman.

Bini spoke to Jaén and told him who Alberto Ríos was. She showed him photos of him dressed as a soldier, and a copy of the Uruguayan document that proved he was Orlando Ortega Ortiz, newspaper cuttings that spoke of the man with the three Os, Captain Horror. When Pepe asked where she'd got her information from, she said she couldn't reveal that, and Pepe left it at that. She said only that at the time of the accident she didn't know who Alberto Ríos really was.

To make sure Jaén was really on her side, she told him that after knocking the cyclist over, Alberto refused to get out and fled the scene without offering him any help. And his ghost began to torment her. It visited her in dreams to ask her to see that justice was done. And as she could no longer stand the remorse, she was going to confess the truth, but she wanted to reach agreement with Pepe.

Indeed, Pepe didn't see her go with any men over those days. After getting Alberto Ríos's ID in order to note down his details, Pepe gave the key to Bini. All he ever saw of Alberto was his photo; and he couldn't confess the truth, because that would go seriously against all his commitments. After declaring that he himself saw him and checked him into the hotel, he had of necessity to keep on lying. And that was what he promised Bini: if someone questioned him, or summoned him to make a statement in court, he would pretend to recognize him as the guest he saw that day.

But the entire success of the frame-up depended on a convincing performance from Bini. For the show before the court, you'd make her learn by heart a very strict libretto that was easy to memorize. You thought that in order not to make a mistake, she should adhere strictly to the facts of what she herself really saw, except in one small detail: Alberto Ríos, not you, would be at the wheel of the murderous car. And you invented an ingenious little trick so Bini wouldn't make a mistake. You forbade her to call you Aldo. You would invent a bedroom name, darlin', ducky or something like that.

The next day you decided she could call you Tito. You said that was what your close family called you. But Tito is also another name for Alberto. So when she gave her evidence in court, everybody would identify Tito with Alberto. And by employing that little trick, it would be very difficult for the little thing to put a foot wrong.

You reckoned she'd be ready in a fortnight. You imagined that if she always called you Tito in this period, either to your face or when she spoke about you with other people, she would soon forget Aldo. And if she weren't ready after a fortnight, you'd take a month. When you got back to Europe, you'd ring her and give her practice in calling you Tito.

But before you left, you made her repeat ad nauseam and down to the smallest detail what Bini and Tito experienced together the day of the highway accident.

As she would be telling the pure truth, what she said would coincide with the findings of the forensics people, which would endorse her statements.

As for the reason for her confession, she would tell a little lie: tormented by visitations from the dead man, she'd gone to her godfather so he could call on Orula to mediate. And the Lord of Oracles ordered her to go and make a full confession; because that was what Baltasar París's ghost demanded.

From the first rehearsals, you thought Bini's commitment wholehearted. She was not worried by the fact she might go to prison for a few months. She'd taken on your cause and revenge for Teresita as issues of her own.

Her generosity and solidarity were moving. She was enthused by the idea of putting the monster inside and enabling the worldwide denunciation of his crimes to go ahead. Her own imprisonment was not important.

Nobody would save Three-O. However much he denied staying at the Triton and wearing those shoes, the stories told by Bini, Jaén and the maid would be enough to sink him.

Bini would seem the ingenuous, frightened believer who repents and confesses to her crime; and Alberto the cynical foreigner who refuses to confess. That alone would guarantee he'd be sentenced. You took care to check up and were almost definite he would spend two years in jail.

But things didn't turn out as you'd predicted. According to what Pepe Jaén told Bini, when the Florsheims left the maid's hands, they began a lateral movement that led to a district police station. They changed owner several times. It was incredible how those shoes walked alone through Havana. And naturally, as soon as the police found Fefita, whew, right away the names of Bini the hooker and Alberto the foreigner popped up. So the police beat you to it and didn't give you time to complete Bini's training.

When she found out from Jaén that the police wanted to question her, Bini agreed with you that she should give herself up immediately. Otherwise, her confession wouldn't be voluntary and she'd get a longer sentence.

Of course, you couldn't show your face at the station where Bini made her statement; but you found out via Chacha that everything had gone to plan.

You hoped that Bini would be let out on bail, but Gonzalo's lawyer friend assured you that, given that manslaughter was involved, the prosecutor would order her to be kept under preventive arrest. It was an unavoidable routine measure.

In fact, two days later they arrested her, and the next day you disappeared from Cuba. You'd be away for some time. They told you it would be more than a month to the beginning of the case; and your task was to travel the world looking for victims of Orlando Ortega Ortiz, ready not to forget and not accept any full stops. And in the meantime, let the bastard await in prison his inexorable decline.

# Part VII

Part VII

# 24 number 2 building, fourth floor, south wing

As it was extremely unlikely a court would absolve him, it was likely that Alberto's provisional imprisonment would extend to two years. And from the moment he entered the Combined, Alberto bestowed upon himself daily doses of comforting psychotherapy.

'There's always someone in life who'll put the lid on you. That's why you have to learn to be a good loser. And a man who doesn't walks in darkness, like the blind. People with savvy know that. "Skulls don't scream", as your uncle Alfonso used to say...But what an asshole Bini is! Cool it, you idiot, don't get worked up now, there'll always be time to get your own back. Life has its twists and turns. In the meantime, behave intelligently, keep your feet on the ground. Get used to the idea they've already tried and sentenced you.'

The Argentine consul appeared on his third day inside, a pleasant enough fellow, around thirty-five, who regretted he'd been so unlucky over the accident. He showed sympathy and tried to cheer him up.

The Uruguayan Fischer came with him, his partner in

Texinal, an old friend of his brother Tomás, who knew nothing about the role he was playing. Fischer informed him about a Mexican lawyer he'd contracted on his behalf and who was already studying his case. He'd be coming to Havana within the week.

Benefiting from the facilities the consul enjoyed, Fischer also brought him considerable stocks of provisions: six buckets for storing water, his laptop, the diskettes and books he'd asked for, victuals, tea, coffee, and several plastic bottles filled with whisky from his own supply. He also managed a small fan, a folding table and a chair.

Alberto had to work miracles to fit those goods into his tiny cell. Mariano gave him a small cupboard left by another prisoner where he stowed away all his provisions, except for the bottles, which wouldn't fit. He put them under his bed. And he put the computer on the table surrounded by several piles of books, papers and diskettes.

Nonetheless, that influx made his cell a warmer place. It wasn't long before he also got from home a few posters and a couple of arty nudes.

By the end of the week Alberto was feeling much more relaxed. After hitting rock bottom, things improved from day to day. And as soon as he'd got the necessary materials, he began to work on his book, with noteworthy results. He worked from 10 p.m. to 2 a.m., and from 2.30 p.m. to 5.30 p.m.

The hours flew by. A week passed, a fortnight passed, and he didn't even notice. He was short on time for everything he wanted to do.

He did his gym exercises half an hour before the water was turned on; and Mariano gave him passes so he could play *frontón* three times a week for an hour with a group of young guards. That effort kept him in good shape.

Soon after moving into his cell, Alberto found out there was a small group playing bridge – his favourite pastime – at the far end of the corridor he was on. The five of them met every afternoon in cell 4155, which had space for thirty-two beds. They'd place a table in one corner and play from 8 to 10 p.m. when most of the cell inmates were watching television, or were in the games room (officially dubbed 'the participatory area').

As the bridge players were discreet and played in silence, the prisoners who wanted to sleep at that time of night tolerated their presence and didn't protest.

Alberto's appearance in cell 4155 was welcomed with great delight. His presence allowed them to form three well-balanced pairs and even organize a tournament, with no need to rotate around the five of them as they'd done till then.

The level of expertise was pretty high, and Alberto fitted in perfectly. He was seeded third. Only Leo van der Putten, a Flemish Belgian, and Jordi Freixenet, a Catalan from Barcelona, played better than he did.

One hundred and forty-one of the foreigners inside were doing time for drug dealing. Eighty of them were Colombians, mostly young and poorly educated. The rest were South Americans of diverse nationalities, plus twenty or so Mexicans, and about the same number of North Americans and various Europeans, mostly Italian and Spanish.

There were only four Argentines, including Alberto, in the one hundred and ninety-six prisoners in south wing. The most entertaining was a guy from Entrerríos. Naturally, he was another head case, but a laugh and a character. He'd been given twelve years as a crew member of a Liberian boat, who'd been arrested trying to bring in a pile of coke. Like Alberto, he was fond of do-it-yourself psychotherapy, but used other arguments. He'd say he wouldn't do the ten years left because Castro's government would fall first. And he then maintained that when the northern blondies arrived or the Miami Cubans they'd be more understanding in relation to his case. The communists always exaggerated. The coke he was carrying wasn't even for Cuba. It was in transit to Europe.

'Like me, you've had a transit problem,' quipped Alberto.

'That's right, my coke wasn't going to harm anyone here, and I had only four kilos.'

'Is that all?' Alberto wound him up. 'Hell, *che*, how unfair!'

'And I only wanted to earn money so I could feed my children.'

When he talked about his children he started to cry.

Alberto slapped him supportively on the back and made an effort not to laugh in his face. People's attempts at self-deception filled him with contempt, made him want to be sarcastic. And in his opinion most of the prisoners were on that trip.

One of the few who didn't merit his contempt was Servio Tulio, a Colombian in his mid-sixties, who was also caught with a drug cargo on a fast launch. He was another champion of irrationality and lived in a world of his own, but in Alberto's opinion he wasn't prone to self-deception.

'This time I just needed to get rich very quickly,' he explained to Alberto.

Servio Tulio had an infallible formula for making money: dedication to hard work. He made a fortune three times by making savoury rolls and cooking oats.

Alberto remembered the savoury rolls. You bet he did; very popular items in Cali made from yucca flour and cheese and eaten for breakfast. Piping hot from the oven and accompanied by cold porridge, they were delicious.

Servio Tulio made his first fortune at the age of twenty-four; and that was when he got into rearing fighting bulls. It was an old, incurable passion.

'Watching a bull you've reared performing in the ring is really the cream on the cake.'

He made a pile three times from savoury rolls; and three times lost it on his bulls. But he had no regrets. He had three rounds of breeding, each more famous than the last in his country. He was a happy man for thirty-two years. He reacted decisively and courageously after the first two disasters; he found premises in poor barrios and, sure he would make a recovery, shut himself in and made savoury rolls. After working like a mule for four or five years, he bought more land and fighting bulls. Because the same hand that was good at kneading bread was also neat at cross-breeding.

But when his third failure came, at the age of sixty-five, he lacked energy to make another fortune on savoury rolls. That was why he got into cocaine, with the idea of making capital he could then invest in more bulls. But the Cubans fucked him up. His eight-year sentence, with no possibility of remission, gave him little prospect of ever rearing bulls again.

'If I can ever be of help…' Alberto chimed in.

'Off you go and get me a rope to hang myself with,' he replied one day when he was in a sombre mood.

On the third day of his temporary incarceration, the court notified Alberto Ríos that his obligatory defence lawyer had been appointed. But when the lawyer turned up to visit that same afternoon, Alberto rejected him, informing him that he had a Mexican lawyer who'd be coming to Cuba any day now.

Indeed, after studying the case details he'd been sent, the Mexican flew to Havana. He stayed for eight hours and had a long exchange with Alberto, in a cubicle of no. 3 building at the Combined.

'How could we prove,' he asked immediately, 'that the man with the white goatee and long hair, checked in at the hotel with your name, wasn't you?'

'I've told you once, Doctor, they were pure coincidences; they used my ID or another person came by the same name…'

'Another person, with the same name, the same long hair and beard and who gave shoes in your size as a present…? Coincidences don't work very well in court, Señor Ríos; and when they come thick and fast and feed on each other, they are bad news. Believe me, if you've no way of proving you weren't in that hotel on that date, and that the famous shoes weren't yours, then I can see no way I can possibly defend you successfully.'

Before he left, the lawyer deducted three thousand five-hundred dollars for the consultancy and travel expenses, and agreed to return the six thousand five hundred remaining of the advance he'd received from Tomás Ortega. He wrote a cheque to Alberto there and then, and returned the same afternoon to Mexico City.

The most interesting prisoners Alberto met in his first twenty days of temporary imprisonment were some of his fellow bridge players.

Apart from the Flemish Belgian and the Catalan, the group comprised John Volzov, a North American expert in paper manufacturing; Emilio Letelier, a Chilean forestry engineer; and Franco Pippi, a Florentine trader with aristocratic pretensions.

The Fleming and Italian were quite grey and had little to say for themselves. Each was doing fifteen years for murder and both had a long way to go.

Franco Pippi's Cuban girlfriend was to blame for him being behind bars. In a rage at an episode of infidelity, he strangled her; and van der Putten, an accountant for a Belgian firm in Havana, beat the boyfriend of his girlfriend to death. Beat him about the head and neck with golf clubs. He'd caught them fornicating behind a hillock.

Van der Putten was very dour and taciturn. He chain-smoked. He walked along the corridors talking to himself and gesticulating. Or stayed in his cell, where he solved chess problems and studied bridge, the only thing in the world that seemed to interest him. He competed at regional level in his country. He refused to sunbathe in the yard and didn't go to the games room. He spoke only the minimum necessary to survive and befriended no-one.

The Italian was bi-thematic: he talked only about a catastrophe that because of Wall Street threatened international high finance, or about his own genealogical tree. He was a real loner. On south wing nobody understood his financial assumptions; and nobody was interested in his ancestry, which, according to Pippi, included several *condottieri* and eight potato-head Popes.

'That sounds more like Irish stew than a family,' quipped Alberto, when he heard that.

The other three had interesting life stories.

John Volzov was shy and ugly and told his tale with a certain masochistic relish. He departed the family hearth when very young and lived for several years as a hippy in California. His messy clothes made up for his unfortunate physique and allowed him to land the occasional girl. Following the trend, he joined the revolutionary left in Berkeley in the sixties. Though he didn't understand the essence of the Cuban revolution, in those years he supported what was happening on the island and Fidel: at first rather tepidly, though at least publicly. Almost thirty years later, a father of two adolescent children and occupying an important position in the Texas paper manufacturing industry, his support for Cuba was reduced to secretly condemning US dirty play.

And in 1990, on an ill-fated first day of the holidays, when he was to fly from Houston to Miami to meet his wife and children, he began the celebrations by himself very early on. He was very drunk when he boarded the plane and downed another half bottle of vodka on the flight. Until what he could never have imagined happened; when they were flying over Florida, he decided to embrace an air hostess, hold a nail-cutter to her jugular and demand they take him to Cuba.

When the doors of the Boeing opened in Havana, and the security police summoned to meet the plane approached the steps, they were confronted by a bald pate circled with red ringlets, which straightened up to display a glaze of green eyes as bloodshot as a Tartar's, above narrow shoulders, and in the nether regions an obese stomach atop stubby, bandy legs.

That pear-shaped individual, in Bermudas and red T-shirt, waved a bottle on high and launched into a solidarity speech: 'People of Cuba…', etc., etc.

When John Volzov woke from his drunken stupor several hours later, he smiled incredulously. He thought his cell was part of an ongoing bout of drunkenness. But when he discovered he was in Havana, whither he'd hijacked a plane, he almost went crazy. They were also accusing him of assaulting a passenger who'd tried to stop him, only to make matters worse. After being struck on the head with a half-empty bottle of whisky, the man was now in a deep coma in intensive care in a Cuban hospital.

John cried silently for two days, while he wrote one letter after another to beg his wife and children's forgiveness.

Because of agreements on the hijacking of planes, Cuba was to return him to the United States; but when the passenger in hospital died, and as the aggression had occurred on Cuban soil, John Volzov had to pay for this crime first. They sentenced him to eight years, of which he'd already done three.

Volzov finished his story in tears.

'What a ridiculous drama! Only a drunken idiot can get into such a mess!'

Emilio Letelier and Jordi Freixenet were the craziest in the group, and at the same time the most appealing. Alberto enjoyed them in his way, and liked to egg them on.

At the age of twenty-three Emilio graduated in forestry engineering from the University of Chile, and lived for a time working for the FAO in the forests in the south of his country and in Argentina. They sent him to Canada in 1986. It was there he learned bridge, the favourite game of several of his Anglo-Saxon colleagues. It was an ideal game for killing time in northern solitudes. But Emilio never considered bridge to be other that a banal waste of time. He preferred to devote his spare time to satisfying other interests.

As soon as he reached three, Emilio's mother read to him *The Iliad* and *The Odyssey*, and got him to sleep by recounting old Greek myths. And she always declared that those old stories were more beautiful in Greek. But his mother died when he was seven.

And Anna, his Swedish wife, died when he was twenty-five. She was killed in a car accident when they lived in Uppsala.

It was the second hard knock in his life, and he started drinking. He abandoned his work and the area. He turned his back on trees and wood. And on any kind of work at all. He tramped for two years, drunk and in rags, through the north of Sweden; and one day, when he'd been fasting for three and couldn't get a drink, he assaulted a rural savings bank and was given a four-year sentence.

The first six months in prison cured him of his alcoholism. He never drank again. And to fight off tedium and resurrect his mother, he began to study Greek. He studied eighteen hours a day in a psychopathic frenzy. After nine months he learned enough to understand Homeric hexameters printed in bilingual editions. And around that time he conceived of a project that would become his life's ambition.

Endowed with a fantastic memory, he proposed to learn by heart *The Iliad* and *The Odyssey* in Homeric Greek, English, French and Spanish.

After doing his sums, he predicted that in eight years he would be able to surprise the world by trebling the feats of memory of Homeric bards, able to recite the forty-eight rhapsodies and twenty-eight thousand lines that made up both poems. Emilio Letelier proposed to store in his brain four times that: one hundred and twelve thousand lines. A world first.

His lunacy was now irreversible; one day, the very noble, ancient rhapsode's art would allow him to earn a decent living. He would appear on television programmes and in centres of culture throughout the world. He would become famous by reciting batches of lines, from this number to that, whatever he was asked and in whichever language.

And one day he left a free man and they deported him back to Chile.

In Santiago he affirmed his inability to work as a forestry engineer. In fact, he could no longer work at anything. His Homeric endeavours, his only justification for living, threatened to go off the rails. He could perform that feat only in prison, where his roof, meals and time were guaranteed.

Besides, his recent life as a bandit and jailbird frightened his friends and family. They all loathed his physical appearance and ragged clothes. He had got used to being unkempt. And, for heaven's sake, that skin, which hadn't seen the sun for years, sickly, glazed like the belly of a fish…His best friends acted distant when they saw him; kept well away, were all very busy, beset by problems, etc. There was only one, now a prosperous doctor, who took an interest in him; he interned him in his clinic and discovered he was suffering from skin cancer. He was referred to a state dermatologist who informed him that his illness was curable, but required a long, expensive and rigorous treatment.

Emilio was debating for days whether to carry out a serious bank raid, to provide enough money to pay for his treatment; or to shoot himself in the head and put an end to the problem.

He was appalled by the idea of dying a frustrated man, not having been able to memorize Homer. But at that time his medic friend got him to read a scientific article about a new treatment for skin cancer available in Cuba; something that was very effective, or so it said, and in some cases it cured or at least held the illness at bay. They applied a product they'd created, combined with brief daily sessions of sunshine. But the trick was in the fact that the greater vertical nature of sun's rays in the tropics favoured a radiation that was impossible in other parts of the planet. And that strength of the sun allowed a particular balance of infrared and ultraviolet rays to be struck which, together with the applications of their product, impacted therapeutically on one's skin.

Letelier also found out that free socialist medicine in Cuba was also available gratis to prisoners. So he decided to try his luck.

He managed to get a loan to pay for the flight and flew to Havana in a Chilean tourist charter flight at the beginning of 1996.

The very next day, with a plastic pistol he'd bought in a toyshop in Santiago de Chile, he intimidated the woman behind the till in a shop, struck an assistant and carried off eight hundred dollars. He fled, and that same day raided two other shops, where he kicked in windows and frightened the public. In the third, he got involved in a skirmish with an armed policeman, and provoked a shot that wounded a customer.

They sent him down for six years.

When Alberto got to know him, he was in his third on south wing. He'd improved in Cuba. His skin was bronzed and didn't have that cadaverous sheen it had acquired in Sweden. His treatment was very simple: instead of the forty-five minutes' sun enjoyed by the rest of the prisoners in the yard, he was allowed five stretches of fifteen minutes at different times; and with Mariano's permission, he moved around during the day, when he wanted, with no need of a pass, between the fourth and the ground floor. Then he'd head for a small square where he'd recline in his swimming trunks, sunbathe and give his skin the necessary treatment.

Seeing that his Homerically heroic project was gaining ground, and that his illness was under control, Emilio enthused. His good spirits in the bridge school made up for the sourness of van der Putten and John Volzov.

Everybody liked him in the gallery; he joked with guards and prisoners, and spent the day standing in his cell reciting Homer at the top of his voice in his four languages. He had already learned as far as line fourteen thousand three hundred and ninety-seven of The Iliad. When he got to line fifteen thousand five hundred and thirty-seven, the poem's last, Mariano would give him a party.

When he heard that pledge, Alberto offered to help: he would pay for a succulent meal and as much drink as Mariano would authorize.

On the mural newspaper on the fourth floor, south wing, Mariano (who Alberto also thought had a few screws loose) would record daily, in big red figures, the days remaining till Letelier reached his memorable goal. When Alberto first read that piece of news, there were still one hundred and fourteen days to go. They expected to hold the celebration on 5 December.

Jordi Freixenet was another interesting character, the jack-of-all-trades on the fourth floor. A Catalan with very handy hands. He could sort out the plumbing as quickly as the television or a problem with the gas cooker. He knew a lot about domestic engineering.

In 1996, on his first trip as a tourist to Cuba, Jordi found himself listening to boleros in the White Beak Club at the St John's Hotel, where there was an outdoor cabaret. Another, very drunken, rude tourist went a grope too far with his Basque girlfriend, who'd accompanied him from Spain. Jordi's rage was such that the drunk only just managed to clear an eighty-centimetre-high wall, fleeing from the blows raining down. But Jordi's furious right hook hurled him into the void. He'd gone so mental he'd forgotten they were on the twelfth floor.

He was given a four-year sentence and was already in the third.

As with lots of prisoners who suffer from claustrophobia and the wear and tear derived from being immobile, in captivity his old delirious dream of constructing a city where all the streets headed downwards took on another level of intensity. It would be like a huge Roman Coliseum, with a circular base twenty kilometres wide and forty metres high.

Streets would furrow the city going from one point at the heights to a spot opposite at the bottom. That way the inhabitants would be able to move around by bike, or in open-sided cars, which Jordi would design in the style of the trams in Rio. The passengers would travel in them with one leg aloft, and the other on the pavement, in order to push themselves gently downwards…

'But if the streets all slope downwards, why are you going to make people row with a foot on the ground?'

'Come on, dear Alberto; if a street slopes from a height of forty metres over twenty kilometres, it will only have a minimal incline, less than one degree; that's not enough for vehicles to move by themselves. Passengers will always have to lend a helping foot; and ten will make ten legs rowing on the ground, as you put it. If they only move them slightly, they'll make terrific progress. It's good exercise and splendidly ecological…'

'Then what happens when they want to go back to the top?' came the inevitable question from Alberto.

'I explained that to you, my friend: with the help of ponies.'

At the destination point, there'd be a series of wheels activated by small horses, to raise the vehicles on enormous platforms.

And he was going to give Fidel Castro his whole invention as a present.

Jordi wanted nothing for himself.

Alberto put the idea into his head that he should ask Fidel for a decent pension.

'Yes, that's worth considering,' Jordi agreed. 'Why didn't I think of that first?'

'I'm sure he'll grant you one,' Alberto encouraged him. 'And if you ask him, I'm sure he'll even give you a little Cuban island, where you can give your balls a run and continue thinking on behalf of Cuba…'

'Do you reckon so, Alberto?'

'Of course, you idiot; you need to start negotiating with Fidel right away.'

'Yes, but with him personally. Otherwise, nothing will happen.'

'Of course, Jordi, he's the only guy you can trust around here.'

Alberto decided to wind him up and convince him he shouldn't wait till he was free. He should ask for the interview right now.

Jordi promised he wouldn't give his invention to anyone, not to a minister, not to a bureaucrat, not to any academic. He'd trust only in Fidel.

Just like Alberto, Jordi loathed bureaucracy and intellectuals, a string of thieves and lazy gits.

Before his trial, Alberto was under preventive arrest in jail for thirty-eight days.

As part of his therapy, he kept repeating a comment from Dr Pazos, whose liking for cockroaches had led him to praise them as queens of ecology, champion survivors, a most ancient insect that, throughout history, adapted to the most adverse conditions. It could live in torrid deserts and at the North Pole. Everything seemed to point to the fact that it would never become extinct. Entomologists believed that they would survive a nuclear war, laughing themselves silly. Besides, the cockroach had a beautiful scientific name: *Periplaneta americana*.

That was what Alberto wanted to be like; resistant, sporting with adversity; like cockroaches or coral reefs, rock solid amid the worst storms.

Prison? A hoot; and if he succeeded in finishing his book on cruelty, it would be a triumph over himself.

Indeed, prison was moulding his life and his mind to a different rhythm. Even his heart beat differently. He noted that he was more predisposed to reflection, to restructuring his ideas; in particular, his ideas on life and his own self.

After twenty days behind bars, Alberto was convinced he could stand two years. Nothing in the daily routine was intolerable. He suffered no sacrifices, sadness or humiliation. It was very annoying to be without sex, but that would be sorted.

In the meantime, each day he adapted better to his motley milieu, packed with lunatics; it soothed him to listen to their ridiculous dramas with an attentiveness he never allowed others. Among so much *felacio*, he reaffirmed himself as someone chosen by destiny and nature.

On 1 September, after twenty-two days of captive sojourn in the Combined, Alberto Ríos received a visitation from Captain Bastidas.

Bastidas first spoke to the prison authorities, in order to find out through them whether prisoner Alberto Ríos was prepared to see him.

As Alberto wasn't in the hands of the police but at the disposal of the public prosecutor, he could refuse to accept visits of a private nature. He was on the point of saying no, but his curiosity got the better of him.

It was agreed he would see him in his own cell at 9.15.

That was neither usual nor according to the rules. Visits by lawyers or functionaries of any kind took place in the cubicles in number 3 building, second floor, north wing; but that day, at that time, the whole of building number 3 had to stay closed in the morning, in order to implement the bi-monthly programme of fumigation. And Major Mariano Robles Marín authorized the visit as it involved a colleague examining the case. And especially because he expressed his desire to help the man under arrest.

Bastidas arrived at 9.20 in plain clothes.

'Well, Captain, fire away.' Alberto welcomed him standing up, not prepared to offer him a seat till he knew what he wanted.

'I've heard you still don't have a defence lawyer...'

'That's right.'

'I've a couple of ideas I think you should consider.'

Alberto imagined that the policeman would try to fix him with a defence attorney, with whom he'd already agreed a commission. As far as Alberto knew, such levels of corruption didn't exist in the Cuban police, but in Cuba everything was developing too quickly.

'Then please take a seat, Captain…' and he pointed him to the bed.

He tried to appear welcoming.

'No, don't worry. I'm fine standing.'

But Alberto insisted on being nice. He almost pushed him. He wanted to see him seated on his bed.

'Look, I'll sit here, "on the wall of modesty".'

Sitting on the bed, Bastidas looked at him quizzically.

Alberto pointed to the edge of a small wall sixty centimetres high and ten wide, whose only use, as he demonstrated, was to hide those who were crouching down to crap in the lavatory.

'If a policeman spies on me through the spyhole, he can only see my head.'

As he said this, he took a thermos from the foot of his bed and two cardboard cups.

'Some freshly made coffee?'

'No thank you,' replied Bastidas.

Alberto bent down again and grabbed a box of cigars.

'A Cohiba?'

'No thanks, I've given up smoking,' said Bastidas.

Bastidas went to the heart of the matter; despite all the evidence against him, he was inclined to believe he was innocent.

Alberto smiled at him, perplexed. And went on the defensive. This cop might be plotting something else.

'Something tells me that Bini is lying and you're telling the truth.'

'What good news!' Alberto laughed.

After slapping a thigh twice, he took a long draught on his cigar. He expelled a very bluish puff of smoke to his right, towards the only air vent the cell had. In that grey suit, and in cloudy profile with white goatee and locks, Alberto presented an image of saintly sensuality.

He was enjoying his Cohiba.

'I also believe I'm innocent…So that makes two of us.'

He strove hard to show he was in a joking mood, implicitly unworried by prison and his upcoming trial.

'I don't think the court will think the same. The evidence against you is very compelling.'

'So what are you basing your views on, then…?'

'I've observed your behaviour…A guilty person would have acted differently…'

'Can you give me an example?'

'I could give you several, but it's all very subjective, and hardly relevant. They are just small details. After twenty years we police have a second sense…'

'Well, that's great! Can I offer you a whisky, Captain?'

'You've really got whisky here?' And Bastidas lowered his voice and looked rather alarmed.

'I swear I do, my consul has behaved like a mother to me; he brought the entire stock of whisky I had at home.'

'Your consul has acted like a mother…' Bastidas repeated, glancing round the cell, highly intrigued, 'and the chief warder like a very consenting father.'

'Yes, like a father…I expect he also thinks I'm innocent.'

And he guffawed once more.

'So, then.' He lowered his voice again. 'Will you have a whisky?'

'All right, pour me a whisky.'

Alberto kneeled down nimbly by the foot of the bed, stuck his hand underneath and took out a wrinkled plastic bottle and two cardboard cups.

'Twenty-year-old Ballantine's,' Alberto boasted.

He poured out the shots, handed Bastidas his, settled back on his low wall and raised his glass as if offering a toast.

'I'm delighted you're convinced I'm innocent….'

'I didn't say I am convinced; but I'm inclined to think you are innocent. To be frank, I'd not put my hands in the fire for you…'

They looked at each other silently for a moment.

'…but I do know a lawyer who might. He's a very special individual, and in my view the only person in Cuba who could take on the case with any likelihood of success.'

Only then did Bastidas raise his glass, but only to down the whisky in one gulp.

Alberto looked at him in surprise.

'Would you like another drop?'

'Yes, please fill the glass up.' And he held it out.

Alberto filled it to the top and saw that his pulse was firm, that he didn't shake like an alcoholic. And once again, wow, he downed his poison in one gulp.

Alberto opened his eyes wide and smiled in praise.

'Nothing wrong with your pipes…but they say you can't have two without a third.' And held out the bottle, which Bastidas hadn't given him time to put the top on.

'No, thanks.'

Alberto inspected the skin of this policeman who drank like crazy. He looked for the broken pores of an alcoholic, but found that his skin was smooth. He didn't have a ruddy nose or cheeks either.

A strange fellow. Perhaps he wasn't the crook he'd first imagined; but a *felacio* of rare distinction, whose conscience obliged him to offer a disinterested hand, beyond the realm of duty. And he decided to find out what manner of policeman Bastidas was and what he was really after.

'OK, I'm listening, in what way is this lawyer friend of yours so special?'

'Among other things, because whatever the accused says, he always knows whether he's dealing with an innocent man or a liar. And if he agrees to defend you, it will be because he believes in your innocence. He has his own methods to avoid making mistakes.'

# 25 dr azúa

Dr Azúa was black, forty-eight years old, almost two metres tall, and weighed in at one hundred and twenty kilos; but didn't look fat and could claim to be thirty-five.

Between the ages of ten and twenty-five, when his father was still alive, Azúa resided in Europe and India: three years in Paris, four in Moscow, three in Rome, five in New Delhi. From very early on he felt a vocation for medicine, and turned out to be exceptionally gifted in that respect. He had a divine hand, full of magnetic powers, which he cultivated here and there in itinerant mode, rather off the top of his head, and with little to no theory.

Nonetheless, the only serious studies he followed on his definitive return to Cuba were in law. The wandering life, enforced on him by his father's diplomatic profession, prevented him from studying medicine; and on his return to Cuba, at the age of twenty-five, he preferred to study law via the route of open examinations. And once he had graduated, he devoted himself wholeheartedly to his special talent as a defence lawyer.

263

Bastidas, a good friend of Azúa from his time in Moscow, had informed him of his niggling feelings about Alberto's case.

The first consultancy session was held in one of the cubicles set aside for lawyers. Azúa had already read the statements given by Bini and the two employees at the Triton.

After the introductions, when Bastidas withdrew, Azúa sat back in his chair, which he pushed against the wall, and shut his eyes.

'Talk to me. Give me your version of the facts.'

Alberto's version took only a few seconds.

'I was never with Bini in a car that wasn't mine. I never wore two-toned Florsheim shoes. I never stayed at the Triton Hotel. Everything she attributes to me in relation to the accident with the cyclist is untrue.'

Without opening his eyes, Azúa told him: 'Keep talking. Tell me everything you remember about your relationship with her.'

Alberto then related how they met at the marina in October 1998. She wanted to learn how to surf and he wanted to fuck her. He would invite her to his house or yacht for these flings. And he always paid her. She was mad, amusing and very good in bed. He told him of their last encounter in the Tocororo, the previous call, the story of the dream, the lottery and the theft of his ID card.

Azúa listened, eyes shut, mouth open. The whole time his head swayed slowly like a pendulum.

When Alberto finished his account, Azúa opened his eyes and started to rub his hands gently together.

'That's fine, sit down here,' said Azúa.

He stopped rubbing and pointed him to his own chair, which he placed in a corner of the cubicle, tight against the wall.

Azúa sat down opposite and got Alberto to bring his knees together, so they were between his own.

Alberto obeyed, quite apprehensive and highly intrigued.

'Give me your left hand.'

He was somewhat embarrassed by the situation, and by the serious way the fellow was engaging in his various manoeuvres, but decided to follow his lead.

Alberto stretched out an open hand and Azúa placed it palm downwards, on the palm of his own right hand, which he rested on his knee. Then, he raised his left arm and stared at his watch.

'When it can't stand any more, take it away,' Azúa told him.

'When it can't stand what?'

'You'll soon see,' replied Azúa keeping his eyes on his watch.

Indeed, before ten seconds had passed, Alberto's hand began to give off more and more heat. Soon, he couldn't stand the temperature and took his hand away.

'God, how did you do that, Doctor?' And he bent over in alarm to look at Azúa's very red, open palm, as if to make sure he wasn't hiding some gadget.

'Don't worry, I'm finding out if you told me the truth…'

'But you almost incinerated me…' joked Alberto, intrigued by the arts of this black wizard.

'Shhh,' interjected Azúa, frowning. 'Give me your other hand, and don't worry, because this time you're not going to burn.'

Alberto obeyed. Azúa gripped his right hand; it was very warm but bearable.

'Look at a spot on the ceiling and stare at it.'

Alberto focused on the corner to his left.

'Answer my question without taking your eyes from that spot: were you with Bini at the Triton?'

'No.'

'Did you ever wear the Florsheim shoes?'

'No.'

'Now, look into my eyes.'

Alberto saw him lean his body slightly over towards him, with a welcoming expression and the hint of a smile on his lips.

'Look into the centre of my eye...'

From that distance the cornea looked whiter and very shiny.

'Who was driving the car when the cyclist was knocked over?'

'I don't know. I wasn't there.'

'What motives might Bini have to declare against you in this way?'

'I don't know. I can only suppose that the guy who knocked the cyclist over is paying her to put the blame on me.'

'Keep looking into the centre of my left eye.'

Azúa held on to his hand for a few seconds more, moved slightly over to him and clasped his knees between his own. He stared at him for a few moments, unblinking, looking grave. Finally, he let go and put a hand on his shoulder.

'Bastidas is right. Bini is trying to pin the collision with the cyclist on you.'

Alberto was in a state of wonder and started to cherish hope.

They had a second session the day after. Straight away, Azúa was like a bucket of cold water.

'I must be candid. I've listened several times to the statements made by the girl and the other two; when I compare them to the information gathered by the examining magistrate, I can see it's going to be very difficult to defend you. If the three witnesses keep to their statements during the trial, I'll be able to do next to nothing. The evidence against you is very strong. They'll very probably sentence you to two years in prison...'

'How probably?'

'Ninety or so per cent.'

'What can we do?'

'I'd prefer to disentangle myself from the case, because I

can't see that the defence stands a chance. Our only hope is for Bini to contradict herself before the court; but in the recording she's very coherent and self-confident, so don't build up your hopes.'

'I'm prepared to pay whatever fee you ask for.'

'That is a secondary matter. Besides, I'll only charge if you are absolved. And I must tell you I'm only taking the case on for ethical reasons.'

'What ethics?'

'The only one there is: if I, a man convinced of your innocence, won't defend you, who will?'

The fact that he wouldn't accept any fee if he didn't secure his release showed that Azúa wasn't the bandit he thought he was to start with. Bastidas couldn't be either. And if the black with his witchcraft and strange games could fix it so Bini made a mistake and proved his innocence, he would be most delighted to pay him whatever he asked for.

What if Azúa failed and they sentenced him to jail?

All he could think of at the moment was to send what he would save on Azúa to pay for a killer to settle accounts with Bini. He could contract Pizzaiolo, for example.

But that task would be for later.

The best thing was not to set his hopes too high and continue the psychotherapy. With Mariano on his side he knew that prison was tolerable. Now he should concentrate on his work and finish *Fruitful Cruelty*.

# Part VIII

Part VIII

# 26 a mistaken diagnosis

Aldo returned that night to the Triton determined to confide in Aurelia no more, after her exaggerated alarums and excursions when she found out about the accident. Nor in Gonzalo, naturally, and he discarded both as possible collaborators in his plans against Three-O.

Over the two days when they didn't meet up again, Aurelia predicted that that bitch Bini would be the ruin of Aldo. She began to mortify herself, and to mortify Gonzalo.

Her duty, as a professional and Aldo's friend, was to open his eyes; and even if it pained Aldo, if it ended their friendship, she'd tell him to his face what she thought of Bini. In particular, she should tell him how ridiculous he'd look if he married her, or took her to Italy. Aldo couldn't go on mixing that whore up in whatever way he was unravelling his Pygmalion complex. He should see her for what she was: a ruthless tart who went to bed with anybody for money. No matter whether it was an impotent old man, a fat fart or a stinking drunk.

Aurelia's aggressive attitude placed Gonzalo in a difficult

situation. He didn't dare argue with her on her specialist ground. Aurelia was one of the most intelligent women Gonzalo had ever met in a long interaction with intelligent women. And she might know lots about psychiatry, but he couldn't share a view that so condemned and rubbished prostitution. He felt such a lack of empathy verged on the unprofessional.

But these days it was dangerous to argue anything in favour of Bini in Aurelia's presence. She was unmovable, both as doctor and woman. She was intent on destroying the false image Aldo had created of Bini.

Gonzalo would have preferred to show him with the necessary tact how ridiculously he was behaving; but he knew that alone wouldn't shift him. Nor did Gonzalo believe that Bini was a ruthless whore.

For fuck's sake, didn't Aurelia realize that a young, pretty prostitute like Bini wasn't forced to bed loathsome guys? She was much in demand, and could allow herself the luxury of choosing her clientele...

As an expert, Aurelia was not unaware of the fact that very few women functioned like men; namely, that they could gain sexual enjoyment with any lover they liked physical contact with, without any pretence of spiritual love. But as Aldo's friend, she hated to see him involved with a woman like that, a whore into the bargain, both ignorant and common. It was the last straw to contemplate marrying her. If that marriage took place, Aldo would face ridicule and upsets. And Aurelia would strive to stop it. Clinically and humanly, that woman was a piece of shit Aldo didn't deserve.

Gonzalo disagreed. A couple of years ago, he had been seduced by a pupil who, rather than answering his questions in written exams, would dedicate erotic poems to him, and thrust him into an illicit adventure that allowed them to get better acquainted. The lass confessed she got the hots with one guy today, another tomorrow, and enjoyed herself with both, yet neither provoked those elevated feelings poets sing of. All she required was to fancy the guys. And it wasn't just because she wanted good-lookers. Sometimes she was attracted to one by his ideas, or the amusing way he spoke; or an ugly but virile man, or one with a gruff voice. And she rejected certain men for their epidermis. She didn't know why, but the mere thought of touching some made her feel like sicking up.

Gonzalo had well-founded reasons for thinking that Bini belonged to that class, and not the loathsome category Aurelia imagined. Well, OK, he could agree that in an egalitarian, paternalist society like Cuba, a young woman who doesn't study or work and prefers to prostitute herself is generally of low moral fibre. But not always. There existed unlucky beings that were victims of their own histories and families. It wasn't the same thing to be a great-granddaughter of an insurgent general in the War of Independence, granddaughter of a sugarocrat, and daughter of two university academics on the anti-Machado left, like Aurelia, or be the great-granddaughter of slaves and, four generations ago, of mountain peasants, stultified by their isolation, in-breeding, illiteracy and other cultural handicaps.

And besides, all societies have their high priestesses of love, sacred prostitutes, like those who practised in the temples of Aphrodite, Astarté or other erotic deities. Bini was one of those who delivered themselves up; and while she was with a guy, customer or not, she performed like a woman in love. She possessed that gift. In that furtive episode on his birthday, Bini got the hots for him just seeing him tango. And as she was a generous woman, she felt his momentary emotion and nostalgia and got turned on. Why not see that as the reaction of a healthy, noble, supportive love? Why did those Christians always see genital relationships as something dirty? No, it wasn't right to accuse her of being filthy or mercenary, because of the way she surrendered herself. Why condemn her like that?

Yes, but what about the horns she'd inevitably plonk on Aldo?

Oh.... That was another side to the problem.

★

On the public holiday on 26 July, after recharging his batteries at the Triton for two days, Aldo returned to his original idea of talking to Gonzalo and Aurelia about Three-O. He would confess the whole range of his plans. He called them to set up a fresh meeting at their place.

He could rely on Gonzalo; and Aurelia was an intelligent, sensitive woman and just had to understand his situation. And if she understood, she'd support his plans. At any rate he could bank on them not betraying him.

Aldo dived in and showed them his photographic documentation on Three-O, Orlando Ortega Ortiz, the Uruguayan of the three Os, Captain Horror; and sketched in his sinister curriculum. He related the episode on Lavalle and Talcahuano, after leaving the cinema; their arrest and transportation to the EMA, where Teresita had died. And without going into details he told them how Three-O had led several sessions of torture involving himself.

Finally, he revealed everything he'd ever hatched against him. First, he wanted to shoot him in the street, but then confronted the problem of how to get a weapon; afterwards, he'd thought of impaling him, until he realized that would be more than he could handle; and finally, he opted to put him in prison and in the meantime set up a trial in Europe.

He praised Bini's out-and-out solidarity. It was really moving. She'd taken responsibility for stealing Three-O's ID card, with which he checked in at the Triton, thanks to the complicity of Bini's long-time friend, Pepe Jaén, a totally trustworthy individual.

Gonzalo blanched.

Aurelia couldn't believe her ears.

'And yesterday, Bini gave the Florsheims to a chambermaid, in order to get them off our hands. We needed a witness, for when Bini confesses that the shoes belonged to Three-O.'

And he showed them the wig and goatee he'd worn in the hotel in order to pass himself off as his enemy.

'Bini will sink him when she makes her statement. And now I'm training her to call me Tito…'

It was all too much for Aurelia, who jumped up.

'You've gone mad,' she exclaimed in horror.

Gonzalo also looked very worried. In his opinion, Aldo should settle for executing the bastard in the street.

'And you can count on my help. We'll see what's the best way to get a weapon; but trying to blame the guy for things he didn't do will backfire on you and cost you dear…'

'It won't backfire…'

'Don't be mad, Aldo,' insisted Aurelia. 'Any small technical error can betray you.'

Aldo was very stubborn.

There would be no technical error. Everything would be based on the evidence of the check-ins at the hotel, the statements of the two employees, and Bini's declaration.

'I'm sorry, Aldo, but what I like least about all this is that Bini is involved and that you've implicated a friend of hers…'

It was time to tell Aldo what was what.

'…you can't imagine what kind of woman she is.'

'If you're going to tell me she is a whore, it's not news.'

'Well, I'll tell you again, so you really take it in: yes, she is a whore; but I don't want to talk about her; it's you I want to concentrate on.'

When Aurelia lectured him on his Pygmalion complex, he listened in silence. He seemed interested and rather surprised.

Aurelia tried to be didactic and simplified her exposition.

Aldo shook his head and smiled.

'Your piss is missing the pan, Aurelia…' he said, almost sarcastically. 'I'm sorry, but your diagnosis…'

'No need to say you're sorry. Day in day out my patients tell me that my diagnosis…

'But, *che*, Aldo, you never listen to anyone and you always imagine that you alone…'

'I don't imagine anything,' Aldo interrupted her testily; 'I know what my problem is. You are the ones who know nothing.'

Aurelia looked at him in a blind fury.

'But...how dare you...?'

Gonzalo gave her a dig with his elbow, stood up and shouted: 'Please cool it!'

Gonzalo was afraid she'd go too near the bone.

'Anyway, Aurelia, I'm grateful,' replied Aldo, in a more conciliatory tone, but looking daggers at her. 'I know you're doing this out of friendship, to help me...but you're mistaken...'

'Look, Aldo, all my patients...'

'Aurelia, you're not the first psychiatrist to give me advice... I've been having treatment in Rome for years.'

Neither Aurelia nor Gonzalo had imagined that. They thought Aldo was such a positive, well-balanced man.

She half closed her eyes and looked at him suspiciously. She seemed taken aback.

'I see Dr Troccoli...Do you know him?'

'Yes, he's a distinguished authority. We met at a congress.'

'You don't say?'

'Two years ago, in Brazil.'

'Well; as for my relationship with Bini, Troccoli has more information at his disposal than either of you...

'I'm referring to information about me, my real pathology, which isn't what you suppose,' he told Aurelia. 'Because it's not about my complex about my age, which does exist to a certain extent, but something much worse, that's been torturing me for twenty years.'

Aurelia looked at him reproachfully and waited for him to reveal all.

'I like little girls,' Aldo said finally, emptying, almost in a rage, his half-full glass of whisky.

Aurelia arched her eyebrows, but managed to curtail her

shocked reaction halfway. Could she have been so mistaken in her diagnosis? She rapidly readjusted, relaxed her facial muscles and threw herself back in her chair. In a few seconds she'd adopted the imperturbable façade of an experienced professional, those for whom *nihil humani sibi alienum putat*, etc., etc.

A paedophile? Aldo, a paedophile?

Gonzalo shook his head to chase off an obscene image. A pair of hands stripped the skin from his temples, from his ears. That was what he used to imagine as a kid when he read horror stories.

Aldo was sixteen and La Negrita twelve. She'd been raped by her stepfather in Jujuy at the age of eight and ended up one fine day as a servant girl with Aldo's family, him being a young, very nice lad and a virgin to boot. She'd done quite some mileage for her age and taught him amusing positions and games. She was very confident in the efficiency of her fellatio and bet money with Aldo: 'I bet you can't get to ten,' she'd tell him, and would start counting while she kissed and kissed. Or she'd pirouette around and take up positions that made him laugh. At the same time she was gentle and very tender. In her way she was in love with Aldo.

They satisfied their desires almost on a daily basis. Aldo lived his life looking for an opportunity to escape to the shed with La Negrita, and masturbated between encounters, thinking about her.

His mum caught them one day and sacked La Negrita. Aldo never saw her again. His mum gave him a book published by the Jesuits so he could grasp the extent of his impurity. Aldo resisted during a month of abstinence before relapsing into sin by touching himself and thinking of La Negrita.

On holiday in Montevideo, reluctantly, just to follow the crowd, he agreed to visit a local brothel with a group of friends. He was left completely cold by the fat thirty-year-old whose room he'd entered. He was so disgusted by those enormous, flaccid breasts, her strident laugh, heavy breathing and filthy language, that he didn't even get undressed. He paid her and left totally repulsed.

In subsequent years he suffered other failures with prostitutes. And by the age of twenty-three, when he had his first adult woman, he still masturbated daily thinking about La Negrita. Until that moment, his entire libido was linked to her dark skin, fleshy, fleshy lips, slanted eyes and mischievous sweetness, which made their trips to the shed such a thrill.

In the next ten years, he had three very normal relationships with a partner. The last one was with Teresita, until they were taken to the EMA.

'Five of them raped her, in front of me. And then…I don't want to think of the beastly things they did to her. Three-O grabbed me by the hair and dragged me close up to look. "See what you can expect, *felacio*," he would say.'

When they entered the EMA, Three-O took his watch; left him barefoot in midwinter, because he liked his shoes, which were a perfect fit; and to spare his life, demanded a sum of money that forced him to sell his share in the ownership of a clinic.

When Aldo regained his freedom, he was thirty-three, and for a long time he couldn't have sexual relations. He was depressed by the memory of being sodomized by Three-O; or when he was forced to worship his rooster tattoo, or lick the mud off his boots, or run and bark on four legs while he and the other executioners laid bets. Time and again the image of Teresita crossed his mind: raped, tortured, racked by the pain from the teeth of the mice trying to escape from her vagina; and when he tried to have sex again and tried to come, he failed several times. Then he started to masturbate again thinking of La Negrita. According to the explanations of his Italian psychiatrist, his horror at his experience in the EMA made him regress to adolescence in order to find refuge in memories of a healthy, innocent sexuality. And the years passed, and he could no longer have normal relations with a woman. Not even when he fell in love with Giuditta, a phenomenon who stopped the traffic in Rome. He required the memory of La Negrita to get an erection and orgasm. But things weren't easy. Sometimes he couldn't concentrate. The mental effort exhausted him; and over time, the image of La Negrita finally wore thin after he'd overused it with Giuditta.

'Around that time, after I'd divorced, I went to Thailand, and out of curiosity, or perhaps driven by my subconscious, I went into a de luxe brothel in Bangkok; I ended up making love to a thirteen-year-old girl.'

He was aroused by her dark skin, her negligible breasts; and felt he was with La Negrita again.

This image from Thailand accompanied him for a couple of years, in his relationships with adult Europeans. Then he had a Turkish girl with similar traits in Munich.

When Aldo became aware of his paedophile dependence, he started to reproach himself. How could these poor girls excite him, who were themselves victims of the monstrousness of society? What wretchedness of his own led him to enjoy what deserved only compassion? Something very base and twisted was lurking in his erotic apparatus.

His psychiatrist finally hit on a sound explanation. Aldo was also a victim, a raped being, whose girlfriend had been murdered after he'd been forced to witness the worst possible humiliations and tortures. The girls in Bangkok and Munich were beyond redemption; they were probably prostitutes from the moment they opened their eyes. But he wasn't a paedophile monster excited by their defencelessness and wretchedness. He was using them only to renew his erotic memory of his youthful love for La Negrita. Hadn't this been the refuge he'd sought after being humiliated at the hands of Three-O?

And then suddenly, Bini.

'She was the first adult in twenty years that I made love to without thinking of a young girl. When it happened, I couldn't believe it...I'd found an antidote for my aberrations...'

When he returned from his first trip to Havana, his psychiatrist recommended he establish a permanent relationship with that woman.

'The fact is that her attitude in bed, the things she says and does are those of a ten-year-old; because that must be her emotional age.'

Bini also aroused in him an unsuspected vigour, an ability to come back for more, that he'd never enjoyed even in his youth. And another positive novelty, after two months of his relationship with Bini and thinking only of her, which came effortlessly, was that he began to function with other adult women.

'Don't you understand? With Bini I stopped being a monster. Why should I worry if she's ignorant, tacky, a whore...! Do you think I don't know those things? Or do you think I should live on appearances, marry a chic, cultured lady, and carry on with my aberrations?'

He looked at them defiantly.

Aurelia thanked him for confiding in them, and recognized that, indeed, Bini could be his salvation. But it was stupid to marry her.

Aldo was drinking a lot and the alcohol was beginning to take its toll. Suddenly he started to cry.

'Three-O killed Teresita and it was my fault.'

Because if Aldo hadn't kicked him in the balls when he'd insulted her, nothing would have happened. He took them both to the EMA out of pure spite, because neither he nor Teresita belonged to any revolutionary group.

'And Bini wept when I told her this story. And twice spontaneously offered to help me. Can't you understand why I adore her? Please don't speak badly of her.'

Gonzalo recovered his sense of humour. He quipped he could not but revere St Sabina, after the miracle she had performed.

Aurelia got up and kissed him.

'You've convinced me, you're quite right,' she told him, and went off to the kitchen to sort her ideas out, with the excuse that she was getting something to eat.

After he overcame his shock and the momentary repugnance he'd felt at Aldo's confession, Gonzalo retreated into his sense of humour.

He calculated at the top of his voice that if they sentenced Bini to six months in prison, Aldo would miss out on enjoying her some four hundred and fifty times in that period. And that was based on three shaftings a day, a very modest estimate after Aldo's recent performances.

Did such abstention represent a threat that he would relapse into paedophilia?

No. Hadn't he just told them that he had only to think of her in order to function with other women? Well then, he should see Bini every month, refuel his erotic images, and then go back to Italy and his natural milieu. But he shouldn't be so silly as to marry her…

'Come on, she's twenty-nine and you're fifty-five…What do you want? To turn into an antlered deer from the tundra?'

According to Gonzalo, Aldo should pay a monthly visit to Cuba. And he'd renew his batteries after a single weekend with her. He'd break all his records on these weekends. Would return to Rome with his brain cleansed of impurities and stuffed with images of Bini, which would recharge him in case he felt like making himself available to Italian women.

Gonzalo's jokes dispelled Aldo's gloom. And before he left, he got the couple to agree to don a disguise and anonymously deliver compensation to the cyclist's widow.

'Yes, of course, you can count on us.'

# 27 *ius iurandum*

The court appointed for 'Case no. 610 in 1999, against Alberto Ríos and Sabina López', in its preliminary discussions with the police magistrate, recognized that the two accused provided very different versions of the facts. Sabina López Angelbello admitted that the cyclist had been knocked over and her own involvement; but Alberto Ríos denied the version presented by the young woman, and accused her of lying in order to prejudice him.

'Given the opposed interests of the two accused', it was agreed that each should have their own defence lawyer.

Dr Godoy, the duty lawyer appointed to defend Bini, studied the dossier put together by the police, read the statements and concluded it would be an easy case; his client would be absolved, or at worst sentenced to a few months in prison.

Bini's formidable performance, rehearsed ad nauseam, also convinced Godoy of her innocence.

For his part, Azúa couldn't flourish before the court his infallible paranormal talents, his gifts as a seer and wizard, as the only source for his conviction that Alberto Ríos was an innocent man. He would look ridiculous. Nor could he use either hypnosis or magnetism in the courtroom. If he did try any of that, Bini's defence would protest and the court would defer to them.

His only hope was to make Bini fall into a trap, to confuse her, to force her into self-contradiction or apparent self-doubt. He would attack her in beliefs that Azúa was sure he knew well. There lay the only ray of light.

Bini came to the trial wearing the colours of Yemayá, but in a childish outfit. Although Aldo had left more than a month earlier, he'd seen to everything. He'd even chosen her hairstyle and clothes: white trousers, tight fitting at waist and hip, but loose farther down; and a sky-blue, broad-sleeved lacy blouse, tied at the waist. He got her to wear Shirley Temple plaits, and white medium-heeled, lace-up shoes. Nobody, to look at her, would think she was a hooker.

The general public was not much in evidence in the courtroom, as was usual for traffic crimes: two employees from Texinal, and a few friends and relatives of Bini. The witnesses called by the prosecution and defence included Pepe Jaén, the maid from the Triton, Captain Bastidas and a few experts from the CCL. In all, with the tribunal, defence lawyers, prosecution and the public, only some twenty people filled the room.

Prompted by the chair of the tribunal, the secretary read the charges against both of them. Then, as they began a review of evidence, witness and accused had to swear the appropriate oaths. The experts who had studied the details of the accident were unanimously of the opinion that the person driving the car was the one wearing the Florsheim shoes early that morning. And they based their opinion on an indisputable fact: in the attempt to avoid colliding with the cyclist, the driver of the car had had to swerve to the left, and brake on the mud adjacent to the drain, where he'd left his shoe-prints.

'And did you find traces of footsteps that side?' the prosecutor asked one on the forensic witnesses.

'Yes, Comrade Prosecutor, a few.'

'Can you indicate which?'

The forensic expert leaned over a portfolio of drawings and extracted a sheet.

'Only these…' And he exhibited outlines which he affixed to a blackboard with a couple of tacks.

'Could you describe what this is?'

'They are footprints A, described in our report, and which correspond to the Florsheim shoes, presented here as evidence.'

'Any detail of particular interest?'

'Well…I would advise you to observe that in this case' – and he used the pointer to indicate an incomplete footprint – 'the person driving the car, when getting out on this side, first rests the toe of his shoe on the muddy ground. That is quite logical, given where the car stopped and heeled over on a pile of mud, against the flow. That person, who was wearing the aforementioned shoes, must have stretched his left leg out in order to get some purchase on the ground; and one can see here that he first put all his weight on the ball of one foot, in order to be able to get out. Then here, and here, he takes two steps with the whole foot, as can be seen from the well-defined print of the heel…'

'And, Lieutenant, how do you account for the presence of prints B, attributed to a woman's trainers, which appear around the body, but are absent from close to the vehicle?'

'Because when getting out on her side, the person wearing the trainers rested her feet on the cement of the road, and the prints were immediately washed away by the rain and passing traffic.'

Then the prosecutor questioned Alberto Ríos: 'What have you got to say about the evidence brought by the forensic experts from the Central Laboratory for Criminal Investigations, which accords with the statement made by the accused Sabina

López, according to which she got out on the right and you on the left?'

Annoyed, his eyes blazing, Alberto responded haughtily to the prosecutor: 'I have to say that at no time did I get out of the vehicle on the left or on the right; because to get out I'd have had to have got in, and I never did, as I've stated repeatedly.'

They listened to the statements from the other forensic experts for almost an hour, and they all brought data that supported Bini's version. Fefita and Pepe Jaén's lapidary statements followed on.

The maid didn't say for sure that Alberto was the same person she saw with Bini.

'No, comrade, I couldn't swear to it, because I was never close enough to see his face properly; but if it weren't that gentleman,' and she pointed at Alberto, 'it was someone very similar.'

'What's your evidence for saying he was very similar?'

'It was his tall build, his white hair and beard...'

'How far away was he?'

'From the end of the corridor to the door to Room 322. Which is to say,' Fefita pointed to a door, 'from here to that door. And I saw him again, when he got into the lift.'

On the other hand, Pepe Jaén swore that the accused man Alberto Ríos was the same person who checked in on 24 July, to Room 322 at the Triton Hotel.

'Could it be that somebody, who was not the accused , but who was in possession of his ID card, could have checked in at the hotel?'

'Well, comrade, to tell the truth, it's not impossible, but only if the receptionist doesn't check the photo. And I can assure you I always do. It's routine for me. One can be busy doing something else or distracted, but when one gets documentation, the first thing one does, quite mechanically, is to open the page with the photo and check that the customer...'

'You cynic! How much did they pay you?' roared Alberto.

'Silence!' replied the chair of the tribunal, slamming his hand down on the bell.

He was already waving an index finger at Alberto, but added nothing when he saw that Azúa quietly chided him.

Alberto decided to shut up, and for the rest of the hearing just shook his head and burst out laughing.

The prosecutor's questioning of Bini reached its climax when she declared that Tito was at the wheel of the car at the moment of the accident.

And she was telling the truth.

'And who is this Tito?' interjected the prosecutor.

'That man there…' Bini lied for the first time.

'I would ask you to call the accused by his correct name,' the chair of the court admonished her.

'Ay, no, comrade,' she protested, getting into a huff. (Aldo had insisted that under no circumstances should she let herself be swayed. She should keep using the nickname of Tito at all costs.) 'It's the only thing I can call him. What's wrong if I call him Tito?'

'It's not correct; you should call him by his name,' the chair insisted.

'Ay, Comrade Chair, you're makin' it very difficult for me. I'm so used to calling him Tito, and if I have to remember what he's really called, I'll get into a tangle in what I'm saying…'

The chair gestured impatiently, shrugged his shoulders and decided not to insist.

'All right; carry on.' And he dropped a resigned fist on the table, with a barely audible 'Cunt rules'. The colleague to his right ducked his head to chortle behind some papers.

'Proceed, proceed,' insisted the chair.

Then, as Tito wouldn't let her drive, she stood on her head in her seat from pure rage, began to pull faces at him and annoy him; but her rage soon subsided and she started fiddling with him again.

Her play-acting and the deliberately risqué nature of her

account led to titters round the courtroom, and the chair of the court had to intervene and call everybody to order. But those who heard her felt she had told the truth.

Finally, she described her sexy little games as the cause of the accident and related how she jumped into the back seat and began to tickle Tito, and him laughing all the time, and stroking him, and when she threatened to describe the nature of her caresses, the chair of the tribunal asked her to omit the detail, while the other members of the court started taking notes, or coughing, or suddenly took out handkerchiefs and blew their noses.

At this point, after her daring, comic and piquant description and pretence of naïveté, she began to sob, just as they'd rehearsed, and to blame herself for her pranks and groping which had led to Tito knocking the cyclist over.

It was a brilliant performance. Standing up in front of the dais, she projected an image of gauche innocence.

Alberto Ríos listened in amazement to the 'Tito' Bini imputed to him with such cold-blooded cynicism. As she piled on the detail, Alberto could only glare and shrug his shoulders. He tried to smile sarcastically but it came out as a tragic grimace.

The impact on the whole courtroom was tremendous.

At the end of the first day, Azúa confessed his pessimism to Bastidas: 'She hasn't left a single chink where I can get at her…She's obviously been well trained.'

In fact, Bini had prepared herself to present an image of an irresponsible, rather stupid tart with a heart of gold; a crazy dame who acted recklessly, out of simple religious motivation, even though it might harm her.

And she was a big success.

The character and *mise-en-scène* created from the outset the effect of overriding veracity that Aldo had envisaged.

On Monday, 20 September, when the second day of questioning

began, everybody thought that a prison sentence for Alberto Ríos was a foregone conclusion.

In order to reconstruct the moment of the collision, Bini merely recalled what she saw: when the cyclist crossed in front of him, Tito tried to swerve to the left to miss him, but couldn't stop the right mudguard from hitting him. The car lurched slightly, skidded on the cement, and she thought they were going to turn over. They slid several metres on two wheels, but Tito finally struggled to right the car and brake on the edge of the kerb, next to a cement post. The car twisted round, and Bini stood up very solemnly to show in what way, lifting her left knee slightly and bending her torso to the right.

Her mimicry triggered a ripple of laughter round the room.

On the dais there was another bout of ahems and coughing.

When the laughter stopped, the chair informed the accused she didn't have to enact the vehicle's twists and turns.

'Very good, Comrade Your Honour.'

Fresh laughter.

'Ay, I'm sorry! Comrade Chairman,' Bini corrected herself, after a furtive whisper from the verbatim secretary typing away at her side.

When she addressed the court, Bini was a frightened little girl: she put her hands over her mouth, opened her eyes and bit her nails.

Except for Azúa, Bastidas and Alberto Ríos himself, nobody in the room imagined it was pure premeditated play-acting.

'Let the accused continue,' the chair ordered.

'And that's why Tito had to get out on tiptoe...I got out on the other side and we both ran through the rain, to help the man, but he was already dead. Tito got to him first and felt his pulse...'

'You pathetic liar!' bawled Alberto as he punched his seat with his fist.

He was sitting at the other end of the same bench, from which Bini had got up in order to make her statement in front of the dais where the judges sat. As a preventive measure, they had placed three uniformed guards between the two accused, equipped with tear gas and truncheons.

'Ay, Tito, my love, we must tell gospel here...!'

Alberto went bright purple. He sat down, on the point of collapse, wiped his brow with a handkerchief and responded to comments that came from the head guard seated behind him. He nodded, somewhat calmer.

'Let the accused continue.'

Bini, who had started to cry, dried a few tears and continued.

'Well, Tito felt the man's pulse, and bent down to listen to his heart, and signalled to me that he was dead; and that we couldn't do anything to save him; he said the best thing would be to leave as soon as possible.'

'Was it raining?' asked the prosecutor.

'Yes, Your Honour...errr...Comrade, yes, it was raining lots, and we got back into the car.'

'You each got in through your respective doors?'

She tried to remember.

'No, there was a lot of mud on the driver's side. Tito got in from my side an' then me got in a'ter him.'

That was the conclusion reached by the forensic experts, after analysis of the prints. It confirmed that the accused was telling the truth.

The greatest tension during the hearings for 'Case no. 610 in 1999' came at the end of that second day, when Dr Azúa was questioning Bini.

When she stood in front of the tribunal again, Azúa approached her, stared into her eyes and stepped back slightly. He chose to position himself midway between her and the dais.

Azúa thundered forth his resonant sentences, without a microphone, and with a number of telling remarks.

'Are you a believer?'

The huge black, with his electrifying gaze and unexpected question, upset Bini; but she kept calm.

'Yes, I'm a believer, and what about yerself?'

Azúa and a section of the public burst out laughing.

'Order in court,' and the chair slapped his hand down on the bell. 'The lawyer asks the questions here. You, the accused, only have to answer. Proceed, Doctor.'

Still smiling and looking amiable, Azúa addressed Bini: 'Indeed, you should only provide answers; but on this occasion I will answer that, yes, I am religious. And can we know which religion you profess?'

'I believe in God, and my saints.'

'Are you pledged to a particular saint?'

'Yes, I've pledged to Yemayá.'

Murmurs round the courtroom.

Azúa now summoned his most sonorous tone, while he swung his torso round, so the whole room would hear: 'And would you be prepared to swear before an image of Yemayá in this courtroom, to the effect that everything in your recent statement was the whole truth?'

'I protest!' Bini's defence lawyer, Godoy, almost catapulted himself from his bench.

'I will remind Dr Azúa that the accused is already under oath,' said the chair of the tribunal, a rather pompous, rhetorical sexagenarian lawman. 'Please proceed.'

Azúa swayed his head for a few moments, hands on waist; then threw his arms up theatrically and dropped them down in disappointment. Finally, he turned to the tribunal's table: 'As a defence lawyer, and in particular as a believer and citizen of this country where freedom of worship exists, I consider it my right to ask for an extra oath…'

Azúa now spoke as emphatically as he knew how, and his voice trembled with indignation.

'…with all due respect to the magistrates, I beg that, before you refuse my request, you allow me to define the parameters I want to set for the oath of the accused, and likewise, to state my supporting arguments.'

The chair of the tribunal was about to reply but restrained himself when another of the magistrates whispered to him. He bit his lip, twisted his jaw, took off his glasses and looked at the ceiling for a few seconds. He gave the impression that he was counting to ten. Finally, he turned round for a brief confab with the two colleagues to his right, repeated the motion to his left, and when they all were in agreement, announced: 'The court considers it necessary to deliberate on the situation that has been created, and has decided to suspend today's session. The hearings in this case will resume on Wednesday the twenty-second, at two in the afternoon, in this same room.'

Dr Azúa was an atheist; but his scientific interest in paranormal activities, and the orientation of his aesthetic calling towards Afro-Cuban culture and traditions, led him to the Yoruba religion and the Palo Monte.

The Palo in particular, with its animist rites, provided him with fascinating materials for his research into phenomena of collective hypnosis associated with rhythm, magnetism, clairvoyance, hysteria, etc.

Azúa thought that attacking Bini in her beliefs was a possible way to throw out the damning evidence against his client. He would try to place her in the dilemma of either swearing a lie or refusing to swear. If she refused, her credibility would be reduced, even though the court would pretend the contrary. If Azúa could move the ground she stood on, she might contradict herself before the raft of trick questions he'd prepare for her. But to that end, he first had to get the agreement of the court not to oppose his request for a second oath.

In principle, there were no legal obstacles, but it was something so unusual in the annals of revolutionary justice that the court might refuse.

Hence Azúa opted to reveal himself publicly as a believer, as a son of Obatalá, pledged to his saint, all of which was true. He wore a white necklace, with coloured beads, which gleamed against his dark shirt-front.

It was the year 1999 and religion was on the up.

It had all begun in the early nineties, thanks to the activity of a few North American Protestant groups. Led by Lucius Walker, a black pastor who campaigned against the blockade of Cuba, solidarity crusades were organized. In the United States and Canada aid was collected in the form of medicine, clothes, computers and food which the frontier authorities would not let through to Mexico, because they were destined for Cuba.

A little earlier, in 1996, several pastors staged an 'evangelical fast' on the frontier, as a protest against the government ban on their entering Cuba with humanitarian supplies. Nevertheless, the enemy press denounced the fast as a diabolical hunger strike, IRA-style. The Reverend Lucius Walker, a man of average height and looks, lost sixty pounds in weight, but earned much more in the veneration he accumulated in Cuba.

The doughty pastors unleashed a wave of sympathy in very few years. The most significant repercussion was a notable strengthening of Protestant churches based in Cuba. This increase caused a stir in Rome, and the Holy Father was quick to formulate the odd declaration of solidarity against the US blockade of the island. A convoluted diplomatic fencing match ensued between Cuba and the Holy See, culminating in Fidel's visit to Rome and His Holiness's trip to Havana.

The increase in religions in Cuba reached a point that would have been incredible ten years earlier, and several renowned Catholics from the world of science and culture and three Protestant pastors were elected as deputies to the National Assembly of Popular Power.

The *babalaos* and *tatas paleros*, priests of the African religions, met thanks to these winds of tolerance and openness. They aspired to join on an equal footing in the dialogue between the communist government and high-ups in the Christian churches visiting the country.

Didn't they have as much, if not more right?

The religions of African origin are, without a doubt, the most popular with the Cuban people and have by far the most followers. Nobody could deny the deep mark they have left on music and what's most essential in the arts, on the stage and in the national literature.

The paternalist Cuban government, always zealous in its wish not to discriminate against blacks and their culture, began to feel under heavy pressure, especially with a papal visit imminent, when *he* would not agree to speak 'on an equal footing' with representatives of 'prehistoric superstitions', which was the view of the Holy See in respect of *babalaos* and *tatas mayomberos*.

As part of the defence of his client Azúa intended to exploit government paternalism in the face of the Christian clergy's contempt for Afro-Cuban religions. If it was possible for him to create sufficient ideological hesitation at the heart of the court, it was possible they'd agree to the oath.

It was the only hope as far as his defence was concerned, and that was what he told his client. He assured him that the majority of those who pledge to a saint, which assumes a considerable economic sacrifice, really do believe; and a faithful believer would never invoke his or her personal deity in order to swear an untrue oath. That would put the pressure on Bini, unless she'd spent out on a saint for superficial folkloric reasons, which might be the case. If the young woman was concealing a disbelieving nature, and dared to swear a false oath, then there was nothing doing. Neither Azúa nor anyone else could spare Alberto a two-year prison sentence.

From the beginning, Alberto agreed to Azúa's plan. He was resigned and passive and agreed that asking Bini to swear this oath was the best way to channel his defence; but now the trial had begun, and after seeing the extreme cynicism she displayed in the courtroom, his hopes were few and far between. If the court authorized the oath, the lying bitch would swear without batting an eyelid.

The fucking whore, cold-blooded liar, the brazen…!

After the second session, he was sure he'd lose and resumed the labours of self-suggestion he'd already engaged in. He'd have two productive years away from it all. He would withstand the test and emerge strengthened. Prison would be no tragedy. He'd practise gymnastics in jail and also exercise his brain. He would transform it into a fertile organ, with a discipline he'd never achieve in a regime of freedom, where he'd yield to the call of his hedonism.

On this occasion, he would turn adversity to his advantage. He would continue to be a positive man. Prison would strengthen him.

At the end of the day, he'd be fifty-eight when he came out. A man as healthy as himself, who played sport as much as the younger generation, could aspire to live into his eighties.

No, come what may, he'd not let himself get depressed.

'Weep behind the screen,' his father would say, banning any lack of good spirits from his family.

Two lay judges and three jurists made up the court. One of the lay judges, who had been in the military, was a fundamentalist believer in the revolution; and from the start was opposed to any extra oath-swearing, particularly before a *santería* image.

The other layman, a cultured old communist, declared himself incompetent in such doctrinal matters; but revealed he would accept the majority opinion.

Among the lawmen, there was a Catholic; another, the youngest, was a brilliant professor of penal law, who believed in God, but didn't worship or accept any church; and the chair was a devoted follower of José Martí, a positivist, liberal, honest revolutionary, who confessed that he was fond of the odd antiquated theory, including Marxism.

The former soldier, a dark mulatto, was of the view that to accept an oath invoking Yemayá would be a retrograde concession and a dangerous precedent...He spoke well, with gentle humour, but was definite in his belief that they should accept no oath beyond the normal one, in the name of the law.

'It would be dangerous to mix religion up in this,' he commented.

'On the contrary,' argued the chair of the tribunal, who'd clearly had a change of mind. 'I think in the current climate it might be the right political step.'

'And would hopefully set a precedent,' said the law professor and young judge in support. 'A good sixty per cent of the lumpen element we see round here are santeros...What's so wrong in having them swear by their saints? Besides, the oath that counts for us is the one she gave at the start.'

'Just what I say,' said the older lay member.

The discussion was brief. The chair, the young professor and the old lay communist voted in favour of accepting the oath.

At the suggestion of the chair, with an eye to covering their backs, they would ask the lawyer Azúa to give reasons for his request.

'And if the accused refuses to swear?'

'She'll be within her rights; and Azúa must give his word that if she refuses, he won't be able to ask her any questions about her beliefs.'

'Yes, he must give his word.'

New Dawn had only one precinct where the female prisoners received their visitors. There were six tables, each with four chairs.

When Godoy the lawyer appeared with Juan Pedro, his goddaughter breathed a sigh of relief.

The lawyer advised Bini to refuse to swear this oath, if Azúa asked her to. But she opted to consult with her godfather, and asked for him to be brought to the prison.

Godoy spoke to the captain who acted as if she were in charge. The visitor was the godfather of the woman under arrest, Sabina López, and he'd come to see her because she needed to consult him. Given the private nature of this visit, Godoy asked whether there wasn't a more private place. The boss woman recommended they took the table in the corner. If they spoke quietly, nobody would hear their extremely private exchanges.

Juan Pedro agreed to officiate in that place, where other visitors already took up two tables. He asked Godoy to leave them alone, and withdrew with Bini to the corner they'd been designated; but he didn't sit at the table. He took the rectangular mat he was carrying rolled up under his arm and spread it out on the ground. He sat on it with his back leaning against one of the walls, as one has to do in order to enter into contact with Orula. He put on his white cap, took out the *écuele* and placed over his spread-eagled knees the card with its mysterious oracular tracings, where Orula would express herself.

Bini, in trousers, sat at his feet, her legs crossed; and informed him almost inaudibly over half an hour as to what had happened in the accident; and she railed against Alberto Ríos and his crimes; and finished off by revealing to him how Aldo and Teresita suffered when they fell into his hands.

At the end of the day, Bini needed to know whether Yemayá would be offended if she invoked her name to witness a lie, or would approve and help her condemn that monster, guilty of so many crimes, for which he'd never been punished.

Juan Pedro listened to her, head lowered. When Bini finished, he initiated a long, unintelligible invocation in Yoruba, and immediately began to consult Orula.

He placed some pebbles in Bini's left hand, for her to pass over to her right hand, move them between both hands and finally cast on to the sacred cardboard diagram.

After each of Bini's throws, Juan Pedro would note down in a small book the disposition of the stones. Finally, he picked up the *écuele*, a necklace, whose beads, according to the way they fell on the card, would recall a series of sacred feats within the Yoruban pantheon. That is the oracular fount through which Orula, through the contorsions of the *écuele*, has recourse to some chapter, sentence or thought, the reading and interpretation of which will allow the *babalao* to grasp the message.

Dr Godoy, who observed Juan Pedro consulting a written text, thought how Orula was more serious than Apollo, whose messages reached Pythia alive and kicking.

When the third session opened, the chair of the court recalled the previous events. And went on to read the following note:

> This court has decided to listen to Dr Ramón Azúa Patterson, in cognizance of his request to support the need for an extra oath to be sworn in this room; but it reminds him that the accused, Sabina López Angelbello, has been under oath from the start of this case, and that is the only sworn oath we will have regard to. Dr Azúa is reminded moreover that if the additional oath before a religious image is allowed, the accused may refuse to swear if she so wishes and without that affecting the credibility of her statements. For his part, the learned Azúa must give his word that if the accused refuses to swear the requested oath he will refrain from asking questions relative to her religion or beliefs.

The president took his spectacles off, put the piece of paper on their table and addressed Azúa: 'Will you abide by the conditions, Doctor?'

'Yes, I will, Comrade Chair.'

'Alberto Ríos's defence lawyer may speak.'

Azúa abandoned his table, with a roll of card in his hands, and walked over to his usual position, equidistant between the public and the dais.

'In legal history, from times most ancient, the religious oath has been an instrument of intimidation to prevent witnesses from lying. And I say it was intimidation because it was so in olden times and still is today. Greeks, Egyptians, Babylonians and almost all ancient peoples who developed a judicial process forced those in dispute to swear on a deity they worshipped, knowing that if they committed perjury, they would be victims of their fury and reprisals. Nothing could be worse than the malevolence of an outraged divinity...'

The chair of the tribunal was observing him and was imperceptibly agreeing, with that look on his face of 'Yes, and I can see where you're coming from'. But when Azúa looked straight at him, he averted his gaze or pretended to take notes. Azúa knew they were going to authorize the oath.

Azúa's powerful voice and excellent diction had already captivated his audience.

Rumours about the unusual nature of this case had spread around the legal circuit. Azúa's latest eccentricity was all people could talk about; and now the room was packed with students and jurists.

'...but in Cuba, the oath that is required in the name of the law, without any invocation of a deity, is quite useless as an intimidatory device.'

At that moment he turned to point to Bini.

'In the case of the accused, Sabina López, who has even been to prison before, I fully suspect that she experiences little fear before the law in the abstract, and without too many qualms can swear a false oath.'

'I protest,' interjected Godoy. 'Our colleague has no reason to personify his criteria through my client.'

'Just make your case without allusions to individuals,' ordered the chair.

Azúa shut his eyes as if to rein in a gesture of annoyance and continued. 'In any case, learned sir, I can affirm that the majority of believers, whatever their religion, will lie with greater facility after swearing an oath in the abstract than if their holy beliefs have been invoked. And, in my position as an individual, as someone who practises the same religion as the accused, I find myself in an uncomfortable situation. The statements by Sabina López, José Jaén and Josefina Albarracín, plus some evidence obtained by the police forensic team, condemn my client. But my own saints have revealed to me that his feet and the shoes produced as evidence have never made contact; that neither did he stay in the Triton Hotel; and that Sabina López is lying in order to incriminate him. And now, not as a lawyer, but as a believer, if Sabina López, daughter of Yemayá, swears here, before her image, that she has told the whole truth, I would be inclined to believe that I am mistaken. In this respect, I have already spoken to my client, who is agreed that if the accused is amenable to swearing this oath, then I will be unable to defend him, and consequently, he will declare himself a guilty man, in order to bring matters swiftly to a conclusion.'

Every jurist present realized that Azúa's ploy demonstrated a magisterial double game. If the young woman didn't swear the oath, her refusal would be seen as fear or a guilty conscience, and would impact on the final verdict; not against her, but in favour of a much more benign sentence for Alberto; and if Sabina López swore the oath and the Argentine admitted his guilt, on the one hand a few doubts would be sown, but by accepting the charges, he would go some way towards attenuating the severity of the final verdict.

The court's deliberations were brief: no more than nodding heads and an exchange of whispers. Finally, the chair gyrated his neck to the microphone, cleared his throat and, when there was silence in the room, he declared: 'The court has resolved to authorize Dr Azúa to ask for the requisite oath. Let the case continue. Would the accused, Sabina López Angelbello, be upstanding.'

There were smiles and expressions of satisfaction across the courtroom. The Azúa show gained in suspense.

Accompanied by an usher, Bini walked to the microphone, where she remained standing, hands behind her back. This time she sported a blue turban. Her belt and shoes were also blue. She was wearing a white two-piece, a long, flowing skirt down to her ankles; a square neckline and shoulder pads lending her an elegant air.

'She has never been so beautiful,' thought Pepe Jaén.

As soon as Azúa saw her in those colours, he told himself his client was on course to lose. That profusion of blue and white indicated that Bini was at peace with her saint.

Would she dare to swear the oath?

Could he have been mistaken about Alberto? Till that moment he'd not doubted he was innocent...

Yes, but he'd put his hands in the fire for that girl; he couldn't imagine she was capable of perjury.

Well. The matter would be rapidly resolved. He walked over to within a few steps from Bini, stared at her and did something that nobody was expecting: he removed the white necklace of Obatalá from his neck, held it in his right fist and whispered a short prayer. He then unrolled the card and displayed to the courtroom the image of Yemayá. And in a stentorian voice, replete with ominous vibrations, he almost shouted his question at Bini: 'The accused, Sabina López Angelbello, daughter of Yemayá: do you swear on your health and your life, witnessed by this image of the Divine Queen of the Seas, She of the Five Names, that the man who knocked over the cyclist Baltasar París was the accused Alberto Ríos, with whom you stayed for a few days at the Triton Hotel?'

The day before, the divine Yemayá, through the mediation of Orula and her godfather's hermeneutics, communicated her will to Bini. Juan Pedro was referred by the *écuele* to a Yoruba book of wisdom from which he extracted three aphorisms:

'Fire dies, but the red on the parrot's feather never dies';
'A rope can't leash the sea';
'The way is open to the dog'.

Juan Pedro found that Orula had been as clear as crystal:

The red on the parrot's feather was the blood spilt by Alberto, for whom there could never be forgiveness or oblivion. He must pay for his crimes.

With the mention of the sea that couldn't be leashed, Yemayá was alluding to herself: the sacrilegious Alberto Ríos would not be able to escape her severe justice.

The third saying was the most explicit and straightforward: the dog was Aldo, who, guided by Yemayá, had sniffed out the criminal hiding in Cuba. But Bini showed him the way. And by prophesying that the way was open for the dog, Yemayá indicated that Bini, as an agent of justice and a way to truth, could invoke the saint with a lie, in order to punish the criminal.

Juan Pedro's rapid exegesis dispelled all Bini's qualms. She was the way for the dog, the receiver of divine permission, to carry on lying in court. And she smiled gratefully to Yemayá, such an understanding bearer of justice.

'Yes, I swear by Yemayá that Tito knocked over the cyclist and was with me at the Triton.'

Azúa bent his head and gestured emphatically with both hands, to indicate he'd completed his defence.

That same afternoon, Alberto accepted the charges in the presence of the public prosecutor and admitted he was guilty.

The verdict was published the following day. Bini was sentenced to six months in prison, for complicity in the crime by fleeing the scene and not helping the dying man; and Alberto Ríos to two years, for manslaughter, and also for fleeing and not helping.

# 28 a good, if eccentric, listener

After each trial hearing, Alberto was taken back to sleep in his cell at the Combined. But he didn't let the other prisoners ask questions. On those days he shut himself in and read and wrote, and didn't even go into the corridor. He even refused acrimoniously to discuss the case with the guards who tried to sound him out.

And when he was definitively returned to his cell, with a two-year sentence, he tore up his diary and told himself that from 22 September he should advance only two basic goals: to make his stay in prison a positive experience and whip into line the other prisoners' discipline as best he could.

He'd stop that bunch of mental defectives he'd got to endure for two years from fucking him up. He needed to implement a strategy so he'd be in total control of this great expanse of time and small spread of space.

Naturally, at the centre of his prison activities would be the work on his book. Raquelita took pity on his plight, agreed to field his questions and seek out information she would then fax or e-mail via Mariano. And after reading the first chapters of his manuscript, Dr Pazos expressed an interest in following its progress closely.

In his cell, Alberto could devote no more that six or seven hours a day to the book. He worked with heroic concentration and ended up exhausted; but achieved a level of mental health comparable to that of the common criminals, who spent eight or ten hours in the prefabrication plant.

It wasn't easy to fill your time up in prison. Alberto slept well for six hours, and occupied four or five in the yard, at the gym, on the track, eating, and playing bridge; but that left another eight or so to kill. He dedicated part of that time to reading fiction, newspapers and magazines. He passed on watching videos, which he'd have had to see with other prisoners.

What most relaxed him was listening to stories. They were sometimes real tear-jerkers, but entertaining all the same. Some of the natural storytellers projected the best film scenarios imaginable.

The need to kill time encouraged him to think and be patient, even with books. After many years, he discovered he could read poetry again. He was mesmerized by Whitman, Rilke and Darío. And experienced something similar with novels.

In the mid-eighties, when he'd made two attempts to re-read *Les Misérables*, he'd given up after a few pages. That novel, which he'd worshipped as a kid, at forty bored him with its slow pace, didacticism, abuse of omniscience and unnecessary description of landscapes, buildings and furniture. After seventy years of film, the narrative rhythms of his favourite eighteenth- and nineteenth-century novelists seemed clunking and facile. But the rhythm of the Combined allowed him to enjoy again Fielding, Hugo, Dickens, Stendhal, Tolstoy and Manzoni. In a few weeks he became more tolerant as a reader, and also as a listener.

The long day on south wing, particularly with nightfall

imminent, sharpened the prisoners' eagerness to tell tales. It was a way to escape yourself. And an urgency to dust off memories energized the telling; lent colour.

The Colombian Servio Tulio, with his bullfighting follies, savoury-rolls enterprise, disputes with his son and bloodcurdling childhood in Tuluá, fulcrum of the violence in Colombia in the fifties, produced, according to Alberto, the best contemporary narrative. Fucking hell, if only some of those pen-pushing South Americans could write with the drama of those oral tales.

He also liked to listen to Casimiro, a cook and blubbing liar from Entre Ríos. His life was a cascade of tragicomedies. Alberto wound him up. When he saw the tears well, he'd feign sympathy and enjoy what he considered to be excellent vaudeville.

Gradually he got to know other storytellers: a Peruvian reliving his adventures in the Amazon jungle; a Puerto Rican dandy; a Korean vet and former car salesman in Japan; a Panamanian pickpocket and junkie, who'd spent several months in a Cuban hospital on a detox course and wanted nothing from life but the next fix. There was also a Bolivian who'd emigrated to Buenos Aires, a footballing gigolo, who spoke with a real BA accent and a joke a minute; and Alberto laughed a lot with Paisa, another Colombian from Medellín, a fund of wisecrack comparisons, which all started with 'more': 'more tangled than wrestling octopuses', 'more difficult than lining up ten monkeys for a photo', 'more lost than Lindbergh's son', etc.

At Mariano's suggestion, Alberto made an impressive donation to the south wing library, and for those who could read English, he put into circulation some thirty bestselling thrillers he'd bought in hotel shops and tourist centres in Havana.

And very quickly, through his changing-mood tactic, he soon sorted it so that nobody bothered him. Anyone who

tango for a torturer

tried to accost him, even his storytelling friends, he'd fend
off with brusque remarks and bad-tempered grimaces. It was
clear to all that Alberto was good and generous, but was also
eccentric, very irritable and unapproachable. He always looked
down when walking along corridors, frowned and stared at
the ground, so people couldn't even bid him good day.

Mid-October he sparked off the only incident of his stay
in prison, with a Colombian drug dealer, dubbed Jairo, who
insisted on badgering him. He always wanted to ask something.
After sending him packing a couple of times, Alberto got
embroiled in a third, very sharp exchange with the guy, and
swore at him. From then on Jairo began to provoke him and
whisper insults after him, when they bumped into each other.
But one day Alberto recalled he was a black belt and gave him
a display of karate-do that put him in hospital. And that row
enabled him to broadcast loud and clear, as he performed an
exhibition of *sukis* and kicks to Jairo's face, that he needed to
concentrate on his business, because he was writing a book
that forced him to meditate night and day, whether in the
corridor, in the yard, shitting in the bathroom, or sleeping in
the dining room; anyone who spoke to him and interrupted
his thought processes earned his displeasure; and if he
persevered, a flurry of punches as well.

Mariano had to intervene, and when Jairo, the instigator of
the row, found himself threatened with solitary, he decided to
forget Alberto. That was the end of that.

The prison suffered from a surfeit of lunatics, and the
prisoners, even the most violent ones, learned to respect
Alberto. So all newcomers to south wing soon discovered that
he was a nice fellow, but obsessed by the book he was trying
to write, and that you couldn't talk to him. You had to let him
be. When he felt like conversing, he was really friendly and
very generous; he would give out cigarettes and cakes and pay
for medicine in dollars for some inmates who fell sick; but if

you spoke to him, he became as prickly as a porcupine and kicked you.

Consequently, when he wanted to listen to stories, he chose one of his good storytellers, and took him to his cell, naturally with Mariano's permission. He'd sometimes gather around him three or four prisoners with whom to converse and drink coffee.

And every fortnight, on a Friday, Alberto enjoyed his day in the medical wing, where he welcomed the little whores contracted by Texinal.

By November, his life was proceeding as planned: everything was under control.

It would have been self-deception to think he was happy, but he was pleased enough by his first three months in the Combined. He suffered only from a few of the many shortages that wore down the majority of those inside.

# 29 bife chorizo

*Bife chorizo*, or *bife de chorizo*, doesn't taste of *chorizo*. Its taste, shape, and cut have nothing remotely in common with a *chorizo*. But in Buenos Aires that's the name given to a lump of almost half a kilo of beef, cooked on embers, one inch thick and so tender you could cut it with the back of your knife. It's served on a wooden board that has an indentation at one corner. The indentation is for the diner who prefers to season it with *chimichurri*, a seasoning made from Mediterranean herbs, oil and garlic. But even without the seasoning, with a pinch of salt and the juices it exudes when you attack it, for any Argentine carnivore a *bife chorizo* is the best roast meat in the world; and when outside his fatherland, an Argentine yearns for his *bife de chorizo* and is inconsolable. Any other meat in the world pales in comparison, be it the best entrecôte, *filet mignon, fiorentina*, sirloin, T-bone, or whatever variety of beefsteak, chop or barbecue joint.

One day, when Gonzalo was alternating between guilt at obesity and carnivore nostalgia, complaining that the meat

ration offered in the best Cuban restaurants never went beyond
three hundred grams, Aldo remembered that the staff in the
Argentine embassy received, via Aerolíneas Argentinas, various
meats cut at source; and he started to test out the waters to
see whether he might extract a few *bifes de chorizo* in order to
give Gonzalo a surprise. At the time he was planning a dinner
in honour of Bini, who'd done only two months in the New
Dawn. Aldo was going to use the occasion to announce his up-
and-coming marriage and honeymoon in Italy. And he made a
note in his diary, so he didn't forget when he met the consul,
who'd asked to see him over the next few days.

In September, Aldo's construction firm got permission to
build two hotels in a Camagüey tourist complex, on the strip
of coast known as the Queen's Gardens. Aldo had persuaded
his partners to take on the very low-profit contract, because it
would be the start of future, juicier deals in Cuba. He got the
responsibility for on-site supervision, so his visits to the island
were also justified by a work content and brought him some
profit.

The Bini effect continued to work its therapy with pleasing
novelties. In Spain, while moving his case on against Three-O
and the call for his extradition, Aldo had some very positive
experiences.

In Madrid, he had a sudden attack of desire for a sexy call
girl who'd been pointed out in his hotel. And for the first time
in his life, he performed with a woman he'd hired in cold
blood.

'Great, guy; fucking great: you're as hard as a teenager,' the
girl urged him on.

On successive days he tried out others and it really did work
fucking great.

Incredible. He finally enjoyed and came effortlessly. He did
what one would expect from a healthy man of his age. He now
fearlessly welcomed women in. When they were next to him, in

his hotel room, he flirted a bit, chatted, drank and let them get on with it. He closed his eyes and gave himself up to fantasies that no longer centred on little girls. Bini occupied his entire amorous space.

According to his Roman psychiatrist, the blessed Bini wrought miracles in the cure of his paedophilia. He should cherish that girl; cherish her like the apple of his eye. And he convinced him it would be dangerous to bring her to live in Italy. The change of country and atmosphere could transform their playful relationship into something else and ruin it completely.

Gonzalo had already argued something similar.

For his part, Aldo knew he would never adapt to life in Cuba. The crazy rhythms of the tropics were for crazy times, for holidays, for when you weren't working and wanted to let off steam. He'd never put into practice the idea that sometimes lodged in his head, of selling up and taking root in Cuba. He wasn't Juan Pedro, Bini's *babalao*, able to be very happy whenever he could get a good cigar, or share a swig of rum, or listen to the birdsong in his yard, convinced it was celebrating his good works and expressing the contentment of his dead. Many Cubans like him, thanks to an elemental, ever-present sensuality, could enjoy life in the midst of shortages unacceptable to a middle-class European.

Forget it. It would be a leap in the dark to abandon the dizzy pace of business life in Italy, to surrender to hedonist retirement with Bini. It was quite evidently a nonsense. It was very late in his life to steer in such a different direction.

Was he being a coward? Was it philosophical blindness?

In any case, his youthful flirtation with Eastern spiritualism was a thing of the past. At fifty-plus he wasn't now going to forgo the anaesthesia of the competitive life, and the goods and sweet comforts of the rich in the First World.

He reckoned that Gonzalo wasn't far wrong in his suggestion of a moderate transoceanic polygamy.

'You know, you're right; it would be a real privilege.'

Yes, but not the way Gonzalo was proposing, a weekend a month. Aldo much preferred a week with Bini every two months.

'Try it out for a couple of years, see what happens; and if it works, there are many possible variations...'

'You're right; time will tell...'

But neither Gonzalo nor Aurelia could dissuade him from marriage. They'd marry and he'd take her to live with him for at least three months in Italy. He had to repay her for her anger in solidarity and the tears she had shed when he told her about the tragedy with Teresita in the EMA. There was no way he could compensate her for her immediate support in putting the bastard inside. And besides, Bini was the woman he had most fun with in bed.

Of course he would take her!

Gonzalo didn't need to persuade him he should marry *and* keep all his wealth and property in his name.

'Of course, *che*, I'm not that stupid...'

Aldo had befriended the Argentine consul, a pleasant, amusing man, whom he met by chance in a reception at the Italian embassy. They hit it off as fans of Boca Juniors. In due course, they nibbled their nails together in the ambassador's residence in front of a televised cup final in Argentina. It was there that Aldo ate his first *bife de chorizo* in Cuba. Argentine meat, an Argentine cut, delicious.

And on 14 November, when he went for his appointment with the consul, to seek advice on importing wood from El Chaco he was wanting to use in the Camagüey project, he sounded out the chances of getting some *bifes de chorizo*. And something unexpected happened.

'How many, more or less?' asked the consul.

'We'll be six,' answered Aldo.

'You'll need five kilos or so, so as not to run short...'

'Yes, that's what I reckoned.'

'I'm out of *bife* at the moment, and everybody else must be in the same state, till the next flight; I'm not sure how to get that amount…' He pressed his intercom button and a female voice piped up. '*Che*, Sarita, when's the meat coming for Alberto Ríos?'

When he heard that name, Aldo's ears pricked up.

The consul listened, uttered a couple of monosyllables and hung up.

'Look,' he told Aldo, 'a stack of *bifes* is arriving on the next flight ordered by a compatriot. All I can promise is that I'll talk to him…'

'Who is this guy?'

'He's in jail; but he wants to give a party and sent an order for one hundred and twenty kilos of *bifes*…'

'A party? Where's that going to happen?'

'In the slammer, where else?'

'And is that possible?'

'It seems like a joke but it's true.' The consul laughed. 'The poor fellow is in prison because he killed a cyclist on the highway; but they put him in a wing reserved for foreigners; and it's more like a club than a prison.'

'You don't say…!'

'It's incredible but the guy seems really happy.'

'I can't believe you, Consul! How can a guy be happy doing time?'

'No kidding, Aldo, I went to see him on Tuesday. He says the slammer is the best thing that could have happened to him. They put him in a cell by himself, and he's working on a book he always intended writing. They let him bring his own supplies in, he drinks and chomps whatever he wants, plays *frontón*, lays women and has got a pile of crazy buddies in there. There's even one who sings tangos. He says he'd stay four rather than two years if he could.'

'And why's he giving the party?'

'He didn't tell me the reason; but they're doing it big time, meat from Argentina and booze galore; they're hiring dancers and musicians and...'

The consul remembered something and activated the intercom. 'Sara, before you go, call Texinal, ask for Emma and put her through to me. Thanks.'

And he turned to Aldo and pointed to a paper on his desk. 'It's going to be some party, they're even hiring a clown and a magician. He asked me to call his firm, so they do the contracting.'

Aldo read on the sheet of paper: 'Policarpo the Clown and Maguncio the magician, phone the Artex Agency'.

They joked a while about the Cuban prison system and agreed to meet a few days later. The consul would negotiate with the prisoner over the next forty-eight hours, and was sure he'd let him have five kilos of *bife de chorizo*.

The fucking bastard... So he's happy, is he?

On his way back, Aldo frowned as he drove.

Nevertheless, when he got out on 21st Street, he seemed less tense. He smiled at the old concierge, stroked a little boy on the head who was coming out of the lift with his mum, and pressed the button for the tenth floor.

When he placed the key in the door, Aldo was sure that Orlando Ortega's happiness would be very short lived. He'd ensure it soon turned to angst, insomnia and fear; and he'd ensure that the party changed into a real wake. He'd just had a really funny idea. He'd also ring Artex and ask after Maguncio the magician.

Following on from her good behaviour and the extensive confession she'd given during the trial, plus her impeccable work rate in the sewing room, Bini's six-month sentence was reduced to two, and she came out a free woman on 22 November. Aldo, who flew to Cuba the day before, was waiting for her at the exit, with a bunch of flowers.

'Just like the films!' Bini shed a large tear. 'That's why I adore you so.'

Nobody had given her flowers before.

The second surprise was that everything was ready for their wedding on 15 December in Havana. And on the 16th they'd go to Italy for their honeymoon.

The announcement was made during the meal promised at Gonzalo and Aurelia's place. The consul had got the *bifes de chorizo* a couple of days earlier. Bini's father and godfather were also there with their wives.

The meal was a great success. Gonzalo came back for seconds twice and downed a litre of wine; and the Cubans admitted they'd never eaten such juicy meat.

# 30 a trying visit and an innocent joke

On 21 November, when only two weeks were left to the day when Letelier the Chilean met his target of memorizing *The Iliad*, Mariano began the preparations for the promised celebrations.

Alberto came up with several ideas and offered to cover the costs.

It was also agreed to invite a classics professor from the Faculty of Philology, to inform those present about Homer's cantos and their relation to Letelier's feat of memory.

When Alberto suggested that Gardelion sing a few tangos, Mariano added Gentle, an excellent black tenor who, despite his nickname, was doing thirty years for multiple murders. Mariano would also get a guitarist to accompany them both.

Alberto suggested including some comedy acts to fill in the spots between Letelier and the musicians; and Mariano immediately recommended Policarpo the clown and Maguncio the magician; both were fantastic, and let's hope they're not on tour. Alberto agreed to contract them. The people from his company would see to the details.

Mariano also thought about contracting the Folkloric Troupe of Cuba.

'The important thing is for it to be a good party; and forget the expense, Mariano. I'll see to all that.'

Fucking hell, what a great character Alberto was!

Mariano had never known a prisoner like him, solvent, enterprising and generous all in one.

'A pity they only gave you two years!' he quipped gratefully.

Letelier's party created such great expectations among prisoners in south wing that they were counting the days already. And there were still eleven to go when Alberto received the news one day that Dr Azúa wanted to see him. He was waiting in a cubicle in the administration block. Mariano expedited a pass and Alberto went straight off without a guard.

What can that black want after all this time?

'I saw Bini yesterday.'

'Bini! You don't say!'

'She asked me to talk to you.'

Alberto stared at him, intrigued, and shrugged his shoulders.

'She's terrified because Yemayá appeared to her in a dream.'

'And what does Yemayá want? To send me her best wishes?'

'Don't mock. This might help you.'

Azúa's somewhat wild stare provoked a degree of anxiety.

Alberto raised his arms as if in disbelief.

'Please, Doctor, don't fuck me around with more crazy stories. Bini's dreams don't deserve my time or your trip out here…. I don't believe in idiot things like…'

'What you believe is of no matter,' interjected Azúa, throwing himself back in his chair. 'I for one do believe in dreams and I've still not given up hope of proving your innocence, and believe me, Bini is regretting…'

'Regretting what?'

'That she lied at the trial. She's ready to put things right in public.'

Alberto scrutinized him for a few seconds. A shadow of incredulity, a flicker of suspicion, passed over his half–closed eyes before he finally smiled stiffly and signalled a truce with open palms.

'All right, Doctor, this is beyond anything I could ever imagine; I'm sorry, I'm all ears.'

But he remained on the defensive and Azúa could see that. He leaned forward, elbows on the table, hands intertwined, speaking softly and conspiratorially.

'I was a little put out by our defeat in court…' he began, his eyes lowered. 'But I kept my faith in your innocence; and, as you are aware, I know the religious scene in my country, inhabited by people who do what they are bid in their dreams.'

Azúa broke off and looked almost blankly at a wall.

'And…?'

'At the moment Bini is torn by a guilty conscience.'

'And given the display of cynicism she gave in court, do you really believe that craven crawler's got a conscience?'

'"Man is a creature who crawls between heaven and earth", according to William Shakespeare,' Azúa replied wearily.

Alberto smiled and gestured to him to go on.

'Fine, a good quote; I'm listening.'

'And just as well; because the worst step is the one yet to be taken.'

'Not such a good quote; but do go on.'

'Bini says she's had the dream three times, and you can maybe help her to decipher it.'

'You don't say! Me the oracle?'

'O, O, O,' and he made a round shape with his thumb and index finger. 'What does the letter O three times mean to you?'

''The fucking bitch, the fucking whore. Where can she have

got…'Who else is behind her? What the hell are they plotting? Intimidation, bribery?

While he frowned and pretended to rack his memory, Alberto stared at the ground. He tried not to get angry. He was of course not going to reveal to Azúa the initials of his name.

'Three Os…?' repeated Alberto. 'No, Doctor, they mean nothing to me…Why does she think they're to do with me?'

Azúa cleared his throat, looked at him, but kept quiet. Was he trying to detect a lie in his eyes?

What if he grasps your hands and ask you what the three Os mean?

Take it easy, you idiot, you've no reason to be afraid. If he asks for your hands, you just act as if you're offended and don't play his game.

'And do the letters E, M, A…mean anything to you?'

While he was shaking his head, his skin bristled and his ears burned. He must have gone very red or very pale.

Azúa now looked at him feigning indifference.

Fucking hell…Can this black be in…

'Bini first dreamed the name. She saw it in letters…'

'My name in letters?'

'No, Yemayá's, white letters on a blue background…She's says it's the first time she's ever dreamed her in letters. She'd previously only seen her image. And she says that the name then lost the first Y and the syllable "yá" at the end. But the three letters E, M and A stayed put.'

Alberto didn't believe in seers or prophetic dreams. Someone must have passed his real initials on to Bini as well as the acronym for the school. And that someone knew what he did to the prisoners there.

And did that black, who was so intelligent, really swallow the story about the dream? Wasn't he also in the swim?

The uncertainty from his first day inside returned. He could no longer rest, read or work on his book…He could expect only sleepless nights, hours of worrying…

If it's the same people from Montevideo, why don't they snuff you and *chao*? What shit are they planning?

They only want you to know that they know…

Yes, of course…they want you to doubt, to suffer because you don't know…

Fucking hell, the same game you played with your prisoners.

And what the hell's the black to do with this? Is he an accomplice?

And Bastidas as well?

A plot with Bini, with Jaén, right from the start…?

And once again Azúa's loud voice: 'But the Three-Os business is more interesting.'

'Three Os,' Alberto corrected him.

He was pleased he'd kept his self-control and could still joke.

Azúa ignored him.

'She says you appeared to her with your hair close cropped; and you had three red Os tattooed on your forehead.'

'And couldn't they be zeros, or some other symbol…?'

'Exactly what I asked, but she described a written O, with a little squiggle on its right. You appeared to her three times; and she says the first was on the night of the final judgment.'

'That sounds very apocalyptic, Doctor.'

'You're right.' Azúa laughed. 'The night after the final hearing; and then twice more.'

Alberto kept shaking his head thoughtfully.

'I'm sorry I can't help you, but I'm as much at a loss as she is.'

'She got it into her head that those letters contain a message, and as soon as she got out, she went to consult her godfather…'

'Oh, so she's out already?' choked Alberto.

'She got out yesterday, and the first thing she did was to go and see her godfather, who consulted Orula, and she predicted blood.'

'Really, Doctor, do you give any importance to all this?'

'Yes, I do; and the godfather summoned the dead, to see if anyone could help interpret the dream.'

A shudder, a sudden wrinkling of the scalp, a contraction of the diaphragm...

Azúa seemed blacker than ever. His skin gleamed.

Alberto discovered that a 'box of the dead' was for drumming an invocation; and that during the drumming for Bini, a spirit rose up in the godfather's eldest daughter and revealed very concrete things. It was a Congo slave, killed rebelling in the nineteenth century, very fond of being invoked from the boxes and drums in that Regla back yard.

When the girl possessed was questioned, as her shoulders shook violently, very hoarsely and in Congan babble, she foresaw that the only one able to interpret those letters was the prisoner of an oath.

'Bini almost fainted when she heard the Congan; and now thinks Yemayá is upset with her because she used her name in an oath...'

'Is that what she told you?'

'No, but I'm sure that that's what her affliction is, and we should use it to our advantage.'

'But how can she feel remorse? Didn't you say that her godfather authorized her to swear the oath?'

'A *babalao* can be fallible. He's not the Pope.'

Alberto, who'd gone deathly pale, didn't know what to think.

'And she sends word that if you can unravel what EMA and OOO are, she's ready to do anything to really help you.'

'And your interpret...?'

'Yes,' interjected Azúa. 'My interpretation is that she's shocked, dead scared and ready to go back on her perjury in court.'

No remorse afflicted Bini. Those who'd bought her off had invented the dream; asking him for help in interpreting the dream was an excuse so he knew that they knew. Worst of all, even Azúa was playing along.

In the ensuing days, Alberto didn't add a single sentence to his book. He wasn't in the mood to go down to the yard, to play *frontón* or bridge. They had tracked him down and planned to shit on him. And Bini had been part of the plan from the start.

Could they have knocked a cyclist over just to put him inside?

Ridiculous. The Montos and Tupas kill cops, not cyclists. Quite simply, Bini swiped the car, killed the cyclist by accident, by herself or with someone, and they decided to put the blame on you. You're done for. They've got you fucked. The strange thing is they prefer to keep you in the slammer and didn't rub you out when they found you... They must be hatching something much worse.

Ever since he'd touched Cuban soil, Alberto had never known such days of anguish.

There was still more than a week to go to the party, but the preparations were going full steam ahead.

From the moment Letelier came into south wing, Mariano had taken to him. And recently he had looked after him like one of his own; put him on show, celebrated him, spoke to his children about him as a paragon of virtue and true grit; gave him generous free passes which the Chilean spurned, because he wasn't interested in freedom.

Touched by Letelier's Homeric lunacy and a sincere admirer of his heroic memory, Mariano saw that party like his daughter's coming of age birthday party. And like all fathers, who really love a son, he was grateful to Alberto. Thanks to him, his idea of organizing a humble get-together in homage to the Chilean had mushroomed into something never before seen in south wing, despite the exceptional regime he offered the foreign inmates.

For his part, Alberto, who was paying for excellent victuals and entertainment, had also given his time, energy and intelligent ideas. According to Mariano, he deserved a reward, because as José Martí said, nothing is so base as ingratitude.

Mid-November, Captain Inocente, secretary to the prison director, who was much amused by Mariano's paternalist excesses, and knew with what panache he was planning Letelier's party, plotted with his boss to play a joke on him worthy of medieval executioners.

With the director's agreement, Inocente faked the photocopy of an Interpol document, sent from Sweden, to the Cuban Ministry of Justice, demanding the extradition of Letelier, accused of five rapes and the murder of children he had buried in the garden of a house in Uppsala.

On Saturday, 27 November, when they had everything ready, they called Mariano to the boss's office, and when they showed him the photocopy, he blanched. He looked as if he was going to blub.

Immediately, he couldn't get any words out. He threw away one almost whole cigar and lit another.

'As you will understand, the party must be suspended; before the other prisoners find out, the Chilean must be put into solitary.

'From today,' added Inocente.

Monosyllabically, jerking his head in approval, Mariano let Inocente and the colonel philosophize on the enigmas of human behaviour; and that prisoners are prisoners; and are in prison for good reason; and that the worst one can do is to feel affection for them...

Mariano looked time and again at the document as he ran his fingers through his hair. And time and again he shook his head disconsolately. In seconds, his face glazed over. His eyes darkened. You could see him suffering.

The sadism of the director and his lackey lasted some ten

minutes. When they saw he was near to breakdown, they confessed to their joke.

Mariano looked at the colonel and Inocente, not knowing whether to be relieved, offended or confused. But his indulgent nature prevailed. After five minutes and a couple of shots the colonel poured him, he tore the photocopy up and rolled it into a ball, which he threw angrily into the wastepaper basket.

His good spirits restored, and to get his own back for their abuse, he launched into a eulogy of inmate Alberto Ríos. He finally asked the director to grant him a day out a week.

The director gave him verbal authorization; but reminded him of the rules: no prisoner, however exemplary his behaviour, should get a pass before he'd done his first six months inside.

'Alberto can't get a pass till February ninth, but I wanted to give him his first this next weekend,' persisted Mariano.

'I won't sign any pass for the Argie before February ninth but if you're so keen on this guy, you take the risk and let him out; but you heard me, I don't know nothin'; and if anything happens, I'll crucify you. You got it, Mariano?'

Alberto accepted that the brain had a paranormal dimension, not properly studied by modern science. He was aware of seriously scientific papers documenting the existence of certain involuntary telepathic activities that were falsely attributed to clairvoyant phenomena. He knew that thought is energy, and as such a highly organized form of matter. He didn't doubt, for example, that Azúa himself possessed a most highly endowed organism. He had himself experienced the high temperatures his hands could generate. And was in no doubt at all that he could call up special powers that convinced him of his innocence in the case of the cyclist who'd been knocked over.

Why not accept, then, that Bini had a highly endowed brain with access to truths that were blocked to others?

And what if she'd been sent his initials and those of the school via some mysterious conduit?

It is well known that strange waves exist, phenomena of animal magnetism that to this day scientific knowledge has been unable to systematize...

Don't be such a mug, Butcha' – he used to use his family nickname in these reproachful monologues – the only thing that is objective and scientific here is that they've tracked you down and are going to piss on you.

He couldn't swallow a tall story like that, no way.

What bastards had contracted Bini? Who wanted to piss on him? When and how?

All Alberto knew was why.

A heavy weight threatened to fall down and crush him. They wanted his head. But how did they want it?

On the fourth day after Azúa's visit, uncertainty weighed on him like a ton of lead. He felt the same as his prisoners of old. Theoretically he was familiar with the phenomenon. He had studied it and taught it in his courses. And couldn't forget the threat.

A headache, a persistent fever in the temples, began to harass him. But it wasn't a high temperature. It was fear.

Fear is the raw material of a good persuader, the *felacio* Mitrione would pontificate.

After that lethal visit, Alberto managed only snatches of sleep. He hardly ate. A few more days of such anxiety, and he'd go crazy.

Within a week, he started to ramble, to think of escaping, and to conceive of impossible arguments to rid him of his past guilt.

He realized he was suffering the effect of an XF.

They could ambush him; kill him. Yes, he'd always understood that. To an extent expected it. Someone who recognized him could torture him viciously; but it had never occurred to him that one day he would be subject to a violent spot of XF.

In the specialized language of prison psychology, XF represented the emotional situation of a political prisoner who knows he has been caught because the police have uncovered his subversive actions; but the prisoner doesn't know how much they know, how they found out, who in his group talked; and above all, he doesn't know what reprisals they intend taking.

The striking aspect of this situation is that XF (Xenophontic Fear) provokes strange psychological defensive reactions, with serious consequences for logical thought. The prisoner, as was now beginning to happen to Alberto himself, spends several days hallucinating about escape, manically and minutely planning an attempt; or concocts utopian arguments with which to trick his interrogators, to avoid torture and regain his freedom.

When introducing the concept to his intermediate classes on persuasion, Alberto used to quote a passage from the *General Cyropaedia* (Gamma, 1, 23), where Xenophon states that humans suffer more from the fear of torture than from the torture itself.

And experience with techniques of persuasion in numerous prisons on the planet shows that XF produces two stages in seventy per cent of cases of political prisoners: first, 'defensive irrationality', when the prisoner elaborates impossible escape routes, and 'collapse', which takes place without any physical intimidation, at the end of forty to sixty days. He can't resist, can't fight off the obsession. And one day calls the jailer, talks endlessly and becomes an informant.

XF is not a very frequently used technique, because it can't be applied when there are actions under way and it's urgent to get information from a single prisoner. But today it's applied rigorously when several members of one subversive group are caught, and the confessions under torture of the first two or three provide the necessary information. To carry on torturing the rest of the group is in these cases uneconomic, because the 'subjects who have been successfully XF'd' can be completely de-ideologized and turned into informants in the pay of the police, destined to infiltrate their own subversive group or others. Alberto perfected the XF technique on Tupamaros and

Montoneros in the seventies, and wrote an article for the journal *Intelligence*, in which he set out 'an evaluation of eco-suasion' used in twenty-two experimental cases. The article unleashed a polemic in the pages of that journal. Specialists from Langley participated, some of whom had nothing but praise for the then Lieutenant Orlando Ortega Ortiz.

But he now found himself in that unaccustomed situation, and could already recognize the first symptoms of the 'defensive irrationality' stage.

His only solution was to escape from prison. Logic said no, but his XF said yes, it would be very difficult, but it was his only possible salvation, because if they were talking to him about the three Os and the EMA it was because they already had their sights trained on him, and were ready to shoot.

By 26 November, after his second day of hunger strike, Mariano, who was very worried, visited him in his cell.

Was something the matter? Why was he no longer playing bridge, going down to the yard, playing *frontón*?

Alberto blamed it on a pain in his heel, nothing serious, and a flu-ey feeling, for which he'd take aspirin. It was just passing aches and pains, he'd soon get over it; meanwhile, he was benefiting from his confinement to move his book on.

Mariano calmed down, but on the 30th, when the guards told him that Alberto was still keeping to his cell and not working on his book, but spending almost the whole time lying on his bed looking at the ceiling, Mariano went back on to the offensive. He didn't think Alberto was suffering from a normal crisis suffered by inmates. He decided to give him some good news to see whether or not it raised his spirits.

# 31 news from madrid

From their apartment on 21st Street, Aldo and Bini enjoyed splendid views of Havana.

'Wonderful: three hundred and thirty degrees of uninterrupted vistas...' repeated Aldo, whenever he praised their location to a visitor.

'Sea included,' added Bini in her capacity as co-host; and she would point contentedly towards the elegantly neo-classical National, against a background of the Malecón, which was visible to the Castle Point, slightly foreshortened by the distance.

Aldo felt good in Vedado. Walking its streets was like being at home. It was quite strange and made him think of his childhood. It wasn't that Villa Urquiza resembled Vedado. It was rather the sense of a barrio unfinished, a kind of identity arising from the urban shambles and mixture of eras and styles; lots of big houses, flaking walls, tree roots bursting through roads, potholed pavements, and on rainy days limpid puddles littering the highway. Some tall buildings marred the really central area.

They were a few examples of gringo grandiosity, already built when 'the Comandante came and ordered a stop to be put'.

When Aldo first focused on the panorama from the top of his terrace, he remembered the song by Carlos Puebla. Throughout Latin America his generation had sung it from 1959 in acts of solidarity with Cuba. It was also an unusual song. It was perhaps the first political text of the Cuban revolution set to music and, while preserving the festive spirit of the Cuban *son*, it attacked the Batista government, its conspiracies with the mafia and property speculation of the fifties: 'They thought they were here to stay/in their apartment blocks/and the people in their torment had just perished'.

That first round lumbered Havana with the thirty-five floors of FOCSA, that ugly prison bird with its wings unfolded; and also the insipid box of the Hotel Capri, the property of Santo Trafficante managed by George Raft; and the Habana Riviera, belonging to the Jewish mafia, the headquarters of Meyer Lansky in his final years; and the Free Havana, which the Hilton chain put the last touches to a few months before Fidel descended from the Sierra Maestra with his host of bearded warriors.

As well as the three hundred and thirty degrees of landscape, 'sea included', that apartment offered the charm of an east-facing terrace, where a pleasant breeze always blew on hot days.

Aldo had sounded out the possibility of buying the apartment; but it wasn't legally possible; and he didn't want problems. Nonetheless, he managed it so that the owner, a seventy-five-year-old, childless widow, rented it out to him for one pretty low annual payment, two bedrooms en suite, a dining-cum-living room and the magical terrace. Aldo also got the owner's permission to make a few small improvements.

He would thus install a grill with pump and pulleys to roast his meat Argentine-style; and while he was building, he also erected a rustic oven in order to cook his own bread and pizza on stone.

And when Bini left prison, Aldo granted her some of the

wishes she'd expressed: a piano installed on the terrace, protected from the day-time sun by a canvas awning, and from the rain by waterproof sheeting; and a futon so they could make love under the stars; and in their bedroom, a one-hundred-and-ten-inch screen, and a king-size bed with a red silk bedhead.

Bini was well used to wishing in vain, and Aldo's gesture, even though he'd made no promises, made her cry. Quite uncanny.

'And I've got another little present you're going to like.'

He made her shut her eyes and placed a small box in her hands.

She opened it and found a key.

The key to a car!

'Really? A car for me?'

'A Japanese model, a Subaru Vivio, and this as well,' and Aldo handed her a sheet of paper.

It was the receipt for a course of driving lessons.

She leapt round his neck. Clasped him round the waist with her legs, smothered him in kisses, and knocked him to the ground.

'And where's my car?'

He took her by the hand and pointed it out from the terrace. It was a tiny yellow car.

'Ooh, it looks like a little egg.'

They were soon downstairs and she kissed and hugged her little egg. Fondled and stroked it.

Aldo had to drive her to Siboney again so she could try it out.

'All right. Just a trial drive.'

And he extracted a pledge that she wouldn't try to drive it till she'd passed her driving test.

'By Yemayá?'

She hesitated, her face darkened, but she swore the oath.

'By Yemayá.'

★

When Bini agreed to go to prison, she didn't do so for Aldo but rather because of the sudden, anguished hatred she felt towards that brutal abuser who tortured and disappeared Teresita.

When she saw how pleased and grateful he was when he welcomed her out of prison, how generous he was towards her, the trouble he took to make her happy, she wondered yet again whether she shouldn't try to live with a guy like that.

Yes, but…what about the horns?

Well, she'd see. For the moment, she'd go along with him in the wedding plans, in getting papers and being able to travel easily. A little trip to Italy wasn't a bad idea anyway, to get a feel for democracy and human rights.

She could now invite her friends and musicians to the terrace to have drinks and great musical nights out; or could watch videos on the big screen, hugging Aldo; or receive her friends in her new bed, drawing on a cigarette-holder, wearing a lacy dressing gown and draping her hand over the silk bedhead, like a movie star.

Nonetheless, as soon as she started her driving lessons, she began to lose her interest in travelling to Italy. If she had her way, she'd not abandon her little egg for a single moment. She spent the day memorizing the traffic code. For the first time in her life she studied seriously.

On the night of 30 November, the thermometer on the terrace showed twenty-five degrees. Aldo didn't want to go out and suggested they took advantage of the fine weather to watch television in the open air and eat pizza.

'But first I'm going to eat you,' she said, and forced on him a long lovemaking session under the stars.

Bini woke up hungry for pizza at 4 a.m. He too was hungry. He rubbed his eyes, yawned a couple of times, and asked for some coffee.

She went to the kitchen and came back with two cups.

He was waiting for her on the terrace, with the oven already on.

At half past, while Aldo was kneading his pizzas, Bini trundled out the television on its stand.

The oven was soon spreading the ineffable aroma of seasoned wood when it mingles with the night breeze, enriched by olive oil, tomato, cheese, basil and garlic.

Bini was savouring a seven-year-old rum and Aldo playing with his pizza spatula when they heard the whistle of the fax.

Aldo finished taking the pizza from the oven, went into their bedroom, picked up the fax, walked into the sitting room and took a bottle of red wine from the cupboard. Back on the terrace, he put his glasses on and read the message.

When Bini sat on the bed, waiting for her tray of pizza and wine, Aldo declared: 'It's all ready in Madrid. The lawyer's asking me if he can present the case to the Spanish courts.'

'And what are you going to do?'

'I don't know yet. I've got to think it over…'

He put the fax down, took off his glasses and picked up the spatula.

'Have you ever heard of Maguncio the magician?'

# 32 a pass in the right direction

At 9 a.m. on the 30th, after a shitty night, Alberto was ruminating, and staring at the cell of his ceiling.

Suddenly, the Judas-hole opened and the guard told him that Mariano wanted to see him in his office.

When he saw him come in, he didn't even bid him good day: 'Get ready, because we're leaving tomorrow at eight.'

'For a …ride?'

'Well, I mean, a day's leave. You shouldn't get this till February, but you're coming with me tomorrow.'

'Really?' and he felt his heart thumping.

'Fuck, Alberto! Have I ever let you down?'

'No, but I can't believe it…' Sudden hope, fear and euphoria, a unique opportunity, a rush of ideas, Nene, the yacht, but where will I find the petrol?

'…and…when do we come back?'

'I'll stay out to the evening, but you've got to be back here at eight am. It's a twenty-four-hour pass.'

★

Back in his cell, he shook nervously. He couldn't go back to bed. For a few moments he recovered his muscle tone. The hope of making his escape was a stimulus, like an injection in the vein.

Fucking hell, if he got that leave and was left alone for twenty-four hours...

Mariano took Wednesdays and Saturdays off; and if he took up the offer of his car, he'd have transport guaranteed every Wednesday at the same time.

It took Alberto two hours to hatch his plan: he'd look out his firm's lawyer and Nene and use them to prepare his escape. He should proceed cautiously, so nobody rumbled his scheme.

He hardly slept. He sat at his computer and jotted down the details of his plan.

From the day Alberto was imprisoned on 9 August, his yacht *Chevalier* had become the responsibility of Dr Dionisio Paredes, a lawyer and covert partner in Texinal. Paredes too was fond of water sports. From prison, Alberto signed a document authorizing Paredes to use his yacht whenever he wanted.

Till the end of July, for looking after the yacht's engines and acting as pilot for Alberto, Nene earned one hundred and fifty dollars a month; but as soon as he was put inside, Paredes the lawyer informed him that from then on he'd get only fifty dollars flat for spending a day a week on maintaining the *Chevalier*, and when Paredes required him as a pilot or mate, he'd pay him cash by the hour. And till the beginning of November, with the fine weather, Paredes went out sailing every weekend. He loved deep-sea diving, and his two adolescent sons went with him.

That 1 December, at 8.03, Mariano drove through Post 1, with Alberto next to him. The guard kept a copy of the pass and handed the original to Alberto: the safe pass signed by Major Mariano Robles Marín, with the prison stamp, authorized him to stay out until 7 a.m. on 2 December. It wasn't the guard's business whether Alberto had done the necessary six months to get a pass; and without comment he signalled to the gatekeeper to let them through.

It was a rather cloudy day, but the sea was calm. According to his diary, it still wasn't winter; nor was it autumn, judging by the lack of wind and the searing hot sun. Anywhere in the world, that was spring.

'What are you going to do today?' enquired Mariano.

'Give my sceptre an outing and drive around Havana.'

'I advise you not to do both at once....'

Alberto looked at him, perplexed.

'You know, don't go bonking in a car and knocking over another cyclist.'

Alberto laughed loudly. Mariano was witty, even seemed intelligent. Perhaps it was only a façade. You couldn't be intelligent and so cosmically naive.

On the rest of the journey, Mariano rattled on about his daughter's wedding coming up on Saturday.

'Why didn't you tell me?' protested Alberto.

Mariano shrugged his shoulders.

'Where's the party being held?'

'At my mother's house, in her big back yard.'

'Can you give me the address?'

'No, I can't. I forbid you to send any presents.'

'But Mariano, *che*, I thought we were friends...'

'Don't get things wrong, Alberto. In the jail, with the other prisoners, I can seem as such; but if you give me a present, it will get out sooner or later, and that can harm me.'

'But I can give you money and you...'

'Don't fucking go on, Alberto.' Mariano shouted indignantly. 'Friendship is one thing and bribery another.'

Alberto clammed up.

Ay, the guy's worried about honesty...! He's got a cheese bap for a brain...Fuck him. It's his loss.

'But don't take it like that, Mariano...I only want to...'

'Shit, Alberto, let's change the subject. Look how beautiful the sea is.'

Since Mariano had mentioned the sea, Alberto was on the point of saying it was the only thing he missed in prison; but he held back. He shouldn't mention the sea. Nobody should be reminded that he owned a yacht anchored at the Hemingway Marina.

After he came out of the Havana tunnel, Mariano was going to head to Santos Suárez, and he suggested Alberto got out in Prado, where he'd get a taxi home more easily.

Within half an hour, Alberto had had his first deep bath for four months. He went into his bedroom, where he had to switch off the air-conditioning; he put on a dressing gown and spent a while stroking the silk beading of the lapel. He drank a glass of icy white wine and then called the Texinal offices to get them to send his car. After four months of living without furniture, shut up in a cell with an uneven floor and bumpy walls, he relished the forgotten routine of opening his sandalwood wardrobe. Felt the smooth sheen of the blond wood, the scent from the drawers and the cool temperature of the shirts piled high with manic tidiness.

His greatest pleasure was to sit at the wheel of his convertible. He remembered the first time he'd driven a motor vehicle. It was in the countryside, a John Deere tractor, belonging to his uncle Alfonso. Moving that weight with his own hands and feet, steering it, driving it round a corner of the field... Another ineffable sensation he was now recovering. He'd been driving cars for thirty-five years. And before going to prison, he couldn't recall a week when he'd not driven. First, the cars of the Uruguayan police. Then, in Florida, he'd bought an old banger. And that was what he did everywhere he lived. Until in 1977, in Buenos Aires, he got his first new car, with the cash he'd extracted from that *felacio*, imprisoned in the EMA.

★

He found Dr Paredes in an office at the Ministry for Foreign Commerce, where he worked as a consultant.

Surprised by the visit, and rather confused, the lawyer managed only a welcome smile.

'How did you fix it? You've not been inside for six months...'

'The prison cops have fallen for me...What can I do?'

And he related his close relationship with the man in charge of his wing, his gratefulness for his support for the party, and his economic contribution to the needs of south wing.

'Besides, he's not afraid I'll run away: he knows that the best thing that could have happened to me was to be put inside...'

And he emphasized what Paredes knew, how pleased he was to be shut up; the adventure he was into; the picturesque characters he'd got to know. The break in the habits of decades forced him to think new things, even about himself, and to review some ideas he'd thought good but which were now out of date.

'Just today, when I was telephoning from my house, soaking in my bath, I finally concluded that we human beings don't know how to live; we only value what we have lost.'

It was a commonplace, but Dr Paredes was a common man; he nodded, philosophically engrossed, as if he'd just heard something really profound.

'Yes, Doctor, I've had a son and sown lots of seeds; but in order not to pass unnoticed through this life, I need to write a book. It's an old frustrated dream; and I'm going to bring it to fruition, thanks to this glorious Cuban prison.'

A fresh philosophical coating for an old banality.

*Felacio* Paredes was easy meat.

'But just imagine, Doctor, free again, the whirlwind of life, and especially in this country, with the women you've got here, this climate, this sea...' And he paused for a long time, his head lowered. 'This sea I need so much...'

'Yes, I understand...'

'It's the only thing I miss. While we're on the subject, how are you getting on with Nene?'

'Wonderful, as I told you: he's very hard working, responsible and punctual; and he keeps the yacht up to scratch.'

'Have you used him as a pilot?'

'I always do, just as you recommended. I never put to sea without him.'

'And how much do you pay him when he goes out with you?'

'Three dollars an hour.'

Alberto calculated that Nene, apart from the fifty dollars a month, could be earning fifteen or twenty dollars every time he went out with Paredes. Every month, even if he worked each weekend, it was much less than the hundred and fifty steady rate he got from him.

'Not bad,' said Alberto thoughtfully; 'but the poor guy is fucking short of cash, he needs to repair an old vessel that's laid up in Cojímar, and it's costing him a pile…'

'I didn't realize; he never mentioned anything…'

'He's very reserved about his own affairs; but he came to see me the other day in prison, and asked me to give him a hand. He wants me to give him permission to go deep-sea fishing, once a week, so he can sell the fish and help himself. I said he could.'

'That's a nice gesture on your part, and I think the lad deserves it.'

'Yes, he's been very straight with me, very loyal, and it doesn't cost me to give him a hand…So, Doctor, when he asks, please sign a permit for him for the marina authorities. He'll give you a call one of these days to get your agreement.'

'Fine, he's got my telephone numbers.'

That same afternoon, Alberto looked out Nene.

According to the agreement between Alberto Ríos, the public prosecutor and the authorities at the Hemingway Marina, the *Chevalier* could go out to sea only when authorized by Dr Dionisio Paredes. If Nene, despite being a permit-holder as a skipper of short-haul boats, needed to take the yacht outside the quays of the Hemingway Marina, to test out the engines or whatever, Paredes had to authorize him in writing; but in fact, while Nene didn't go far, or stay for long outside the inlet, the marina authorities turned a blind eye. Nene, who had been a coastguard, knew the men in the nearby barracks. They all trusted him.

Nene lived in Old Havana, on the corner of Alcantarilla and Alambique. He, his wife and two children lived in a big colonial house that had been recently repaired. Alberto went by his house twice that afternoon, but Nene wasn't back. And his wife didn't know where he was.

He turned up at night, at nine. When he saw Alberto, he looked surprised, but not as pleasantly as Dr Paredes.

Ever since Alberto had been jailed, Nene had been earning less, but hadn't had to swallow so much bile from that bastard, who humiliated him at the least opportunity.

He cordially detested him. But after working for Alberto for a year, he'd been able to repair his house and win a couple of rounds in the unequal contest between providing treats for the children under the Special Period as well as basic necessities like clothes and shoes. Alberto was one of so many bitter cups a man had to drink if he was going to live decorously.

All smiles now, Alberto greeted Nene effusively and asked after his children's schooling and praised the coffee brought by his wife.

As soon as they were alone, Alberto went directly to the point interesting him: 'Would you like to earn a hundred dollars every Wednesday?'

Nene raised his eyebrows at such a foolish question and stared at him, his shoulders slumped.

'On Wednesday, weather permitting, you'll pick me up off the Miramar coast. I'll be floating there with a whore at my side. I spoke to Paredes and he'll give you the permit for the authorities. Ring him tomorrow and agree a time. I told him you'd asked me for the yacht to go fishing once a week because you were hard up and wanted to help yourself out by selling the fish you caught.'

And he spun him the same yarn as he had Paredes: he was very happy in jail, was making good use of the time, writing his book, blah, blah…

'You can't imagine what it means to me, Nene. I've been dreaming of writing this book for years…'

El Nene went on the defensive. Alberto never spoke to him so plainly, so confidentially. He wanted something.

'…and I had to get banged up to get stuck in. The truth is it's not really like being inside. I'm having a great time. I only miss the sea and fucking more often. They only let you see a woman once a week. So, every Wednesday, which is going to be my leave day, between ten and two I'm going to have my fill of sea and pussy. You get me, Nene?'

'Yes, of course, Señor Ríos, I…anyway…'

Alberto didn't let him speak. He started to explain his personal bonds with Mariano, who was very supportive, etc., who, among other things, had allowed him an exit pass two months in advance. He was his best friend, a real brother; but his authority didn't extend to letting him on board the yacht. That was an issue for the public prosecutor.

'That's why I've come to you, and it's just between us two.'

'But that…could be very…'

'Don't be a dick-head, Nene!' he scolded him. 'You'll be fine. They didn't find us out before and they won't now. What might happen to you? Nothing. You just say you didn't know I was banned from sailing in my yacht, and *chao*. Your only crime will be helping me take whores on board. At most you'll get sent down for a day; but so you don't lose out, I'll give you another three thousand dollars right now, on top of the hundred a week.'

And he started counting out the hundred-dollar bills.

Nene couldn't believe his eyes. The patriarch did his sums. The husband remembered his wife's birthday. The dad thought of the bicycles promised to his kids.

Naturally, he accepted.

On Wednesday, 8 December, at 10 a.m., weather permitting, Alberto would turn up with his siren on the beach on 34th Street, in Miramar. There they'd both put on their wet suits and flippers, would pick up their snorkels and goggles, and swim offshore for five hundred metres, but never moving away from an imaginary line that was an extension to 34th Street. That was where they'd wait for the *Chevalier*. Alberto and the girl would wear little red caps so Nene could identify them.

And the next day, at 6 a.m., before returning to the Combined, Alberto would drive by and pick up Nene in his car, and take him to the Marina. Nene would go in by himself, and extract from the yacht the two isothermic wet suits, goggles and snorkels, which they'd take to Alberto's house. So they'd be to hand the following Wednesday.

# 33 homage to a rhapsode

The party would start at 8.30 a.m.

Alberto got to the leisure area around seven, and immediately put the television on.

The west of the island was still dotted with friendly suns. There were also some little white meringues that augured light storms and choppy seas in the eastern provinces, but no danger to smaller vessels.

Perfect, if only the weather could keep like that for another three days.

A summer sun shone down on the whole area around the Caribbean, the Gulf of Mexico and the Yucatan and Bahamas channels. No tropical storm was brewing; there was no high pressure over the oceans and the 'brutal, turbulent North' was totally calm on the political and meteorological fronts. That week, the US was not starting a war, or laser–bombing anyone. Nor were cold fronts circulating over its territory which might threaten the blue of the Cuban sky in days to come.

Perfect.

After listening to the weather bulletin, Alberto headed into the kitchen.

The Colombian Servio Tulio had been kneading bread rolls since 5 a.m. and preparing the porridge for the one hundred and fifty invited to the party.

If I get out at eight, I'll be in 34th Street by 9.30. If I reach 34th, I'll swim to the point. If I swim to the point, I'll get on board. And if I board my *Chevalier*, it will be bye-bye, Cuba dear…

The prisoners were asking about the magician and the musicians who'd been contracted. And from the previous evening unconfirmed rumours had been circulating that if participants were well behaved at the party, the three bottles of beer promised could multiply. There was talk of five, of seven…

Some people, who'd already sold their quotas a week before, were engaged in exchanges, transactions and bargaining, for cigars and food.

Letelier, the man under homage, was to say a few words and take part in a café debate, but nobody knew how that would work. Many enquired whether in a café debate coffee would be served.

From the previous day Mariano had been accompanying the video director and his crew to film shots inside the prison and in particular Letelier's cell with its thirty-two beds.

When the much-trumpeted professor of classical philology appeared at 8.30, the guests were already in their seats in the main room.

In the centre there was a table, higher than the rest, where Letelier sat, flanked by the professor and Mariano, on whose right sat Alberto.

When silence fell, Mariano got up to announce the café debate would take place immediately after breakfast.

Immediately, six volunteer prisoners, including Servio Tulio himself, served each guest three savoury rolls, gave them the choice of a cup of hot chocolate, with or without milk, or real cold porridge, with or without milk.

When the guests, all rather suspiciously, except for the Colombians, bit into their first bread rolls, people laughed and made loud noises of approval.

In the midst of such breakfast abundance, Alberto stood up to say a few words in praise of the delicious flavour of that 'dish, a tasty mouthful kneaded from cheeses and yucca flour', and called for applause for the selfless Servio Tulio, who'd been battling away in the kitchen by himself from five in the morning to prepare almost five hundred bread twists.

It was never known whether the thunderous applause that erupted was thanks for Servio Tulio, to praise the savoury bread, or for eloquent Alberto, the virtuoso − sponsor, as Mariano would say − behind almost every titbit at that party.

Alberto beamed contentedly. His escape plan, which seemed more and more feasible, reduced his XF and kept at bay the phantoms that had been pursuing him ever since Azúa's visit.

Suddenly, he decided to liven up the breakfast and took the microphone in order to relate − and why not? − Servio Tuliuo's singular history, his alternating peaks and troughs, his hard grind to re-emerge time and again from nothingness thanks to savoury bread, only to ruin himself once more by rearing fighting bulls; but between bankruptcies, he rubbed shoulders with millionaires, bullfighters and celebs; and Alberto's account animated Servio Tulio, who launched with his usual verve and wit into the tale of when his fighting bulls won him the favours of Amparo Arrebato, a celebrated dancer and the most renowned, most coveted courtesan in Cali, and, whenever he got drunk, he evoked his first visit to Cuba, at Christmas 1957, when he was twenty-four. Stinking rich, he'd splashed out on the greatest binge of his life, at the Tropicana Cabaret, under the stars, always in the company of two or three of those black beauties who were expensive, flighty and unforgettable; they were the best days God had given him, and ever since, on every

New Year's Eve, wherever he was celebrating it, in toasts and speeches he'd always asked St Judas Thaddeus to allow him to see the year 2000 in Havana. His eyes dampened and, straining a smile, he concluded: 'And you see, St Judas remembered me, here I am, and only a few days to go.'

The threat of a storm of tear-jerking led Mariano to interject and give them all a surprise, and, after signalling to a server, he declared that the guests would now savour, also thanks to Alberto Rios's kindness and generosity, a delicious Cuban coffee, quite unblended.

Three hundred incredulous eyes then saw the prisoners acting as waiters come in carrying their jugs on high. The room filled with that unique, unrivalled aroma, of real, unblended coffee, freshly percolated through cloth filters.

Among the majority of inmates originating from coffee-producing countries, Caribbeans, Colombians, Central Americans, Brazilians, particularly those with no family in Cuba and left to their own devices by miserly consuls, there were those who tasted the sublime, one hundred per cent pure potion from their childhood, so unlike the wretched bilge water served up in the Combined, and crossed themselves, gave thanks to God and thought of the mums they had abandoned, mums who brewed the best coffee in the universe.

Three Greeks hooked up arms and began to dance, like Zorba. And the eight Italians present, children of that nation of artists and sybarites that civilized Europe in coffee creation, sipped and savoured, rolled their eyes and held their breath, wept in unison, and experienced the fourth dimension.

But that was only the beginning; because the waiters returned with baskets stuffed with cigars and distributed the best Cuban brands: Montecristo, H. Upmann, Cohiba, two small packets a head.

Alberto's generosity – he'd spent a hundred and eighty dollars on cigars, three hundred and twenty on coffee and almost four hundred on chocolate, cheese and yucca for breakfast – sparked off applause and praise. The room was euphoric. Nobody, not even the guards, remembered a moment like it, in any other prison. South wing was living a dream. Mariano looked at them and smiled quietly, proud as could be. From the other end of the room, Gardelion roared that in twenty years inside he'd never known a party like it.

'Fantastic, *Garufa*,' and he blew out clouds of smoke.

Most of the foreigners had never had two boxes of cigars in their prison lives. No one was expecting such a generous share-out of the most coveted, most smuggled item, a real money substitute in their daily comings and goings. Every partygoer was now a rich man. In prison annals no such bonanza had ever been recorded.

And now, Alberto Ríos, with the right granted by the fact he is the principal sponsor of that collective epiphany, gets up to applause and asks for silence to introduce Mariano, who begins to read a speech prophesying future redemptions for prisoners, and Alberto, with his mind on weather reports and sea currents, and how all the inmates must see their time inside as a new start, life allows for many unexpected turns, and Alberto, thinking whether the port authorities, whether Nene will put in enough petrol, and what he will say when he appears by himself, without a whore in tow, and how every inmate must be confident that a door always opens for men ready to mend their ways, and how Emilio Letelier was an example of worthy struggle against adversity, such tenacity, transforming the setback of time in prison into a moral victory, a victory for culture and the spirit, an incredible feat memorizing the twenty-four cantos of *The Iliad*, applause, whistles, hurrahs, GET UP...AND SING, GET UP AND SING, and Mariano, pointing out that Homeric cantos are cantos that go unsung, and Mariano's hands begging for silence, and that's enough racket, and rushing to finish his speech, and finally introducing the words of the man being paid homage, and Letelier takes the microphone, gives thanks for the party, particularly to Mariano and Alberto, who have taken so much interest, but he, in truth, isn't used to public speaking, and his emotion at such an expression of friendship prevents him from speaking, he's not prepared anything, is at a loss for words, then a Salvadorean raises a hand and asks him to explain what on earth are cantos that go unsung, and what was *The Iliad*, and then another prisoner, a taciturn North American who spoke good Spanish, explained highly succinctly the central story of *The Iliad*, and another prisoner enquired how long Letelier had spent learning those cantos by heart, and when he said nine years, there was a round of exclamations, confabs and chatter, and someone else asked what benefit would Letelier get from it all in the future, and Alberto answered for him and explained that when Letelier left for a free life, he'd live like a nabob, because as he was able to repeat the verses in ancient Greek and translate them into four languages, he'd get a load of contracts to appear on television or at cultural centres throughout the world, and it was then that Letelier began to get appreciative glances from his colleagues, who, for the first time, attributed some common sense to him. And when Alberto began to calculate aloud what anyone could earn as a professional Homeric rhapsodist, Letelier asked for the microphone to clarify that, beyond any material gain, it all had a much greater value for him, because just as Servio Tulio reckoned the best part of his life was that New Year's Eve in the Tropicana, the best of his was his childhood by his mother's side, when she read to him Homer's cantos and taught him Greek and told him all the old Hellenic myths, which he got her to repeat again and again, and when he didn't go to sleep with the story of Oedipus, it was with the labours of Hercules, or with the adventure of the Argonauts, or Theseus and the Minotaur, or the apple of Discord, and to go back to those stories was like recovering his mother, and the tenderly maternal leitmotif now began to dampen a few eyes, and a Mexican raised his hand and said his mum had also told him some very old stories of the Mayas and Pancho Villa and he wanted to know why those stories told by that Chilean's nice mum, like the one about that apple, were so brilliant, and the others chorused, GET UP AND TELL IT, TELL IT, TELL IT, and as Alberto and Mariano smiled intently, everybody demanded the story of the apple, and the banging of cups on tables got louder and louder, THE APPLE, THE APPLE, well, all right, here's the story, and according to Letelier's mum, the person really to blame for the Trojan war that's recounted in *The Iliad* was Discord, and the professor underlined the fact that she was a twin sister of the god of war, an infamous harpy and notorious spoilsport; and Letelier, that's right, in effect, it was Discord's idea to roll a golden apple along the wedding table where all the gods from Olympus were banqueting, inscribed with the motto 'For the most beautiful!', and three of the goddesses present, Hera, Athena and Aphrodite, each very vain, began to pull at the apple and fight, until King Zeus, to avoid another terrible set-to with the Olympians throwing chalices of ambrosia at each other's heads, decided to appoint as arbiter one Alexander, alias Paris, young son of the king and queen of Troy, renowned as the most handsome man in the world. And so the three goddesses, guided by Mercury, went to Mount Ida, to ask for Paris to give a verdict, and they started preening themselves and insulting each other in front of him, and each one attempted to bribe him. Hera offered him the reward of being master of the universe if she were the most beautiful; Athena offered to make him invincible in combat; but Aphrodite was more psychologically astute, and offered him the hand of Helen, the most beautiful of mortals; Paris immediately consecrated her as winner.

From that moment, Hera and Athena swore to hate Paris and the city of Troy for eternity, and to fulfil her pledge, Aphrodite got Paris to seduce, rape and carry off to Troy the beautiful Helen, wife of the powerful King Menelaus.

As soon as they learned of the adultery, Hera and Athena made the heart of Agamemnon, the outraged husband's brother, seethe with hatred; and persuaded Achilles, Odysseus, Ajax and

Diomedes, and the most valiant Achaean princes, to march against Troy, destroy it, killing and enslaving men and children, raping the women and reducing them to slaves. It was the only way to clean the stained honour of Menelaus Atreus.

Letelier was animated, looked transfigured. When he spoke, he gazed upwards, like Jorge Luis Borges, who always focused his blind eyes on the muses residing high in the ceiling. And, emotionally charged, a hypnotic aura radiating from his demented eyes, Letelier silenced the chatty, partying prisoners, who now listened enthralled to the fate of Troy, the birth of Paris, the sacrifice of Iphigenia, Agamemnon's return to Argos, Achilles' anger, and then went on drinking real coffee and smoking great smokes on this their best day ever behind bars.

Servio Tulio asked whether the Minotaur was connected to bullfighting, and once again it was the guest philologist who related the myth of Theseus, and when he remarked that he once threw an ox over a temple, a tremendous debate ensued as to whether the legends of the ancients were more beautiful as told by your mother when you were a kid or as told by those gringo films, all shooting and chasing, that are also a pack of lies, but wrapped up as if they told the truth.

When Letelier finished, he was greeted by rapturous applause and shouts of encore. Nobody imagined that the café debate, transformed into myth-telling session, would go on past midday; so, in order to continue with the programme, Alberto introduced Gardelion and his guitar accompanist, and Gardelion said that to carry on with the theme of that Señor Homero, whose surname people never mentioned, he was going to sing 'Malena', a tango by another Homero, by the name of Manzi, and then came 'Sur', and almost at the end, when they sang shoulder to shoulder, Alberto was suddenly mortified again by the thought that if he made his yacht escape on the eighth, Bini would go unpunished. He wouldn't be able to throw back at her the heap of shit she'd landed on him; but there would be a time to deal with revenge and whores.

As soon as he landed in a safe spot, he'd contract Pizzaiolo, a freelancing Argentine killer, based in Miami, very professional, clean jobs, expensive but perfect. Pizzaiolo could come to Cuba as a tourist and cut her to ribbons; there'd be an extra job, to order a giant pizza to be sent to the undertakers instead of a wreath with cheesy letters saying: 'Chao, Bini: we're quits. Deep condolences, Alberto Ríos'; and he laughs and remembers the Donald Westlake novel he'd read a few days ago which told of something similar. It's the first time he's laughed so freely for a long time, and now, seeing Gardelion make way, to a round of applause, for Gentle, who starts on his round of boleros with 'Two Gardenias', Alberto decides to go to the kitchen to inspect the *bifes de chorizo* turning on the spit.

Half an hour later, when the first round of cold beer is being taken round the tables – a historic event – and they immediately unload on to aluminium trays those colossal chops, each weighing a pound, the prisoners look at each other, look at the meat, smile and look at one another again, smell, and when they lower their heads and start chomping that meat, the tenderness of which most have never tasted before, and savour, and swallow, and cut and fill their mouths with chips and lettuce, a dramatic silence descends, and, as in Homer's Agora, the smell of rich cow fat sends mortals into ecstasy and honours the gods, but Blind Homer and Homero Manzi are a thing of the past, and now there's applause for Gentle, but the dramatic desires aroused by those *bifes* put nobody in a mood for boleros, there are but lowered heads, which chew and chomp.

Alberto looks on approvingly, not because the sight pleases him but because he notes that chewing is a repugnant, cruel act, and an excellent example in the animal kingdom of the close relationship between cruelty and survival.

The inmates still wrestle with their *bifes*. Though stuffed, they eat on. They engorge like boa constrictors, and when the second can of beer is served, a concert of sighs and disgusting belches lauds the excellence of the repast.

Policarpo the clown makes his entrance and the diners laugh and take small sips of beer so it lasts longer, and after the clown's act is done, around 3 p.m., they serve a third beer and drummers and dancers appear and perform some Afro-Cuban numbers, and the singing and percussion enter the bloodstream and heighten the feelings brought on by the beer and bring on thoughts of women and parties, and immediately the magician Maguncio is introduced, who enters juggling pins, plates and balls, and then embarks on a round of mental tricks and mathematical calculations at supersonic speed, and for his grand finale he asks for three volunteers to come up and act as his helpers.

He gets one to blindfold him, another to open a small case and the third to get out a virgin pack of cards and break the seals. At once, the first helper takes from the pack all the fives, jacks, queens and kings; the second shuffles; and the third gets another three spectators to take one card each, and show it to the rest of the gathering.

One selects a three of hearts, another a six of diamonds and the third a ten of clubs, and Maguncio, still blindfolded, announces that he will take from the same pack numbers that when added to the cards already extracted will make ten, and Jordi, the Catalan, gets up to say that's impossible, because in the pack there's no card that added to ten makes ten, and the magician gesticulates angrily and impatiently, strikes his forehead, and says sure, señor, the gentleman was right, he'd forgotten to take out the tens, and without letting go of the pack or removing his blindfold, he puts his hands on his hips and gives a little kick of disgust, but finally opines that he won't let such negligence spoil his act, and will find a solution, somehow or other. That's why he is a magician, right? And he lifts the pack up high above his head, shuffles it at the dizzy speed of a conjurer, and asks his helpers to cut three times. Finally, he places the pack on a small table, fans out the cards face down and, looking at the ceiling with blindfolded eyes, he slips his hands over the backs of the cards and extracts a seven of hearts which, added to the three of hearts held aloft by one of the prisoners, makes ten; after the first round of applause, there is a second, when the magician takes out a four for the six of diamonds; and then a silence follows, as they wait for the promised contrivance to solve the problem of the ten of clubs.

After passing his hands once more over the fanned-out cards, but without touching them, Maguncio says no, the card he wants isn't there; but that anyway he can feel the card is there, in the possession of someone in the audience, and, gesticulating theatrically like a blind man, he turns round and starts to walk with a hand outstretched, palm cupped outwards, like a radar antenna, till he stops in front of Alberto Ríos, and declares he has found the missing card.

What's the name of the man sitting opposite my palm?

Several voices reply that it is Alberto Ríos.

And Maguncio asks Alberto Ríos to look in his back pocket, where he keeps his handkerchief, to see whether there isn't a card there.

Alberto feels his pocket, and breaks into an admiring smile, which suddenly broadens into a guffaw of amazement: his hands are holding an astounding, never-before-seen zero of clubs, which added to the problematic ten, completes the series.

But when the magician asks Alberto to show the card around, he sees painted on the back three Os that are dripping blood, and beneath them the acronym EMA.

Alberto took refuge in the bathroom, feeling dizzy and sick. By the time he returned, the magician had gone. The literature professor was starting on his introduction to Letelier's feat of memory.

Alberto sat back in his seat, where he remained silent, looking but not seeing the rest of the show.

When the fuck did the magician put that card in his pocket?

Perhaps when Servio Tulio was speaking. Or Letelier, when he was already sitting behind the table. The magician could have stopped behind those completely open-backed chairs and slipped the card into his very loose prison uniform trousers without anyone noticing. Anyway, someone was telling him through the three Os of his initials and the EMA acronym that they knew about his past.

His enemy would go on playing cat and mouse with him, planned to intimidate him, depress him with conjectures and fear, torture him from a distance. And he was succeeding…He anticipated an inexorable relapse into XF.

While the prisoners were applauding the news of a fifth beer, Alberto thought that whoever had intrigued with Bini, and perhaps even with Azúa, and naturally with Maguncio the magician, was an enemy to be respected.

He calculated that eleven days had passed since Azúa's visit on 24 November. If that was the frequency with which they intended to remind him of his past, they were going to be disappointed, because after just two more days he'd be out of Cuba and out of reach. And then nobody, not even his brother Tomás, would know where Orlando Ortega was living, nor under what name.

Turning over his fears and hopes of escape, he saw nothing of the Letelier show, the recitation before the cameras and admiration and applause of his colleagues in captivity of dozens of verses in Greek and Spanish.

Then Mariano revealed the grand finale, everybody present would get a cardboard box with a buffet supper and two cans of beer to consume in his cell.

Alberto could hardly manage a jaundiced smile at the generalized antics around the tables.

And as in the hecatombs of the Achaean warriors, that night to be remembered, 'nobody went without their fair share'.

But Alberto Ríos refused his.

Maguncio the magician's trick had taken his appetite away.

# 34 scent of a dog

Alberto tossed restlessly into the early hours. He didn't get to sleep till five o'clock.

When he woke up at 7.15, he felt ravenous.

Unusual. He generally woke up not feeling hungry. But a lot of meat one day called for more the next, especially as he'd not eaten supper.

He rushed to get to the kitchen before 7.30, when they stopped serving breakfast.

He got his tray at the window and headed into the dining room. He walked head down, self-engrossed, looking as off-putting as ever, in order to deter any attempted approaches. No doubt the party was the talk of the prison, and he wanted to ensure that nobody accosted him in this respect.

By himself, in a far corner, his back to the room, he rapidly downed his breakfast and returned to his cell to get the balls so he could practice alone on the *frontón* court. He picked up his pass in the office and walked down the four floors.

The clear sky and lack of wind soothed him.

And he began to hit the ball furiously around the empty court, till sweat streamed down.

At nine he went back to the fourth floor, exhausted and out of breath. He washed himself with the water he'd collected in his bucket and stretched out to think about the only thing he was capable of thinking about.

Who was sending him those messages? Could it be only one guy? A subversive who'd survived? The relative of somebody who'd bought it? The brother or son of someone disappeared?

Could it be several people? Was it the same people who twice tried to kill him in Montevideo?

How had they come across Bini?

What revenge were they planning?

How'd they tracked him down?

Had his brother Tomás said too much? Or could it have been Soria El Negro?

Tomasito and El Negro were the only two people in the world aware of his imposture.

Perhaps it was some bolshie or Montonero who'd infiltrated the Argentine Foreign Office or police; but he could know only that Alberto Ríos was not Alberto Ríos. If Soria or his brother hadn't sold out, nobody could know that Alberto was Orlando Ortega's false identity.

And while he was rambling, he heard the Judas-hole to his cell open and the guard announce: 'Alberto Ríos, you've got a visitor in administration.'

Alberto got up and went to the office

'Your consul's waiting for you,' an officer told him. 'Here's your pass.'

Alberto walked to the cubicle, and, indeed, behind the glass, as usual, was his consul come for a short visit.

He passed beneath the glass a list of the things he'd brought him that Texinal had sent, and which he'd just handed over at the parcel room for checking.

The consul smiled as he listened to the summary description

Alberto gave him of the party; and as he was departing, he said he would be leaving something for another compatriot in reception.

'And I've got a surprise,' he announced as he stood up. 'Bianchi came with me and is very grateful and wants to meet you, and do anything to help you, in fact...'

'Who's this Bianchi?'

'Bianchi,' his consul repeated, 'the guy who asked for the *bifes*...He came with me and I already got him a pass from the office...'

'Oh, of course, I'm really delighted...'

'He's waiting for me to leave so he can come in....'

'Yes, wonderful, tell him to come in...'

What a windbag that consul was!

But he couldn't insult him. This Bianchi man had shown he had style by sending him that box of cigars and vintage whisky, as thanks for the *bifes de chorizo*.

As he saw him coming in, he stood up, and from behind the glass, smiling politely, invited him to take a seat.

'Thanks for coming to visit, Señor Bianchi, sit down, pleased to meet you.'

'The pleasure's mine. You can't imagine how I'm feeling.'

'You don't say!' Alberto smiled, feigning alarm. 'You like visiting prisons?'

'When it's to see a compatriot, of course...'

After hearing that, he decided the fellow was an idiot or a hypocrite, and was surely after something. Business with Texinal? More Argentine meat? What the fuck did he want?

'I'm glad of your support,' said Alberto.

'I'm so pleased to meet you again after...' Aldo started to calculate '...twenty-two years.'

As soon as Bianchi said 'meet you again', Alberto felt on the defensive. And mention of twenty-two years wiped his smile away. The fellow was referring to 1977 when, yes, Alberto was living in Buenos Aires. Who the hell was he?

'I don't understand...' said Alberto, exaggerating his surprise and staring at him.

'Don't you remember me?'

Alberto knitted his brows and narrowed his stare. Let him be an old Argentine soldier, not a prisoner.

When he saw himself being examined like that, Aldo almost dropped his friendly smile and put on his ogre's face; or looked at him from afar and posed in profile to jog his memory; or spun round like a top, Fred Astaire-style. Or almost left straight away. What the shit was he doing there, wallowing morbidly in the delights of looking that bastard in the face?

'No, I really don't remember you,' replied Alberto, and he looked at him again, genuinely intrigued; but neither his name nor his face meant anything to him.

'Make an effort; my name is Aldo Bianchi.'

There were so many Aldos and Bianchis in Argentina...

And he didn't feel afraid. How strange! In that situation, he should. But he kept calm.

'OK, where was it you met me?'

Aldo kept smiling and staring. 'On the corner of Lavalle and Talcahuano.'

'Lavalle and Talcahuano?' repeated Alberto. 'I'm afraid that doesn't ring any bells either...'

'Come on, Orlando, make an effort: take a good look.'

By now Aldo wasn't reproaching himself for his playing sadistically with his victim. He accepted that was his intention, and nothing else. And he was enjoying what he was just about to say. Yes, enjoyment, pleasure, no stupid guilt trips. And *chao*. It was what he wanted, and why not?

When he heard himself being called Orlando, strange to relate, his blood didn't turn cold. His pulse didn't quicken, nor did he blanch.

He just stared and stared at Bianchi.

He realized that he was prepared; for years he'd been

expecting the day when exactly this would happen. Right. That someone would suddenly emerge threateningly from his past.

He'd got it now. The man in front of him bribed Bini, Jaén and the chambermaid. Sent messages via Azúa and the magician. It was *him*. And he'd come to settle accounts.

He couldn't identify him, didn't know who he was; but it was *him*.

He experienced two seconds of cold resignation, which the imminent danger had brought on before.

It was a breakdown in his nervous system, a halt in his emotional current deactivating his red lights. The machinery of his brain stopped to recharge before engaging in the difficult task of reorganizing his panic and rage, and sketching in a route to safety.

What did Bianchi's visit mean? Could he have come to denounce him?

He'd clearly not let on to the consul, who'd introduced him a few minutes ago, as good tempered and friendly as ever.

Was he planning to divulge his past? Would he do it today? Would Mariano find out? The rest of the prisoners? The whole of Cuba?

Would Mariano isolate him? Would he stop his days out?

Could Bianchi know he got days out? Could he know his next one was in forty-eight hours' time?

Aldo stared back at him for three seconds, and now his lips wore no smile.

'We met on Lavalle and Talcahuano, but we had regular contact in the Navy Engineering School. We would see each other every day.'

'Were you in the armed forces?' He let slip the foolish question.

'No, Orlando Ortega, you were the one in uniform…Stir your memory, *che*.'

Orlando instinctively began to articulate a gesture of shocked denial, but prevented himself in time from committing an 'overflow'.

*De abundantia cordis os loquitor.* He speaketh from the bottom of his heart. Every qualified interrogator knows this saying. Knows it and learns to make the most of it. A prisoner who's faced with clear evidence, who kicks out against it, lies and denies the undeniable, commits an 'overflow', a blind defence mechanism that places the interrogator in a position to denigrate him and destroy his morale; with the result that he manages to extract a more complete and trustworthy confession.

Orlando opted to look at the floor and keep quiet. From that moment he would react only to one end: he'd strive at all costs to keep Bianchi calm and not rush him into denouncing him today or tomorrow. If he could get to his real identity, there'd be a greater chance of dialogue and of reading his game plan. Immediately, rather than denounce him, Bianchi wanted to play at cat and mouse. In that case, he'd immediately pretend to be very scared and anxious and would try to follow his drift, to amuse him. Or perhaps it would be better to pretend he'd repented, that he was tormented by religious remorse; make him understand he intended killing himself because he couldn't stand the weight of his guilty conscience; or tell him of his decision to join a monastic order, like the man who dropped the bomb on Hiroshima. Perhaps Bianchi was looking for the grave of a disappeared. Or the name of another persuader. Perhaps he needed him alive, and was prepared to negotiate. For the moment, he needed to extract information. It was vital to find out Bianchi's immediate intentions. Did he have other accomplices in Cuba, apart from Bini? Had he also bought off Azúa?

Aldo saw him look down and took a piece of paper from his shirt pocket. He unfolded it and stuck it up against the glass, then tapped twice to get Orlando to look up and read.

It was the photocopy of a Uruguayan ID card, for one Orlando Ortega Ortiz, with a ten-year-old photo and his fingerprints.

Fuck, he was caught. If he wanted to escape, Mariano mustn't see that photocopy in the next forty-eight hours. Otherwise they'd compare those fingerprints with the ones in the ID office and would simply look and see they were the same. It would mean Mariano would authorize no more day passes, and that he wouldn't be able to escape in his yacht. It also meant that because of the crime of entering the country with a false identity, his sentence would be increased; and that this Bianchi, and his accomplices, because he no doubt had them, would let the rest of the prisoners know about his past. That would force Mariano to isolate him to stop them from killing him. Orlando Ortega Ortiz knew only too well that matricides, rapists and murderers of children, police stooges and torturers survived in no prison anywhere in the world. And that total isolation would be the death of him…

He was surprised he was so calm, and heard his own response: 'And who are you?'

'My name is Aldo Gelasio Bianchi, but you used to call me the Dog in the EMA…'

It all came back to Alberto; yes, of course, Gelasio *Felacio* the Dog.

Fuck, fucking fuck, what bad luck…! He'd made him run on all fours, made him bark, and lick his boots clean. And even fucked him.

'…you did horrible things to me, remember? You killed my girlfriend, Teresa Villavicencico… You ordered her to be put on that machine that sucked out her entrails.'

Of course he remembered. And behind the smoke of the Camel cigarette that Bianchi lit up, Alberto remembered other columns of smoke, emerging in the distance, like the branches of a bramble, from a huge tip in Avellaneda, smoke concealing the sun in a cold sky, beyond the barbed wire of the trenched field where they finished off and buried the people they'd done to death in the Engineering School; on his orders, his students had gang-banged her, and she'd then died of an electric shock, because Soria El Negro overdid the electric prod, and he remembered her being thrown into the grave with the others; but he'd kept Bianchi, who was into nothing subversive, inside for a time, before finally caning him for a heap of dosh and then letting him out…

'You used to call me Felacio the Dog, and made me lick your shoes clean; the very shoes you'd stolen from me when you put me inside. Remember?'

Yes, Alberto remembered. They were very soft leather casuals. He liked them as soon as he saw them and they were a perfect fit. Fitted like a glove. And, of course, Bianchi knew they wore the same size and had used that to fix him with those Florsheims.

'I was just following orders, for heaven's sake; I sincerely thought you were a dangerous plague, and they ordered us to eliminate you or destroy your morale…'

'Don't try it on, Orlando, you liked seeing us suffer… You had a good time, and in my case you knew very well I wasn't plotting anything… You put me inside because I kicked you in the balls. And you killed me and you tortured me like a subversive, and I had to give you a fortune so I wasn't killed. You left me without a cent, Orlando Ortega…'

Yes. That was how it had been. First he'd fucked him in front of the others. Then he'd organized the famous 'derby of pansy dogs' – they'd forced Bianchi and the other prisoners to run naked on all fours, and all the officers in his group laid serious bets like at an English dog track; and when his money was at stake and the Felacio dog wasn't winning, he kicked the hell out of him till he cried. Fuck, why did it have to be that guy who tracked him down in Cuba? What bad luck… It would be difficult to convince this fellow that he'd repented.

'What I never understood is why you haven't killed me…'

'We took shots at you twice in Montevideo…'

'Why didn't you do it here when you had me on a plate?'

'It would have been a waste to have just shot you. At first I thought of kidnapping and torturing you, but I realized it was beyond me. And then I thought of something better. Look, just read this. It's a present from me.'

Aldo walked some four metres to the window, from which a uniformed guard was watching them, and put the paper in the turning device. The guard picked it up on the other side, examined it on both sides to make sure a razor blade wasn't stuck to it, skimmed over the text, and with a flick turned it on to Alberto, who got up to collect it.

It was a flysheet that had appeared in *Brecha*, a left-wing Uruguayan newspaper:

A REQUEST FOR THE EXTRADITION TO
SPAIN OF MAJOR ORLANDO ORTEGA
Accused of crimes against humanity

This newspaper has it on very good authority that two citizens with Spanish nationality, previously resident in Argentina and Uruguay, formerly left-wing militants in both countries, have contracted a famous Madrid lawyer to petition the Spanish parliament for the extradition and subsequent trial of Major Ortega, now hiding under a false identity in a country in Latin America.

The two petitioners, who prefer not to reveal their names yet for strategic reasons, state they were direct victims of the tortures that in the sixties and seventies the sadly famous Captain Horror used to inflict, in the dungeons at the Cilindro building and the Navy Engineering School; and both have in their possession official documents and various statements in support of their accusation, and likewise enjoy the total support of various international and River Plate organizations, in defence of human rights.

Major Ortega already got scent of this at the end of 1997, and disappeared from his home in Montevideo without leaving a trace; but according to our source, in whom we have complete confidence, Major Ortega has been residing ever since in a Latin American capital city, the name of which we cannot reveal. He was planning to live there and enjoy the fruits of his considerable, fraudulently accrued fortune, something he'd been doing until very recently; because the curious aspect of the case is that Major Ortega was arrested on a minor charge (of complete insignificance compared with ones he used to commit on a daily basis), which will keep him in jail until the middle of 2001, and, of course, stop him from disappearing again or putting himself out of reach of justice.

Our newspaper will shortly confirm this sensational, welcome news, and will then take the opportunity to detail everything that our informants are now keeping under wraps.

Orlando finished reading the flysheet, gestured contemptuously and put it to one side.

'Did you visit just to bring me this?' And he directed his first look of defiance at Aldo. 'Sooner or later, they'd have informed me. I suppose you've other reasons for coming...'

'Other reasons?' Aldo smiled again. 'Perhaps. Maybe I couldn't resist seeing the look on your face when I tell you that the second article they mention will be published in Montevideo on the eighth. And I wanted to see you here now, because very shortly you'll be in a high-security cell, isolated from the other prisoners; and under a regime that will only allow you visits from your lawyer, consul or a relative.'

And he stared at him smiling sardonically.

Orlando suppressed his feeling of terror. He felt his ears were on fire. But he kept calm. He repeated to himself that he wouldn't give up hope till the eighth.

'And as they say in what you just read,' Aldo continued, 'they will report you as living here under the false identity of Alberto Ríos; and I can also reveal that on Tuesday morning the Spanish lawyer mentioned will be coming to present his request for your extradition…'

Orlando remembered how the flights from Spain always land at night. Sparks of hope still glinted.

'Well, you happy with what you see on my face?'

'I confess you're a little disappointing. I'd have liked you to have vomited from fright. But you probably don't know what to expect…'

'Yes, death awaits me at my own hands. I've always known that. And by the way, could you grant me a favour?'

Aldo went on the defensive. 'That depends.'

'How did you find out I got put inside?'

'My sense of smell…A dog's never lets him down. Anything else?'

'Why didn't you kidnap me? What did you get out of the palaver over the dead cyclist?'

'It's a long story. I told you I didn't feel able to torture you…And when I still didn't know what to do with you, Bini and I knocked the cyclist over; and it was then I had the idea of making you pick up your bill…'

'A piddling revenge…I'm not suffering at all in here.'

'My revenge isn't the fact you are inside. Two years won't pay for a single fingernail you extracted…My revenge is for you to get a long sentence, and I'll make sure that in every prison the inmates know who you are, so you have to live in isolation, as will happen here.'

'Yes, I'd imagined something of the sort.'

'And as the laws of Cuba only kick in against crimes committed on its territory or against its citizens, I wasted almost three months in Montevideo and Argentina trying to find out if you'd tortured or disappeared any citizen from this island.'

'No, I didn't see to any.'

Aldo recalled how Spanish whores use the euphemism 'to

see to' when referring to their work with their customers. Curious how Uruguayan torturers also used it to talk about their prey.

'I knew setting up an international campaign and an extradition request wouldn't be easy. I had to speak to lots of people, turn over all kinds of history, look for your victims, and persuade them to act without fear of reprisal. And as soon as I unleashed the hunt, the world police mafia would find out; that would put you on your guard and you'd escape me in Cuba as you did in Uruguay. On the other hand, banged up here for two years, you'd give me time to get things moving, and no danger you'd get away again...'

'Yes, I understand.' As if it didn't relate to him. 'A good plan. Congratulations.'

'Thank you.'

'And are you sure the Cubans will extradite me?'

'No doubt about it; I've already sounded them out. They don't like torturers.'

Orlando smiled half indulgently, like someone who understands and forgives this dislike of Cubans.

'Well, well. And while we're at it,' he blurted out, giving him a glassy look, the first Aldo thought appropriate from a sadist, 'aren't you scared the Uruguayan or Argentine police mafia won't want to get even with you? They might think you'd develop a taste for dusting down old cases, and decide to do you in so you can't stir any more.'

'Yes, it has crossed my mind, but I'm not scared.' He stood up. He was beginning to feel loathing. Curious it had taken so long.

According to Aldo, the Madrid lawyer would arrive on Tuesday night; he might present his request on Wednesday morning, the very day his leave began. It was to be supposed that the lawyer wouldn't act before nine o'clock. The news would spread like wildfire and Mariano would be one of the first to find out. But with a little bit of luck, the bureaucracy at the Ministry of Justice, or Foreign Affairs, or whatever Cuban body received the declaration, would delay in communicating it; or if the lawyer showed up with his papers long after nine or hopefully in the afternoon; and if the weather came good, and Nene as well, Orlando by this time could be in the Yucatan Channel, enjoying the fresh air miles away from the Cuban coast. During the night or the morning of the ninth, he'd get to within some thousand metres of the Cancun coastline; would abandon the *Chevalier*, and swim in his wet suit to the beach, where he'd be just one more winter tourist. He'd just take his underwater fishing equipment so he could conceal his diskettes with the material for the book, Alberto Ríos's passport and his credit cards.

And within a few hours, Alberto Ríos and Orlando Ortega would both disappear for ever among the twenty million inhabitants of Mexico City. And a couple of days later, he would buy himself a new name and passport, and that would be an end to it.

He watched Bianchi stand, give him one last, almost pitying smile, and then turn round to walk to the exit.

Nonetheless, Alberto hadn't given up hope.

Nor that Aldo Bianchi and Sabina López Angelbello might soon be among the plankton. Pizzaiolo would deal with them, and perhaps before too long.

# 35 god, the authorities and the weather

On 8 December, according to the report the night before on television, weather conditions were going to be excellent: 'A clear sky over the whole of the island; an average temperature of twenty-four degrees in the western provinces; a calm sea, no dangers for smaller vessels.' Couldn't be better!

Nevertheless, Orlando Ortega endured a sleepless night. Two dangers threatened: first, that as a result of some move outside the official channels, the prison authorities had already been informed of the Spanish lawyer's arrival in Cuba with his extradition request; second, that Aldo Bianchi might discover that on 8 December he had a pass out and would be in the city with full freedom of movement.

In the first instance, for security reasons, the director of the Combined would veto Mariano's issuing of more passes to inmate Alberto Ríos; particularly as, by granting them, Mariano was violating a regulation, as he'd already explained. And if such an irregularity got as far as the general prison authorities, the shit from the fan would also hit the colonel, for having turned a blind eye.

And they wouldn't just withdraw Alberto Ríos's pass for that day, but every pass, even those he had a legal right to later on, until he could refute the irrefutable accusation about his false identity.

And in the second instance, Bianchi would imagine that the fake Alberto Ríos, now aware his enemies were plotting to put him behind bars in a solitary security cell for the rest of his days, would try to escape from Cuba at any cost; and naturally, to prevent that, Bianchi would alert Mariano, and he'd withdraw his passes. Perhaps he'd already called him that very night. And Mariano would cancel his leave. He'd do it as a basic precaution, even if from the onset he didn't believe Alberto Ríos was a fierce wolf in sheep's clothing, as Bianchi would claim.

By 6 a.m. he'd exhausted his ability to think. He shut his eyes, but couldn't sleep; his ideas were still going round, tied to a cruel wheel.

If Bianchi and his people were intending to mount a big international outcry, like over Pinochet, it wouldn't be at all surprising if the lawyer and even Aldo Bianchi had given an interview to the Cuban press before they made the formal request for extradition.

Or perhaps what the Uruguayan newspaper had published on the eighth in the morning had already been broadcast on international TV channels, or via the Internet. And the spectacular, juicy, paradoxical morsel of gossip about the famous Uruguayan torturer, a prison inmate into the bargain, hiding in Cuba under a false identity, would spark off endless commentaries. Radio Jeta, Radio Bemba or Boca – radios with lots of Lip and Mouth – would immediately inform their listeners in the Combined, and they included Mariano.

Moreover, Bianchi may have made some comment to the consul when they drove back to Havana together. Given they were such friends, and with the official announcement imminent in forty-eight hours' time, it was very possible Bianchi may have broken the news. After all, it closely involved the consul. He'd not realized the wool had been pulled over his eyes, and had been made to look a right fool.

It was difficult to believe the consul would broadcast the gossip from every street corner; but you couldn't guarantee he might not try; or decide to make fun of himself during cocktails at the embassy, relating the case of an Uruguayan prisoner who pretended to be Argentine, and how he, like an idiot, had spent several months running errands for him and visiting him in jail, out of solidarity with a fellow countryman who'd fallen on hard times.

If such were the case, the exchanges recorded by any journalist, gossipy diplomat or state security policeman could reach the Public Prosecutor's Office or the penal institutions; and once the wasps' nest was disturbed, they'd settle on the ears of the colonel or Mariano.

Fate was pursuing him from behind various parapets. Even if Bianchi kept completely mum, the consul or his secretary might ring the Texinal office just to coordinate visits to the Combined or the delivery of his supplies, as they usually did. In such an event, they might say that the previous week Señor Ríos had presented himself in person, because now, blahblahblah, he got a twenty-four-hour pass every week. And then the consul might comment on that to Bianchi; and right away Bianchi would alert the prison director to cancel all his passes. That would be fatal; as would be any contact between the consul and Mariano.

As far as Orlando knew, the diplomat hadn't spoken to Mariano that week. He even remembered how, when he was going from number 2 building to his appointments with the consul and Bianchi, he'd seen Mariano leave Administration and drive his car towards the exit. It would have been difficult for Mariano and the civil servant to see each other that day, or the day after. And even during the visit, everything seemed to indicate that the latter knew nothing of his false identity.

What would he say when he found out? And he tried to imagine him attempting to give the affair a comic twist: 'And just imagine, I felt for the poor guy, in jail because of a traffic accident, and it turns out he's a Uruguayan cop, and professor of torture…'

'A professor of cosh and prod…', and he remembered how a wit at the EMA had given him that nickname inspired by a tango called 'Cosy Pro'. Not even his own students were convinced of the scientific nature of their profession. For Christ's sake, he was a specialist in the disciplines of persuasion! And for years while he taught courses, he'd burnt the midnight oil studying, he'd attended seminars, symposia, refresher courses in Langley, in the Panama Canal Zone, in Colorado, in Devil's Horn, so he was up to speed with the latest technology.

Some softies were horrified, but war had always existed. Why so much fuss! Victory was not won only with arms but with information, and one of the best sources of info was an enemy in captivity when subjected to various techniques of intimidation. 'Twas ever thus.

At a quarter to seven, after an hour with his eyes shut, he finally got some rest. He'd surely got big bags under his eyes; those undesirable little black wrinkles under his eyelids.

Nevertheless, he felt calmer, like a soldier when the day to join battle finally comes.

At the time, the small ventilation hole in the ceiling through which daylight entered served as an escape hole for the pessimistic spirits he'd built up during the night.

At seven sharp he heard the usual sounds of the guards changing. It was one hour to the time when he could leave. And though the meeting with Mariano was at ten minutes to eight in his office, he calculated that he could stay in his cell for another quarter of an hour. At any rate he wouldn't go for breakfast. He had time on his hands. And was worried about meeting up with Mariano. From just looking at him and observing his attitude when he said hello, Orlando would know whether a problem existed or not. And a childish feeling of cowardice kept him in his cell. He wanted to defer the encounter with Mariano for as long as possible.

Ten minutes more. Yes, he'd wait ten minutes before he went out. And he forced himself to think of the positive aspects of his plan.

He imagined his escape working perfectly, crossing the Yucatan Channel and swimming to the coast of Mexico. Good. What would he do once he'd landed?

Naturally, the Cuban police and Interpol would alert the Mexicans about this prisoner on the run. He should prioritize getting another false identity, to travel the world. He also had friends in Mexico. And money would make it easy for him to get documents.

Good. Given he had the necessary papers, what should he do next?

He could go to Uruguay. They couldn't extradite him from his own country. The law protected him. A national plebiscite protected him. All the military active during the years of the dictatorship, persuaders included, had been declared unimputable.

If he returned to Uruguay, he'd have to subject himself to an execrable routine that he'd already fled once. He'd survived two ambushes in Montevideo and wouldn't let there be a third time lucky. In Cuba, on the other hand, he'd never moved under escort, always scared and looking out for the fateful bullet. Cold, windy Uruguay, and its mere three months of sailing and beach season no longer interested him.

Money would enable him to find the definitive bolthole in this world. Curaçao? Jamaica? Guadeloupe? The Cayman Islands? Maracaibo? Cartagena? Veracruz?

True enough, but he'd require facial surgery and new papers if he were going to hide in a country in the tropics and live without fear. Perfect papers beyond suspicion, obtained without intermediaries who couldn't keep their mouths shut. He no longer trusted his brother or colleagues in the south. Involving Soria el Negro had been a mistake he wouldn't make a second time. From now on, he'd travel alone, like the Jackal.

As a precautionary measure he decided to have breakfast.

When he was past the main danger point, and outside waters under Cuban jurisdiction, he'd feel very hungry. And perhaps there was nothing to eat on the yacht; but it wasn't very sensible for him to eat anything right now before swimming five hundred metres.

At 7.25, when Orlando Ortega was carrying his tray to the refectory, he saw Mariano in the distance leaving his office. He seemed to be in a hurry. Mariano also saw him and stopped next to the glass window, in order to wave some papers at him. He acted as affably as ever. Before going on his way, he threw up five fingers and then three more. To confirm he was expecting him at the agreed time.

Phew! What a relief! His pass still worked. He could now be sure Mariano knew nothing. Not yet.

At 7.40 he returned to his cell to put on the civilian clothes Mariano had given him permission to keep there, in order to avoid the weekly bother of going to change in the store in building number 1.

Now wearing brown casuals, khaki trousers and a greenish shirt, he headed to the office area. Ever since they'd both been organizing Letelier's party, Mariano had ordered the guards to give him access to his office, whenever he wanted.

At 7.50, Orlando sat down on a bench in the corridor, to wait for Mariano.

At 8.05, when they left number 2 building together, there was indeed a clear sky and an early morning sun was beginning to warm the car seats.

With one hand on his plastic packet and one foot on the running board, Orlando turned round and looked over his shoulder at the sun.

'Come on, get in...What are you looking at?' Mariano harassed him.

'The sun.'

'Hell, it's not as if we've stuck you in some dismal dungeon...'

Orlando was hoping to follow the movement of the sun westwards. Throughout the afternoon, he'd keep it in front of him. The sun would guide him to his freedom. Then he'd watch it set, disappearing into the sea, or behind the Mexican horizon. The difference was, he thought, as he settled down next to Mariano, that the same sun would come up the following morning, but Orlando Ortega Ortiz would have disappeared for ever.

They passed through Post 1, and Mariano drove towards the coast.

'I called your consul yesterday afternoon, but he'd already left...'

Mariano kept a keen eye on the road and broke off when they overtook a lorry that was polluting the atmosphere. He didn't notice the sudden look of fear on Orlando's face on hearing that.

'...and I called him again today at eight thirty but he still hadn't got back.'

The fucking bastard! Just as well...

Orlando looked to his right and pretended not to be very interested.

'Why did you need him?'

'We need some medicine for Casimiro...He's got kidney problems and the doctor prescribed a drug the public health service is out of. We need to order it from outside the country...'

Casimiro was the cook from Entre Ríos. As an Argentine, he could ask for help from the consul, but Mariano thought that if he asked Alberto, it would all be that much easier.

'I've got to go to Santa Fe and the embassy's on the way... Will you come with me?'

'Just give me the name of the item and I'll order it from my office,' replied Orlando.

'All right, if you think...I'm getting rather embarrassed at all the help you're giving me...'

'But it is for a fellow countryman of mine, isn't it?'

They drove through the Havana tunnel, turned along the Malecón towards Fifth Avenue, and drove its whole length. Orlando tried to get out at the roundabout by the old Dog Derby Stadium so he could get a taxi to Atabey, but Mariano insisted on taking him to his front door.

'Hey, if you can, do sort the business for Casimiro,' he reminded him as he bade him farewell.

'Yes, of course, I won't forget.'

And he took the piece of paper on which Mariano had jotted down the medicine's name.

At 8.55 Orlando entered his house.

After twenty minutes, a taxi picked him up at his front door. He was wearing bermudas, beach sandals, T-shirt and baseball cap. In a sailor's bag, he carried his wet suit, flippers, his snorkel and goggles. He checked that he was carrying his passport, credit cards, two hundred dollars in cash and the diskettes with the material for his book.

It was all he needed.

He looked up at the sky and saw that it was clear.

He remembered a bullfighting poster from the Franco days on which a bullfight, in a provincial ring, was advertised on one condition: 'If God's willing, the Authorities aren't opposed and weather permitting'.

He looked back at the sky.

In terms of God and the weather, his flight seemed feasible. And the authorities, for the moment, weren't giving any signs of life.

Good. On with the motley.

At 9.35 Mariano got a call from the colonel while he was driving.

'Where's the Argentine?'

'I dropped him off at his place a few minutes ago.'

The colonel started shouting angrily. 'Go and get him! Get the fucking police to go as well and take him back to the Combined.'

'But...Colonel...'

'It's an order. Carry it out, you idiot,' and he hung up.

And when Mariano informed him at 9.50 that the guy had disappeared from his place, the colonel ordered him to search heaven and earth.

The Argentine was an impostor, a torturer, not even an Argentine, a fucking bastard who'd entered Cuba on false papers. And this time it was no joke mounted by Inocente. They'd just called from the Ministry of Justice to tell them of the situation. And he, Major Mariano Robles Marín, should know that he was number two on the list of assholes in Cuba. Because he, the colonel, occupied number-one spot. What got it into his head to allow Mariano to break regulations? How the fuck could he have authorized Mariano to act the angelic prison guard taking his prisoners out for rides? What excuse was the colonel going to invent when his superiors put the squeeze on his balls for giving out undue leave?

Texinal? Yes, perhaps he'd gone to their office for Casimiro's medicine but, fucking hell, weren't there any telephones in that barrio? Maybe farther on, and Mariano, driving slowly, looking at both pavements, weighing up where to call from, stopping by a mansion with an acrylic advert hanging down its façade, going in without a by your leave, demanding a telephone, yes, to make an urgent call, uptight, breathless, and a telephone directory as well, yes of course, it's my pleasure, Major, and the secretary a bit embarrassed, hesitant, and hello, and Mariano discovering that Señor Ríos had indeed been at Texinal ten minutes earlier, but had left for an appointment at the Argentine embassy, and back to the directory, dialling quickly, the consul, please, it's Major Robles, and the consul, hello, who's that, sounding reserved, as if on the defensive, and Mariano, that it was Major Robles, the warden of…and the consul, yes, yes, of course, I'm sorry, Major Mariano, naturally, yes, and the consul had just spoken to Aldo Bianchi, who desperately needed to talk to him, Bianchi?, Bianchi?, who was Aldo Bianchi? And the consul explaining he was a former victim of the torturer, who was not Alberto but Orlando Ortega, who wasn't Argentine but Uruguayan, a real bastard, yes, yes, Mariano already knew all about that, how disgusting, and the consul went on and on, a bastard who deceived everyone, and Bianchi had gone to see him in the prison two days ago and revealed to him that he'd been tortured by him, for the sole juicy pleasure of giving him advance warning in person of the declaration against him to be presented in forty-eight hours, an international hue and cry, a request for extradition, a trial in Spain, and a very worried Bianchi wanting to locate Major Robles, Alberto now a known torturer had got leave, and now the fellow could imagine the ton of bricks about to fall on his head, life imprisonment, isolation, knowing he'd never get another pass, would use that same day to make his escape, a mistake giving him passes, and Mariano was in the shithouse, what a stupid mistake, the yacht, yes, his yacht, a very serious error, and it was 10.03 a.m., he needed to speak to the Hemingway Marina immediately.

The man in charge of frontier guard post number 17 got the call at 10.12.

The authorities at the Hemingway Marina informed him

that the *Chevalier*, a yacht under the French flag, had left its jetties at 8.50. It was perhaps being used for an illegal exit. It was urgent to track it down and stop it leaving Cuban waters. It might be too late but every attempt should be made. The marina authority took responsibility for capturing and boarding the said vessel. For the immediate operation, requested by the head of penal institutions, coastguard headquarters would send them at any moment the official order, duly processed. But there was no time to waste. The yacht, which left the quay with one crew, was sailing quite legally; but as far as the marina authority was aware, the owner, the Argentine imprisoned in the Combined, hadn't been seen there. Of course, there was always the possibility he'd secretly entered the marina precinct in order to make a clandestine departure; or perhaps, according to Mariano, he'd try to board the boat at some other point on the Havana coast.

At 9.55 Alberto got out of a taxi on First Avenue and 34th Street. He walked the sixty metres to the sea, and was pleased to see there were no bathers on the wall where they usually clustered in summer.

A calm, transparent sea, no wind, a minimal, lazy swell, twenty-seven degrees in the sun, ninety-three per cent humidity, the Cuban winter was a joke. It was the ideal summer for many countries located above thirty-five degrees north, or below thirty-five degrees south. But Cubans feel the cold and foreigners don't swim off the little barrio beaches.

That coast, free of prying eyes, made things easy for him. In two minutes he had donned his wet suit, flippers and googles. Tied a red kerchief round his head pirate-style in the absence of a cap…and like a duck to water.

According to his calculations, if he swam gently, he'd cover the five hundred metres agreed with Nene in some twenty minutes. As he wore flippers, he didn't need to use his arms. He carried a harpoon in his left hand and a fishing knife in his right. He buttoned on to his right forearm a waterproof sleeve attachment, the pockets of which carried his documents, two diskettes, some money and credit cards.

It was all he needed.

And he hadn't swum a hundred metres when west–north–west presented him with the unmistakable, encouraging silhouette of his yacht the *Chevalier*, its black–fringed grey hull, its elegant, lively prow punctually furrowing the sea with good memories and greater expectations on course to its appointment.

Nene, who sailed from the Hemingway Marina at 8.50, arrived close on a level with 34th Street early on. He passed by for the first time at 9.45. He trained his telescopic sights on the beach, but saw no trace of Alberto Ríos. Ten minutes later he was back, but nothing doing.

He was rather worried, and went on till he was level with 20th Street, which he recognized by the blue building of the Ferreteros Social Club, and swung back upwater. And this time he did make out someone swimming with something red on his head. As soon as he got a good focus, he recognized it was Alberto.

What about the girl he was supposed to be bringing?

He probably couldn't find a whore who could swim. Or had agreed to pick one up at another point along the coast, where the yacht could dock.

As he helped him on board, he noted he seemed strange and nervous. And once on deck, he started looking towards the coast. He examined it inch by inch.

'Where's the hooker?'

'She refused to come at the last minute,' Orlando replied bad-temperedly. 'She can go to hell! Point the prow towards the *beril*, I want to dive around there. I'm really crazy to see the platform seascape again.'

The *beril*, a Cuban fishermen's name for the edge of the sea platform surrounding the island, is a nautical mile away, and the yacht would get there in a few minutes.

When Nene calculated they were near the sharpest decline, he reduced their speed to a minimum and asked him: 'Is this where you want to dive?'

Orlando hadn't taken his wet suit off.

That was normal, if he intended to swim in the cold waters of the *beril*. Orlando Ortega didn't reply; he opened one of the pockets on his forearm and extracted a transparent nylon bag, tied round with a thread. He undid the knot and extracted some hundred-dollar bills.

'I agreed to give you a hundred dollars every Wednesday, right?'

Nene nodded, intrigued, as Orlando counted out the bills.

'…six, seven, eight, nine….And a thousand.'

He put them back in the bag and handed it to Nene, who still had a hand on the wheel, and turned to point his binoculars first south-east, and then south-west.

'I don't understand…' Nene stammered, looking at the dollar bills through the nylon.

'What is it you don't understand, Nene?'

'The thousand…?'

'Do you know why I'm giving you all this?'

Nene shook his head, nonplussed.

'Because of the fright I'm about to give you now,' and he unsheathed the knife.

Nene gave him a terrified look.

'Take your shirt off.'

Nene obeyed. Without letting go of the bag of money he took off his shirt and stood there in bermudas and slippers, his torso naked.

'Dive into the sea.'

'Here…?' Nene, frightened, looked towards the coast.

'That's why I'm paying you a thousand, Nene. Go on, dive.'

Nene understood. Alberto was going to escape from Cuba and prison.

He'd swum fifteen hundred metres to the coast lots of times, but never unarmed.

'Give me the harpoon.'

'No, I need it. Go on, dive, for hell's sake.'

What could he do?

Nothing, only what the mad bastard ordered him to do.

And when they asked him? And if they accused him of being an accomplice?

No problem, he'd tell the truth…Not the whole truth, naturally. He wouldn't mention the dollars.

It never once entered his head to resist.

Why? It would be absurd. Besides, Alberto was a *karateka*, bigger than he was, and armed…

He bit on the bag determinedly and jumped into the sea.

They didn't bid farewell to each other.

There were no tender or harsh words. No gratitude or reproaches. Each looking after himself. Each had coincidentally helped the other.

As he flailed around, he heard the din of the engines gathering speed again. The yacht began to move into the distance. From the noise, Nene reckoned it would soon hit top speed. A pity about the petrol he'd not charged him for. Some Italians had given him half a tank and he thought he'd cover that with Paredes. Some eight hundred dollars all in all. But, of course, he wasn't going to mention that after he'd given him a thousand.

While he flailed on, he didn't know whether to feel happy or regret the loss of his main source of income.

On the one hand, he'd never have to put up with the Argentine again. Although he'd behaved better towards the end and he accepted that he was generous with the bucks, he was one hell of a bastard.

Yes, he cursed him; but was happy with the loot he'd collected.

Of the three thousand he'd got the week before, half had already gone on cement, wood, belaying pins, flagstones, tiles and paint. The house would be like new. He intended to use the rest to repair his boat engine and the woodwork on the prow. And when he was able to fish again, he'd at least make sure the kids got their grub and would always have something left to sell under the counter. And now with this extra thousand he'd buy the air-conditioning his wife wanted.

He flailed on more enthusiastically.

Now the scare and surprise were gone, he had no regrets.

On the contrary, he'd drink a bottle of vintage rum tonight. He'd celebrate getting rid of the Argentine and his humiliations. The past was water under the bridge. And while he swam, he told himself it wasn't from lack of courage that he'd tolerated that bastard; it was to make sure there was grub and clothes for the kids and wife, so the roof didn't collapse on them.

What any good father would have done.

At that moment, a hum approaching from the west, and as he turned, fuck, the coastguard launch!

It was steaming along at full pelt after the *Chevalier*, which still hadn't disappeared over the horizon.

Would they catch him?

Of course, the fellow was getting out of nick. That was why he was looking so scared in every direction. And the fact is he can't escape. You don't play with an armoured launch…

Fuck, and what will happen when they ask about you?

Alberto will say he forced you to jump…

And when they catch up with you, what are you going to do with the dollars? You won't let them catch you like a dumbo clenching the bag between your teeth.

He thought of a quick solution and went to it straight away.

He undid the string, rolled the bills up and placed the wad at the bottom of the bag; manipulated the spare nylon until he'd tied it tight with a big knot. Then, inside his bermudas, tied the end of the string to the loose material of his jockstrap;

and tied the other end to the bag, and twisted it twice under the nylon knot.

It dangled there like a third testicle.

It couldn't fall from there.

And nobody would think of that hiding-place, except someone who knew his crotch well, and noticed an increase in his genital area.

The only thing still frightening him was that Alberto might say he'd paid him four thousand dollars to help him escape from Cuba. In that case, he'd admit to the payment, but say it was just to allow women on board.

And he kept thinking that, in the worst-case scenario, the balance of his relationship with Alberto Ríos still left him favourably in the black.

When the frontier police launch appeared to his left, Orlando was still three miles inside Cuban waters.

When he spotted them in the distance, it was only a couple of gauzy wings; a white, spectacularly symmetrical V, with a gleaming, frolicking dish in the middle.

The December sun created mirages on the very calm, quicksilver sea. Then, when he heard the hum, he knew it was the moment of truth. The symmetry was advancing on him. The mirage, now visible at its centre, was a reality full of content: a speed launch, equipped with multiple weaponry. He stared and stared. He knew resistance was futile. That fatal launch represented his return to the Combined, extradition to Spain and life imprisonment.

Such bad luck.

The authorities had decided against any bull running that day.

# 36 memory

When he was back in his cell, the guard informed him that for the moment he had to stay there. He found it almost bare. Orders from the top: no more computer, radio, or extra food and drink.

They handed him a list of what they'd taken to the store and he signed on the dotted line. They left him only his clothes, a few books and writing materials.

He stayed quite calm for two days.

The die was cast.

He wasn't sure what might happen. Nothing good, that was for sure. Given the extent of the hue-and-cry Bianchi was proposing, the news would spread into every corner. Everybody in the Combined would know. To protect him from the other prisoners, the authorities would be forced to isolate him. Proof of that was that they no longer allowed him to go to the yard or leisure area. Not even the dining room. The guard brought him his food on a tray four times a day.

It was useless trying to conjecture. He fell into a state of apathy, into a strange absence of despair. It wasn't worth bothering to think through the detail. It was a waste of time trying to guess his future. At the moment he felt sleepy. Whenever.

On the morning of his third day like that, Mariano had him brought to his office. There were threatening nudges, furtive looks and whispers from the prisoners who were leaning against the wall waiting for lunch. It was the first time he'd walked along that corridor escorted by two policemen.

Not one prisoner spoke to him.

They watched him walk by in silence.

He walked down that same corridor, his eyes on the ground as usual, but next to the grille leading to the administrative area, he saw Letelier, who always smiled his way and made some friendly remark; but this time, the Chilean looked at him as if he were a stranger, with a deliberate coldness.

His encounter with Mariano in his office was less uncomfortable than he'd expected.

Mariano was bent over his desk, jotting something down. When he saw him come in, he neither greeted him nor offered him a seat. He handed him a document.

The thirty-four-page document, published in Buenos Aires, was a CV for Orlando Ortega Ortiz, with photos from the sixties, and a detailed account of his theorizing and practising of torture in different countries of Latin America. From what he could see as he skimmed it, it contained statements from his victims and diagrams of some of the tortures he'd organized.

'This arrived a couple of days ago and I think half the world has read it...' commented Mariano.

'Naturally.' Orlando smiled. 'And for reasons of security, you'll have to put me in solitary...'

'Yes, until you get a fresh trial...'

'And will Cuba agree to the request for extradition?'

'Most certainly; but you'll first have to see out your sentence here, plus whatever's added for the other things...'

'What might they be?'

'Falsifying public documents, illegally entering the country, and attempted escape.'

'And how long will I get for that?'

'I don't know; speak to your lawyer. I called you to sign this, if you're in agreement,' and he handed him a page of writing.

To avoid lots of comings and goings and more hearings, given the clear proof that existed, the public prosecutor's office enquired whether he was prepared to admit his guilt in relation to the crimes of forgery and illegal entry into the country. If so, they could make an immediate start on the trial for attempted escape.

'No, I won't sign this without consulting my lawyer.'

'Very well,' said Mariano, and turned round to the policeman who'd brought him there. 'Take him away. He's been allocated CD 440.'

When he heard that number, Orlando could no longer control the expression on his face. In his struggle to avoid surrendering to despair, he'd nurtured a secret hope that he'd be moved to another prison where nobody knew him. He knew that the CD section comprised the 'disciplinary cells', used not only to protect certain prisoners, but to contain the most dangerous elements, who stayed there in total isolation.

When Mariano saw his cheeks suddenly collapse, he remembered Mortimer, a thirty-year-old English suicide victim he'd been fond of.

Mortimer had slashed his veins in his disciplinary cell. Mariano regretted the death of that good man, who, like so many prisoners, had travelled a thorny path from orphan child, delinquent adolescent, violent adult, gunman, inmate, to murderer of another inmate, and a thirty-year sentence.

Mariano blamed himself for that suicide he felt so intensely. He reproached himself for not having known how to handle Mortimer's crises and aggression. But if Alberto killed himself, his only regret would be the extra suicide they'd add to his professional record. But Orlando Ortega, the individual depicted in that gloomy document and the indictment presented by the Spanish lawyer inspired only a wish to forget him as soon as possible, a wish that one had never known him at all.

When the guard grabbed his elbow to take him away, Alberto started to say: 'Anyway, I'd like to thank you for what you did for me…'

Mariano didn't need to speak to shut him up. His look cut him dead; and sustaining its severity, he focused on the guard and made a gesture like Pope Wojtyla at his absolutions, which really meant: 'Get him out of my sight. Take him away, for hell's sake.'

On his third day of solitary, his head was bursting. He couldn't sleep. Couldn't read. Couldn't concentrate.

He was allowed out of his cell only between 10.30 and 11.15 to take the sun. They took him handcuffed, sat him on a bench and tied one foot to a continuous metal bar. They placed six other prisoners in similar conditions but at a safe distance. One of them was clearly Latin American and spoke to himself all the time, making the occasional but very distinct gesture. A very young black gringo, wearing a woollen hat, swung from fits to a schizophrenic rap Orlando couldn't understand. Maybe he was improvising. He must be in a nearby cell, because Orlando could hear from his own some of the high notes that sounded like an engine in pain.

The gang include one who seemed really contrite and totally resigned. A fair-haired lanky lad also caught his attention, one he recognized as having arrived in the same lorry with him and Gardelion. The guy now smiled at him lasciviously and threateningly. Alberto recalled his stay in Lima, when he'd dress up as a rich young thing and swagger effeminately into stinking bars, under the bridge, by the Rimac, and bash up layabouts. If anyone looked at him like that blondie, he'd batter him to pulp. He remembered a *cholo* Indian who started smiling at him like that and making obscene gestures. He kicked his face to pieces till he'd erased all his features. And he did it without any real rage, just for practice and to feel good. And also because when he'd bruised someone, he banged *chola* Indians more pleasurably.

When he'd done a week of solitary, the new lawyer came to see him. They took him handcuffed to a small room inside the high-security wing. The lawyer advised him to sign the declaration of guilt for using forged documentation and making an illegal entry into the country. Orlando agreed.

All he wanted to find out from that lawyer was how much they'd add to his present sentence and what the likelihood was that the Cuban government would accede to the extradition request.

He could get a further four years for the three new crimes; together with the year and a half left of his current sentence, he'd got five and half years left in Cuba.

'And in what conditions?'

'The same as now.'

'And could I be moved?'

'Impossible; this is the only prison in the whole country where foreigners are kept.'

The following day he signed the papers for the public prosecutor's office and started to think about the most practical way to put an end to it all. He opted to tear a sheet up and weave his own rope. He calculated he could take a leap from the little lavatory wall with a rope tied to the ventilation vents in the ceiling.

The small grille was about two hundred and fifty centimetres from the ground; and he measured one hundred and sixty to his Adam's apple. So he had ninety centimetres in which to hang himself. If he wanted his body to hang some thirty centimetres from the ground, he'd need only sixty centimetres of rope, to which he should add fifteen to allow for tying it to the ceiling and thirty-five for the strangling device, slip knot included.

Yes. He'd need to weave a one-hundred-and-ten-centimetre-long rope. That was easy. The sheets provided were two metres by one and a half. He calculated that from each sheet he could get fifteen strips ten centimetres wide and two metres long; that would give him five twists just over a metre long. If that weren't enough, he'd need only to tie two of these twists together to obtain the length he needed. In order to hang himself, he'd climb on the little wall of modesty. In his case, it would be the little wall of death, ha ha ha, and weep behind the screen.

If he stretched out his arm, he could reach up two hundred and thirty-five centimetres, which, with the seventy-five of the wall, would make it easy to tie the rope to the ceiling. Then he'd put the rope round his neck, and tie his wrists with one of the five twists he'd prepared beforehand. He'd jump up as high as possible in order to break his neck. That way he'd fall more heavily.

Life's a waste of time, he hummed.

He liked the songs of Pablo Milanés. They always said such intelligent things.

The idea of hanging himself had come to him on Thursday. He turned it over for a couple more days, but couldn't think of anything more feasible and sure. He'd have preferred to bleed to death, but how? He couldn't sharpen the end of a spoon in order to slash his wrists. The guard brought him his food on a plastic tray, with just one very blunt, brittle plastic spoon that they always took back at the end of the meal.

He also thought of hitting himself with a lethal karate chop, but he doubted it would work.

On Saturday afternoon he came to a decision. He'd weave his twists that night and hang himself in the early hours of Sunday.

When the guard took the dinner things away, he expressed his surprise that the prisoner hadn't eaten anything.

'Anything wrong?'

'I'm tired of eating beans and hake.'

The man shrugged his shoulders, picked the tray up, the cardboard cup, the plastic spoon, and left without replying.

Orlando thought it was worth killing himself so as not to have to eat any more of that bilge. He remembered, nevertheless, that when he was still living as an optimist in south wing and giving himself survival psychotherapy, he quite liked the beans and hake.

And when the man departed, he felt at peace again.

Human life was a waste of time. And so was his.

Tens of millions died in the Second World War. As they did building the Great Wall of China, and the pyramids of Egypt... And when the plague was doing its worst in the Middle Ages.

At 5.10, one minute before jumping from his little wall of death, when he was tying his hands behind his back, the rope already round his neck, he evoked yet again the image of his sister Marujita, on all fours, and of his father possessing her in his dressing room. He was fifteen at the time and Marujita was sixteen.

And he wondered yet again whether Captain Horror was spawned from the genes of that turbulent father, or from the hatred he felt against the world, from that moment when he saw them together, or from his relief after he'd hacked them to death, days after, in the small family chapel.

They found him at 7.15. His feet hung a mere ten centimetres from the ground.

# Epilogue

# 37 brum, brum, brummmmmmm

'The Forum and Coliseum? Those piles of stone? No, I don't like them...'

'And what did you like most about Rome?'

'The racing cars, the money-making machines, human rights...'

'What an idiot!'

'*É una stronza!*'

Impossible to converse with.

Aldo's friends in Rome could express only horror and anger.

'For God's sake! What does he see in her?'

'She's got a good butt on her...'

'But that's all she has: a butt. He didn't need to go to Cuba for that...'

'And didn't need to marry her...'

He started to weary of Bini by the end of the first month. His psychiatrist and Gonzalo were right. She wasn't the same in

Rome as she was in Havana. Without the aroma of the tropics, without the heat and humidity, everything was different.

Bini was like rum, tasty in Cuba and insipid in Europe.

Without the madness and total relaxation that imbued Aldo's excursions to Cuba, Bini wasn't Bini. Her delights diminished.

The best would be to see her regularly in Havana. He had only to imagine her there, in her element, with her godfather and irrational childish ways, to desire her again and ignite his engine. Afterwards, he found it easier to cool his ardour in the company of others.

In order to make love with Simonetta, Aldo had evoked, with resonant and repeated success, their wedding party in Varadero, when Bini, in almost naked rapture, rode astride a tame dolphin. Their undulating movements, twists and turns in the swimming pool, transformed into precise caresses, exactly where she liked caresses, and the subsequent playful leaps and shakes, and her plunging up to her waist, even her neck, galvanized his erotic memory. In sky-blue bra and panties, lasciviousness itself, Bini was Ogun in the colours of Yemayá.

Nobody seeing her that night would ever forget her. She bit her lips, writhed on the dolphin's back. My God…! Then she climbed out of the swimming pool, eyes lusting, took Aldo by the hand and urged him to go to bed with her. The dolphin was about to send her into orgasm. She'd imagined she was riding an enormous phallus; but refrained from coming in front of her dad and Pepe Jaén: she didn't want all the guests to discover she was so whorish, ha ha ha, and had had it off with a fish. Even then her godfather Juan Pedro had given her a pasting. What did she think she was doing parading around in bra and panties? Was she drunk? Had she no respect for people?

But the life they both now led in Italy didn't encourage Bini to get up to her tricks, the divine tricks that so fed Aldo's libido.

Ever so disappointing. At home all she did was watch telly, the stupidest programmes, horrible musicals, ridiculous games, and the shorts with telephone whores aimed at nocturnal masturbators.

When Aldo took her to visit the forums, the Coliseum, Trajan's Column, she said the things from yesteryear bored her. What most set her alight in Italy were cars and human rights. And money-making machines.

Although she had no need, whenever she walked by a cash machine she'd take money out. Then give the notes back to Aldo, so he could put them back in her account. She couldn't restrain herself; putting the card in, keying in and watching the notes come out was pure joy, magic. She was now somebody else. She was no longer the girl down on her luck, with Dad at war, a bitching mother, patched hand-me-downs, bad teachers, reform school, jail...

Keying in on the cash machines made her feel she'd been compensated. She now lived in a democracy and enjoyed human rights...

'What? What? What's that about human rights?'

Naturally. The fact she could exercise her human rights made her forget the poverty of her childhood. Just key in a secret number, whoosh, a tangle of cables started whirring across the world, declaring that she, Bini López, existed. Uh-huh. They recognized her in the banks. She now lived in a democracy and had democratic rights, like the women in her films, all with their own car, mobile and credit card...

Aldo stifled the first guffaw, and then the impulse to reason with her. But he said nothing. When they got back to Cuba, he'd contract a good history teacher for her.

Bini's incredible ignorance, which in Cuba made him soft hearted, now began to exasperate him. Particularly when he was falling in love with Simonetta.

Yes, he needed to send her back to Cuba. But as he'd promised three months in Italy, and she'd done only one...

When that Ferrari Testarossa sidled slowly down the Via Veneto, steered by a twenty-year-old Sophia Loren, Bini realized why she'd come into the world.

As José Martí said, children were born to be happy. Something she wasn't; but now, with a rich husband…

The red Ferrari. That was what she wanted from life. It was the ne plus ultra, the desideratum, paradise in red.

That night she dreamed of Changó driving the Testarossa. Oh if only she could…!

If some day she could drive a buggy like that, she could die contented.

How much would a Ferrari Testarossa cost?

She did some sums for the first time.

Would it cost much more than the Little Egg?

Probably if she sold the Little Egg and the medallion…

Aldo had had a cameo brooch made up for her as a wedding present, with the image of Yemayá cut on an enormous aquamarine. The whitest ivory emphasized the charms of her black skin. And Bini discovered that the medallion, as she called it, cost more than the Little Egg. And the Little Egg cost eleven thousand bucks. Probably, if she sold both, she'd have enough to buy herself a Testarossa.

Engrossed in his own affairs, Aldo explained bad-temperedly that a Ferrari Testarossa cost more that two hundred thousand dollars.

Bini thought such a price was a violation of human rights and shed a furtive tear…It was then the penny dropped for Aldo, and he regretted his lack of affection.

Poor thing. She'd done so much for him, and now he was mistreating her, falling in love with another woman, trying to detach himself from her…From a woman who had not only restored him to normality, but had done time for him – more than for him, for a just cause. If all human beings in this world acted with the same sensitivity and courage as that ignorant whore by the name of Bini, sure there wouldn't be so many running sores.

Oh, no…It wasn't like that. He was exaggerating.

He adored her. Yes, he sometimes became impatient, but he'd never abandon her altogether. He would still see her. But she now belonged to his past.

He thought of renting a Ferrari and taking her for a drive.

Impossible. He needed to slave away for fourteen hours a day on his backlog of work, and devote his odd idle moment to Simonetta.

Suddenly a providential solution came out of the blue.

Paolino would be the ideal person: serious, honest and also obsessed by sports cars.

He slept on it and awoke with his mind made up.

He got to his office earlier than usual and summoned Paolino to tell him he intended welcoming in the new millennium with some charitable works: he was going to give Paolino a month's paid holiday and lend him a Ferrari Testarossa.

'That would be great! Unfortunately, Ferrari stopped making the Testarossa years ago.'

'That's true, but I know an agency where they rent luxury cars and they've got two Testarossas available.'

Paolino couldn't guess what the leg-pull was all about.

'I'm serious, Paolino. I want you chauffeur my wife until February the twenty-ninth…'

Paolino gave him a look of terror. Date already fixed? So it wasn't a leg-pull…

'I want you to show her Florence, Bologna, Venice, Milan, Turin, Genoa, Monaco, Marseille, Paris, Barcelona, and be waiting for me in Madrid on the twenty-ninth of February.'

In Madrid Aldo would take over the Testarossa and Paolino would fly back to Rome by Alitalia.

'*D'accordo?*'

As far as Paolino was concerned, seeing himself spared his desk and on full pay sitting behind the wheel of the car he worshipped for a month, with that fantastic black woman, staying in luxury hotels all expenses paid, was as unthinkable as seeing Signor Bianchi don a kimono, take a sword from his desk drawer and behead his secretary.

'Do you have a credit card?'

'Yes, sir…' and Paolino stared at him anxiously.

He still couldn't believe his ears.

'Perfect. I'll credit you with thirty million lire so you can see to all the expenses of hotels, restaurants and drives; you can give me the bills at the end. Now go back to your desk, sit down, take a deep breath, then a tranquillizer and rest assured that this is no joke. Then go and see to the details with Signora Vittoria. She'll look after the hotel reservations, the car-hire contract, the insurance, everything in your name and Bini's. And when you've finished with her, come straight back here.'

He picked up the telephone which had started ringing and dismissed Paolino with a peremptory gesture.

There were still surprises in store for Paolino.

After half an hour, when he'd spoken to Signora Vittoria, he returned to his boss's office.

'Make sure the door's shut…'

Paolino obeyed.

'I want Bini to drive, but be very, very careful. And I've chosen you because I trust you as a person and as a driver. If anything happens to her, your head's for the chopping block. You can let her have the wheel, but only on motorways; and watch it, don't let her order you to drive too fast. Don't let her do more that one hundred and fifty. And, in particular, never let her drive in cities. You understand?'

'Yes, of course, I'll see to all that, Signor Bianchi.'

'Good, get ready to leave the day after tomorrow…And remember, never more than one hundred and fifty and only on motorways…'

'Rest assured, Signor Bianchi…'

'I'm not at all assured, Paolino…Not at all. She'll put pressure on you, and she's good at that…'

'But I swear I won't give in. I'll tell her I'm carrying out orders, that I could lose my job…'

'Don't start swearing oaths, Paolino, she can be very capricious and persuasive. And one other thing, nobody in this office, or the whole of Italy, must find out I ordered you to take my wife off on this jaunt. The details are just between Signora Vittoria, you and myself. If you blab, you really will lose your job. I'm warning you.'

Paolino promised he'd be more tightly sealed than an Etruscan urn.

In Madrid, in the wake of the Pinochet affair, at the end of October 1999, Baltasar Garzón the judge declared he was taking out actions against ninety-eight Argentine soldiers and civilians, linked to the dictatorships of Videla, Massera and Galtieri. Dr Garzón accused them of terrorism, genocide and torture, and stated that the Law of the Full Stop was a legal aberration, contrary to all international treaties.

The news reached Aldo's ear subsequently that several of those characters were directly connected to the horrors perpetrated in the Navy Engineering School.

That was the reason why he intended to be in Madrid on 29 February. A friend of his had fixed an appointment with Dr Garzón, and he would be present too.

His idea was to introduce himself as a victim of the EMA torturers. He'd take a copy of the pamphlet with the illustrations and wretched account of the crimes of Major Orlando Ortega Ortiz. He intended giving him confidential but well-documented information, which he himself had gathered against the former Uruguayan torturer; and would offer wholehearted collaboration in his realistic initiative.

Aldo hoped to see photos of the Argentine soldiers accused of participating in the EMA whom the judge had in his sights. And he'd perhaps recognize among them two faces he'd never forget, but whose real names he'd never known.

One of them, the one they called El Negro, was a swarthy, hairy-skinned fellow who dragged his R's and spoke with a northern accent. He was Orlando's main acolyte in the torture chambers. Incredibly flat nosed, chinless, sunken eyed. Unmistakable. After a quarter of a century, Aldo would recognize him from any photo.

The other, the one they dubbed the Hot Prod, who'd never fade from his memory, was the one who most enthused over Three-O in his rituals with his cock-a-doodling rooster; and who acted as referee and bet-collector in the pansy dog derby.

Aldo would have preferred to forget the EMA and its victims for ever; but his debt to the memory of Teresita meant he must help Judge Garzón.

Paolino drove as far as Florence. She observed him and took a deep breath. She melted at the mere thought she'd very soon be driving that red beast that was so handsome and powerful. Brum, brum, brummmmmmmm went Paolino as he took the gentle bends on the motorway at two hundred and twenty kilometres an hour.

In Florence they went shopping, visited two cashpoints, dined in a trendy trattoria and went early to bed.

She drove the whole way from Florence to Bologna. She told Paolino that it was the happiest day of her life and he had his fifth erection.

In Venice they had a ride on a gondola and visited shoe shops, and she even managed some red trifles that matched the Ferrari Testarossa.

As they were leaving a service station, where he took back the wheel and gave it another irresistible brum, brum, brummmmmmmm, she also felt inspired and pinched his thigh.

Paolino had his sixth erection at the wheel, but held back.

She watched him drive and was filled with admiration. Paolino was ugly, big nosed and skinny, but was transfigured when behind the wheel. His features were all magnified. She saw him all scarred with a kerchief round his head, like a pirate.

Days later, when they were entering Milan, he did another brum, brum, brummmmmmm and navigated a roundabout so elegantly she could no longer restrain herself: she undid her belt, knelt on her seat and bit him on the shoulder.

When they were close to the Duomo, he pointed out a cashpoint.

While she got out to exercise her human rights, he entered a chemist's and bought a box of one hundred and fifty Rooster-brand condoms.

With its virile crest and boastful chest, the rooster winked at him and gave him an encouraging smile.

When he got back, Bini stroked his groin.

Paolino could hold back no more.

'Let God's will be done...'

He was sorry for Signor Bianchi's sake. He had done everything humanly possible...

That night, in Milan, the rooster preened its chest and sang several times. Not at La Scala, but inside the Ferrari parked in the vicinity of the Piazza Castello.

In Turin Bini exercised her human rights at three cashpoints and at night reinforced them dancing at an elegant nightspot with the friends she had made at the hotel. And she discovered that Turin was the Italian city that manufactured most cars, and that aroused her. When they left, she insisted on driving.

'Ay, Paolino, no one will ever know...'

And who could resist being ear-nibbled, Thai-massaged and French-kissed in a Ferrari Testarossa, as the shadows fell over the foothills of the Alps.

It was the first time Paolino had broken the pledge he'd made to Signor Bianchi.

The second was when he allowed her to drive on the Ligurian coastal roads near San Remo at two hundred kilometres an hour.

They flew some one hundred and twenty metres before falling into the sea. Two fishermen from the area gave them up for dead. But it turned out the Ferrari was amphibious and, after gliding down, it slid along a good way before sinking.

He emerged, very battered, very bruised, but with nothing broken.

She suffered a fractured tibia and her fourth vertebra was dislocated.

When they embarked in Fiumicino and landed at Rancho Boyeros, Aldo carried Bini lovingly in her arms. She said no way would she ride in a wheelchair.

A month later, her leg was still in plaster and her neck was immobilized by a brace. But she got better by the day, thanks to the miraculous massages of Dr Azúa, her great friend and accomplice from months ago, ever since he'd found out from Aldo and his documented explanations the justice-bearing purpose of their montage against his former client. And after Bini had felt his hot, magnetic fingers on her skin, she'd only accept treatment from that huge black, who was so like her father.

When Aldo told Juan Pedro of all the adventures with the Testarossa, and started making fun of Bini and her childish ways, and how she'd wanted to sell her Little Egg and the Yemayá cameo brooch in order to buy one of the world's most expensive cars, the *babalao* gave his interpretation of what had happened.

'Of course,' he affirmed, 'they fell into the sea because she'd offended Yemayá. The saint must punish her. And if Bini sell that medallion, sure she not come out alive.'

Fiction
Non-fiction
Literary
Crime

Popular culture
Biography
Illustrated
Music

# dare to read at serpentstail.com

Visit serpentstail.com today to browse and buy
our books, and for exclusive previews, promotions,
interviews with authors and forthcoming events.

---

NEWS · cut to the literary chase with all the latest news about our books and authors

EVENTS · advance information on forthcoming events, author readings, exhibitions and book festivals

EXTRACTS · read first chapters, short stories, bite-sized extracts

EXCLUSIVES · pre-publication offers, signed copies, discounted books, competitions

BROWSE AND BUY · browse our full catalogue, fill up a basket and proceed to our **fully secure** checkout – our website is your oyster

## FREE POSTAGE & PACKING ON ALL ORDERS ANYWHERE!

---

## sign up today and receive our new free full colour catalogue